SOMETHING YOU ARE

Hanna Jameson wrote *Something You Are* when she was just seventeen, and at the age of twenty-one had already drafted two sequels. She has lived in Australia, travelled Europe, Japan and the USA with bands such as the Manic Street Preachers and Kasabian, and has worked for three years in the NHS. She is currently studying American History & Literature at the University of Sussex.

HANNA JAMESON

SOMETHING YOU ARE

HEAD of ZEUS

First published in the UK in 2012 by Head of Zeus, Ltd.

This paperback edition published in the UK in 2013
by Head of Zeus, Ltd.

9 7 5 3 1 2 4 6 8

A CIP catalogue record for this book is available from
thes British Library.

Paperback ISBN 9781908800633
eBook ISBN 9781781850503

Printed and bound by CPI Group (UK) Ltd, Croydon, CR0 4YY.

Head of Zeus, Ltd
Clerkenwell House
45-47 Clerkenwell Green
London EC1R 0HT

www.headofzeus.com

Acknowledgements

Thank you to my mum and dad, Paul Davies for being a genius, and Jemma Pascoe and Jonathan Sissons for impeccable taste in music and literature. Also, thanks to Nick Cave & The Bad Seeds, Leonard Cohen, Elliott Smith, Radiohead, Nirvana, Smashing Pumpkins, and Boy Cried Wolf, for the constant soundtrack to writing this one.

'I did it all myself'
Spike Milligan

So I have no real culture. I am a monster. There are others whom I could be with, but I don't want to be.

Kirsten Bakis, *Lives of the Monster Dogs*

PROLOGUE

2000

There were three of them, standing on the corner between the main road and my house. I knew they were going to stop me. Around here, you just knew these things. My estate lurked in your peripheral vision like an abusive partner, silent until it lurched into spates of motiveless violence.

'Hey!'

I avoided eye contact.

'Oi! Oi, Nic!'

It would have been unwise to carry on walking so I stopped a few feet short of the tallest boy in the grey hoodie.

'All right.' I nodded, not too familiar but not abrupt.

Night was falling, casting long shadows across the pavement and making the boys' already dark skin appear almost black. They looked about thirteen, even the one who was taller than me, though they might have been younger.

'Got any money? My brother needs some fags.' The tallest jerked his head at one of the smaller kids.

'No, just on my way home.'

They made no indication of moving so neither did I. Four pairs of hands drifted into pockets. I had nothing. I had the sense to glare, but felt closer to vomiting or passing out.

'You've got a funny surname, in't ya?'

Silence.

'Cariana? Bit gay.'

'Caruana,' I corrected him.

'*Caruana...*' he drew out the syllables. 'Like *marijuana*?'

'Yep.'

A red Honda passed by. I felt eyes scan the scene from behind a pane of glass and then they were gone.

'I'm going home, lads,' I said, dropping my gaze and taking a step forwards.

'Na na na, mate.' The tall kid stopped me with a hand to the chest. 'Na na na, I asked you whether you had fag money, mate. Nic, mate. Nic, that's you, right?'

'Fuck's sake, I don't have any money on me!' I took my hands out of my pockets to gesture and he punched me in the face.

The street became sky as two of them tackled me around the waist. The back of my head smacked against tarmac and hands went into pockets. I kicked out and connected with shins but I could hear them shouting.

'Stay down! Stay down or I'll shank you, I'll fucking shank you!'

I froze, flat against the pavement with rainwater soaking into my back. It could have been an empty threat but I wasn't going to take the chance. They searched my pockets, relieving me of my mobile while I looked up over their heads at the darkening cloud.

'Take that off,' the tall one said, pointing at my watch, my dad's watch, black leather and silver numbers.

I hesitated and one of the smaller kids kicked me in the ribs.

'Do as he says, bitch!'

'Or we'll fuck you up!'

'Just take the phone,' I said, wondering if I would ever reach my house.

This time the kick was in the face. I spat out blood and rolled on to my side to let it fall to the pavement. They would kill me over the watch; these kids would kill over a postcode.

'All right, fuck, *all right*!'

I tried to undo the buckle with a trembling hand, praying that it was enough.

'Hurry the fuck up!'

The tall kid grabbed my wrist and I saw the knife, an evil fucker of a stiletto blade. I panicked and lunged for the handle. An arm crushed my neck but I couldn't let go. If I let go I was dead; another statistic, a face in a newspaper next to an embarrassingly optimistic list of my aspirations.

At first I thought I was just punching him, slamming my fist against his chest so that I could breathe again, but when he let me go and I was still holding the handle I realized what had happened.

He looked at me with dead eyes. Huge flowers of blood blossomed and spread across the front of the hoodie, bleeding into each other.

The other two kids started to run.

'I'm... fuck...' He turned and tried to limp towards the main road.

'Wait! No, wait!'

I dropped the knife and followed him as he dropped to his knees by the kerb. I crouched beside him and searched his pockets for my mobile.

'Wait, just wait...' I didn't know what I was saying. Words kept tumbling out without coherence.

'I want my mum...' He started crying, holding his stomach. 'Please, you have to get my mum!'

There was blood on the handset as I tried to dial 999.

'Please...'

'Wait! Wait, just wait!'

The line was ringing and ringing and the tarmac I was kneeling on was slick with blood and rainwater.

'Emergency services—'

'Hello? Hello! I need... I need a—'

The kid wasn't speaking any more.

'Hello? Sir, hello?'

I thought I was just punching him.

'Oh God...' A hand went to my mouth to hold back the bile and the tears came instead. 'Fuck.'

'Hello? Can you hear me?'

I ended the call and struggled to my feet. The street was empty but that was to be expected. People would have turned their backs or disappeared into houses. No one wanted to go to court. No one was worth that.

I wiped the blood off my hands on to my shirt, and zipped up my jacket as if it would hide the stains.

I thought I was just punching him.

I went to take him by the shoulders to get him out of the road, but he was too heavy. I could only manage a few steps before having to drop him. He looked his age now, despite his size. His face was that of a child's.

For a few moments, I was torn between trying to lift him again and running back to the knife.

I ran.

The blade was red all the way up to the handle.

It was surprisingly light when I picked it up. It had gone into him so easily that I hadn't even noticed, like sliding it into butter. I retched, threw it away from me and heard it clatter against a drain.

I started walking, faster and faster, towards my house. The buckle on my watch was loose and I slid it back into place. I

4

couldn't believe how close I had been to getting home; five minutes later or earlier and this wouldn't be happening.

I made it to my front door without seeing anyone else and wondered how long it would take for someone in the surrounding houses to phone the police or an ambulance. I couldn't steady my hands enough to get my key in the lock so I knocked instead. For a second I worried what Mum would say about getting blood on the carpets.

I was only seventeen. That kid had been younger.

By the time my brother answered the door I found it too difficult to speak.

'Tony...' I choked.

'Jesus, fuck, Nic!' He grabbed at me, searching for the wound so that he could stem the blood, and paled as he realized it wasn't mine.

'Tony, we need—'

'Oh, Jesus Christ...' He leant out and scanned the street.

'His mum!' It was all I could get out through the tears as he dragged me inside by the front of my jacket. 'Please, we have to get his mum!'

CHAPTER ONE

2010

The first time I killed someone I wasn't paid for it. Like many other kids I drifted into my career by accident, because it was the first industry to offer me money, because, with my record, nowhere else would have offered me any.

I turned right off Marylebone High Street and into a road of detached houses. Like the stockbrokers and accountants still in their offices I didn't have to be working, but I had dragged myself out of a shallow sleep on my sofa and into my car when Pat Dyer had called and offered me a job.

I pulled into a lay-by, got out into the excruciating cold and squinted at each front door. His daughter had gone missing, apparently. I didn't know much about Pat, having only been introduced once in passing. I knew more about him by reputation, but they were all the same, these types: clever, self-important, predictably psychotic.

A gust of wind went through my coat and I gritted my teeth as I walked up to Pat's house. I noticed, as I knocked, that any space where grass or flowers were meant to be had been covered with concrete.

A blonde woman opened the door and I faltered.

'I'm... Hi, I'm Nic, Nic Caruana.'

She looked at my hand with her arms folded, before shaking it. Her wrists showed traces of white scars and she had the most desolate eyes I had ever seen. Pat sounded like the type to have a model wife, and she stood at least two inches taller than me.

'Um, Pat called me over,' I said.

'Oh.' She stood to one side, mimicking a smile. 'Great.'

I'd almost rather have stayed outside.

'Look, I know this is awkward but Pat left about five minutes ago,' she said as I walked in. 'I'm Clare, I'm his wife. He said... Well, he said to tell you anything you wanted to know.'

There was a slight accent to her voice; definitely Scottish.

I felt wrong-footed by the change in plans. It wasn't that she was a woman, but their tendency towards overt displays of emotion made me tense.

'When was the last time you saw her?' I asked, driving past the possibility of small talk.

'This morning, when she left. She was meant to be back by four.'

'You know, she's probably just at a party. Most of the time when I get called out to things like this I end up driving a sorry kid back from a rave somewhere.' I smiled. 'You know, begging them not to throw up in my car.'

'Maybe, but I don't think so.' She returned my smile, but with the expression of someone who knew I didn't have kids myself. 'What do you do again?'

'Private detective of sorts.'

'Oh really? I heard you track people down?'

'Yeah, I do that.'

'And make them pay for things?' Not once did her eyes leave my face. 'Pat's words.'

'I...'

'I see.'

'That's quite a... general description of my job.'

'Well, PR has never been Pat's strong point.'

'Yeah, well, most people quite like their kneecaps.' I regretted the low shot and looked back at the front door, willing Pat to return. 'Sorry.'

'Don't be sorry.' Contrary to my reaction she didn't look bothered. I had misjudged her in assuming she didn't know a lot. 'I don't like you. I didn't like you as soon as I heard Pat call you.'

I wasn't sure whether to be bewildered or amused. 'That's OK.'

'Do you want to sit down?'

All of their furniture was a little too big for the house. The gold-rimmed mirror hanging in the hallway gave the impression you were sharing the space with too many extra people. In the living room the sofas were leather and the TV and computer were unnecessarily large. In a few years I could see us watching screens projecting life-sized images; no distinction between fiction and ourselves.

I sat on the edge of a sofa and Clare leant on the arm of another. She had tried to dress down the grey cocktail dress with a cardigan, and she wasn't wearing any shoes. Maybe it was just her height, but she had quite a daunting presence for a woman.

'We called her friend, the one she was meant to be meeting, and according to her she never even arrived,' Clare said.

'Where were they meeting?' I asked, glad to be back on solid ground.

'Tottenham Court Road tube station, I think. They might have been catching the tube from there, I don't know.'

'Did you try calling her?'

'We both tried but she never picked up.'

'What's her friend's name?'

'I don't think you should know.'

I found it hard to meet the suspicion in her face. 'I won't hurt her.'

'You're not with the law.'

'What difference does that make?'

'You don't have anyone to tell you when you're going too far.'

'Why do you think I need someone to tell me?' I asked.

'Everyone does. And if you didn't you'd probably be working with the law rather than outside it.'

I smiled. I couldn't help it even though it would seem patronizing.

'You don't have a very high opinion of people, do you?'

'No, just you.'

'OK.' I inclined my head. 'So I'm not allowed to know her friend's name?'

'No.'

'Did she have a boyfriend?'

'No, they broke up a while ago.' She sat down and pulled her legs up on to the sofa.

'Am I allowed to know his name?'

'No.'

'You ever give people a chance?'

'Do you?'

'Fair enough.' I shrugged. 'Can I see a picture of her?'

She looked at me as if I had asked for pornography.

I spread my hands. 'I can't find her if I don't know what she looks like.'

After a small hesitation she stood up, walked over to one of the bookcases in the corner and took down a framed photo. The girl in the picture looked like a dark-haired version of her mother, I thought, with harder features that reminded me

9

more of her father. There were the same high cheekbones and dancer's posture that Clare had, but she was nowhere near as interesting without the scars.

'What was she wearing this morning?'

'She was wearing her black and white striped top. Um... jeans, black boots, high heels.'

I decided against asking to keep the photo and handed it back. Clare replaced it on the bookcase and next to it I noticed a sculpture of a woman's body, legs twisted up behind the head, the face featureless apart from an open soundless scream where the mouth was meant to be. It didn't sit comfortably with the rest of the room.

I caught her eyes, tensed and looked away. 'Look, do you mind if I go and speak to some people? I'll call Pat on his mobile but it's probably best I start trying to get some leads.'

'It's what he's paying you for.'

'Try not to worry too much. You know, I'm sure she's fine.'

She nodded. 'She'd call if she was.'

I was about to leave when I caught myself in the doorway, turning back. 'Sorry... What's her name?'

'Emma.' Her face was all shadows and grief, as if she already knew her daughter wasn't coming back. 'Her name's Emma.'

My breath froze in the air on the way back to my car. I could have gone home, but it was a job and sleep was overrated.

I wanted a closer look at her hands.

The level of cold on this night was oppressive and vaguely threatening. I let myself into DC Geoff Brinks's house through the back door. Due to his late-night cigarettes it was never locked.

You would never guess that he had two children, I thought as I sat down at his dining table in the dark. Usually you could see the telltale signs, like drawings stuck to the fridge or family photos, but his house was as void and grey as the man himself.

It was later than usual, a little while after midnight, when I heard him coming down the stairs. I could have given him some warning but where was the fun in that?

Brinks switched on the light and let out a high-pitched cry as he fell against the wall.

I swear this never stopped being funny.

'Evening, sunshine.'

'Fuck! Fuck... *Fuck*, Nic!'

'If you don't lock your door one day you'll get unlucky and it won't be me you find down here.'

'Lucky, pfft...' Brinks, his T-shirt and boxers hanging off the bones jutting out of his hips, crossed the room to the fridge and got out a bottle of Carlsberg. He was slight to the point of emaciated, with small rat-like teeth and slick hair. 'You're lucky I don't sleep in the buff, mate.'

'There would be *nothing* buff about that, mate.'

Brinks sat down heavily across the table, making me want to stand up.

'This has to stop,' he said, rubbing his finger across a stain in the plastic tablecloth.

'Well, when you start locking your door I might start knocking.' I winked, not able to resist fucking with his head. 'Meet the missus, eh?'

'No, not just that, I mean this.' He gestured at nothing. 'I mean this whole thing.'

I snorted. 'And you think I have nothing better to do with my time than cultivate new contacts?'

'Come on, Nic—'

'I need to be kept up to date on this case.'

'Nic—'

'*Stop* bleating my name like some fucking woman!' I reached into my khaki bag and dropped a wad of notes on to the table. It was more likely to shut him up than words.

He looked up from the money, as pale as the notes. 'What case?'

The token pretence at integrity was disgusting. I wanted to smash his head into the fridge and leave him choking in a pool of his own blood but it wouldn't be fair on the family upstairs. Brinks would do anything for money. I doubted it would take much for him to let me do that.

He coughed and fear flickered across his features. Sometimes I wondered whether he could see my thoughts betrayed on my face.

'What case?'

'It's not a case yet, but it will be soon. Do you know who Pat Dyer is?'

He took a gulp of beer. 'I want to say arms dealer...'

'Yeah, he lives in Marylebone. His daughter went missing today.'

'Yeah, I know of him. Daughter is about sixteen now, right?'

I hesitated, surprised at myself for having not asked. 'Um, yeah.'

'How long has she been gone?'

'Since this morning. She went to meet a friend and never arrived. Parents only found out a while ago.'

'Don't want her gone another twelve hours, do we?' he said, looking at me over the huge shadows under his eyes. 'You know I'll only be brought in if we find a body?'

'I know.'

'Ever the optimist.'

I shrugged. It seemed pointless, hoping she would be found. The only alternative I could think of was that her friend had lied. It didn't fit though. Her friend would have covered for her otherwise.

'I'm gonna need things like CCTV footage, case notes, photographs, the usual.'

'Do you have a description?' he asked, counting the money left on the table.

'She's got long dark hair, blue eyes, mole on her neck along her collarbone.' My mind was full of bin liners and mottled skin, blood under broken nails. I wondered how much money it would take to make Brinks do that to someone. 'She was wearing jeans, black high-heel boots and a black and white striped top.'

'Getting ahead of ourselves a bit, aren't we?' he said, rubbing his eyes.

'If she turns up alive it'll be a nice hundred pounds to lose.'

'Point.' He pinched the bridge of his nose as I stood up and wandered towards the door. 'Seriously, this has to be the last time.'

'Heh, whatever.' I smiled back from the doorway. 'Like you have a choice.'

'I'm serious…'

'Thanks, Geoff!' I called back, already outside.

'Go to hell, Nic.'

I dialled Pat Dyer from a petrol station while downing an energy drink in my car, not expecting an answer. It was well into the early hours of the morning and stress was weighing on my eyelids.

After a few seconds Pat answered. There was a dim rumble,

13

as if he was driving. It was the third time I'd spoken to him, but the picture that was starting to form in my mind was of a man who didn't tolerate contradiction or competition. He spoke like someone who was not only unaccustomed to interruption, but on constant lookout for anyone who seemed as though they might try.

'Yeah?'

'This is Nic, Nic Caruana.'

'Oh yeah? Clare said you were following some leads?'

'Well, it's hard to tell at the moment but what was the name of Emma's ex-boyfriend?'

'Danny Maclaine. Don't worry about him though, I've just seen him. Got a few leads of my own, you know.'

'Do you mind if I talk to him anyway?'

Pat went quiet for a while.

'He doesn't know anything,' he said, sounding competitive.

'I'd still like to talk to him.'

'Believe me, if he knew anything he would have told me.'

'Sure thing, but I like to check these things out myself.'

He waited for me to relent, but I was more at ease with silence than him.

'Fine,' he said. 'But he doesn't know anything.'

He gave me an address in Edmonton and hung up.

I turned the car around, thinking that she was already dead. I tried switching on the radio and grimaced at the onslaught of drum 'n' bass before switching it off again. When I stopped at some traffic lights I shut my eyes for a moment, jerked myself awake and drew a star in the condensation on the window.

She's already dead.

The upper windows of the house in Edmonton were blocked with mattresses. Danny Maclaine answered the door with one

14

eye swollen shut. His jeans were too baggy and his hair was on the verge of dreadlocks. A ginger cut-price Kurt Cobain.

'Are you Danny Maclaine?'

'Fuck, I already told him I don't know where she is!'

'I just want to talk to you.'

Danny turned his head side-on to look at me. 'Who are you?'

'I'm working with Pat. Don't worry, I don't think you know where she is.'

'So she really is missing then?'

'Yeah, since this morning.'

'Fuck…' He jerked his head. 'All right.'

There was only one lamp in the living room, one sofa, one table, no TV. He sat down carefully, an arm around his ribs. Someone in the street was playing Deftones too loud and a group of lads were shouting their way past the window. On the floor at his feet was a bag of pills.

'When did you last see Emma?' I asked, standing in the doorway.

'About three weeks ago, maybe four, I don't know.' He picked up the bag of pills and let me decline one before knocking back two for himself.

'How long were you together?'

'A year. She was cool. We were together since she was fifteen. Her dad never liked me though, mad bastard.'

My eyes fell across the bruises and split cheek. 'He gave you quite a going-over.'

'Well, he's been waiting for an excuse for long enough.' He shifted on the sofa and looked up at me as if he was about to share something important. 'Look, she's not the sort of girl who would pull a fast one on her parents. She's a good sort, really. If she's missing it'll be… it'll be something.'

'I don't want to jump to conclusions,' I said. 'Any idea where she would go? Places that she used to hang out?'

'Only the usual places, clubs and stuff…' He shrugged, leg jigging. 'They were only places she would go with me though, cos of her age. I don't know where her new fella would be taking her.'

The music stopped but the shouting continued.

'She had a new boyfriend?'

'Just from what I've heard,' he said. 'She was seen out with another guy.'

'Do you know his name?'

'No.' His eye narrowed for a moment. 'I don't even know what he looks like.'

The shouting outside stopped.

'She's… she's probably dead, isn't she?' he said.

I knew he wouldn't appreciate a lie, even if it would have been kinder to give him one, at least for now.

'Maybe. Maybe not.'

He nodded and sat back, one eye staring ahead.

'I need to go but I may need to speak to you again.'

Danny didn't say anything else. He was rolling himself a joint when I left.

CHAPTER TWO

I glanced at my reflection in the overhead mirror again and pushed it away, embarrassed that I cared.

I was an odd-looking guy by my own admission. An Italian father and Scottish mother had given me features that had taken years to grow into, and even now they remained uneasily arranged on my face: a Roman nose, pale eyes and aggressive teeth against a natural tan. My hair was still short, but starting to hang like Lennon's during his fringe phase.

I sat back in the driver's seat, grimacing.

Across the street the front of Pat Dyer's house was grand and sombre. Everything about it said fuck off. Pat's Mercedes wasn't in the driveway and he wasn't answering his phone.

I got out of the car, eyes on the living-room light.

I called Pat.

Nothing.

I called Pat again.

Nothing.

Fuck.

I walked up to the door, rang the bell and listened to footsteps coming swiftly from the living room. When she opened the door she didn't bother to hide her disappointment.

'Oh, it's you...' She stepped back, masking the worry with contempt, charcoal shadows under her eyes. 'Have you found anything?'

'Nothing yet.' I hesitated, until I realized that she wasn't

17

planning to invite me in again. 'Listen, I need to search Emma's room. If it's OK with you, of course.'

She said nothing.

'OK, well, let me phrase it another way,' I said. 'I'm going to search her room, because that's what I'm being paid to do. You can be OK with it, or not. I actually don't give a shit either way.'

I expected her to slam the door in my face but she stood to the side.

'Fine.'

I stepped inside and turned. 'Look, it's just—'

'Don't worry, I understood you the first time.'

There was nothing I could say to make the atmosphere easier, I realized. There never was. With my job I only ever met people at their worst; racked with grief or spite or a petty need for revenge.

I walked up the stairs and heard her say, 'It's on the left,' which was as close to an endorsement as I was going to get.

When I switched on the light the first thing that hit me was the realization of how young sixteen was. The walls were baby blue and covered in posters cut from magazines. I didn't know who any of the men were and figured I wasn't missing out on much.

I glanced back as I heard Clare coming up the stairs. 'I'm going to need to move some stuff.'

She shrugged and leant against the doorway.

I tried to forget she was there as I started working my way methodically around the room. First I checked the usual places; on the top shelves of the wardrobe and under the mattress. Burglars used the same logic; anything of value was either high or low.

In her dressing table I found a diary and address book.

'That's private,' Clare said.

I raised my eyebrows at her as I sat down on the stool, picking my way past the lock with one of her hairpins. I scanned the most recent entries, saw a few names and put both the diary and address book in my pocket.

'Do you know if Emma had a new boyfriend?' I asked, looking at the photos stuck around the edges of the mirror.

'No.' She hesitated, as if she felt guilty for asking. 'Have you seen...? Did she?'

'Possibly.'

'Oh.'

Emma looked like the sort of girl who knew too many people, I thought. One of the popular kids, with so many acquaintances that she wouldn't be able to tell which ones were friends.

'I thought she would have told us,' Clare said. 'She tells us everything.'

'With all due respect, that's a myth.'

It was too quiet and the room was too bright.

I reached forwards and ran my hands down either side of the mirror. My fingers brushed against something Sellotaped to the back and I stood up to peel it off. It was a bag of white powder.

'No, she wouldn't...' She stepped into the room.

I put it in my pocket along with the diary and address book. 'Don't worry, it might not even have any relevance.'

'It's relevant to me.'

I looked back at Emma's bedside table and saw on the digital clock that it was almost three in morning.

'I'm going to go home,' I said. 'I think I've got enough information to get started. I'll call round tomorrow... or later today, I mean. Hopefully Pat will be back by then and if the

19

police find anything in the meantime I'll know before anyone else.'

'Are you just going to take those?' She indicated her head at my pocket. 'She might come back and if she sees we've...'

I didn't say anything.

'I get it,' she said. 'You don't think she's coming back, do you?'

'No, I'm just doing my job.'

She looked me up and down but she seemed too tired to argue further.

'Fine,' she said.

'Cool. I'll check in later.'

I brushed against her shoulder as I walked towards the stairs, but her arms were folded and the scars on her wrists weren't visible.

My mobile started vibrating in my pocket. It was Brinks, and I already knew what he was going to say. He wouldn't call me at this time of night unless it was from a crime scene.

'Yep?'

Brinks sounded as if he was walking, heavy breaths sending white noise down the line. 'We've got the guys from Family Liaison heading over to the parents now. Poor bastards are going to have to identify a body.'

'You found her?'

'Her... it, whatever. If it wasn't for some of the clothes you described I wouldn't even fucking know.'

'Is it bad?'

'Bad? More like unrecognizable. Seriously, Nic, shot and beaten to fuck.'

My thoughts went to the girl's face in the picture frame; red, purple and smashed. I avoided looking back up the stairs at Clare, but I could feel her expression searing straight through me.

'Who found her?'

'Taxi driver. I'll give you the names and statements as and when.'

'You sound spooked?'

'Yeah, well, you're not here. We'll catch up later; I'll give you some photos and stuff. Just thought you should know.'

'Thanks, I suppose.'

'Laters.'

In a moment of sheer dread I considered carrying on down the stairs, leaving without meeting her eyes and pretending the last thirty seconds hadn't happened. I put my phone in my pocket, with the diary and coke, and looked up at her.

She took a breath and a few of the waiting tears worked their way out. 'Who was that?'

'Listen, don't panic,' I said, marvelling at how ridiculous it sounded. 'Listen to me. In a couple of minutes some officers are going to arrive and ask you to go down to the hospital to identify someone. Can you get ahold of Pat?'

'I've tried, he's not answering...' She came down a few steps. 'What do you mean *identify* someone? You mean they've found something, don't you?'

'I don't know yet.'

Why had I come back? Why hadn't I just stayed in my car? Why hadn't I just stayed at home and avoided this mess?

She came closer but still stayed above me. 'Don't *fucking* lie.'

It would be an insult to deny it. She knew more than that. It was admirable that she found the control to keep talking, even with the tears rolling down her cheeks from red eyes that the grief hadn't yet caught up with.

'I think it's her,' I said, softly, as if that would make it easier. 'Is there any other way of calling Pat?'

She looked away. 'He's not answering. Neither are his friends.'

The tears were still coming but it was just formality, an imitation of a natural reaction to cover the shock.

'How are you sure?' she asked.

'The clothes, he said.'

'Right...'

For a second, I was worried she might faint.

I heard a car pull up outside and she put a hand to her eyes. 'Oh God, where the fuck is Pat...?'

There was a knock, a pause, and then the sound of the doorbell. I moved aside so she could pass me, rubbing her eyes as she opened the door.

The officers were in uniform, young and grave.

'Mrs Dyer?'

She nodded but said nothing. She didn't invite them in so they carried on talking.

'We're very sorry, but we need either you or your husband to come with us to identify a body that was recently found.' The officer glanced at me over her shoulder, hovering three steps up, trying to stay out of sight. 'If both of you—'

'I'm not Pat Dyer,' I said quickly. 'I'm... a friend.'

I could feel the fear emanating from her in cold waves.

'Do you have any way of getting in contact with Mr Dyer?'

'No,' she said. 'No, he's not answering his phone.'

'I can drive you,' I offered. Why, I didn't know. It came out like an attack of Tourette's.

She wasn't looking at me but she nodded.

It was quarter past three.

Welcome to hell, indeed.

We were taken to the viewing room. Hospitals all had the same smell as prisons. I looked over my shoulder out of habit, into all the rooms, sizing up the inmates as I had in juvie.

Clare hadn't spoken in the car and she didn't speak now.

The outline that we could see through the pane of glass, under the white sheet, looked smaller than I had expected. I felt sick all of a sudden. She might have looked older in the photograph but she was only a child, really. They always looked their age when they were dead.

They pulled the sheet back and Clare recoiled.

I stepped forwards. The first thing I noticed, which drew me towards the glass in fascination, was that her face was gone. This wasn't the usual purple bruising and fractures; it was total obliteration. I tried to focus on the point where her jaw ended and her neck began but, even with the blood cleaned away as best they could, I failed to find it.

Clare had only needed to look once.

She started crying with her back to the glass and I stayed silent, hanging back. I had tried my best to warn her of what she was going to see in the car but she probably hadn't heard me.

The officers moved away to give us space that I didn't want.

'No no no no no no…'

I saw her knees buckle and managed to get to her in time to slow her descent to the floor. I was on my knees, holding her and unable to stop. I felt her tears stain through my shirt. It should have been Pat here instead of me and I hated him for it. Hate, fear and some alien feeling caught in my throat, making it hard to breathe. I went on to autopilot, doing what

23

I thought other people would do with another man's wife shuddering with grief in their arms; stroking her hair, soft as I had thought it would be; saying, 'It's all right, it's all right, it's all right, it's all right...' even though it wasn't. It was never going to be all right.

I didn't know how long I went on telling her that before I saw the officers returning and knew it was time for us to go.

'Come on, let's go home.'

No response.

I glanced at the officers, nodded as if to say 'Give us a second' and took a breath.

'Hey,' I said, looking down at her. 'Hey, um... Clare.'

She looked at me but there was only a flicker of acknowledgement in her face.

My breath stopped in my chest and I swallowed. 'Come on, we need to get you home. Can you stand for me?'

Slowly, she nodded.

I helped her up and half walked, half carried her out.

In the car there were no words from either of us. She rested her forehead against the window, watching yellow lights go by.

The clock on the dashboard said 05:48.

As we approached the house I saw that the Mercedes was back. I opened the car door for her and walked her to the front door. Pat answered on the second ring of the bell, stood up too straight in his suit, looking as though he was trying his hardest not to lean on anything.

Clare left my side and slapped him.

He didn't say anything, didn't even meet her eyes.

She looked him up and down, her lip shaking, and walked inside.

I could still smell her perfume on my clothes.

Pat took a long breath through his nose and said, 'You Nic?'

I nodded. 'I'm sorry.'

His face contorted. 'You can... you can go... I'll call you.'

As I walked back down their path I inhaled deeply, trying to clear my head. An unforgiving wind started howling and when I got into my car the temperature read −4. No one was going to find comfort tonight.

CHAPTER THREE

When I woke up I could feel sunlight on my face and my eyelids were encrusted with sleep. My shoulders were aching, propped up with cushions, and when I managed to prise my eyes open I realized I had fallen asleep on the sofa.

I sat up and Emma's diary slid off my stomach on to the floor.

'Ah, fuck.'

I looked at my watch.

'Wo.'

It was almost midday and the shock propelled me to my feet. I wavered, blinking, until the room came into enough focus for me to locate my mobile on the coffee table. There were no messages from Russia. My flatmate, Mark Chester, had been away for over a month now and I only had five texts to show for it.

I turned in the direction of the kitchen for coffee, decided that I didn't have time, and went into the bathroom instead. It wasn't good. I had a meeting with Edie Franco about a new job in forty-five minutes, and turning up looking like the casualty of a cheap stag weekend wasn't how I wanted to project my professional image.

'Jesus…'

I dashed some water on my face, took off my shirt and noticed I'd written something on the back of my hand.

'Who is K?'

A recent section of Emma's diary came back to me.

'Went for another p/u with K. Imagining Dad's face, LOL.'

I looked at the reminder again before washing it off, and sprayed some deodorant over the lingering smell of sweat and perfume.

Edie Franco owned one of Mark's favourite nightclubs: the Underground. Direct, impossibly blonde and built like a Valkyrie, she came across as the sort of woman with whom you would be lucky to survive a sexual encounter. She was winking at forty, but you couldn't tell.

I was half an hour late but, as I should have expected, she was later. I managed to drink two cups of coffee at the bar before she arrived with a gust of sleet and freezing wind. She was wearing a red coat that covered everything down to her knees and her handshake was more of a firm stroke.

'I missed those swimming-pool-blue eyes!'

'Edie.' I pulled away briskly after she kissed me on the cheek. 'You want anything to drink?'

There was no apology for the time. 'Coffee, black.'

I nodded at the barman. 'I'll have the same.'

'Move to the sofas?' She indicated her head and started walking.

I followed her to a spot away from the doors and sat down opposite her. It felt better to have a table between us.

'Haven't heard from you in a while?' I said.

'Life's been sweet, what can I say? You get married, you have a kid, you open a club, you think about another kid...' She crossed her legs, slipped off her coat. 'Get divorced, call up a beautiful man... don't worry, that's not where you come in...'

The barman came over and put down two coffees.

I looked at mine, smiling, but didn't touch it. 'I'm, er... sorry to hear that.'

'Sorry about the divorce or the beautiful man?' She raised her eyebrows and her expression became coy, wide eyes blackened with theatrical make-up. 'Well, sometimes people just grow away from each other, or too close to other people, or several, whatever.'

I smiled.

'You ever wanted to have kids, Dominic? Pass on that hot side-profile?' She turned her head so I could admire hers, the same nose and full lips.

'Looks better on you,' I said, picking up my coffee.

Another festive song was playing. I looked up at the fake holly pinned to the spirit shelf. There was still a month to go but Christmas was everywhere.

'Sad, isn't it? Working over Christmas.' There was a pause as she followed my eyeline up to the lights. 'Sometimes the evenings look so beautiful from my office I can barely stand to walk home alone... I rarely do, that's probably why we're here, huh?'

'Sidney.' It had dawned on me what the job was. *Who* it was. 'It's Sidney, isn't it? Something to do with the divorce?'

Silence.

I shook my head. 'Damn, Edie, you know I don't like to—'

'You don't like to know why. Isn't that how you work?'

I put the coffee down, too high on caffeine already and unable to look at her directly. 'Domestic disputes, come on, I thought you were above this sort of thing?'

'He wants my son. What am I above? Love?'

I pointed a finger. 'Now *that's* what I don't like to work with!'

'I can't go to court.'

'You mean you w—'

'I can't go to court!'

'You—'

'I *won't win*!' Her fist slammed on to the table and coffee dashed across the polished surface. 'I… won't win.'

The background chatter waned for a moment and I looked over my shoulder, worried about how much attention we were drawing to ourselves.

Edie sat back, touched her hair and looked at the spilt coffee. When she spoke again every word was controlled.

'I won't win in court.'

'You're the mother, you always win.'

'I won't.'

There was an intensity in her face that I found difficult to match. It was why she was such a good businesswoman; every expression was inherently threatening.

'Why?' I asked, even though I didn't want to, even though I could have done it without knowing.

'He had someone follow me, for quite a while, recording… things. If it gets out, which he has threatened it will, I'll never see Scott again.'

'So what do you want me to do? Just destroy the recordings?'

'I'll pay for whatever you need to do to stop them getting out. *Anything*. Understand?'

I nodded.

'You want anything upfront?'

'No, it's all right.' I picked up my bag and got out ten pounds for the coffees.

'Who are you walking home with?' she asked.

I shook her hand and smiled when she held on to it for much longer than was necessary. 'I'm not going home, and I could do without any dodgy internet tapes.'

'Worked for Paris Hilton.'

'I'll give it some thought.' I kissed her hand. 'Merry Christmas.'

Red Café, Kentish Town.

I stirred four sugars into my tea with a stiff shoulder when my mobile rang.

HARRIET MOBILE.

I ignored it. I always did my best to ignore my sister and it wasn't difficult. She spent most of her time on the floors of council flats injecting smack into her thighs.

My older brother, Tony, was also unreachable but for different reasons. He was flying helicopters in Afghanistan and rarely found the time to call. The last time he had tried I had been on a job and had my phone switched off, and since then I'd heard nothing.

It was for the best really, that we had grown so far apart as adults. We all had our shame to hide. Namely the fact that despite our relatively privileged upbringings, fully functional parents and decent educations, our method of rebellion seemed to be single-handedly fucking our lives up.

Brinks arrived with rain and grease in his hair.

'Why here?' he asked, shaking water off his coat.

'They do great sausage sandwiches.' I pushed one of the plates across the table at him. 'Cumberland, they use.'

Brinks put a folder down next to the plate, fidgeting in the chair. 'I got some of what you wanted. Most of the photos and some of the initial statements.'

Already Brinks was earning his money. The man was a natural double agent and I wouldn't be surprised if there was an extensive list of people paying him for information. If he was classier, less desperate and more educated, he could be doing a lot more with his talent.

30

I flicked through the folder but decided against taking out the photos yet.

'DNA?'

'I'll let you know.'

My hand hovered over the folder again. 'Toxicology?'

'Shit, it's early days, Nic, calm down.'

I warmed my hands around my tea. 'Can you talk me through the statement? Taxi driver, you said?'

'I can't give you his name yet, not until we've charged him or released him, but he's a strong suspect even beyond what we'd assume anyway. And there's no point looking at me like that. I'm not going to tell you because I'd actually like a chance to question him before you' – he gestured in mid-air – 'do your thing.'

'Do my *thing*?' I raised my eyebrows even higher. 'What? Strut my funky stuff?'

'Stop being a dick.'

It was like winding up a precocious child. I got out my tobacco and started rolling a cigarette. 'Have you talked to the parents yet?'

'I actually just came from there.'

'And?'

'To be expected. Mother's a state, the father's aggressive; all in all not the nicest way to spend the morning.' He looked out of the window at the rain. 'How well do you know Pat Dyer?'

'I wouldn't really say I *know* him.' I started dissecting my sandwich with the cigarette behind my ear, willing him to shut up and leave me alone to look at the folder. 'Seen him around a few times but nothing intimate, if that's what you mean.'

'Oh yeah?'

I couldn't help smirking. 'Stop trying to talk like a DCI, Geoff, it really doesn't suit you.'

Brinks looked back at the window with hurt pride in his eyes. Looking at him was like watching for the onset of rigor mortis in a living human.

I asked, 'You want some tea?'

'Fuck you.'

He got up and walked out.

The man behind the counter brought over another mug.

I smiled at him and got out the photos, face down. When I was sure no one could see them but me I turned them over one by one and ran my eyes over them in detail.

One of her hands had fallen open around a can of Pepsi. None of her nails were broken but her chest was concave, collapsed, as if someone had stamped on it over and over. Her face was the same and her neck, crushed. There was something about the lack of blood, and the way her body had fallen, that made me uneasy. I would have expected more from a head shot.

Everything about it looked rushed, amateurish and chaotic. Why hadn't the killer disposed of her clothes properly for a start? Why leave her in a place that was so easy to access? All that had shielded her from the end of the alleyway was a scattering of bin liners and a skip. She'd been dropped there with the carelessness of someone throwing away dead batteries.

My mobile started ringing and I put the photos back in the folder.

'Hello?'

'Is this a good time?' Pat sounded more docile than he had a day ago.

'Fine, fine.'

'Can you make it round to mine?'

'Are you sure you don't need more time to...?'

'More time to what?'

Silence.

I faltered. 'What time is best for you?'

'Anytime. I'll be here.'

For a second, the dislike gave way to pity.

'OK, I'll be over in a couple of hours.'

I hadn't expected a call this soon. Denial didn't usually set in this early, but Pat struck me as the sort of person who powered through life that way, dealing with adversity by filling his schedule and frantically ticking days off the calendar.

I put the folder into my bag to look at later, wishing that I had switched off my phone and let Edie walk me home.

CHAPTER FOUR

Pat answered the door with a glass in his hand and stubble on his chin.

I suspected that the clear liquid wasn't water. 'You wanted to talk?'

'Yeah... yeah, come in.'

The air inside the house was thick and hot. Pat went into the huge kitchen and refilled his glass. He hadn't changed out of his suit; it was more creased and carried a heavy stench of smoke.

I dropped my bag by the door and followed.

'Want any?' he asked.

'Bit early for me, thanks.'

'Bet you've seen the reports and all... in your line of work?' Grey eyes glared over the rim of the glass. 'You've seen the photos?'

'I've seen a few. Most of it I haven't been able to see yet.'

'But you've seen the photos?'

I knew what he was thinking. No father would ever want another man to see his daughter like that.

'I'm sorry,' I said.

'Oh, that's nice,' he sneered. 'I've always wondered about your types. Do you enjoy looking at stuff like that?'

I stayed silent but my chest tightened.

He was rubbing his eyes, trying to rub the image of his daughter out of them.

'How's your wife?' I asked, the question like a lead weight on my tongue.

'Upstairs.' He didn't answer the question but refilled his glass, downing it and refilling it again. 'Did you see what he did to her?'

'I know, it's sick.'

'Fucking *cunt* puts his hands on her... on my baby...' Downing the glass and refilling it with shaking hands. 'I want you to find him. I'll pay you anything, I just want you to find him.'

Any words of sympathy or comfort were strangled. It wouldn't help.

'Do you want some coffee?' I asked in an attempt to defuse the atmosphere.

He nodded, fingering a notch on the edge of the dining table.

I put the kettle on and opened the window to let some fresh air in. The anger and the fear were clamped around my limbs like a straitjacket.

'Do you know if Emma had a boyfriend?' I opened cupboards, searching for sugar.

'She broke up with Danny.'

'So she wasn't seeing anyone new?'

'No...' He shook his head, picking at a splinter. 'She would have mentioned it.'

'What was her friend's name?'

'It was Jenny who she was meeting, Jenny Hillier.'

'Do you mind if I speak to her, just to ask her a couple of questions?'

He shrugged, his finger bleeding. 'Sure, I can give you her number.'

I nodded and strained the coffee.

'Black,' Pat said. 'Just black.'

'Shall I take one upstairs?'

'Whatever. She won't speak to you.' He didn't seem to care. I hovered with two coffees in my hands.

'I'll find him,' I said. 'I don't want more than twenty grand, I'll find him.'

'Don't kill him.' Pat looked up from his coffee with blank eyes. 'You won't kill him until I see him. I want to make him hurt, I want to make him fucking *bleed*.'

'I know.' I glanced upwards again and indicated with the coffee. 'I'm just going to…'

He waved a hand, apparently losing interest in my actions.

I left the kitchen and went upstairs; pictures glared at me from every wall. All the doors were shut apart from one, which was ajar. There was no light inside. I nudged it open with my shoulder and she looked up sharply from where she was sitting on the floor beside the bed, knees brought close to her chest.

'Sorry… It's er, me. I was just bringing some coffee.'

She didn't acknowledge me but looked away again. Her clothes were unchanged but she looked thinner under them. Still the grey cocktail dress and cardigan, still dressed for the missed social occasion.

'Can I get you anything else?' I came inside and put the coffee down on the dressing table. 'Something to eat?'

The side of her face was shiny with tears and the blue eyes were shot with red.

I couldn't put my arms around her this time, not like before, so I sat down beside her instead, mirroring her pose. A few minutes went by before I realized how cold it was. I reached up past her and held the cup of coffee in front of her face.

'You should warm up,' I said.

Eventually, when I refused to move, she took it without looking at me and rested it on her knees. When she brushed her hair behind her ear I noticed a new bruise on her wrist next to the old scars.

I stood up, went back downstairs and saw that my bag had disappeared from where I had left it by the door. I stared at the doormat as if it might appear, rerunning through the memory of letting it drop from my hand.

I whirled around, thinking of the photos, and saw Pat sitting at the kitchen table. As I came closer I saw them, spread out in a collage of blood and open wounds. Pat was leaning over, looking far too closely, eyes right up against the glossy prints, against the bin liners and blood and naked skin that he had once called his daughter.

My bag was by the foot of his chair.

I saw his fist tighten around the glass as he heard my footsteps.

'Hey!' My hand went for the photos.

He grabbed the front of my shirt and the glass hit the floor.

'Fucking *what*!' he snarled.

I slammed his arm into the granite worktop and twisted it up behind him. The alcohol gave me the advantage over his superior height.

'Don't touch me again.'

'Fuck off,' he spat through gritted teeth.

My heart was pounding. 'Don't you *dare* fucking touch me again.'

'I won't! Get off!' Pat wrenched his arm away, swaying. He put a hand to his mouth and vomited a dark grey mixture of vodka and bile into the sink.

I gathered the photos and picked up my bag.

Pat leant against the counter, his lips resting against his fist and his eyes on the window. He was shaking.

'I'm... sorry,' I said.

It took him a while to speak.

'No one's fault but mine,' he replied.

I was parked on a kerb in the Audi, blowing cigarette smoke out of the window in the direction of Edie's house. It was a stylized, calculated assault of modernity, very much like the woman herself. It was all glass and right angles; so modern it was almost ironic.

At least it used to be her house. I doubted whether she still lived there. I didn't know what time Sidney usually got home, but I had no better way to spend the afternoon. He might have been out, taking his son somewhere, maybe visiting family...

Best to have nothing to lose.

That was how I had always done things. Apart from the firearms and the roof over my head and other transient objects there was nothing to become attached to. Friends and relatives and children were for people who could hold a conversation for more than ten minutes without wanting to beat the other person into the floor, who could handle small talk and network and do all of the things people were required to do in social situations.

When I had finished my third cigarette I switched my phone back on to keep myself amused. I sank down in my seat, put my feet up on the dashboard and scrolled through text messages.

The writing on my hand was still visible.

'Who is K?'

Thinking back to the photos now, and the blood, I was almost certain Emma had been moved.

The phone started vibrating and I answered it because I was too bored to ignore it any more.

'Hey, it's me.'

'Yeah, I know.' I shut my eyes at the sound of my sister's harsh cockney twang. 'What do you want, Harriet?'

'Er, I need a favour…'

'How did I guess?'

'I'm not doing too good. I had this fight and I got fired and… I just need a little bit of cash. Just a little bit; I'll pay you back, I promise. It's just until I find another job.'

It was almost funny, the regularity and predictability of these requests.

'Why were you fired?' I asked.

'It wasn't my fault.'

'It never is.' I rubbed my eyes. 'So what happened to the last five hundred I gave you?'

She hesitated. What was most insulting was that she didn't even bother to sound convincing. Like other addicts I had come across she didn't speak for herself any more; everything she said was a stock phrase used on everybody in order to get what she wanted. When one didn't work she moved on to another.

'Um… well, I had to pay off a few debts, and—'

'Don't give me that shit, it went to your fucking dealer.'

There was a silence.

'I only need a couple of hundred, just to pay off this debt and pay my rent and then I'm done, I promise. Oh come on, it's not as if you need it!'

She had managed to go from self-pity to excuses and then on to anger in less than a minute. I had the option, as I did every time, to tell her to piss off and make her own way, but even as I entertained the thought I knew it would never happen. I hated her sometimes, most of the time these days, but not nearly as much as I hated myself for giving her the money.

'Yeah, you're always a couple of hundred quid away from being *done,* aren't you?' I said. 'It would be nice to hear a promise from you one day that I think you might actually keep.'

'Oh please, I really need to pay this guy off and I don't have anywhere else to—'

'OK, Harriet, *OK.*' I just wanted the call to be over. 'How much do you want, two hundred?'

'Er, could you make it three?'

I shook my head, fist tightening around the wheel. 'Fine, three hundred. You can come and pick it up yourself, I'm not gonna waste any petrol money on you.'

'Thanks, Nic, I promise—'

'Whatever.'

I ended the call. Our parents gave her money too; it wasn't just me, but that didn't make me feel much better. Sometimes I caught myself wishing that our childhoods had been harder, more traumatic from an early age. I wished that Dad had been stricter or Mum had drunk too much, that either of them had done anything to unburden us of the responsibility for how our lives had turned out. It wasn't their fault, none of this was, but that was the problem.

Tony was the only one who refused to pay. I knew she had stopped asking him years ago, way before he went to Afghanistan. She had stopped seeing him because he was of no use to her, and around the same time I had also started avoiding him. I suspected the real reason was that he reminded us too much of our own failures, but I didn't like to dwell on it.

Sidney's car pulled into the driveway across the road.

It was half past four.

I memorized the number plate and watched Edie's son, Scott, walking up the drive holding a gym bag. He looked in his early teens and held himself like his mother. Sidney was tall, Scandinavian, square-jawed. From the one time I had met him in Edie's club a few years ago I remembered that he was quite softly spoken for someone with his build.

I checked my watch again, just to be sure. Time was almost an obsession to me; it had to be, in my line of work. Nothing was more crucial than timing.

Two more minutes had passed.

It didn't look like an easy house to break into, I thought. Someone would have to let me in, or I'd have to find another method of coercion...

I started the engine and pulled away.

CHAPTER FIVE

I dreaded going back to that house, but Pat wasn't answering his mobile so I had no choice. I stopped at a petrol station and tried to eat a bacon sandwich while sitting half in and half out of the driver's seat. Seeing my reflection in the rear-view mirror made me think of my mum and 'Dominic, you don't eat properly!'

I should call her, I thought, but the token gesture wouldn't make much difference. I should have been a better son in many ways.

I put the rest of the sandwich on the passenger seat and lit a cigarette instead. When I had finished that I lit another and smoked it as I drove, CD player off, radio on, 'education cuts', flicking ash out of the window and thinking about the scars on her wrists. Clare turned into Emma, Emma turned into blood, into darkness, into weeds and crushed Pepsi cans.

As the house came into view I exhaled, looked in the mirror and looked away just as quickly. I stopped, rehearsing half-formed questions as I got out and walked up to the door with my eyes on the windows.

I rang the bell and waited.

Rain started to soak through the back of my coat.

'He's not in.'

The life was drained from her skin; brittle cheekbones showed beneath clingfilm.

'How long will he be?' I asked.

'He usually comes back for lunch. You can wait if you like.'

I would rather have waited in the car but it would have been rude to refuse.

The air was stale and dust floated in the shafts of light. In the kitchen she turned to face me and her voice was heavy like the air.

'Do you want a cup of tea or something?'

'Yeah, sure.'

'How do you...?' She swallowed, the words coming out in fractured sighs. 'How do you take...?'

I was about to tell her not to worry about it but she was already crying. *Fuck, she's crying.* I resisted the urge to panic and took an involuntary step forwards.

'Um...' I implored my brain for something appropriate to say but came up with nothing. 'Hey, come on.'

'I'm sorry,' she said, over and over through her hands. 'I'm sorry...'

I touched her shoulder, stepped closer and stood with my arm around her until the tears subsided. It wasn't until I felt her start to calm down and I moved away that I realized how tense I was.

'I'm really sorry,' she said again, sitting down at the dining table and holding the palm of her hand against her forehead. 'I just keep crying all the time, I can't... stop crying, it's pathetic.'

'It's fine.' I folded my arms and smiled awkwardly. 'I don't really want a cup of tea.'

She laughed, or at least made the brief motion of laughing.

I watched the rain hitting the windows in grey sheets and sat down with her.

'Has anyone been round?' I asked.

'Just a few friends and Pat's friends, people he works with.

I don't know why they bothered, it's not as if any of them actually know her…'

'Can I let some air in?'

She shrugged. 'If you like.'

I stood up and opened all the windows. Breathing in their house was like inhaling sand.

'So you're working for Pat now? Officially?'

'Yeah.' I spoke down at the worktop. 'I know you don't like that.'

'No.'

I looked up and she was still watching me.

'You'll find him?' she said. It was more of a statement than a question.

'That's what I'm being paid for.'

'And what then?'

I struggled to look at her and was perplexed as to why. Something about her induced an overwhelming sense of unease. There was guilt there too, which I wasn't used to.

'I know what you do,' she said.

'It's hardly recreation. I do what I'm good at, like Pat does.' I met her eyes again and they were blank. It was a cheap shot to take. I didn't know if it was shame that made me redden. 'I just do as I'm asked.'

'What you're paid to.'

'Exactly.'

It sounded more defensive than I intended.

Silence.

'Emma didn't have a boyfriend?' I asked, for what felt like the thousandth time.

'She broke up with Danny. She didn't mention anyone else.'

'No one?'

44

'I don't think so.'

'Can I go over this again? You both called her but her phone was off?'

'Well, it was ringing but she never answered.'

'Right.' I paused. 'If it's OK with you, I'd really like to ask Jenny Hillier a couple of questions.'

Her eyes were full of fury when she looked at me again, so much so that it almost made me take a step back.

'How did you find out her name?'

'Pat told me.' I chanced a smile. 'No subterfuge involved. I'd tell her I'm a private detective working on Pat's behalf and ask her a few questions about when she was due to meet Emma and if she saw or heard anything suspicious. That's all, I promise.'

I doubted that my word would be worth much to her.

She watched the tabletop, picking at the same splinter that Pat had. 'Well, you'll get her number off Pat anyway.'

'That wasn't why I was asking. If you don't want me to speak to her then I won't.'

'What you're paid for, right?' There was a hint of sarcasm in her voice.

'Within reason.'

'There's nothing *reasonable* about it.'

The bruise on her wrist had faded, I noticed. My gaze moved from her hands to her neck. Every part of her looked so fragile. Her daughter had been the same. I could see the blood from those scars on her wrists against translucent skin, bruises on her neck…

I caught her eyes and averted mine, tasting copper on my tongue.

She took her hands off the table.

'Maybe you should come back later,' she said.

'Yeah, maybe.' I picked up my bag and felt dirty for looking at her again. 'So I'll ask Pat for Jenny's number then?'

'Yeah, you do that.'

I wasn't sure how to leave, standing in another man's doorway, thinking about another man's wife with the taste of blood in my mouth.

'You should eat something,' I said.

'He's not paying you to care.'

I hated the contempt in her tone, hated that it stung. I walked back to the car with my head down against the rain and I had no idea why she made me feel so much shame.

Pat sent me a text while I was driving, asking me to meet him in some bar in Victoria where I guessed he had been for most of the day. As I was reading it I almost mounted the kerb and some woman started shouting at me.

I didn't want to go, but I had little choice. I drove there because he was paying me, and struggled to park.

When I found Pat inside he was going through his iPhone, and he barely looked up when I stood beside him. The place was crowded, full of university students and draped in silver tinsel, but there was a respectful space around us. Pat commanded that sort of reaction.

'Why wouldn't she have tried to call me if she was in trouble?' he said.

'Sometimes people panic. They don't react how they should.'

'I'd be the first person she'd tell if someone had been giving her hassle, I know I would.' He searched his Received Calls again and clenched his fist around the phone. 'I'm her *father*, for fuck's sake!'

'You want anything else?' A girl with metallic red hair leant across the bar.

'Yeah, another vodka and orange.' Pat pushed away his empty glass without looking up, scrolling through the list of numbers until he surrendered to the fact that what he was looking for didn't exist.

'Soda water and lime, please,' I said, smiling and handing her a fiver.

She gave me the once-over and moved away.

'Nic,' Pat said, taking off his suit jacket and laying it across the bar. 'You know sometimes I call her mobile seven or eight times an hour just to hear her voice, you know, asking me to leave a message.'

It was hard to hate him at times like these, despite his superiority complex and the vacant despondency in his wife's eyes.

'It's normal, I think.'

'Have you ever lost anybody? I mean, do you have kids?'

The answer to both was no, but I suspected that wasn't the answer he was looking for, so I lied for the sake of normality. 'Lost somebody, yeah. Kids, no way.'

'Makes sense, I suppose. But you know, you go through all these things, falling in love, getting married and all… that.' He gestured in the air with his drink. 'But until you have kids… When you have kids, if you do… you'll be fucking shocked at the capacity you have to love something.'

He ran a hand through his hair.

I nodded as if I understood, but of course I didn't. I understood pain, could give a master class in it, but this went beyond that. It was like a virus in the soul, something that killed you slowly from the inside.

'You do coke?' He met my eyes for the first time since I had come in and his pupils were fiercely dilated.

'Not while I'm working.'

'Then you smoke,' he said, indicating his head.

I nodded and followed him outside the doors of the pub where we lit our respective cigarettes. It was drizzling. Across the street there was a scattering of blue and red Christmas lights. The only times I had taken coke were with Mark, in our flat before nights out, or wedged into the cubicle of a nightclub toilet, but there were easier habits to maintain. My sister was better at that sort of recreation, but it seemed a sad thing to do alone.

'All right, Pat?'

Pat looked up without a flicker of recognition at the young man who had approached us.

'All right... er, mate. How are you?' he said with the grace of a seasoned celebrity.

'Oh never mind me, how are you doing? I heard about your daughter, man, I'm so sorry. It's horrible, just horrible.' The guy nodded at me, pulling a beanie hat down over his ears.

'Oh.' Pat managed to tighten his lips slightly in an imitation of a smile. 'Thanks.'

'You got anything on who did it yet? The filth find anything?'

'No.'

There was a silence.

'OK, er, well, I hope you're OK and everything. I hope your missus is OK too.'

Pat nodded.

'OK, well... see you around.'

We watched him leave. It occurred to me that for every client and lackey Pat must have a dozen enemies.

'Do you know anyone who would hold a grudge against you for any reason? I asked, taking long drags to combat the cold. 'Someone you had a fight with? Anyone who would want to get to you?'

'It's crossed my mind.' He exhaled for a long time. 'Thought it was only a matter of time before you asked me that, but still seems easier not to think about it, even though it might help... It wouldn't make it easier if it was random, *easier* isn't the right word, but to think that someone might have done this because of me...'

He shook his head and dropped his cigarette to the ground.

'I have other leads to follow,' I said. 'If you want more time.'

'Time, huh...' He snorted and turned to go back inside.

I stayed, watching the drizzle turn into a dense mist. Paul McCartney was playing from a Wetherspoon's nearby and I couldn't listen to it for long. It was too early; festivity forced on us to try and dilute the hopelessness of things.

I stubbed out the remains of my cigarette and went back inside, feeling short of breath.

I only caught a few words of the argument before reaching Pat, who was face to face with some college student with a fucking awful haircut and an upturned nose.

'That's my drink you've got there,' Pat said, taking his suit jacket off the bar and putting it on.

The kid frowned at him and replied in a painfully thick southern accent, 'No, I think you'll find it's mine.'

'No.' Pat's voice was a growl, full of nicotine and coke as he buttoned the jacket and pulled up his sleeves. 'I *think* you'll find it's mine. You preppy cunt!' he added as an afterthought.

'I don't think so.' The kid glanced at his friends and actually dared to smirk, looking him up and down again. It wasn't his fault, really. He had no idea how much danger he was in.

'Put it down.'

I glanced downwards and saw Pat's fists shaking by his sides. I wanted to warn him off but I was too conscious of the crowd.

'Put it *down*,' Pat repeated.

'Now look here—'

Pat took him by the collar and yanked him away from the bar, ignoring the stunned expressions following him out. The drink hit the floor by my foot and vodka and orange flew over my shoes.

I pushed through the mass of people.

'Pat!' I shouted as I fought my way out of the front doors. 'Pat, leave him! Leave him!'

Pat threw the kid to the pavement and stamped on his arm until I heard it snap.

The kid was screaming so loud that it drowned out the traffic. There was a collective gasp behind me from the windows and the doorway and I froze, loath to get involved.

Pat kicked him once and then lifted the kid up by his shirt and punched him, again and again and again until there was so much blood I couldn't watch any more.

'Pat!'

I caught his arm and was dragged forwards with the momentum of the next blow. My feet left the ground for a moment and I was whirled around in mid-air. When I hit the deck I stumbled backwards over the kid on the pavement. I landed on my back and a car passed behind my head close enough to make everything blur with adrenalin.

As I scrambled to my feet Pat pushed me away, almost sending me back into the road. His eyes were black. 'Fuck off!'

I punched him across the face, hoping that the shock would be enough to make him stop.

He held his jaw for a moment, not taking his eyes off me, but when he straightened up I could see it was over.

I backed away slowly and crouched down to help the kid to his feet. There was blood everywhere, distorting his facial features, and his arm was held at a strange angle across his chest.

'Come on, come on, up you come.'

The screaming had stopped and been replaced with gasping. When I took his other arm around my shoulders I could feel him quivering.

No one had followed us outside. No one had dared.

I walked the kid inside and ordered him an Irish whiskey from the same barmaid, who regarded me with wide eyes. I couldn't resist smiling at her as I took the drink.

'Drink that,' I ordered as I sat him down at the back of the room.

He took a gulp and started coughing. 'Fuck... fuck, he broke my fucking arm!'

'Calm down and call 999. You got off lucky.' I leant in slightly across the table, so that no one else would hear. 'If you press charges and fuck with him again in court, I doubt you'll be so lucky next time.'

I patted him on the cheek, straightened my coat and left with my head up. It wasn't as if anyone here knew who I was.

It didn't take long to spot the silver Mercedes and I crossed the road after a hundred yards. It was only then that my breathing started to return to normal and my muscles began twitching from the sudden action.

I brushed ash and rainwater off the back of my jeans

Pat was sitting with his hands around the wheel, unmoving, and I got into the passenger seat beside him.

Silence.

'So, your place or mine?' he said.

'You can't drive like this.'

'I can do what I like.'

'You'll kill someone.'

'You care? Ironic.' He looked sideways at me, smirking. 'Can't believe I let myself take a punch from a guy with a mullet.'

'It's not... Ah, fuck it.'

I sighed and leant my elbow against the window. When I looked at Pat again he was observing the blood on his knuckles, hands still around the wheel.

'Give me the keys, I'll drive you back.'

'Like fuck—'

'Shut up and give me the keys.' I held out my hand.

After a small hesitation he got them out of his pocket and opened the door. 'Should have known you'd be a tricky cunt with a surname like yours.'

By the time I had returned to Victoria to pick up my car dusk was falling. It was only four o'clock. Brinks had sent me a text so I took a detour on my way home and parked a little way up his street.

A procession of charity workers, a woman with five or six little ones, was moving down the road from door to door. The smallest kids, who looked about four or five, were dressed as angels, probably to take advantage of December being so imminent. I watched them for as long as social appearance would allow before getting out of my car, thinking about what Pat had said. I found the idea of my life being so dangerously intertwined with someone else abhorrent.

Brinks was smoking outside his back door when he saw me appear in his garden.

52

'For fuck's sake!' He hastened away from the door to the side of the house where I stopped and loitered in the drizzle. 'She'll see you if she looks out of the window, you know.'

'Aw, you're ashamed of me?'

'Fuck off.' He ushered me back into the alley beside the house, where we stood beside a muddied yellow tricycle.

'I got your message saying you wanted to meet,' I said.

'And you thought you'd come to my *house* again?'

'Well, yeah.' Hands in my pockets, shivering. 'What have you got for me?'

Brinks's indignation didn't last long. It never did.

'I couldn't get you much. We've interviewed the girl she was meant to be meeting, Jenny Hillier, and her story checks out. Her grief seemed genuine enough; we don't think she's lying.'

'What was her story?'

'That she was meant to be meeting Emma outside Tottenham Court Road tube station so they could go to a friend's house. Emma never turned up and her mobile was switched off so she assumed she was ill and went to the friend's house on her own. She didn't know anything about the situation until Pat called her in the evening looking for Emma.'

'Anything else crop up from the post-mortem?'

'She hadn't been drinking and there was no evidence of drug use either.' He blew smoke into the wind, into my face. 'There were two semen samples.'

The silhouette in my mind became two. It was a horrible image.

'Really?'

'Mm, sick fuckers. Doesn't fit with the taxi driver though, if there were two. There's been no sign of an accomplice with this guy.'

'Can I have his name yet?'

'Ha! No way.' He made a smirk look painful. 'Another thing, there have been investigations into officers taking backhanders recently and there are a couple of eyes turned in my direction. It's a hot subject in the press and I know the superintendent is looking for someone to make an example of.'

It was a tired story, one I heard at least once every few months.

'Do you want more money?' I asked.

'I don't *want* anything.' His face was drawn, cheeks sunken above the cigarette. 'I just want to stop.'

'You can't, I've already paid you.'

'You can have it back!'

If I wasn't mistaken he looked on the verge of tears.

'You can't,' I said, perturbed by his expression. 'You've made your choice. I can't afford the hassle of finding someone else connected with the case.'

He opened his mouth as if to say something else and thought better of it.

There was nothing else he could say, in the dark and the yellow glow filtering through from the pavement, in the wind and the grey rain and blood on both our minds.

'Still,' he said eventually. 'The best we can do is hope she was shot first.'

'Oh yeah, that'll be a consolation for her parents... No fingerprints?'

It seemed futile now, this endless asking of questions.

'Yeah, but nothing that gives us any leads. Unless we have suspects we have nothing.'

'Someone must have seen something.'

'No, no.' He shook his head with a wry smile, and slowly

kicked the tricycle away, as if we were contaminating something innocent. 'People turn the other way.'

I knew what he meant. That wall of silence. That huge fucking insurmountable wall of silence and the closed curtains when I'd stabbed that kid. Banging my forehead against bloody bricks and lies and self-preservation...

'Thanks for your help,' I said.

'Mention it.' He stubbed his cigarette out against the wall. 'Don't come to my house again.'

I walked away through the side gate and across the road to my car.

Eight o'clock, four weeks before Christmas and the road was silent. Nothing but a few sad wreaths hung in doorways, the rain and silence.

Too much silence.

CHAPTER SIX

My flat was empty. I dropped my bag by the door and fell back on to the sofa. It was too big for one person, too sparse and full of blacks and whites, but there were rarely two of us.

After a while I got up, made a cup of tea, remembered that I should eat something later, and sat down with a notepad and pencil. I hadn't been allowed to keep the photo of Emma and my head hurt with all the names and faces crammed into it. I could feel the dull, deeply embedded ache at the front of my skull.

'Emma Dyer', I wrote.

'Pat Dyer'.

'Clare Dyer'.

I paused.

'Jenny Hillier'.

'Danny Maclaine'.

I tore off the list, ran my palm over the next page to remove any dust and sharpened the pencil. From the image of the photo in my memory I traced the outline of her face first, the clearest thing in my mind, then down to her neck and the mole on her collarbone. Her jawline was delicate and defined, like her mother's. Her hair came down over her right shoulder and was brushed behind her left ear.

It was something I had been aware of from a very young age: the ability to remember images in infinite detail and replicate them in pencil or charcoal. This usually wasn't necessary and was relegated to a hobby, but at times like this it was useful. It was also nice to know I would never need to carry around a notepad, like some hippy arts student.

My mind went blank and I sank into a semi-conscious trance as I spent the next two hours filling in the white space with her eyes, nose and the chip in her front tooth that made her smile just less than perfect. She had very defined eyebrows.

A few times I realized that something was wrong, that her eyes were too wide, too sad, and erased them.

My phone vibrated in my pocket, bringing me back into the room. I rubbed my eyes and read, SO VERY, VERY FUCKING COLD. BACK IN A FEW DAYS, DON'T DO ANYTHING I WOULDN'T DO. SCHASTLIVO! M XXXX

I couldn't help but smile at the prospect of Mark breaking the silence in here again, especially so close to Christmas. I opened the laptop and quickly Googled the Russian. It meant 'Be happy!' He had used it before but it was hard to remember.

My phone started vibrating again and I glanced at the clock before answering it. I recognized the number.

'Hi, Mackie. What's up?'

'Five grand if you get over here right now.'

Despite being quite a reputable drug dealer in his time, Mackenzie Woolstenholme's voice had never lost the nervous and hyperactive edge of a teenager talking to adults he didn't know.

'Everything all right?'

'Can't call anyone else over, this is a fuck-up, Nic, a real bloody fuck-up...'

'Slow down, what's happened?'

'I can't say over the phone, please, I just need someone I can fucking trust—'

'Jesus, all right. Give me a vague idea?'

'*Please*, please, I'll explain... I can't... Fuck, ten grand! Ten grand, if you like, just *get the fuck over here!*'

It was going to be horrific, I could tell. When you had seen the worst of what could push people to this kind of undignified desperation it became fascinating to see how it differed from person to person.

The image that immediately came to mind was a few months old. I'd sat in the corner of a lock-up smoking and waiting for Mark to finish pulling a paedophile's toenails out for a job, so that we could make it to the cinema in time for the trailers. I finished three cigarettes and the man didn't make a sound, enduring and resigned. Even Mark had looked impressed.

'OK, I'll come over now.'

'Oh God, thank you, thank you so much... I'll meet you outside.'

I ended the call and made sure I'd packed the boot of the car for all eventualities before I left: tape, hacksaws, gloves... I tried to remember the man's name as I drove, the man who had stayed so terminally silent, but it escaped me, like the rest of them.

Mackie appeared outside his house in the glare of my headlights, loitering at the side of the pavement with his hands clasped across his chest like a hitchhiker seeking penance. He was an unfortunate-looking man in his early fifties, but had always made up for his lack of aesthetic value with inane chatter and an ability to call anyone and everyone 'mate'.

I got out and he was at my shoulder, lip trembling through the stream of justification. 'Don't judge me, Nic, mate, please. There's no one else I could've called.'

'Ah, I've seen it all before.' I smiled, masking my curiosity as best I could. 'What happened?'

'I went to work and...' He led me up the front path and inside the doorway, looking up and down the road before shutting the door on us. 'When I came back... I can't go in there, I can't.'

The hallway smelt of smoke and dimly of incense, along with something else. An African mask leered down from a wall.

I followed the direction of his gesture to the living-room door and left him standing there, breathing through his teeth. The faint faecal smell became stronger.

I had an idea of what I was going to see. Whether it was an accident, suicide or the meticulous arrangement of a psychotic, they all looked the same after a while. There was rarely any identity. Body parts became no more than pieces of DIY shelving. You could see what they could have been and what they used to be, but we were all just wood and polystyrene.

'*Jesus!*' I opened the door, retched and had to look away for a moment, a hand over my mouth and bile burning the back of my throat.

Behind me Mackie was watching through his fingers, shaking his head.

'Jesus fucking Christ...'

The naked thing sitting on the right side of the leather sofa was the same shape as a man, but so much liquid strained the skin that every limb had become misshapen and balloon-like. It was riddled with broken blood vessels, shimmering where too much pressure had forced splits and caused unnameable fluid to ooze its way out.

Over its head was a plastic bag, misted and grey with death rasps, and on its feet, ankles bulging over the chic lines, was a pair of black stiletto heels.

'That...' I said, swallowing. 'That is quite fucking disgusting.'

'You can't tell, I fucking mean it, you can't tell *anyone*!'

'Why would I? I don't know who he is,' I said, dragging my eyes back to Mackie, who was shuddering with his hands over his eyes. 'Damn, it's not the most dignified way to go.'

'No, I mean you can't...' He was almost in tears; a hideous sight on any man. 'You can't tell anyone about me, about *this*.'

When it dawned on me what he was saying I couldn't help but laugh. Between this and the stilettos I was beginning to feel as though I was on a twisted hidden-camera show. But it was a refreshing novelty; it wasn't often I was faced with something I hadn't seen before.

'My God,' I said. 'You've got a dead fucker in heels in your living room to clean up and you're more worried about people knowing you're *gay*?'

'It's not fucking funny!' he spat, jabbing a finger. 'You think this is a joke?'

'Well, Mackie, come on...'

I sighed, eyeing the thing on the sofa and trying to gauge just how much mess the decapitation was going to make. It was too big to heave into the car in one piece. The smell of excrement overriding the copper and semen was bad enough.

'He's been here all day, has he?'

Mackie nodded. 'He was sleeping, so I just left. I don't know when it happened.'

'OK, can you go into the kitchen and put your clothes in a bin liner? All of them.'

It had clearly been here for days. Fuck knows what had actually happened, and fucked if I was going to ask. I turned, desperate to get outside.

'Where are you going?'

I opened the front door, grimacing. 'To get some tools.'

*

Mackie stood, naked and shivering, in the kitchen to avoid getting forensic over any more of his clothes, while I sawed off the most ungainly limbs in the living room.

The majority of the floor around the body was covered with sheets of plastic and duvets from upstairs, but I knew it was going to be daylight by the time we stopped scrubbing every surface with chemicals. Every time I pierced the skin more liquid seeped out and to make things even more fun Mackie had vomited all over the hall when the shock had caught up with him.

I wrapped an arm in more bin liners, put it in the suitcase behind me and tried to blow my fringe off my forehead. His left hand had swollen over a wedding ring, I noticed.

My back ached from being hunched over for so long and the extra layer of the clear poncho was making me unbearably hot.

'Eh, Mackie!' I called, sitting back on my heels to take a few breaths and eyeing one of the stilettos. His feet had swollen so much that I was unable to get them off. 'You don't want to keep the shoes, do you?'

Silence.

I regretted making the joke. 'You guys properly involved?'

'Don't take the piss out of me!' he shouted back, his voice drenched in fear and humiliation.

'I'm not! Just... making conversation.' I put down the saw and leant back on my arms, sitting back up when my muscles complained. 'I'm not taking the piss, accidents happen to everyone. I've seen all sorts, I could tell you some stories...'

There was a silence that I waited for him to break. A mental image of him having a moral meltdown and sprinting from the kitchen to turn himself in prompted me to call, 'Still with me, Mackie?'

Silence.

'Don't mess with me, fella.'

'I'm here.'

The acknowledgement allowed me to relax. I looked around at the stained sheets and the man's head, mouth still gaping against the plastic, lolling back from an armless torso like a broken deckchair. I was glad Mackie was in the kitchen; I didn't need to see myself through someone else's eyes right now.

'We worked together a bit,' Mackie said from the kitchen. 'If it's just blow-jobs and stuff, that's not even like being properly... you know...'

'Gay?'

'Shh! Are you fucking crazy?'

I snorted. 'You live in a detached house, calm down.'

'Well, it's not the same.'

'Blow-jobs and stuff, with a guy, that is gay. Or bi-curious, whatever...'

'Bi-*curious*! You a fucking issue of *Cosmopolitan*?'

'You *are* a fucking issue. Oh look, I'm in here, right now, cleaning up one of your issues!' I picked up the saw again. 'You're gonna stay here while I take the car out, all right? Did anyone else know he was here?'

'No, how stupid do you think I am?'

The question hung in the air for a while. I got back on to my knees and tried, once again, to ignore the smell.

There was a sniff from the kitchen, a choke, a sigh caught in his throat. The noises weighed heavily on the silence and I coughed, hoping to disperse the atmosphere.

There was a tattoo on the man's forearm. Of what, I couldn't work out, but I didn't want to know any more.

'Can you stick the radio on in there?' I called.

As the house was abruptly invaded by Blondie's 'Call Me', it occurred to me that Jenny Hillier had lied.

CHAPTER SEVEN

Eleven in the morning.

No sleep.

I dashed some cold water on my face from the kitchen tap and dialled Jenny Hillier's number. I had only left Mackie's an hour ago, drained and dressed in a new set of clothes from the boot of my car.

'Hello?'

'Is this Jenny?'

'Yeah, who's this?'

I took a breath. 'Hey, my name's Nic Caruana. You don't know me but I got your number off Emma's mum, Clare.'

There was a pause as she registered what I had said.

'Oh, OK, what's this about?'

'Emma's dad, Pat, has asked me to help find out what happened to Emma and apparently you were going to meet her that day, is that right?'

She sounded wary. 'So you're the police?'

'No, I'm not the police, I'm kind of a private investigator. I'd just like to ask you some questions about what happened.'

'I didn't see her.' This time there was a hint of panic.

I softened my voice. 'I know you didn't, I know. I just need to get all the details so I can help Pat Dyer. You know the police aren't really very forthcoming with their findings so I need to do everything from scratch.'

I guessed that as a middle-class teenager she was going to be fashionably anti-establishment.

'Well... if it'll help, I can't see any problem.'

I walked into the living room and picked up the drawing of Emma. 'Are you free today?'

There was another pause, loaded with suspicion.

'You can meet me anywhere that's convenient for you,' I said, folding the picture into quarters. 'A café? Bar? Wherever you want.'

She seemed reassured at the mention of a public meeting place and thought it over for a few seconds.

'Well, I'm out in Leicester Square later with some friends so... how about opposite the Häagen-Dazs place, you know that? I'm gonna be a couple of hours and I've got to be home by five... My mum, you know, since the... thing.'

'Sure, sure, that's fine. I can be there round four?'

'Yeah, that should be OK.'

I put the picture in my bag. 'That's great. I'll be wearing a black jacket over a red shirt, so you can recognize me.'

'Right, OK.'

'Thanks, Jenny, you're being a great help.'

I put the mobile down and inspected my hands, dry and cracked with chemicals. It crossed my mind to call Edie Franco but I decided against it. Even though it felt like neglecting my other job, I didn't want anything more to think about.

I stood shivering in Leicester Square for ten minutes watching the crowds. A group of Hare Krishna monks passed me, in pale robes. I'd seen them many times before and they always looked so content. It must be nice to devote your life to something other than your own pointless survival, relieve yourself of the weight of self-doubt and life's big questions.

'Er, Mr...?'

I turned and found myself looking at a young girl dressed in a denim skirt and footless tights. Her hands were in the pockets of her coat, probably around a rape alarm of some kind.

'Yeah, hi, Jenny.' I smiled. 'I'm Nic. Do you want to walk?'

I indicated my head and we began walking in the dying light.

'So you're a private detective, right?' Jenny looked me up and down with all the bravado of youth. 'I thought you'd be taller.'

'Yeah well, we don't all wear trench coats either.'

'And you're not working with the police?'

'No, I don't like to. I don't really trust them, to be honest,' I said with a roll of the eyes. 'Neither does Pat, that's why he hired me.'

She nodded. 'OK, so what do you want to know?'

'How long did you wait for Emma before leaving?'

'Um, probably about twenty minutes.'

'Did you try calling her?'

'Yeah, but I couldn't get through.'

'Switched off?'

'Yeah.'

I looked ahead again. Everything was lies or silence.

Jenny seemed to sense the change in mood and glanced at me. 'What?'

I stopped and met her eyes. 'Look, I don't want to scare you, but I know that's not true.'

'What do you mean?' She became defensive too quickly, far too quickly. 'What, are you saying I'm lying?'

I tried not to sound too confrontational but I was tiring of her front. 'Yes, but that doesn't bother me, Jenny, it really doesn't. I'm not the police. I'm not going to tell your parents or shop you for obstruction of justice. I just want to know what you're not telling everyone.'

She folded her arms. 'How do you even know if I'm lying or not?'

'Her mobile wasn't off. Her parents called it about ten times and it was on. You didn't try to phone her or you would have known that.'

Her eyes widened and for a second I was frightened she was going to run.

'Don't even think about it,' I said, dropping the act. 'You wouldn't even have time to shout for help.'

I could almost see the cogs behind her eyes whirring as she tried to think of a get-out. She started to back away and there were too many people. If the stupid brat ran she would vanish.

'No,' I said, taking her arm and jerking her forwards. 'Look, I don't give a shit about you, this isn't about you, it's about Emma. If you tell the truth now you'll never see me again. If you don't, you're going to wish you'd talked to the police when you had the chance.'

She was shaking. 'I'll... I'll scream...'

I sneered, 'You think I haven't heard that before?'

'Please... this guy...'

'Who?' I tightened my grip on her arm, backing her to the edge of the walkway. I was close; I could see it in her expression. 'Emma's new boyfriend?'

'He'll kill me...'

'He'll be the least of your problems if you don't.'

'Oh God... OK...' She put a hand over her eyes, trying to twist her way out of my grasp. 'OK, his name is... it's Kyle, Kyle Browning.'

Who is K?

'Kyle Browning?' I nodded, prompting her to elaborate.

'He was... he was some guy Emma was seeing, and she didn't want her parents to know so she told them she was meeting me instead. Oh shit...' Her lip trembled. 'Let me go... please, *please*...'

'In a minute. Why are you scared of him?'

'He was just dodgy. Emma knew it, which was why she never told her parents. She was meeting him somewhere near Peckham and she had me cover for her. He was into drugs and all sorts... he was just really bad news.'

I let her go and looked left and right in the semi-darkness and glaring neon lights.

'Do you have money for a taxi home?' I asked.

She started crying. No one gave us a second glance.

I got out my wallet and handed over thirty pounds. 'Look, get a taxi, OK?'

Her fingers closed around the money but she couldn't look at me.

'I'm really sorry about Emma,' I added.

'Right... yeah.'

She looked her age, I thought. Emma hadn't.

As I got into my car I saw Jenny hailing a taxi further on down the road. I watched her until the vehicle had disappeared from sight. It was nice to know that someone's daughter was getting home safely.

When I let myself in there were suitcases and a pair of black Dr Martens in the hall.

I smiled and turned into the living room. The record player was on for the first time in weeks and Mark was sprawled across the sofa. He looked like Sid Vicious without the hard edges, with green eyes and an unnervingly symmetrical face.

I thought he was asleep but he opened his eyes. ''Sup?'

'Yo, homedawg.' I smiled. 'All these holidays and you never tan.'

'I work out of the sun.' He showed his canines and sat up.

'How did it go?' I walked into the kitchen and put the kettle on. 'Did it go OK?'

'No scars worth mentioning.' He stood up and stretched, six feet tall and spider-like in skinny jeans and leather. 'It was mostly talk. Some intimidation, nothing heavier than that. What about you?'

'You know about Pat Dyer's daughter?'

'Only from your texts and stuff.'

'He's paying me to find the guys that did it.'

'I always thought he needs a slap.'

'You *knows* it!' I snorted. 'Have to give him the benefit of the doubt though. She was his only daughter and if you could have seen what those guys did to her… It's horrible. Shame his wife had to see it.'

'Clare, isn't it?'

'Yeah, Clare.' Her name felt different on my tongue than others.

'I remember her vaguely. Very beautiful.' He frowned. 'Good at her job. You know she's a model? And a dance teacher.'

'Really?'

'Stunning woman…unbelievable presence.' His eyes lingered like a caress. 'I missed you.'

'I missed you too.' I rolled my eyes. 'I wasn't the only one. Every time I came home there was another message from that Calvin Klein model guy… I can't remember his name.'

'Lance? I must catch up with him. He was… energetic.'

'I know. I was trying to sleep next door, remember?'

He spread his hands with a coy smile.

I noticed the dried blood beneath two of his fingernails and inclined my head.

'Back at work already?'

Mark followed my gaze to his hand and inspected it, scraping away the stains with his thumbnail. His fingers were decorated with tattoos, most of them Russian. There were many more hidden beneath the shirt and I noticed a new one nearly every time he returned from abroad.

'Aha, yes… Property developer in the first-class lounge. He flipped the finger to one of our waitresses.' He grinned. 'I may have caught up with him in the bathroom after we landed.'

I shook my head. 'So he'll be nicer next time?'

'Well, *sans* finger, I imagine so.' He chuckled to himself.

'God, you can't help yourself, can you? Poor bugger. What did you do with it?'

'What?'

'What do you mean, what?' I snorted. 'The *finger*!'

'Oh.' He looked confused. 'You know, I can't remember, I had quite a few Bloody Marys. Maybe I… No, I think I must have left it in the bathroom.'

He had never done his job for the money, not like me. He did it because he enjoyed it. He knew that his talent was for inflicting pain and taking life the same way that other people discovered that their calling was in music or sport.

'I was actually going to call you today for a favour,' I said, as Mark inspected his fingernails for forensic.

'Elaborate?'

'I thought you might be able to track down where this guy lives?'

He leant back against the worktop and pulled himself up, cross-legged on the granite. 'Depends how dodgy. Name?'

'Kyle Browning. I wouldn't usually ask you for something so

small but I don't have the time to exhaust all the other sources before I pull in the big guns. I need to find this guy quickly.'

'And I'm your big gun, am I? Honoured.'

'Yeah, that's exactly what you are,' I said, smirking. 'But have you heard of him, Kyle Browning?'

'No, on the scale of things he's obviously not so dodgy that I know of him. He probably works for someone more prominent.'

'You think you could find out quickly?'

'For you I'll find out by tomorrow at the very latest. I'll make a few calls and then, who knows? I... In a bag, I left it on the conveyor belt!' He clapped a hand to the side of his head, beaming. 'At baggage claim, that's it. Watching it go round and round in an old camera case...'

I pinched the bridge of my nose, trying not to laugh.

'Ah, come on, let's go out,' he said, jumping down. 'My body clock needs fucking up.'

Camden was crowded, rows of insects running from one club to the next across the broken paving slabs covered in spit and pools of grey gum. That's all most people amounted to, really. They lived, procreated and died without disturbing the air.

I was on my fourth shot of absinthe and Mark was dancing to Joy Division with some guy I recognized from a billboard. Maybe the same guy as last time, I wasn't sure.

'... There were these black stilettos. Plastic bag and these fucking stilettos!'

'Can only hope I'm having that much fun when I go,' Mark had said.

It was at times like these that I felt at my most omniscient. No one in here knew who I was or that I could kill them if I was paid to. There was a blade concealed in my sleeve at all times, that could puncture clothing and organs in seconds without a cry.

The guy Mark was dancing with would never know that Mark would enjoy his screams just as much as he appeared to enjoy his laughter.

'She has loads of scars on her wrists, you know, like loads.'

'You know that releases endorphins too?'

'So fucking bourgeois...'

'Hey, you can never be too happy.'

There was a guy, a skinhead, watching Mark. He caught Mark's eye and held his girlfriend in front of him like a shield, probably to disguise the hard-on that Mark's lascivious gaze was giving him.

I smiled to myself.

I wondered what Clare was doing.

The night disappeared with the next absinthe. I blinked and the club was replaced by my front door. Hours had been lost inside that shot glass. Mark was laughing at something with an arm around my shoulders, unsteady on his feet. He had never been able to hold his drink. No fat on him.

'Going round and round the conveyor belt, in a fucking camera case... Can you fucking imagine?'

I hoisted him over the threshold and manoeuvred him to the sofa, finding it difficult to stay upright.

'I'm not drunk, I'm just gonna... lie here for a minute.'

The room turned on its side as I collapsed on to the sofa. Mark's head was resting on my knee as he started singing something out of tune. He was still laughing.

We were both laughing but I couldn't remember why.

I was tired suddenly.

I wondered what Clare was doing.

I thought about asking Mark more about her, but he had fallen asleep with smudges of eyeliner under his eyes.

CHAPTER EIGHT

An address in my pocket and a cigarette between my lips.

Driving through Peckham.

Reaching Greenwich, hung-over as fuck.

Rain pummelled the windscreen from white cloud as I parked at the bottom of Shooters Hill. I walked up to a small detached house with my collar up and head down, numb with paracetamol.

I had an address, NI number and a brief description that painted Kyle Browning as a small-time coke dealer. I had suspected for years that one of Mark's sources was a computer hacker of some kind, able to find addresses, phone numbers, vehicles and even medical records. He had never been willing to discuss it, which was fair enough.

There was a footmark in the centre of the door and the wood around the lock was splintered. I kicked some empty bottles off the step and rang the bell. After a few seconds I knocked and the door opened, revealing a small skinny boy who looked as though he had been through a tropical storm.

"'Lo?"

'Kyle around?'

It seemed to take a while for the meaning of the two words to register in his mind.

'... Kyle?'

'Yeah, Kyle, is he in?'

A shrug. 'Guess so.'

The boy jerked his head and staggered away inside, away from the light.

I followed him and shut the door. Through the gloom I could make out young bodies strewn around the hallway and living room in varying states of consciousness. Brittle plastic crunched under my shoes and I looked down to see the fragments of a syringe.

Sweat, piss and vomit hung in the air with the smoke.

'Where's Kyle?' I asked again, fighting to urge to throw up.

The boy turned, rubbing his eyes and brushing a sheet of blond hair out of his face. 'Er... dunno, could be upstairs, I guess? Saw him go up there with a couple of girls last night.'

'Thanks.'

The boy grunted and shuffled into the living room.

I turned around and stepped over the teenagers on the floor before making my way upstairs. I tripped on the frayed rug adorning the landing and craned my head around the nearest door.

'Kyle?'

A dishevelled blond head surfaced from the double bed with blotches of mascara under her eyes. The redhead next to her also stirred, casting a glance in my direction before pulling a pillow over her head.

'Mm, what?' the blonde murmured.

'Kyle Browning?'

'Who?' She blinked the sleep from her eyes and grinned, her eyes glazed. 'Wo, were you at the party last night? Didn't see you, you're hot...'

'Er...' I wasn't sure how to respond. 'Thanks.'

'Come join us.' The girl rolled on to her back.

'No thanks, I've got to find someone.'

I backed away from the door and the redhead raised her

face from the mattress again. I reckoned that they had a combined age of about thirty.

'Kyle?' she said.

I came back to the doorway. 'Yeah, do you know where he is?'

Behind her the blonde rolled on to her side, one hand playing with her bra strap and the other between her legs.

'Yeah… in the other room. Probably tripping out.'

'Thanks.'

The blonde gave me a coquettish wave as I went across the hall to the other door.

I kicked it open.

'What the fuck?'

A young lad with chiselled features and long hair was doing up the zip of his jeans.

One of the naked girls sitting on the bed screamed and pulled the duvet up around her chest. The other one stared at me, a needle sticking out of her forearm and a belt between her teeth, either too shocked or too stoned to react.

'Kyle?'

I saw the guy's eyes dart left and right at the sound of his name.

He glared. 'Who the… who the fuck are you?'

'I'm here about Emma Dyer.'

I clocked the more responsive girl swiping something off the bedside table that looked like a clear packet of pills. But in the moment I took my eyes off Kyle—

I dodged the fist heading for my face and aimed a kick at his shins. I went to kick him again when someone grabbed me from behind. The screaming so close to my ear and the sharp pain across my neck made the room blur. Whoever it was, they were surprisingly light as I whirled them around. It was only when I threw them off my back and turned to land a blow that I realized it was one of the girls.

She was all ribs and backcombed hair.

I averted my eyes but the room was empty, save for the other girl slumped against the headboard. The belt dropped from her mouth and she leant her head sideways against her shoulder, her eyes meeting mine with an expression that said: Like I give a fuck. She had a tattoo of a heart on her pelvis, where the bones jutted out. I'd walked in on Harriet shooting up once, and her face had been the same.

A door slammed downstairs.

I looked back at the girl on the floor, livid.

'Are you a policeman?' she said, shaking, an arm across her chest. 'Because the drugs aren't his, I swear.'

'I'm not the police, fortunately for you.'

'Oh...'

She shifted backwards a little and glanced at the door. It occurred to me that she thought I was going to rape her, and my lip curled at the assumption. She was pretty, but in the most tasteless of ways, like you might catch something. The insides of her arms were yellow with bruising.

'Fuck's sake.' I raised a hand to block the sight of her body and left the room. 'I hope he's fucking worth it.'

On my way downstairs I came across the boy who had let me in, meandering around the hallway sipping tea from a chipped white mug.

'Oh, hi!' he said. 'You find Kyle?'

I resisted the urge to tip the tea over his head and sat down at the foot of the stairs, my hangover catching up with me again.

'No... he left.'

'Oh, bugger.' The boy nodded.

I didn't attempt to hide my annoyance. 'Yeah, *bugger*.'

'You want some tea, man? You look wiped.'

I wanted to reply scathingly, but my irritation dissipated a little in the face of the boy's demeanour.

'Sure, all right.'

The boy smiled and walked unsteadily into the kitchen.

'What's yer name then, man?' he said. 'Haven't seen you round here before.'

'Nic.'

'Cool. I'm Joe.' He poured water into another broken mug and swirled the tea bag around, squinting in the weak light from the window. 'You work with Kyle? You look kinda older than him.'

'No.' I glanced back down the hall and at the cigarette burns on the wall. 'Must've been one hell of a party last night.'

'Yeah, Kyle does know how to throw 'em. Dunno where he gets the money to keep payin' for so many sweets. I can barely afford a fuckin' half-ounce nowadays, I'm fuckin' skint.'

He handed me the tea.

'Coke?' I enquired, remembering Mark's brief description of Kyle's occupation.

He grinned. 'Oh, all sorts. Coke, Es, acid, smack, anything you want. Amazin' really, he has a party like this like three or four times a week.'

I looked down the hall again. That sounded like a lot for a common drug dealer to be paying for on a regular basis.

'Why you lookin' for him anyway?'

Joe sounded as though he couldn't really care less about the answer. He looked harmless enough to be trustworthy.

'It's about a girl called Emma Dyer,' I said. 'Do you know her?'

His face broke into a smile. 'Oh, her – yeah, Kyle used to bring her here a lot. Man, she was wild, I've never seen a girl snort that much in my life. Haven't seen her in a while though. She all right?'

'She's dead.'

He rubbed his watery eyes, taking a while to absorb what was being said. 'Fuck, man… fuck, you aren't the filth, are you?'

'No, I'm just trying to track Kyle down to talk to him about Emma. I think he was the last person to see her alive.'

'Oh fuck, man, fuck…' He rubbed his eyes again roughly, sobering up in an instant. 'You think he killed her or something?'

'I don't know, that's what I'm trying to find out. But could you help me? Maybe give me the name of someone Kyle works with so I can speak to them?'

He had both hands to his head. 'Well… if you want someone who knows where he might be then you can always speak to Matt Masters. He's not here, he's not usually around, but he lives a couple of houses down the road at number three. He knew Emma quite well, he was mates with them both.'

'Is he a dealer too?'

'Yeah. Mostly weed though.'

'Cheers.' I smiled. 'What's your name again?'

'Joe, but everyone calls me Meds cos I have to take injections all the time.'

'Diabetic?'

'Yeah. Sucks, cos, you know, I can't do much of this.' He made a gesture back at the living room. 'Or even drink that much, really. But yeah, all my mates call me Meds.'

I put my cup down on the side. 'Thanks for the tea.'

'No worries, man.'

'Oh, and do you mind not mentioning that you talked to me? It's kinda sensitive.'

'Yeah, whatever.'

'Thanks, that's a big help. Just don't touch the hard stuff, yeah? That stuff fucks with your head.'

He returned my smile with a hint of bravado. 'Yeah, a mate of mine used to say that if you abuse something it'll abuse you back.'

'Your mate spoke a lot of sense.'

'Not really – he's dead.'

There was an awkward silence. I wondered whether Clare had been anything like her daughter at this age, whether the scars had ever been accompanied by a scattering of loose cocaine on a dressing table, empty bottles of Bacardi and the stale smell of too much sex and cum-stained mattresses.

'How old are you?' I asked, not knowing why I cared.

'Seventeen... My mate, he was called Dave. He topped himself last year.'

His matter-of-fact tone made my skin crawl. At least some kids deserved the luxury of a normal childhood, away from all this shit.

'I'm sorry.'

Another house, another kitchen, another apology.

'It's cool, man. It was what he wanted, I think. They said it was an accident but I never thought so.'

I glanced at the door and heard someone vomiting upstairs.

'Look, I've got to go... but take care of yourself. This is a bad scene for kids to get into. Believe me, I know.'

Another shrug. 'Only scene there is around here for us. If you're not doing this you ain't doing anything. But I get what you mean, thanks.'

I nodded and turned towards the kitchen door to leave.

'Hey, I'm sorry about that Emma girl, man. I hope you find the bastard who did it.'

'Me too,' I said.

CHAPTER NINE

Every time I saw my sister there was less of her. She was evaporating under her clothes. There were two or three inches of roots showing beneath the blond. Before the drugs the only thing that had stopped her short of being beautiful was her teeth: Scottish canines like mine. Now she was only twenty-four but looked twice that age.

I watched her for a while from my car as she sat down on the steps leading up to the entrance to my building. She looked down at her fingers and said something to herself under her breath, moving her head left and right as if she was whispering a song.

It took a few minutes to psych myself up for the encounter before I got out and crossed the road. As I got closer I found it hard to hide my distaste.

'Fucking hell, Harri, how's Auschwitz?'

'Did I ask for your opinion?' She stood up, shivering and hugging herself with stick-like arms. 'Let me in, it's freezing.'

She hadn't looked at me.

I unlocked the door and swallowed down the hate and the love and the guilt, the lies, the snide comments, the years of silence and not talking about the past and the drug money, always back to the drug money. It was the only thing left that kept this sick mockery of a relationship functioning.

The lift was out of order so we climbed the stairwell to the top floor. I dropped my bag by the door, glad that Mark wasn't home.

'Three hundred, right?' I said.

'Yeah.' She waited in the doorway and watched as I found my chequebook. 'I need money for the train too, I used up the last of it getting over here.'

'Three-thirty then?'

I crouched and got thirty pounds out of my wallet. It was easier to look down at the bag and the cheque than to look at her. I felt sick to think that she was like this because of me, because I couldn't say no, because it was all that could make her happy.

'How are your personal branch of Santander?' I asked.

'Oh, fuck you.' She was watching the cheque. 'Like you've called Mum lately.'

'Yeah, well…' There was nothing to say to that. 'Anything from Tony?'

'Just a letter, last week.' She indicated her head at the cheque. 'Can I have that?'

'What did he say?'

'Nothing new. Asking how everyone was, misses everyone, you know, stuff.'

I kept hold of the cheque.

She folded her arms. 'He asked whether you had met a nice girl yet, how work was, um… said he missed you, said to look after Mum and Dad, said that he might be back soon but he doesn't want to get his hopes up, blah blah blah, you can have the bloody thing if you like… Can I have my money now?'

My money.

I still hadn't looked at her properly, but I doubted she had looked at me either.

'Still with that dick?' I asked.

'If you mean Garry,' she said, 'then yeah. Why do you care?'

'Well, I never used to think you deserved each other but…'

'No, go on. You clearly have something to say, get it off your chest, why don't you?'

'How long is this going to go on, Harri?'

She looked at me then, with brown eyes identical to our dad's. 'What?'

It hurt to speak to her like this, physically hurt. 'No, come on. How much longer are you going to do this?'

'Do what?'

'This!' I gestured at her. '*This*, for fuck's sake! When are you going to grow the fuck up?'

'What's your fucking problem all of a sudden?'

It was always my problem. Never her fucking problem.

'It's my money you're pissing away,' I snapped. It was easier to be angry about the money than to tell her what I really thought. 'I'm the fucking financial go-between for you and your dealer, that's my problem.'

'Well, fuck you, keep your money then, I'll just get some myself!'

She turned around and tried to slam the front door in my face on the way out.

'No, Harri, wait!'

I grabbed my keys and hurried down the stairs after her.

'Fuck off.'

'Just take it.' I caught her arm on the landing, felt the bone through her cardigan and recoiled before I could stop myself.

She glared at me as if I'd slapped her.

'Take the money, please.' I held the money out. It was all I could do.

'You think you're so much better than me – why? Because you're the one giving me money?' Her fingers curled around the notes and the cheque. 'Let me in on your secret to happiness one day, Nic. I'm fucking dying to know.'

I leant against the banister and watched her go. There was no dignified way I was going to have the last word, so I turned and went back upstairs to the top floor. The man passing me on the way down took two puffs from his inhaler.

The flat felt strange in the aftermath of her presence. These were two parts of my life that would never be reconciled.

To the top floor...

The thought sent a shudder down my spine and I felt sick suddenly.

On the way down...

I ran back to the door, down the stairs, from landing to landing with my head full of white noise and adrenalin. I threw open the main entrance and looked left and right down the road without seeing anyone; no one that looked like him anyway. I tried to remember what he had been wearing, the colour, style, *anything*. He had been wearing glasses... and the inhaler...

His face was a featureless blur.

'Argh, fuck!'

I sprinted back up the stairs and realized that I'd have to pack some things.

How could I have been so stupid? How could someone have caught me so off guard?

When I was back inside I paced from the hallway to the kitchen, scouring for any sign of something wrong. Nothing seemed to be missing. I picked up my mobile and started to text Mark, telling him not to come home, when I spotted something on the coffee table: a slip of paper.

Bring thee to meet his shadow.

I read it again, and again, wondering where I'd read it before, and ran into the bedroom to find my suitcase. It struck me, as I flung open the wardrobe and pulled it down, that no one had been in the stairwell when Harriet had come up.

He must have already been in here.

I glanced at the door, unnerved by the silence, and recovered my automatic from a shoebox under the bed before packing the rest of my clothes.

By the time I arrived at our safe house, another equally stylish flat not too far from our usual place in the West End, Mark was already sitting on the sofa watching TV.

I left his suitcase in the hall, went back down for mine and took Mark's lack of acknowledgement for irritation. I rubbed my eyes, trying to find the words. It had occurred to me on the way here that the man was more likely to be involved with the work I was doing for Edie Franco than Pat's case. It didn't make me feel any better, but it made more sense.

'Hey, I'm sorry,' I said, reddening with shame. 'I must have fucked up somewhere, I don't know who he—'

'Shh.'

I realized that he was engrossed in the news, despite the sound being muted. It was only then that I noticed the protests on the screen.

Above a red and yellow news ticker of current affairs two boys were smashing a reinforced window with blocks of concrete; one wearing black and one green. Their faces were covered. *Cut*, and riot police were lashing out with batons across a metal barrier. *Cut*, and the boys were smashing the same window again.

'Fucking hell,' I said, leaning against the back of the sofa. 'No wonder you couldn't get through Westminster today.'

I looked down at Mark but his gaze hadn't left the screen. His legs were drawn into his chest and his eyes were glassy.

'Jesus, are you all right?'

'It's so fucking wrong.'

'Can I turn the sound on?'

He shrugged.

I sat down and hit the mute button. I read the news, tried to understand as much of it as I could despite the statistics and the pointless rhetoric, but I never engaged with it in the same way Mark did.

'They're talking about *respect*. Stupid *fucking* idiots.' He sniffed and his hands balled into fists. 'I went down there today, for a few hours.'

'What for?'

'You know, a bit of community service never hurt anyone.' He looked up at me. 'You get a lot of groups who take advantage of this sort of thing, neo-Nazis and people like that. A few of them were crowding around this girl, knocked her over, cowardly fuckers, so me and another guy picked her up and got her away. The guy with me was obviously under the mistaken impression the police were there to help and he called out to them, and this young officer just smirked and said, "Well, you wanted free speech."'

When I raised my eyes back to the TV we were looking down from a bird's-eye view. The crowd had become fluid, police distinguished only by the odd neon yellow jacket amongst the black.

'It's just so fucking wrong, what they're doing. Only hits the poor kids the hardest.'

'Speaks the Oxford student with the trust fund,' I said, sarcastically.

'Just because I had it easy doesn't mean I have to become a wanker.' There was a hint of a smile. 'I miss that place.'

How we had both arrived here wasn't a topic either of us talked about often, not that I wanted to. The years I'd spent in juvie he'd spent cycling beside canals, but at least my path was an obvious one; I'd never understood why Mark was here.

'Did you bring any whiskey with you?'

'Yeah.' I went back to the suitcases and found the bottle wrapped in T-shirts. 'Triple?'

'We're watching the prospects of a generation being obliterated, on a widescreen TV, in real time. You bet I want a triple.'

I poured two glasses and sat down beside him. It had started raining outside, again.

'Cheers,' he said. 'You know, when the world ends, if we're around to see it, this is how we'll be watching it too. We'll all be on News 24 watching the mushroom clouds coming towards us… Can you imagine? We'll watch the correspondents cutting out one by one.'

I brought my knees up and rested my forehead on them. 'I'm so fucking sorry about this.'

'Don't be daft, we've all done it.'

'You've never had to move me out.'

He ignored me and slapped the side of my leg. In the ten years we had known each other he had never let me apologize for anything. He was the only person I'd met who looked as if he belonged in his world, as if he had made peace with the spectres of self-loathing, doubt and morality that hounded the rest of us.

Over the rim of his glass he watched the TV with a kind of wistful brutality in his expression as the camera panned over the Houses of Parliament.

I wished that I could clear my mind of the girls. There were too many girls, girls with scars on their wrists and women with death in their eyes and girls without faces left in alleyways.

I considered telling Mark about the piece of paper and the familiar phrase but decided against it, for now.

Bring thee to meet his shadow.

Wikipedia told me it was a line by Edgar Allan Poe, some guy who apparently invented detective fiction. Whoever left the note was obviously some public-school wanker. I wasn't, so I figured I'd track him down the old-fashioned way.

'Will you come to Emma Dyer's funeral with me?' I asked, staring at my drink. 'Just for another pair of eyes, you know.'

'If you like, of course I will.' He paused. 'Why is this job getting to you so much?'

'I don't know.' It was the only answer I had and it was the truth. 'The coldness of it, maybe? Maybe her age? I don't know... How can you tell?'

'We've been in situations like this before and I've never seen you drink a whiskey that slow.'

CHAPTER TEN

I parked my car in a lay-by and hoped that the loitering gang across the road didn't turn it into a bonfire before I got back.

I knocked on the door of Matt's house in Shooters Hill and heard nothing. I got out Emma's address book and tried calling the number tagged as 'Matt', but I suspected that, like me, he would be unlikely to answer to numbers he didn't recognize. Kicking the door through seemed like a good idea at first, but there were too many people in the street. I turned and crossed the road again, planning to wait a while.

The group of boys was still there, watching me and the car they could never afford. They would crash it, set it on fire and destroy as much of it as they could, just because they could never do the same to its owner.

'Hey,' I said, taking them by surprise with the acknowledgement.

The oldest of the group, a black boy with cynical lips on a bike, glared.

'Yeah, you.' I knew they would all be armed. My insides clenched out of habit but I reminded myself I could fight them off. I was armed too, this time. 'You know a guy called Matt Masters who lives there?'

'Who wants to know?' The boy on the bike looked me up and down. His knuckles were worn and clenched around the handlebars.

'He isn't answering his phone and I usually buy off him,' I

said, my hands in my pockets and one around the butt of my automatic. 'Do you know where he might be?'

'No.'

'No?'

'No.'

A quieter voice said, 'What about his crib in Deptford?'

The boy on the bike scowled down at the younger boy beside him and cuffed him across the back of the head. 'You shut up, yeah!'

'What place in Deptford?' I asked.

'Aw, fuck's sake!' The boy stood up straight astride his bike again, regaining his composure. 'OK, you wanna go to Deptford? What you got?'

'How much do you want?'

He gripped the handlebars tighter. 'No, you say!'

'You want fifty?'

He glanced at the rest of the group, flustered. 'OK, OK, yeah. Fifty.'

I got out my wallet and handed the money over.

The boy crumpled the notes up and put them in his pocket. 'Daubney Tower. That's where he keeps most of his gear. We only been over there once when he paid me to shift some stuff for him, dunno if it's still the same.'

'Thanks.'

'Whatever.' The boy raised his eyebrows. 'I never seen people who buy off Matty driving fucking Audis.'

I nodded, half smiled and walked back to my car. They were watching me in the wing-mirror as I drove away.

A discoloured block of grey flats came into view and I found a place to park in its shadow. I looked up at the tower and felt my heart sink at the prospect of knocking on every door.

Putting it off would be pointless, so I got out of my car and found the main entrance.

The concrete was dappled with grey ice.

I picked a number at random and listened at the intercom. 'Hello?'

I raised my voice, guessing that the woman must be hearing-impaired from the volume at which she had answered.

'Oh, hi. I'm meant to be meeting Matt at his flat and I've completely forgotten the number he gave me, I'm afraid.' I added a self-deprecating laugh. 'Can you tell me which one he is?'

'I'm afraid I don't know any Matt, dear, what's his surname?'

I could already tell that continuing the conversation would be pointless.

'No, it's no problem, thanks,' I said, backing away from the doors and starting to think about another way in.

'Eh. Who're you looking for?'

I turned to see a trio of boys, all aged around ten and dressed in a mixture of football shirts. They didn't look too menacing but I still took a step back to keep a sensible distance.

'Matt Masters,' I said, looking between their blank stares. 'Do you know him?'

'Might.' The tallest of the three wiped a grubby hand across his nose; he had a spattering of red marks down his arms that might have been eczema or something else. 'What ye got for us?'

I held the boy's gaze and mentally chalked one up to him when he didn't look away. I got out my wallet and took out a ten-pound note, watching their eyes follow it through the air.

'Do you know him?' I asked again.

'Gi's the money first 'n' I'll tell ye.'

I handed it over, amused.

The boy shifted the football he was holding under his arm to stuff the note into the pocket of his torn jeans.

'Ain't heard of him,' he said. 'Sorry.'

The laugh escaped me before I could stop it.

He frowned as if he had been expecting an angrier response and the other two shifted, looking ready to run should I make any sudden movements. One of them was wearing shorts and the sight was enough to make me shiver.

'OK, fine, you don't know him,' I said, pointing up at the flats. 'But can you get me in there?'

'Might. What else ye got for us?'

Despite myself I took a liking to the kid, so I took out my wallet again. This time I found a twenty. They were just trying to get by, to survive, like everybody else.

'Can you get in there?'

'Gi's the money first, 'n' then—'

'No.' I held a hand up. 'We're doing this one my way. You get me in there, and then I'll give you the money.'

The boy's eyes narrowed.

'I give you my word.'

The boy glanced at his mates and strutted forwards to stick out a hand.

I stared at it.

'When ye promise somethin' ye spit on yer 'and 'n' shake on it. Then ye can't break it.'

He seemed completely serious.

I glanced around the deserted estate before shrugging. 'OK, you're on.'

The boy spat on his hand and held it out.

I followed suit and shook it firmly.

'Right.' The boy brushed past me and jabbed a finger at the intercom, listening for a few seconds. 'Mam, we're back, can ye let us in?'

The locks of the door clicked and the boy pushed it open. He escorted me over the threshold before sticking out his hand again.

'Ye promised.'

I handed over the twenty and turned to the stairs.

''N' by the way,' the boy said, 'I lied when ye asked me that first thing. Matt plays football with us sometimes, and he lives on the eighth floor somewhere. Dunno which one, I never been up there.'

I nodded at him. 'What's your name, kid?'

'Gary Steele.'

I smiled. With a name like that he was destined to become either a Face or a Premiership footballer.

'Thanks, Gary.'

Gary went back outside, indifferent.

I took the stairs two at a time, trying to ignore the smell of acrid piss and damp. When I reached the eighth floor I saw someone had spray-painted 'Muslim Scum' across the landing in baby blue.

I observed it until I left the stairwell and knocked on the nearest door.

A young woman with bleached hair and a smoker's mouth opened it.

'You my one o'clock?'

I faltered. 'Er, no. I'm actually looking for Matt Masters.'

'He don't live here, he's next door.' She inclined her head and gave me a quick once-over. Her clothes were several sizes too small and the bare skin bulged, white and taut. 'You sure you don't wanna come in, it's only a tenner for head?'

I looked past her at the flat, at the toys in the hallway, the dust hanging in shafts of light.

'No thanks, you're all right.'

She shrugged and went back inside to wait for her one o'clock.

I tried the door of the neighbouring flat.

'Yeah, 'lo?' A young lad answered it wearing nothing but a baggy pair of jeans, with dishevelled hair and a scattering of teenage acne across his chin.

I got out my automatic and aimed it between his eyes. 'Matt Masters?'

'What the fuck! Wo, wo, mate, just...' He raised his hands above his head and backed away. 'Chill yeah, chill! Fucking hell, what the f—'

'I'm here about Emma Dyer,' I said as I walked him back into the flat and kicked the door shut. 'Sit down.'

'I ain't this guy you're looking for! Matt... Matt, who?'

'Oh yeah? So you're not Matt?' I raised my eyebrows and took out my phone with my other hand. 'Right, OK, let's see about that.'

I redialled Matt's number, only having to wait a few seconds before a phone began ringing from the bedroom.

'Oh.' I feigned surprise, enjoying the game. 'Oh dear.'

Matt shot a calculated glance at the front door. There was a sound of movement from elsewhere in the flat and I pointed my gun at the kitchen. He leapt forwards to seize my arm and I put a bullet in the wall.

Two more shots went into the sofa and he punched me across the face. I wrenched my arm out of his grasp, losing the gun. It spun across the carpet and I lunged for it, but instead of going for the gun Matt made a break for the front door.

I grabbed the gun and followed him, skidding on the slick floor as I ran into the stairwell.

Matt was flying down the stairs in front of me without appearing to tread on any of them. Every so often I tried to aim but he was too far below. I reached the bottom just as he crashed through the main doors and on to the green.

Gary and his two friends stopped swinging the metal bar they had been playing with and watched, open-mouthed, as we tore across the grass towards them.

'Come here, you bastard!' I stopped and aimed at the backs of his knees, but before I could fire a shot something stopped me.

An agonized cry pierced the relative stillness of the estate. Matt flew through the air as if in slow motion before landing in a crumpled heap a good way away from where he had been halted.

Gary was standing with a blank look on his face. In his hand was the metal bar that he had just swung into Matt's shins.

I approached the groaning tangle of limbs on the ground, staring at Gary in astonishment.

'Who the... who the fuck are you?' Matt said through gritted teeth, hands around his calf and writhing.

'Nic Caruana.'

'Fuck...' His head fell back against the grass.

'Now you're going to sit up, I'm going to give you a cigarette, and then you're going to answer my questions, OK?'

Matt scowled at the boy standing a few yards away, still grabbing at his calf and flushed with pain. 'Why the fuck did you do that, you little shit?'

Gary looked away.

Matt struggled to sit up and accepted the Marlboro Light that I lit for him. He took a long drag and gingerly felt his other leg.

'I've heard of you,' he said. 'So, I suppose you're here to kill me, right?'

'No. Not necessarily. I'm just going to ask you some questions.'

'Oh? Right...' He took another drag. 'Look, you've got no fucking idea of the people involved. You think you're just looking for a kid like me? Well, sorry. There's a reason that stupid bint ended up dead and it's not something you want to be sticking your nose in.'

I lit a cigarette for myself. 'Where's Kyle?'

'Kyle?' He laughed, a high-pitched laugh that sounded a little too hysterical. 'Try under the M4, mate.'

I shivered, feeling the cold more keenly in the middle of the green. 'What do you mean?'

He blew smoke out of his nose, breathing through his teeth now. 'I'm really sorry if you knew the girl or whatever. But you can do what you like, take that kid's crowbar to me again, shoot me, whatever. I'm not telling you anything.'

I crouched, unimpressed by his dramatics. 'Oh yeah?'

'Yeah.' He nodded, his mouth set in a grim line. 'Cos I tell you this, I don't give a fuck who you are, what you've done, or what you say you're going to do to me. I'm more scared of him than I am of you.'

There was no one else around, save for the boys behind me. I stood up from my crouch to address them as they stood in an orderly line.

'I want you to do exactly as I say,' I said. 'Turn around, walk thirty paces and cover your ears. Whatever you do, *don't* turn around, no matter what you might hear. OK? I will tap one of you on the shoulder when you are allowed to turn again. Understand?'

They did as I said without question. When I was satisfied they wouldn't be able to hear much I took Matt by the neck of his shirt and dragged him behind the only tree, out of sight of the flats.

'What're you gonna do?' he cried in mock bravado as I let him drop to the ground. 'I ain't gonna tell you—'

His words were quickly replaced by a scream as I yanked his arm up behind his back and stamped down on the inflexible bone. It snapped beneath my trainer without resistance.

'OH GOD, OH FUCKING HELL!'

'You're going to give me a name and you're going to give me one now.'

'OH PLEASE, PLEASE STOP!'

'A name, Matt!' I crouched again and dug my fingers into the break.

'OH GOD I CAN'T... OH MY GOD OH FUCK!'

He screamed again as I twisted the arm, grinding the splintered bones together and hissing the words into his ear.

'The other arm will go too. You think I won't?'

'FELIX! FELIX FUCKING HUDSON. STOP, PLEASE!'

I let him go as soon as the name came out.

Matt fell forwards, curling into a ball on the ground and hugging his broken arm to his chest. His skin had taken on a grey hue.

'Felix Hudson?' I said. 'You mean the drug trafficker?'

'Me... and Kyle... we did some dealing for him...' he breathed, tears streaming down his cheeks. 'Kyle never said why... but I know he killed Emma... Kyle knew it. That's all I know... I promise, God I *promise*.'

I wasn't sure if I believed him. His finger-pointing seemed

too quick and his pleading too theatrical, but he was hardly in a state to start constructing coherent lies.

'Really? Felix Hudson?'

'I swear, I fucking swear, I fucking swear...'

'If I find out you lied to me, you know I'll kill you.'

Matt somehow managed to laugh through the pain. Laugh or cry. 'When he finds out I spoke to you I'm dead anyway.'

I didn't know what to say, so I left it at that.

On the way back to my car I gave Gary a tap on the shoulder. The three of them took their hands away from their ears, watching me through guarded eyes as I gave them a wave.

Gary paused, before running after me. 'Oi!'

I stopped.

He held out a hand and smiled. One of his front teeth had a diagonal chip.

'I tripped him for ye!' he said.

'Oh really?' My eyes narrowed. 'What do you want now?'

He beckoned with his fingers and I made a show of sighing as I got out my wallet.

CHAPTER ELEVEN

'"Go placidly amid the noise and haste, and remember what peace there may be in silence...

'"Be yourself. Especially, do not feign affection. Neither be cynical about love; for in the face of all aridity and disappointment it is as perennial as the grass."'

It was cold but the sun was out, mockingly.

We stood as far back as we could. My hands were in my pockets and I had spent most of the service scanning the congregation. Mark was by my side, looking like a government official with his hands folded in front of him in respect.

I recognized a lot of the big names: Ronnie O'Connell and his wife, Rachel; Will Mageary and his fiancée, Melanie; and Noel Braben. Even Mickey Everest and a few other bikers had made an appearance.

It was more reminiscent of Pat's funeral than his daughter's.

'Is that the Ambassador for Argentina?' Mark whispered, indicating his head at the man standing not far from Pat.

An older woman was crying. Clare's mother, I assumed. She had the same cheekbones.

Clare seemed dry of tears now, as though she had given up on the token formality. Crying was the easiest part; it was everything else that was harder.

I adjusted my suit jacket for the umpteenth time, thinking, *Bring thee to meet his shadow.*

'You look fine.' Mark smiled behind his sunglasses, still looking ahead as if he was listening to the reading.

'I hate suits.'

'I think you look rather dashing.'

'Well, I think you look inappropriate. Stop fucking smiling, it's a funeral.'

The two women in front of us exchanged glances and I rearranged my face into a more solemn expression. Jenny Hillier caught my eyes for a moment and looked away quickly. Danny Maclaine was standing two people away and I noticed him glancing at me, looking for answers like the rest of us.

I made a mental note to talk to him later.

My breath froze in the air as I watched the coffin, trying not to watch the parents and trying not to hear the crying, trying not to think of the broken body going into the ground.

'"Therefore be at peace with God, whatever you conceive Him to be... keep peace with your soul. With all its sham, drudgery and broken dreams..."'

'God, this is pseudo-religious crap.'

'Give me Rossetti any day.' I was watching Pat now, tall and stoical as a monument. I wondered if the only memories he could find of his daughter now were the ones drenched in blood and two semen samples.

'"Better by far you should forget and smile Than that you should remember and be sad."'

'You're on fire today.' I jogged Mark's shoulder and scanned the congregation for any other familiar faces.

'Do you know a guy called Felix Hudson?'

'Not personally, but I see him in the Underground sometimes.' He indicated his head at Ronnie O'Connell and Noel Braben; Edie's subordinates who were largely left to run the club in her frequent absence. 'Why?'

'I'll tell you later.'

'Might he be the reason we're here?'

I nodded.

'Well.' He raised his eyebrows. 'There was me thinking she wouldn't have known most of these people.'

'Believe me, Felix Hudson was the last name I expected to hear.'

The official had stopped reading.

Mark lit a cigarette as people began to shift and disperse. 'Are you invited to the wake?'

'I think it would be bad form if I didn't go.' I lit one for myself. 'It's all right, there'll be whiskey.'

'Amen to that.'

It was strange seeing the house in Marylebone so full of people. The air was even thicker than last time, but I seemed to be the only one who noticed. As soon as I was over the threshold I accepted two glasses of spirit and downed them both.

I kept myself out of the way for fear of having to make small talk, but most of the people there were too wary of me and of Mark to attempt conversation. Pat wasn't here; his car had pulled away from the others on the way back from the service.

I was starting to feel claustrophobic. 'I need to use the bathroom,' I muttered.

Mark was eyeing the man he had suspected of being the Argentine Ambassador and didn't appear to hear me.

The bathroom in the hall was engaged, so I went upstairs. I locked myself in and dashed cold water on my face, taking deep breaths against the mirror. After I had stayed there for as long as I could get away with I left the bathroom and loitered on the landing listening to the chatter downstairs.

I noticed a picture on the wall: Emma, below the age of ten, laughing in a paddling pool. It was a novelty to think of her as a person before the files and the photos. I took a step closer to look at the one next to it, a black and white portrait. To me she looked around the same age she had been when she died, though I reminded myself she had probably been much younger.

'Hiding?'

I started. 'Sorry, I didn't think anyone was here.'

Clare was standing in the bedroom doorway with her arms folded, wearing a black dress with a high collar and three-quarter-length sleeves. Not long enough to cover her wrists.

Compared to the usual wives and girlfriends I met she was hard to read; in other jobs for other men like Pat I could tell straight away what their women were after. Some of them wanted money, some wanted the status and some were sticking around just long enough to secure alimony. Clare was after something, but it was strange that I couldn't work out what.

'You think you find this uncomfortable?' she said. 'Try being related to some of them.'

I grimaced. 'My family doesn't work well in a confined space either, these days.'

'You have a family?' She seemed surprised.

'I have… relatives.'

'Oh, it's like that.'

'Yeah, it's like that.' I looked for my packet of cigarettes, anxious for something to do with my hands, and stopped. 'Sorry, I'll go outside. You don't smoke, do you?'

'I do anything if it gets me out of talking to anybody for a bit.'

I followed her down the stairs and out of the front door, where she sat on the stone steps leading up to the house. After a second of deliberation I sat down too and handed her my lighter. We watched the traffic for a while in silence until I noticed her shivering.

'It's OK, you don't have to,' she said as I started to take off my jacket.

'It's been pissing me off all day anyway. Take it.'

She put it around her shoulders and returned to watching the road.

I couldn't help looking down at her wrists and the faded white lines. They were self-inflicted, I could tell. It occurred to me that I had never seen her in short sleeves and I wondered if they went any further, up her arms or the tops of her thighs. I tried to work out whether I would feel an indentation if I touched them, or whether the years had smoothed them over by now.

'You don't have kids, do you?' she asked. 'No offence, but you can kinda tell.'

I shook my head, more relaxed with the cigarette and with the alcohol in my system. 'No, no way.'

'If I had any sense I suppose I'd tell you: Don't bother.' She laughed. 'Does that make me a terrible person? I think it does.'

'Not really.'

'Oh, what do you know? People only have children to pass the baton. You hope that you can watch someone else cope with your problems better than you did, but they never do.'

'What do you mean?'

The cigarette went out and she tried to light it again, looking flustered. 'Nothing, I mean nothing. God, I bet people just line up to tell you the worst things about themselves.'

I shifted. 'It's my job to ask questions.'

'Don't flatter yourself. People only talk to you because there's nothing there.'

101

'Jesus, if you think you're so much better than me then why are you out here?' I snapped.

She rubbed her eyes. 'I'm sorry.'

I felt that I was staring too much, from her thin wrists to her thighs to her hands, looking for marks, and I focused on the road instead.

'No... I'm not, actually,' she said.

I shrugged.

'Can I ask you a question? Do you ever ask why they want you to do the things you do?'

I turned and her eyes were dark behind the Marlboro smoke. 'No, but if they want to tell me, which they usually do, then I don't mind. It's not my place to ask people their motives, that's what courts are for.'

'Exactly, that's what *courts* are for.'

I didn't reply but when I looked at her again she was smiling a little. She seemed serious about the things she said, but at the same time I sensed that she enjoyed being antagonistic and did it for sport, because she could.

'Thank you,' she said as she inhaled again.

'It's fine, it hardly costs me.'

'No, not that, for when you came to the house. It was... good of you, I suppose.'

I watched the trees moving in the wind across the road, to distract myself from the vivid memory: kneeling on the floor of the mortuary viewing room, able to feel her tears through my shirt.

'It was no problem, I couldn't just leave,' I said.

Silence.

I suspected we were both remembering the same things.

'Where's Pat?' I asked.

'I don't know. You know, I don't even care any more, really.

But you always seem to be here when he's not.' She gestured for the lighter again and I relit the end of her cigarette.

'Are you Scottish?'

'God, you noticed.' This time she smiled properly. 'I tried to get rid of it when I moved... I thought my accent was pretty much gone.'

'My mum's from Aberdeen,' I said, unsure why I was telling her. 'My dad is from Florence, proper Italian.'

'Tanned at Christmas, there had to be some explanation.'

'Well, that's about as Italian as I get. A big nose, tan... and I'm a pretty good cook.' I touched my fingertips to the offending facial feature and took it away when I brushed against the bruise on my cheek, still fresh from the impact of Matt's fist.

'It's dangerous, isn't it? Every time you come here you have something else...' She indicated her head.

My hand went to the bruise again. 'This wasn't about Emma, it was...'

'Another job.'

I swallowed and tried not to redden. 'I—'

'It's all right.'

'No, I... I'm not thinking of it like that.' The words collided in my throat and I stuttered. 'I'm not... I don't think of her as a job. You know, she's a person, I know that. This isn't me... clocking-in or whatever.'

I took a long drag, desperate to stop myself from talking. It was perplexing how much she unsettled me, how a few seconds of scrutiny from those eyes made my mind grind to a halt.

She didn't say anything else, just finished her cigarette and took off my jacket.

'I should go back inside, make polite. Are you coming? If

103

you're lucky my mum will almost definitely tell you her entire life story.'

I got out another Marlboro and tapped it against the step. 'I think I'll just stay here for a while.'

'I wish I could.' She stood up. 'Thanks for the jacket.'

I lit up again as she went back inside.

I tried to call Brinks but there was no answer.

My jacket smelt of smoke and perfume.

I opened my eyes and the ceiling was too close to my face. I reached out and felt rough wood and splinters, too close, so close I could smell the damp soil and rot, clinging to my nostrils, dense air clogging my lungs.

The only light came in tiny wire-like lines.

I pushed upwards but it wouldn't move. The air was too hot, suffocating...

'Hey! Hello?'

I tried to kick out but I couldn't bend my knees. I was stuck, horizontal and shaking, clawing against the wood until I heard muffled voices from above.

'"Neither be cynical about love; for in the face of all aridity and disappointment it is as perennial as the grass."'

'Hello? Hey, somebody, I'm down here!'

'"Therefore be at peace with God, whatever you conceive Him to be."'

'No, no wait! Wait, I'm not dead!' I started screaming, thrashing in my prison.

'"... keep peace with your soul. With all its sham, drudgery and broken dreams..."'

Too close, too hot, suffocating, rotting...

Someone was puffing on an inhaler next to my ear, a cold hissing sound.

Bring thee to meet his shadow.

A clod of earth hit the lid with a thud, blocking the last traces of light. I looked sideways and Emma Dyer was lying beside me, a neat bullet-hole in her forehead, her wrists slashed and pulsing blood.

'Let me out! Please!'

'"… it is still a beautiful world. Be cheerful.

'"Strive to be happy."'

She looked at me, smiling, her eyes running with blood.

'Nic?'

'I'm not dead, I'm not dead, I'm not fucking dead!'

Hissing, next to my ear, an exhale…

'Nic!'

It took a while for me to realize that it was Mark I was grappling with. Our eyes met and the rest of the bedroom came into focus. My skin was clammy and my muscles were stricken with terror, but it wasn't real.

'Oh fuck…' I fell back against the pillow with my hands to my head.

'You all right?' Mark was sat on the edge of the bed, frowning. 'You kept shouting.'

'I'm fine.' I took deep breaths, trying to stop myself from shaking. 'Just a bad dream.'

'You want some tea or something?'

'Please.' I sat up and shivered as the air hit the cold sweat on my skin.

'Is this about Pat Dyer's daughter again?' Mark asked as he put the kettle on, hair dishevelled and green eyes still squinting from sleep.

I sat down at the kitchen table, glad of the light. The Italian cuckoo clock on the wall told me that it was half past four.

'Why do you say that?'

'What else are you thinking about right now?' He poured two cups of peppermint tea and sat down opposite me. 'Take me through it in detail, I'm curious.'

For a moment I saw the girl lying next to me in the coffin, blood spewing from every orifice. I should have told him about the piece of paper, but of course I didn't.

'I think she was beaten and raped after she was shot,' I said. 'I've been thinking about it, and the scene was just too neat, it was so...'

'Contrived?'

'Staged. There wasn't enough blood. I reckon she was moved.' I nodded. 'Plus, why would Felix Hudson be involved in a random sex attack? He's a reputable guy, not some mindless sex offender.'

'Is he your only suspect?'

'His name came up. The only other two I know of are her tosser of a boyfriend, Kyle, and his friend Matt Masters. There were two attackers but these guys just seem too...'

'Amateurish.'

'Right. I mean, these were kids, Mark. They looked barely twenty and Matt said Kyle was dead.'

He took a sip of tea. 'And she was shot, you say?'

I saw a girl on her knees, a gun to her forehead...

Bang.

'That's not something someone would do if they were out of control,' I said.

'That's an execution,' he said.

I shut my eyes, went to pinch the bridge of my nose and winced as I caught the bruise again. 'Maybe he didn't want to spoil her face too much? If the attack was motivated by infatuation he'd want to look at her face during.'

'Rape is a crime of anger, not lust.' He didn't sound

convinced. 'At least not in this case. All your suspects are too close to her personally for it to be a crime of opportunity, so to speak, from a random stranger. If that was the case you'd be looking for a more distant stalker-type, *and* the attacker would have been too frenzied to execute that type of kill. They would have taken her alive.'

'So why kill her? I mean, I understand that some people have that sort of fetish but this is too professional. It's Felix Hudson, for fuck's sake. I keep thinking I'm looking for a pair of wayward necrophiliacs and I'm not. Why would he be involved in this?' I warmed my palms around the mug again. 'I just don't get it... I mean, it looks like the work of a professional and at the same time a fucking psychopath.'

'Who's to say it can't be the work of both? There were two attackers, were there not?' He sat back, yawning.

There was a moment of silence save for the wind outside.

'What were you talking to Clare Dyer about today?' he asked.

I looked up from my tea too quickly and knew that he would notice. 'What?'

'I saw you two go outside for a smoke and wondered how she was.'

'She's... OK.' I shrugged. 'As OK as she can be in the circumstances, I suppose.'

'You know he hits her?'

I took my hand off the table so that he wouldn't see my fist clench. It wasn't too difficult to feign nonchalance in my voice.

'Really?'

'I got talking to a few people at the wake. Amazing what a bit of alcohol can do.'

I said nothing. They had appeared self-inflicted, the majority of the marks, but it didn't really change anything knowing where they came from. It was none of my business.

I kept my hands off the table.

'It was her mother who told me, funnily enough.' He was watching my eyes as he spoke, like an interrogator. 'She said she's wanted her out of there for years but there's nothing she can do to talk her round. Apparently he put her in hospital once, with—'

'Why are you telling me this?'

A flicker of something like confirmation crossed Mark's face.

'For fuck's sake.' I stood up. 'I'm going to bed.'

'I wasn't aware it was a sensitive subject.'

'Oh fuck off!' I turned, knowing I'd blown it. 'You're trying to manipulate me because you think you can.'

'I was right, though.' He raised his eyebrows, still seated at the table. 'Wasn't I?'

'Goodnight.'

I went back to my room and tried to go to sleep. Every time I shut my eyes I saw the inside of a coffin or the bruises on Clare's wrists, the scars. Every so often I'd sit up, convinced I could feel someone exhaling against my ear.

CHAPTER TWELVE

I waited in my car, drinking orange juice from a can and listening to Radio 2, until I saw Pat leave the house at around eight in the morning. Now that it was December the radio had begun a persistent assault of Christmas songs.

This morning Mark had been in the living room when I'd left, doing sit-ups to Shakin' Stevens. Neither of us had mentioned the conversation of the night before. Like most couples who had lived together for a long time we didn't talk about disputes, although, unlike most couples who had lived together for a long time, we'd never had real disputes.

I looked at my watch. It wasn't Pat I wanted to see; it never was.

After a further ten minutes I got out of my car into the light drizzle, and watched for any sign of movement at the windows as I walked up to the house next door. It was a more attractive house than the Dyers', with hanging baskets full of dejected plants and an ironic sign on the door that said, 'Posh Floor, No Shoes'.

After I knocked there was such a long pause that I started to think no one was in, but as I started to turn back I heard the front door open.

A blonde woman in her mid-forties eyed me without a greeting. She was dressed entirely in white. Attractive, but passively so, like an ornament.

'Hi, my name's DCI Terracciano.' It was a name that had

been linked to my family for almost as long as Caruana. 'I'm investigating a small incident next door, to do with your neighbour, Pat Dyer.'

Pale eyes looked me up and down, hugging a white shawl around her shoulders. 'Yes?'

'Do you know the Dyers very well?'

'We say hello sometimes.'

'Do you mind if I ask you a few questions?'

'My husband's at work.'

'I don't mind speaking to you.' I smiled and showed an ID badge that looked official enough to convince people who had little experience with the law. 'Just a few questions.'

I knew she wouldn't say no. I was dressed smartly. People were too polite and suggestible to say no.

'OK, come in.'

The house smelt of floral air-freshener and the carpets and walls were white. Some of the photos in the living room had two children in them; blonde, like their mother. There was no sign of her husband.

'Please, sit down,' she said. 'Do you want a cup of tea or something?'

'Yes please, er, Mrs…?'

'Garwood, Sara Garwood.'

She went into the kitchen. I noticed that the smell was coming from the lilies by the window. It was nice to sit in a house and feel as though something in it was alive.

Sara returned with a cup of tea and sat down on the sofa, arms still tight across her chest and looking at me past a wave of hair.

'What did you say your name was?'

'Anthony.' It was both my brother and father's name. 'DCI Anthony Terracciano.'

'And what did you want to know?'

'Do you see much of Pat Dyer, apart from saying hello?'

'No, not much. He keeps himself to himself.' She crossed her legs, showing pale skin that looked as though it would bruise easily. 'He works a lot, gets back late most nights.'

'Do you know what he does for a living?' I asked, trying to work out what Sara Garwood's husband did for a living: perhaps a stockbroker or lawyer or something equally emotionless and distant. I suspected that she wouldn't have invited me in if her husband were here, not without his permission.

'No. He wears a suit, but that's all I know about it,' she said without a smile. 'I heard about their daughter though. I went round but I didn't stay long. I suppose this is your case?'

'Um... excuse me?'

'I recognize you, from that night. I looked out and you were leaving with her. I assume this is your case?'

I wished I had handled the question better. 'Yeah... yeah, that's right.'

'Right.'

The expression on her face reminded me of Mark. There was nothing to indicate it yet, but I couldn't help feeling as if she knew I was lying.

'Do you have children yourself?' I asked.

'Three, I had.'

I was surprised; this didn't seem like a house full of children. 'Really? They at uni now?'

'Had,' she repeated.

I glanced at the photographs.

She looked down at her hands.

Everywhere I went there were more dead children.

'I'm sorry,' I said, feeling ill.

'Mrs Dyer was ever so nice when it happened... the car accident.' She was watching the lilies. 'The third, well, he was never... She was really nice when that happened too. She asked me to come over if I wanted to talk about it but I never did.'

'Talking never really helps, does it?' I said.

'I hear shouting sometimes. They'll go a while without arguing and then we'll hear them again.'

'Do you know what they argue about?'

'No, but one time an ambulance came to the house.' She glanced through the window as if it were out there now. 'She broke her arm. When I asked if she needed any help she said she had fallen, but... It might be nothing. I suppose no one would believe a woman any more if she said she'd fallen down the stairs and it was true.'

'Do you think it happens often?'

'I only saw an ambulance once but she has bruises sometimes. That's one of the reasons I don't speak to him very much.'

I followed her gaze to next-door's driveway.

'What exactly are you investigating?' she asked. 'The murder?'

'Well, that, and a disturbance. That was everything I wanted to know.'

'I know you're not the police.'

I put down my cup of tea and met her eyes. All of a sudden it felt as if this could end in so many ways and none of them were good. I didn't make a move though, didn't even blink. What happened next was up to her.

'My father was a DCI,' she said. 'You're not. That's not even a real badge.'

I stared at her but she didn't look away.

'You... let me in,' I said, unsure as to whether it was a question or a statement.

'I talk to ghosts. Do you think I care who you are?'

I looked over the cold surface and wide eyes. Underneath that I could almost see the grief and loneliness and the blood running down the insides of her thighs on to the white carpets.

I didn't have to leave; I knew that.

She watched me, legs crossed, her expression simultaneously expectant and indifferent.

I stood up and for a moment I didn't know what I had stood up for.

She still didn't move.

'I have to go,' I said.

'OK.'

'Thanks for your help.' I looked down at her and she nodded.

She came and opened the front door for me. Up close her eyes seemed even wider, too wide for her face.

'Bye, Terracciano.'

That was all she said before she shut the door

I stood on the doorstep for a while between the white house and the house next door, with an aching hard-on and thinking of dead children, more dead children and mothers talking to ghosts.

I walked down the path and tried phoning Brinks from my car, not trusting myself to go next door straight away.

No answer.

I tried again.

No answer.

'Fuck's sake, you bastard...'

I got back out of the car, breathless and disoriented. My phone vibrated and I looked down to see a text from Edie. I'd

113

been putting off seeing her for days, but now all I felt was relief at the diversion.

CALL ROUND THE CLUB SOMETIME. LOVE AND LOVE, EDIE XXX

It was probably for the best that she had contacted me, I thought as I got back in the car.

On the way to Edie's it occurred to me that I could catch Brinks, and made a diversion to his house.

Closer to Christmas now but there were no lights in these windows.

I waited and watched in my car until I saw Brinks leave the house just before half nine, wearing a suit that looked too big for him and carrying his case as usual. It was like him to sulk, but this stubborn silence was starting to grate on my nerves.

I followed the blue Saab as far as the inner city where it pulled into a lay-by. A U-turn at the next lights and I pulled over also.

Brinks had gone into a café and sat down on a plastic chair, taking off his tie and jacket. He was paler than usual, paler and thinner with larger shadows under his eyes, as if someone had turned up the brightness and contrast.

It was a while before I followed him in. Grease hung in the air like a mist above the orange tablecloths. It was obviously his natural environment.

'Oh, for fuck's sake!' He picked up his case. 'Can't you just leave me alone?'

I had expected a less-than-enthused reaction, but I hadn't expected a reaction of this scale.

'What's going on?' I said.

'Fuck off!'

114

'Why have you been avoiding my calls?'

The lady behind the counter stared but said nothing.

'Fuck you!' he spat, standing.

'Geoff—'

'Fuck you!'

Shrugging on his jacket.

'Fuck you!'

Attempting to get to the door.

I blocked his path. 'Come on, I've paid you! You can't—'

'Fuck the money!' Brinks threw down his case. 'Fuck the money and fuck you!'

Then he was crying, sobbing into his hands, tears running on to the creased white shirt in dirty grey flecks.

I stepped back, aghast. Shouting I could deal with, but not this. I'd rather be faced with violence than tears.

'Come on now,' I said, trying not to let him touch my clothes. 'Come on, sit down.'

'My life... my fucking life...'

'Come on, sit down.' I gestured at the lady behind the counter and mouthed, 'Tea?'

She nodded and left us to it.

'And what the fuck are you looking at?' I snapped at the two men eating breakfast in the corner.

They looked back at their plates and forced chatter.

I sat down opposite Brinks and handed him a napkin. 'OK, stop crying now.'

He wiped tears and snot off his face, still sniffing. 'Fuck... fuck, Nic, I'm fucked.'

'Why?' I glanced around. 'And why are you in a place like this on a work day?'

'It's not—'

'No, Geoff, it is that bad.' I flicked a fossilized baked bean off the tablecloth and took my arms off the table, worrying about catching something.

He wiped his eyes again. 'A work day...'

'What?'

To my horror he started to cry again.

'Oh God, she thinks I'm at work...'

'OK, OK, just... stop.' I leant back and tried to keep the distaste from my expression. 'What do you mean? What's happened?'

'What do you think happened? I got rumbled, that's what happened! That's what I told you would happen but you wouldn't fucking listen!'

The rant ground to a halt as two teas were brought over, and I lowered my voice.

'What happened?'

'I got pulled in, taken to one of the cells, asked a load of questions—'

'About what?'

'People I was talking to,' he said, rubbing at a cigarette burn on the table with shaking hands. 'Photos—'

'Of who?'

'People, just people! Jesus...'

'Did they ask you anything about me?'

'That's all you fucking care about!' he said, looking me up and down. 'No, they asked nothing about you. Happy?'

'Of course I'm not,' I said, softening my voice until I had almost feigned concern. 'What's happening now? Are you being charged?'

'No, I've been suspended. They've offered me a deal though. The only way I'll avoid charges is to give names, give evidence, get more evidence...'

'How many other people were you talking to?'

'Enough.' His eyes filled up again and he sipped his tea to avoid my eyes. 'You don't have kids, you don't know what it's like. I only did it for them, every fucking thing I've done was for them.'

I looked down at Brinks twisting his wedding ring around his finger.

'You're going to have to tell her at some point,' I said.

'How can I?' His voice rose again, becoming shrill. 'How can I tell her? I betrayed everyone I worked with, I betrayed her, for what? For money? Well, I won't have to worry about money any more seeing as I won't fucking have any.'

'Look, calm down.'

'Don't tell me to calm down, it's not your life gone down the fucking pan!'

I glared at the men in the corner again, making sure that everyone was pretending not to listen.

'Is there anything I can do?' I asked, hoping that there wasn't.

'Leave me alone.' Brinks shook his head, resting it on his hand. 'Please, just leave me alone.'

'Is there anything else you found out on the Emma Dyer case that I should know about?'

He glowered at me, lip curling. 'You've got no soul at all, have you? No fucking soul.'

I smirked. 'Don't give me that, at least with people like me you know where you stand.'

'What's that supposed to mean?'

'At least you know what side of the tracks I'm on. What about you?' This time I couldn't hide the scorn. 'I don't champion our glorious fucking system and then take pay-offs from the gutter.'

'I did it for my family – what the fuck would you know about family?'

'Bullshit!' I said, not caring who heard now. 'I know people who would rather go away for a twenty-year stretch than betray their enemies, so don't sit there and talk like you're any better than the people you send to court because they have more honesty in their fingernails than you have in your entire fucking institution.'

Brinks said nothing and I hated him. I hated him and I hated every other suit that spoke as though their hand was on the Bible, preaching integrity and truth when I knew they had bent over and let themselves be fucked, by arms dealers and drug barons and contract killers, to keep themselves at the top.

Whores, the lot of them, useless fucking whores.

'I suppose you want your money back then,' he sneered. 'If you're so into integrity.'

'Keep the money.' I stood up. 'I think you'll need it more than me.'

I left Brinks and the greasy café to go back to my car.

Light reflected off glass from across the road.

Click click click click click...

This wasn't a place for tourists.

Someone had left a note under my windscreen wiper. *No power hath he of evil in himself.* I picked it up, turned to get a closer look at where the clicking had come from, but there was too much traffic and the light was gone.

Closer to Christmas now and there were no lights.

No lights in these windows.

CHAPTER THIRTEEN

'Yeah, I'll be home soon, you head out and I'll meet you there.' I cut the call off and turned the car around, looking forward to a night out with Mark to whitewash my mind.

It was two hours since I had left Brinks and I was stuck in commuter traffic, unable to take my eyes off the note on the dashboard. In the end I had to park the car in a lay-by and take a tube to Edie's club, the Underground. When I arrived a young black girl in a halter-necked gold dress let me in.

'Edie's expecting me,' I said.

'I'm not her fucking PA, sweetheart. She's upstairs.'

I blinked. 'Um… sorry.'

She smiled and indicated her head at the concrete stairs, lit at each side with purple fluorescent strips. The club floor and tables were empty, bowing to a vast expanse of black and grey stage. Exposed copper pipes in the ceiling supported low hanging lamps on lengths of red flex. Red velvet banquettes against the walls made the space feel smaller, and the area around the bar glowed with lamplight reflected off the rhinestone bar-top. It worked. It shouldn't have done, but it worked. It was a stylish place, despite Edie's inclination towards tack; it had everything that was appealing to the sort of people who could afford to go there.

I left the girl and took the stairwell up to Edie's office.

It wasn't often that she was here, as this was only one of the many places she owned. Compared to other places, I knew that the girls who worked here liked and respected Edie. She wouldn't stand for anyone being treated unfairly in business, and wouldn't stand for Ronnie or Noel taking advantage of their positions in the way other club managers would.

I knocked. 'Edie?'

'Come in.'

When I opened the door she was sitting behind her desk, wearing a black leotard and not much else.

'Nic, baby.' She stood up, smiling.

I ducked as something huge and white was thrown at my head.

Motherfucker!

'Wo, Edie, what the fuck!' I dodged to one side, looked down and saw that it was one of her monstrous platforms that had hit the doorway.

'Don't "what the fuck" me!' She was coming around the desk.

'Edie, wait! Wait!'

She swung at me with the other shoe.

'Jesus!'

I grabbed her wrist and she punched me in the stomach, hard.

'Edie, stop!'

I took her other arm and pushed her back, right across the office until she was against her desk. For the first time ever, during the shortest of seconds, she looked scared, and I felt the tremor go through her body. Then it was gone. Her nails were digging into my hands.

'Calm the fuck down!'

My ribs were smarting and felt as though they would bruise. It surprised me that there was actually some strength behind her physique.

'How fucking dare—'

'I don't know what the fuck you're talking about!'

She struggled and aimed a kick at my shin.

'Fuck sake, calm *down*!' I snapped, tightening my grip on her wrists.

'I'm calm!' She unclenched her fists, showed me her palms. 'I'm calm.'

Not sure whether to trust her, I let her go and stepped back rapidly, out of range. She was looking at the floor and I took the moment of respite to check my ribs, my heart pounding.

'I'm calm,' she repeated to herself.

I picked her shoes up off the floor. She was at least three inches shorter without them.

'These are pretty fucking brutal,' I said as I handed them back. 'Where did you buy them, one of those cellars, you know... with all those gimp masks?'

'I had them made.'

'I'm gonna bruise, you know.'

'Like a peach.' She picked up an electronic cigarette from her desk and took a few perfunctory drags. 'Don't sweet-talk me, Nic. Not now.'

'Honestly, I don't know what this is about.'

She adjusted her outfit. There was tension in her shoulders, as if she was deciding whether to continue with her rage. Her temper came and went with a speed that rivalled any man I had worked with. Even now I couldn't decide whether I would be able to go through with fucking her, or if it would feel too strange to be used by a woman in that way.

'I got sent some photos,' she said. 'Photos of you talking to someone. Ring any bells?'

I felt a nagging sense of dread. 'Um... who? I don't know, I honestly fucking don't.'

With a grim smile she walked back around her desk and took a wad of photos from one of the drawers. She put them down and pushed them towards me.

I could see who it was without coming any closer.

The photos were from the alleyway beside Brinks's house. I racked my memory for anything that had seemed out of place but there had been nothing. Thinking of the flashes outside the café this morning made my fists clench. I had been so careful, so fucking careful and now someone was messing with me, toying with me as if I was nothing, nobody.

'It's...' There was nothing I could say without resorting to clichés. 'It's not what it looks like.'

'Bullshit. I've had these checked out, and I've made copies so don't think you can take them and run.'

'Who sent them to you?'

'It was an unmarked envelope.' She shook her head. 'You know, I never thought it would be you, of all people...'

'Edie, you've got to believe—'

'No. No, I really don't.'

I couldn't blame her. In her position I wouldn't believe me either.

'Look,' I said, trying not to sound as though I was begging. 'He helps me with cases, gives me information—'

'I don't want to hear it.' She looked up at me. 'If it was anyone but you, *anyone*, I promise you'd be...'

She couldn't quite bring herself to say it, didn't like to think of herself as someone who did business like me. She had one foot in our world and one foot in what was legitimate, but wouldn't commit to either of them.

I knew what she meant though; that was clear.

I nodded. 'I... believe you. I'll prove this is wrong,' I said. 'I'm gonna get proof that this is fucked up.'

'Fine.' She puffed away on the electronic cigarette and shrugged. 'But for now, you can get the hell out of my office.'

She stared me down, daring me to start something. I pushed away any images of violence, flipping the desk over and causing a scene, turned and walked back into the stairwell. It had to be Hudson, I knew that much, but he seemed more capable of finding me than I was of finding him.

'Fuck!'

I slammed open the fire escape and kicked the wall of the building opposite.

'*Fuck!*'

I looked at my hands, marked by Edie's nails, and thought about Clare Dyer. I had to meet Pat, but wanted more than anything to go home.

CHAPTER FOURTEEN

Pat had scratchmarks down the side of his face; three straight and identical lines. He sat down opposite me in the bar, glared as if I was stupid enough to ask about them, and then ordered a glass of wine from the waitress.

His expression made me feel petulant and I raised my eyebrows over my mug of coffee.

'Angry cat?'

'Too curious,' he said, stonewalling me. 'What did you want to talk about?'

'Do you know what Emma liked to do in her spare time? Did you know her friends well?'

Eyes narrowed. 'What are you trying to say?'

'Nothing, I just want to know.'

'What do you already know?'

'Jesus, will you just answer the fucking questions?' I rolled my eyes, shivering every time the door behind us opened and shut. 'I'm not implying anything; these are just standard questions I need to ask at this point.'

He thanked the barmaid for the wine and sighed. 'She liked lots of things. She danced, like her... She danced a bit, but she was better with books and stuff.' His hand went to his face but only for a moment. 'She liked to go to parties but she didn't usually stay the night. We would always pick her up.'

Whenever he spoke about Emma he squinted down at the table, directing the intensity of his words at his drink. Pat never seemed to wear anything but a suit. I wondered how much he depended on this constant display of importance. Did my jeans look like inferiority to him?

'I didn't know many of her friends, I admit. She went a lot of places and we didn't mind dropping her off but I mean, I work, I'm not home a lot. If you want to talk about her friends I'd talk to her, my... I'd talk to Clare.'

I nodded my way through the name. 'That's cool, I can do that. Look, this is nothing really to do with Emma—'

'What's it to you? It's none of your business,' he said, absently touching his face again.

I hesitated. 'Er, no... I didn't mean that. I was going to ask whether you know Felix Hudson very well? He's a businessman, works in imports, he—'

'I know who he is.' He reddened, jerking both hands down to the table. 'Why?'

I watched his eyes, watched for which way he looked when he tried to lie.

'He's linked to someone important,' I said. 'I was just interested in what you know of him – where he hangs out, if you've ever spoken to him.'

He glanced at the door and across the bar before shuffling his chair forwards a little. 'Only a few times. The last time I saw him, the last few times I saw him in fact, was at the Underground... You know, Edie's place? Of course you know it, I mean, who doesn't?'

'I know it, yeah.'

'Well, the last time I saw him was there. It was about a month ago.' He reflected on the time for a moment, when he had still been a father. 'We had a fight, something pointless, and we both got barred for a few weeks.'

'What was the fight about?'

'You know, I can't even remember. Maybe it was over one of the girls, I don't know. It gets a bit heated in there sometimes, when I've had a bit to drink and when he's had a bit. I had some coke, got aggressive, but it wasn't all my fault.'

'Yeah, right.' It came out more sarcastically than I meant it to. 'You on good terms now?'

'We were never on *good* terms, he's a Grade A fucking psychopath.' He snorted. 'And that's coming from me.'

'What makes you say that?'

'He does things to shut you up,' he said. 'Speaks in riddles, passages from books, recites poems to people while threatening to shoot their kneecaps off, leaves fucked-up notes—'

'What do you mean, notes?' I sat up and wished that I hadn't.

He sipped from his glass but didn't take his eyes off me. 'You know, notes. Bits of paper. He threatens people with them... Don't go around shouting about it, but I only know this because I hooked up with his girlfriend once. When he found out she was cheating on him the first time he left this note with a line from *Othello*. You know *Othello*, right?'

'I couldn't quote it but yeah.'

'"Sweet soul, take heed, Take heed of perjury; thou art on thy deathbed."'

I wished I knew its relevance.

'You know, Othello says that just before he murders his wife, for adultery. She's not stupid, a quick search on Google and she knew what he meant. She said she broke it off quickly after that. Now... now she's just more careful. But Felix Hudson, he's a freak, man. A proper freak.'

No power hath he of evil in himself.

'Right,' I said, trying not to let anything show on my face. 'Right, thanks.'

126

Pat spread his hands. He didn't know how he had helped.

I tried to bring the discussion back to the scratches. 'How are you both holding up?'

'Pfft, what the fuck do you mean, how are we holding up?' It looked as though he was trying to laugh but he only succeeded in twisting his lips. 'Fuck you, you mean how did I get these fetching scars?'

Afraid of talking him out of an answer, I stayed silent.

Pat didn't say anything for an unnerving amount of time. His face was blank, the vacant calm that paralyses the features before an explosion of either tears or violence. I'd have given anything to see what he was seeing.

'She's… hard to live with,' he said.

There was an almost irrepressible urge to smash his forehead into the tabletop.

'She's always liked drama… liked making things hard, but that was one of the reasons why I…' He looked me right in the eyes, shameless. 'She's hard to live with, anyway.'

The disgust must have been visible on my face because he raised his eyebrows.

'I've given you an answer,' he said. 'You don't have to fucking like it.'

The door opened and shut again. A shiver went down my spine.

'Do you mind if I speak to her now about Emma's friends?' I asked, standing.

He smiled at me. The bastard actually had the nerve to smile.

'Look at you,' he said.

I left.

When she answered the door I could tell that she had been drinking, or had taken something stronger. Her eyes were a little too wide, blackened with eyeliner. There was a bruise on her cheek and the nail varnish on her right hand was chipped.

'What?' she said, leaning with one arm up against the doorframe. Her hair was obscuring the wrong half of her face, her fringe across an eye.

Behind her something melancholic was playing.

'Is that the Doors?' I said before I could stop myself, before I realized how ridiculous it sounded.

She looked me up and down. 'Pat's not here, you know.'

'I know. It was actually you I wanted to speak to.'

There was a pause, another scan, and she left the door open as she walked back inside.

I followed her, surprised by how dark the place seemed. The dim lighting didn't seem able to reach the corners of the high ceilings any more. The grandiose ornaments, the mirrors and mock chandeliers, drew longer shadows and looked almost menacing.

It was the Doors, I thought.

Clare went into the living room. 'His voice sounds almost like Sinatra here.'

'It's my favourite actually,' I said, unwilling to come further in.

'I always had this idea, when I was younger, that one day I'd be listening to that bit... you know that bit with the piano.' She stopped by the CD player, the one I hadn't noticed the other times I'd been here, and rewound the track by a few millimetres. 'You know, this bit, coming up...'

'I know it.'

She brushed her hair away from her face with both hands, swayed a little to the rhythm when the piano started, did a measured spin that made her red skirt flare, and stopped, glassy-eyed.

'One day you think you'll listen to it and you'll have one of those stupid clichéd moments, those *epiphanies* about life, and everything will... make sense, make more sense. It really makes you want it...'

When the piano stopped she raised a hand as if to rewind it again, but turned back to me. I wasn't sure if it was alcohol; she wasn't talking like someone who was drunk.

'What did you want?' she asked.

'I wanted to check some things about Emma's friends. Pat said to talk to you.'

At first I didn't think she'd heard me. An expression like disillusionment came over her face and she turned the CD player off. She stared at it for a long time before sitting down on the sofa.

I stayed standing.

'And what if I don't want to tell you anything about Emma's friends?' she said, pushing her hair off her face again as though it was smothering her.

'That's not going to help.'

'I wasn't the one who wanted your help.' She blinked, hard. 'OK, what?'

'Did she ever mention anyone called Felix Hudson?'

'No.'

'Do you know who he is?'

'No.'

There was nothing about him in Emma's diary either. I would have remembered.

'Is that all?' she said.

'No.' I sat down this time, on the adjacent sofa like before.

She stood up sharply with her arms folded. Standing still seemed to be difficult; she didn't leave the spot but her feet never stopped moving.

'You know more about her than me, don't you?' she said. 'You're telling me names that I don't even know and they're involved with her. You're going to give me a list of names and I won't... I'm not going to know any of them. Why don't you tell me about her? Go on, I'm asking you. You're being paid for it, so tell me about my daughter.'

Something about her twisted around the inside of my skull. I wondered if it was just me or whether this happened with everyone. When she looked at you it was as if her eyes were trying to force their way past yours, wind their way inside and take you over like a disease.

There was a glimmer of recognition but I couldn't place it. It raised the hairs along the back of my neck and I felt a shot of adrenalin make my heart beat faster.

'Do you want to see a picture of her again?' she asked, not giving me time to think about an answer.

Without me saying a word she had taken down the same photo frame as last time.

I took it but couldn't drag my eyes from her.

'How did you get that?' I asked, indicating my head at the bruise.

Like Pat she ignored the question, and sat down again, rubbing her eyes.

'I knew most of her friends – the girls anyway, and Danny,' she said.

'Anyone called Kyle?'

'No.'

'Anyone called Matt?'

'God, can you just... stop?'

I stopped.

'I wish I could say that she had... said anything, but... I can't remember. I can't remember or she never said anything.'

She shrugged and her eyes became glassy. 'Please don't ask me any more.'

I looked down at the photo. It was the photo of her I didn't like. There was something in her eyes; a calculated confidence that I found easy to attribute to Pat.

'Was Emma happy?' I asked, perturbed. 'Did she seem happy?'

'What do you mean by that?'

'Well… happy, you know.'

'She's… normal.'

'Yeah, but was she happy?'

'She was *fine*.' She raised a hand and started biting one of her nails.

My eyes were drawn back to the odd sculpture next to the space where the photo had been. It held my gaze for a while, as if a head or some features might appear to give it some meaning, but the top of its neck stayed blank.

'You saw Pat today then?' she said.

I nodded, and it struck me that I had only seen them together once.

She started laughing; a high erratic sound. A few tears found their way down her cheeks and I had a fleeting vision of crossing the room to brush them away.

'It's not his fault, you know,' she said. 'It's not something he can control.'

The words made me feel light-headed with hate.

'It bothers him, when he can't control something,' she added. Her skirt had ridden up across her thighs and she pushed it down.

'That's not an excuse,' I said, aware that I was overstepping the mark.

'And what do you know?' she snapped, standing up. 'God,

131

you're all the same! Why are you under the impression that your opinions matter so much?'

'Was Emma happy?'

'Who the fuck is happy?' She laughed again.

I didn't want to provoke anything; I was tense enough as it was. But I couldn't help it. I put the photo to one side and stood up also.

'Why wasn't Emma happy?'

She waved the question away. 'You don't know anything.'

'I know what you're doing is fucked up.'

'Shut up!' She stepped forwards, got in my face and hissed, 'You don't know *anything* about me.'

'I know that you're lying to yourself.'

The slap was unexpected and it stung like hell. Out of reflex I raised my hand to retaliate and stopped myself, mortified.

'Are you going to hit me back, Nic?' She was breathing hard as if she was steeling herself for the blow, inches from me. 'Would you like that?'

She made it sound like the most inviting thing in the world and I felt faint, not in control of myself. Her eyes were wide, imploring me for something. I couldn't step away from her, couldn't catch my breath. She cocked her head and her expression was loaded with scorn.

'Didn't think so,' she said with a smile. 'You have to be paid to help, right?'

I didn't know what to say.

She turned away and sat down, fingers digging into her temples.

'Get out,' she said.

Before I left I handed her the photo she had taken down, but she didn't even look at it.

Her gaze followed me out.

I had eight missed calls from Harriet and three from my parents. Once I was in the car I called Harriet back, but I knew what she was going to say. In a way I had been waiting for it for years and felt as though I had already grieved for my brother by projection.

Rain was hammering the windscreen and I turned the engine off.

Harriet answered on the fourth ring, sounding hollow.

There was a painful silence where both of us waited; for me to guess or for her to confirm. Eventually the pressure became too much and I cleared my throat.

'Um...'

'You should really call Mum and Dad,' she said.

'When did you find out?'

'This morning. Someone came to the house.'

'How...? How did it happen?'

'Shot down.'

The windscreen was covered in a moving sheet of water, rippling downwards as the roar intensified.

'Nic, promise you'll come. Tomorrow, if you like. I'm going over now but... if you need some time—'

'I'll come tomorrow morning.'

'Thanks.'

There was another silence. This one went on for so long that in the end I hung up, knowing that we had nothing more to say to each other.

CHAPTER FIFTEEN

My Audi sat uncomfortably next to their dark blue Ford.

Before I went inside I took off my Rolex, bought for me by Mark and worn every day since last Christmas, and took my father's old watch out of the glove compartment. It had been repaired three times, had a face of faded old-fashioned numbers and a leather strap that was coming apart in a few places. But he would notice if I stopped wearing it.

Thanks to a series of promotions they had moved to a slightly bigger house in a nicer part of London, but I still didn't like coming back. All I could see was the absence of myself; my room converted into a study and only two pairs of shoes in the porch. It was like looking into a parallel universe where I had never existed, and their lives looked better, less complicated.

It was Mum who answered the door when I knocked. I was hoping that it would be Harriet; it was easier to act in front of her.

'Oh, Nic.'

She flung her arms around me and I already felt as though I didn't deserve it. I hugged her back but it didn't feel the same after all this time. I had known this was going to hurt.

'It was good of you to come, we thought you... Never mind.' She stood back, stroking my cheek. 'Are you all right?'

'God, yeah, I'm OK. What about you?'

'Oh, you know...' She waved the question away and pulled

me inside. 'Go and say hello to your father. I'll get you some coffee, you want coffee? Harri's in there too, go and see her.'

It was her way of coping, talking through everything, keeping the words coming no matter how trite they were. It wasn't surprising, considering that she had to do most of Dad's talking as well.

Mum went into the kitchen and I found myself taking deep breaths as I approached the living room.

I smiled at Harriet first, sitting with her legs up on the sofa. Dad didn't stand up for me and I hadn't expected him to. He nodded at me, muttering my name, and we shook hands as if I was meeting royalty.

Anthony Senior was a stately-looking man in his late fifties. Tony had often joked that the only way to make him feel truly uneasy was to give him a hug, or show any affection at all. It had been funny because it was true, but we all knew that underneath the banter it was pretty fucking sad.

'So where were you yesterday?' he said as I sat down.

'Sorry, I was working.'

'Sorry...' He shrugged. 'This is what it takes, eh? To make you come visit your mother at Christmas. You should be ashamed.'

'Don't worry, Dad, some things never change.'

'Don't give me smart talk.'

Already. He had started it already. The speed of the assault had broken his personal record.

'So how's work?' I asked.

'Understaffed. Overworked.' He waved a hand at me. 'You wouldn't understand. Eh, are you OK for money?'

I could have bought his house from him and still had savings to spare. He knew that, but he asked the same question every time. For years I had been telling them I worked as a

135

freelance consultant, which was almost true. Only Harriet knew better.

'Yeah, I'm fine for money, Dad.'

'Are you sure?' He insisted on pressing me, even though he must have seen my car parked outside.

'I'm OK, honestly. *More* than OK.'

'You always did have a tendency to lie when you were in trouble. You remember his tales, Harri?'

I glanced at Harriet but she had suddenly become captivated by the Father Christmas figurine standing by the fireplace. Tony had stolen it from someone's doorstep one evening, drunk, and fallen asleep on the landing with it in his arms. Since then it came out every Christmas, and if you flipped a switch at the back it would do a dance. I could relate.

Harriet seemed to be counting under her breath, her lips barely moving.

'Business is great, I'm fine for money.'

'Business?' He raised his eyebrows at me. 'Is that what was so urgent yesterday?'

'Well, I had to meet a client. You can't just cancel—'

'I'm not an imbecile, boy.' He took a sip from his drink, probably brandy, and peered over the top of his glass. 'Don't get me wrong, we were always *surprised* you made so much of yourself, but don't tell me about business. I know business.'

After a silence that I didn't have the energy to break, he gestured at me again.

'Are you still living with that… *colleague* of yours?'

'Mark? Yeah, yeah, he's still my flatmate.'

He shook his head. 'Hm… It's odd.'

'What?'

'Your age, still living like… students. Is that not odd? It's not just me. It's strange.'

136

'Why?'

'Well, surely you should be living by yourself or with a… woman, by now? Is it because you didn't go to university, you living like you are now?'

'Look, Dad, just because I'm over twenty-five it doesn't mean the only options are living on my own or with some girlfriend. Why can't I live with a friend? Loads of people do it.' I looked over at Harriet, wanting to draw her into the conversation to take some of the pressure off me. 'What do you think, Harri?'

She stared at me, mortified at the prospect of having to speak.

'Um… Well, Mark sounds cool,' she said.

I saw Dad raise his eyebrows and shut my eyes in despair.

'Not everyone has to follow your schedule, Dad,' I said, listening to Mum clattering around the kitchen and wondering whether any of us were going to talk about Tony, about why I was actually here.

'By your age I was married and your brother could already read.'

'Well…' I reddened in my effort to find a response. 'Sorry I missed the deadline.'

It was uncanny, the way he could always make me feel like a piece of shit for not being more like him. I reminded myself of all the reasons why I hated him, why Harriet hated him, and still felt defenceless, overpowered in the face of his relentless disappointment.

'I'm going out for a cigarette, please.' I fumbled for the packet inside my coat, looking at nobody.

'Outside,' he said.

'I know… that's why I said *out*.'

I walked through the glass doors to the dining room and

let myself out of the back door. There was water running off the roof of the shed in the corner, though it had stopped raining for a spell. My hands were shaking. I had spent whole nights fantasizing about punching him in the face, but I never did, and probably never would.

As I lit my cigarette the door opened behind me and Harriet stepped out with a rollie. She had made an effort for the occasion, tied her hair back and put on a tiny bit of weight.

'Skinning up here?'

'It's baccy, not... wacky.'

'You look nice.'

She shrugged.

'Are they all right?' I asked.

'No. No, they're really not. It's just their way of coping, I suppose. At least Mum was crying and stuff yesterday, but Dad, he's just fucking...' She made a vague gesture. 'I don't even know. He's just been his usual fucking self.'

'Always said we got the talking gene off Mum.'

'That's better though, isn't it? Talking about stuff? I mean, I'd rather that than... *that*. I'd hate to have people wondering what I was thinking all the time.'

There was a silence.

'God, he's such a massive cock,' she said, blowing some smoke rings.

We both looked at each other and laughed. For a moment I felt almost young, but I stopped when I recognized that expression on her face.

'Hey, wait... Are you high?'

She glanced at me with black eyes and sighed.

'You are, aren't you?'

'God, give it a rest, you're like an old fucking woman.'

She put one of her hands out, palm upwards, to test if it

had started raining again. It was hard to know what to say when she didn't look angry any more.

It was a tired argument and the anger had gone stale and turned into doubt. Neither of us had the energy to think up another original insult.

'You know, I can barely remember what Tony looked like,' I said as I sat down on the back step, warming my hand around the end of the cigarette. 'Isn't that fucking sad?'

She shrugged again, her eyes on the back fence, the ivy and purple flowers. If it weren't for the difference in eye colour we'd both look like Dad, but the dramatic features suited her more.

'No point being so morose,' she said.

'This is morose?' I shook my head and couldn't help smiling. 'I want some of the crack you're on.'

'It's good shit.' She raised her eyebrows. 'So, you're still living with Mark?'

'Ha! And?'

'Well, let's just say Dad has started making the connection with you never bringing any girls home.'

I grimaced. 'Come on, you and Tony met that girl once, you know... the one with that weird tattoo from the private school?'

'Whatever, I'd totally approve. You seeing anyone now?'

'Not really. There is this woman...' I replied with a wry smile. 'Well, she's married and it's a bit weird—'

'Married, you say?'

'Yep.'

'Scandal. What's her name?'

'Dave.'

She laughed. It was cool, doing this again.

Harriet sat down beside me and shut her eyes for a long time.

'It's a pity, isn't it?' she said when she opened them again. 'That they had to lose the best one of us.'

There was a stabbing pain, right in my gut, and tears sprang to my eyes before I could stop them. 'Oh God, Harri...'

'It's true.'

'No, I know.'

'You know, I was thinking about giving up. Not everything, but the Class As are too expensive.'

'How can you say that?' I looked sideways at her. 'You're fucking high right now.'

'Duh, of course I'm fucking high right now.'

There wasn't anything I could say to that, so I checked my phone instead. There was a missed call from a number I didn't recognize, and there was a voicemail. I put the phone to my ear.

'Don't bother trying to work out how I got your number.'

I had put a face to the voice before he even identified himself. I had also stood up and, without being fully aware of what I was doing, started walking towards the back gate.

'It's Matt. We need to talk. I'll be on South Bank outside the National Theatre in an hour and a half. It's your choice if you're there or not.'

The line went dead.

'What?' Harriet called from the back door.

I turned and walked back towards her, dropping my cigarette. 'Harri, I've got to go.'

'You'd better be fucking joking.'

'It's really important.' I grasped the sides of her arms, almost like a hug. 'I'll be back if I can.'

Her eyes were glassy with frustration. 'You always do this, you always leave me in the shit.'

'I've got to go—'

'Do you have any idea what it's like when no one else is here?'

'Oh, come on, don't be so dramatic.'

'It's hell, Nic! The way they look at you! It's all right for you, they don't see you often enough to think they can fix you!'

I didn't know what to say. 'I promise… I'll… explain later.'

'Oh, fuck off.' She pushed me away from her and sat back down on the step with her cigarette, shaking her head. 'I knew you'd do this. I knew you'd realize that if you stayed around long enough one of them would see through all your bullshit. Fucking coward…'

Almost shaking with anger, I bypassed her guilt trip and went inside, through to the kitchen.

Mum was boiling something, blurred by the steam. She did look her age now, I thought again.

'Mum,' I said.

'You all right, Nic? Are you hungry?'

'I've got to run, I'm really sorry. Work… It's work.' I spread my hands. There was no way I could make it sound less pitiable, less like I was running away.

'Oh, we hoped you would stay…'

There was disappointment etched across her face. It may have been the steam but her eyes looked glassy. I wished, more than anything, that her expression wasn't so familiar. Even the most basic requirements of being a son, I had failed at a long time ago.

'I'll come back later, if I can… Tomorrow, if—'

'Nic, it's fine. It's work, it's important.' She gestured me forwards and hugged me again. 'Do come back, I don't know how you're getting on these days…'

'I will, I promise.'

She pushed me back to arm's length. 'Make sure you say goodbye to your father.'

I left the kitchen, looked towards the living room, hovered for a moment imagining the scene, and slipped out of the front door into the porch. I could hear the soft tapping of raindrops against the roof before I let myself out.

Dad wouldn't understand, I thought, but at least he didn't know anything different where I was concerned. Harriet was right, really. The spoilt bitch was actually right. It felt almost easier to live up to their expectations than try to exceed them now.

CHAPTER SIXTEEN

I received another text as I was coming out of the underground but I didn't recognize the number. An hour and a half had proved a tighter deadline than I had thought, after trying to find a parking space as close to the city centre as I could before taking the tube. It pissed me off that so many of the most urgent moments in my life were dictated by London's fucking transport system.

I was fifteen minutes early when South Bank came into view through the misty rain, past the myriad of heaving chain restaurants. For a while I'd struggled to remember what Matt looked like. I remembered that he was a screamer. That, and he had bad skin.

I stopped by the shallow steps to the National Theatre. People were streaming inside for a performance. Someone took the back of my arm and I started walking without any resistance, my heart quickening for only a second.

His grip was tight, but there was no power there. He was walking with a slight limp.

We walked to the edge of South Bank where there was a wall, a steep drop, and then the Thames.

'I wanted to show you something,' he said.

I looked at him. What I could see of his face, the part that wasn't obscured by the hood of his coat, was swollen and yellow with stale bruising. I remembered him now, but with the marks and the rough cut across his top lip he looked older.

He handed me a photo.

The younger Matt, the one that I remembered with the spots and without the bruising, was sitting next to Emma Dyer on a leather sofa. Their eyes were red. From the cans of beer down by their feet and the uncomfortable flash reflecting off Emma's legs it looked as if they were at a party. Kyle sat on the back of the sofa with his feet on the cushions next to Emma. All of them were smiling, but looking in different directions; Matt was looking at Emma, Kyle at Matt, and Emma at the camera. There was something a little uneasy about it.

'Kyle carried this around all the time,' Matt said, swallowing. 'I know you don't believe me, but I wanted to say... we didn't kill her. I promise we didn't.'

I noticed that one of his arms was held awkwardly across his chest in a makeshift sling.

He followed my gaze and raised his eyebrows. 'You don't get all the credit.'

I looked at the photo again. Emma had her hair tied back, bringing Pat's heavy eyebrows and aggressive stare into prominence. They looked striking on such an angular face. There was something about her that reminded me of Harriet and I wondered whether that was where she had been going. Fast-forward a few years and would she be the girl with the heart tattoo I had seen in Kyle's house? Slumped against a headboard with a used needle sticking out of her arm...

Like I give a fuck.

When I looked at Matt again he was watching the people going into the theatre, casting his eyes up and down the walkway.

I handed the photo back. 'How did you get like this?'

He sniffed, turning away from the wind so that the rain

stopped hitting his face. 'I jumped out of a window. Or… y'know, through a window. You wouldn't believe how fucking solid they are. In films people just sail on through like it's nothing, but fuck, it… *really* hurts.'

'Why?'

'To get away.' His lower lip trembled and he put the photo back in the pocket of his coat. 'I know I acted like I didn't know what was going on with Hudson… But there's no point keeping that up now, I suppose.'

'Did Felix do this to you?'

'What do you think?' He sniffed. 'Kyle's dead. I suppose I got off pretty easy.'

I looked up and down the walkway. I couldn't help it; his anxiety was infectious.

'How do you know he's dead?'

He ignored the question, leaning against the wall and putting his face in his hands. 'Man, we all fucked up so bad.'

I almost put a hand on his shoulder, but remembered that it was broken. I stood in front of him instead, shielding his tears from passers-by. As always, when I was on to something big, I started to worry about him making a run for it.

'What happened?' I said.

The rain intensified and the roaring wind almost drowned out our voices. Across the water an empty tourist boat was rocking, floating atop the waves like a bloated carcass.

'You know what Felix is into?'

'Drug trafficker, right?' I said, now glad that the wind was protecting the discussion from eavesdroppers.

'Well, yeah, he gets drugs in and then distributes them. That's what me and Kyle did for him, just dealing and picking the stuff up sometimes. We never got paid much, just got to keep some of the gear.'

'And Emma did this too?'

'Ah, she was great, she was a great person… She was just… fucking stupid sometimes, like Kyle… well, like everyone else. She had problems.'

'What kind of problems?'

'At home, with her parents or whatever. It doesn't matter. She hung around with us, took drugs, we all had fun. I…' His mouth distorted the words. 'I can't believe they're both… Both of them, fucking dead.'

It annoyed me when my cynicism was so easily diluted with pity. He just looked like a kid; an inexperienced, broken and lost fucking kid incapable of telling a lie. All the same, his grief was almost irritating to me. It was too melodramatic, as if he was mimicking something he had seen on TV but didn't really feel himself.

'She started coming to a few pick-ups, cos she said she found it exciting and it would piss her parents off. I don't think Felix cared. He knew her dad and thought it was kinda funny… It sounds bad, but at the time it was just a laugh. We had nothing better to do.'

Was that it? I thought. Was it that simple? Was all this shit for boredom? Did I end up in juvie and Emma in the ground because life wasn't offering anything more interesting?

'It was OK for a few months, then this one time we all rock up, coked out of our minds… We were getting the gear out of this container, talking nonsense, and then the bint just freaks out. I mean, screaming, crying, fucking mental. We all come running, Felix is telling her to shut the fuck up, but…'

He looked up and scanned the walkway over my shoulder. Apparently spooked by something, he took my arm again and we started walking. His left leg was stiff, and he was leaning on my arm more than leading me by it.

'There were these... bodies. They looked Filipino or something... And they were all just dead, in this container. Not a mark on them, nothing weird, just like they'd starved or suffocated or something. And... fuck...' He put a hand up to keep the rain out of his eyes. 'She just wouldn't stop... bitch, she just wouldn't stop!'

We approached the steps leading up to the Royal Festival Hall and he pulled us to a halt underneath them, sheltered from the weather. It struck me that he hardly ever said Emma's name.

'We were all telling her to shut up and Felix was telling her to shut up, but she was going crazy...' He spread his hands, as if that explained everything. 'And Felix... He just shot her.'

The silhouettes in my head. Emma. Felix. Head shot.

'And?'

'We were told to fuck off.' He shrugged but his face was strained. Even where his skin wasn't swollen it was red with pent-up fear. 'That was it for us. No more drugs, no more money, just... shut the fuck up and don't ask questions.'

'So you just *left* her there?'

'She was already dead, man. He said he'd deal with it – I didn't know what else we were meant to fucking do.' His hands went to either side of his head again. 'Neither of us thought... It just couldn't have fucking happened.'

The idea of regaling this story to Pat and Clare was making me uneasy.

'Well, it did happen so get it together,' I said, trying to jerk him out of his self-pity. 'Look, when you said Emma had problems, what did you mean?'

'What?'

'You said something about her parents?'

The silence went on for a little too long.

'She got on all right with her dad, I think,' he said. 'But I don't think she liked her mum very much. I never met them, so I don't know.'

'What did she say? I mean, specifically?'

He looked at me as though I was deviating from the script, an expression that made me tense, but he thought it over anyway, as if to humour me.

'Well, she used to say she was fed up with her,' he said, glancing at his watch. 'She said she was a... freak. Weird word, I suppose. "My mum's such a fucking freak," or "I'm sick of her head-fucks." She used to say that a lot; she would say her mum was on one of her "head-fuck trips" or on her "head-fuck routine". I didn't really get it, to be honest.'

'Thanks,' I said. 'I just wanted to know.'

In my mind I could see Clare looking at me and feel that strange sensation, of someone scraping away at the inside of my head. Matt may not have got it, but I did. Or at least I was close. Every time I thought I could see the full picture, the family portrait, something blurred it.

'Do you think...?'

Matt had looked at his watch again, and I spoke faster.

'Do you think that Felix was the one who raped her? Beat her up?'

He was shifting from foot to foot, fighting the urge to pace.

'Matt, come on, stay with me.'

'Felix, he's a... He's a freak. Fuck, I... I don't know. I don't know, we just didn't ask questions. He left a note for us... "Don't ask questions." Don't—'

Someone passed a little too close to us and I saw Matt's eyes following them, the colour draining from his face and hugging his arm to his chest. The footfalls dissipated but he was verging on panic.

Don't ask questions didn't sound typical of the Felix I'd encountered. That sounded amateur compared to the carefully selected literary quotations I'd come across.

'But Felix caught up with you?' I said.

'Didn't I tell you he would?' Matt backed away from me, came forwards again, unsteady on his feet, and pressed something into my hands that felt like a slip of paper. 'This is my number—'

'Matt!' I took hold of his wrists and he struggled against me. 'Matt, come on!'

'No, please, *please*, I've been here too long!'

'Matt—'

'He'll fucking find me!'

I let him go and he staggered away, pointing a finger.

'Don't follow me,' he spat. 'Don't… Don't fucking follow me!'

'I won't!' I held my hands up. 'I won't!'

With a nervous twitch, he turned and walked out into the rain again. He took the steps as fast as his limp would allow, and I didn't follow him. He wasn't telling the whole truth, I knew that; I could feel it in my gut. But I didn't follow him.

CHAPTER SEVENTEEN

'Mum on one of her head-fucks. Can't even be bothered to say anything. FML.'

I reread Emma's diary on the sofa again, and ignored another voicemail from Harriet.

'For fuck's sake, Nic, that phone is surgically fucking attached to your hand, I know you're there! I hope you're coming to the funeral at least… God, you're such a waste of space, I don't know why they bother any more. Just call back, yeah? You at least owe them that.'

I tried calling Matt's number, but there was no answer.

I put the phone down on the table and returned to reading the diary. I had ignored the parts about Pat and Clare before, dismissing them as typical outbursts of teenage resentment, but now they had taken on a new meaning. Frustratingly, Emma was sparse with her thoughts and even more so with her feelings, like her parents.

'Mum and Dad breaking records – 2-hour fight. Fun.'

The front door opened and shut.

I looked at my watch and the faded numbers and broken strap looked alien. I had left my Rolex in the car.

Mark wandered into the room with his eyes half closed. He didn't know about Tony. I hadn't found the right time to tell him and, as with my mum, I had never been able to keep up a façade in front of him for long.

'All right,' I said.

'Tea,' he replied, drifting into the kitchen. 'It makes everything better.'

'Danny couldn't stay round cos of Mum being mental. Fucking hate her. So embarrassing.'

The anonymous text message I had received as I'd been coming out of the underground was a video link. It wasn't from Matt's number; I had checked. I sat up and took out my laptop from under the coffee table. The kettle started to rumble from the kitchen as I typed in the web address, and the traffic outside seemed too quiet.

'Hanging?' I called.

'Bit… Too much too early, I think.' He appeared in the kitchen doorway, rubbing his eyes. 'A few of the Russians are in town and I may have accidentally started drinking at midday.'

'Funny when that happens, that *accidental* drinking,' I said as the screen went white. 'Did you just keep falling on to the bar?'

'It was like my body wasn't my own.'

'We've all been there, man.'

He smiled.

The video started loading. I noticed the account was set to Private and the username to the top left was MrsDyerx. I read it again: MrsDyerx. How the fuck had she got my number? The video was still loading, and I almost gave in to the urge to delete it.

Mark must have seen the change in my face because he laughed. 'Either you just lost something on eBay or saw some *very* shit pornography.'

I opened my mouth to reply but nothing came out.

'Come on, share share, what are you watching?' He bounded across the room and climbed over the back of the sofa to sit next to me.

The first thing we saw was Clare's face, too close to the camera, her eyes cast down and the lens jerking a little as if she was adjusting something. Her hair was loose, heavy around her shoulders, and her fringe was falling over one eye, making her look like a child in the half-light.

Over her shoulder I could see her living room, dimly lit. Something classical started playing.

When she seemed happy with the camera's positioning she stood up, so close that for a moment all we could see were her hips and torso, and then she moved back towards the centre of the room. She was wearing a skirt that barely brushed the tops of her thighs, and a black halter-neck.

I wanted to look at Mark for his reaction, but I couldn't take my eyes off the screen.

My heart was beating uncomfortably hard.

Her eyes were focused above us, on something far away. She pirouetted, twice, hair flying and on the points of her toes. From this angle the scars on her arms stood out bluntly against her skin. There were a few near the tops of her legs that I had never seen before.

'Tchaikovsky,' Mark said with a nod, as if that, at least, made sense.

She dropped on to her feet, swayed, moved back across the room as though her body was nothing more than air or water.

Arms extended, gliding, she stopped and descended into the splits, came back up and spun towards the camera again. When she reached it she dropped to her knees and her face was too close for me. She moved her lips along to the music for a while with her eyes shut, nothing more than 'La la la...'

There was a fight-or-flight shot of adrenalin, as if I was being attacked.

'Hm,' Mark said.

I got the impression he was only making a noise to disperse the atmosphere.

Opening her eyes, she smiled again, and blew a kiss at the camera. There was dark make-up on her eyelids, making them look as though they were set even deeper into her face.

I glanced at Mark and his expression hadn't changed, but I saw a barely detectable frown.

She stood up, let her fingertips graze the hem of her skirt as she brought her arms back up around her head and spun back towards the back wall and the shelf with the statue on it.

I cleared my throat and the noise felt conspicuous. I couldn't help it, but I wished that Mark wasn't here. If he hadn't been watching I could have felt turned on without the guilt. As it was, I focused on the nausea and confusion, because getting a hard-on in front of Mark wasn't the kind of awkward moment I could cope with right now.

Turning, she locked her eyes on me, unblinking. She stood en pointe, extended her leg behind her, held the pose and then dropped back down. Taking her hair in her hands again she spun and then stopped, swinging her hair back and forth as if she wasn't in control of her body any more, as if the strings were pulling her from one motion to the next.

Mark sniffed.

I jumped.

One of her legs came up behind her and she held it there, arms above her head, eyes on the camera.

'Attitude,' Mark said under his breath, in a French accent.

Looking back over her shoulder, she relaxed out of the pose, pirouetted once more, and ran towards the lens until she was lost from view.

The footage froze.

The last thing I had seen was the glimpse of her face. Without speaking I took the mouse and dragged the video back to the last shot. Her expression was blank, and hard with concentration. At the same time, it was the most tranquil I'd ever seen her.

I wanted Mark to speak first.

'I wonder why she had to stop dancing,' he said.

It was the last thing I had expected him to say.

'What?'

'Well, she's still good, isn't she? I wonder why she had to give it up.'

'I...' I had never asked. 'I don't know.'

He took control of the mouse and replayed the video from the beginning. I was glad it had been him to do it, and not me.

We watched it again until Clare was kneeling in front of the camera.

La la la...

Mark paused it and scrutinized her for a moment. It was the first time that I had seen him look perturbed.

'It's a bit weird, right?' I said, jumping on the change in his mood.

'Mm. She's... quite captivating.' He glanced at me, rubbing the goose bumps that had sprung up along his arms. 'What does she want from you? Has she said anything?'

'No. Well... No.'

'Well?'

Thinking about what had happened last time I saw her sent a thrill up my spine along with the shot of unease. My foot started tapping against the floor and when Mark looked down I stopped.

'Did something happen?'

'Fuck, no. I mean... No, not at all.'

'I'm not fucking stupid, Nic,' he said, with a smile.

'It hasn't. Really, it hasn't.' I hesitated. 'That doesn't mean I... that I don't—'

'Want it to. I get you.' He nodded and restarted the video again. 'You know she's playing with you, right?'

We were sitting next to each other this time and both my hands were in sight. I didn't have the energy to be defensive.

'Ha, only child,' he said, as she ran into the camera and disappeared. 'Look at that face.'

I raised my eyebrows at him. 'How can you possibly know that?'

'Well, I spoke to her mother, of course, and there were no brothers or sisters at the wake.' He winked back. 'But seriously, look at her expression, you can spot an only child like her from miles away. You can pick them out in a shopping centre, a football crowd, anywhere... Look at her. That's the face of someone who has got whatever they want, whenever they want, their whole life. Looking like she does... it's even more obvious why.'

There was a silence.

'Why do you think she sent it?' I asked. 'If... she's playing...'

'Well, she is. Look at her.'

'You keep saying that...'

'Because it's so obvious, Nic, fucking hell...' He paused the video, restarted it, and then paused it again. 'Look at her, I mean look at her how *normal* people would. You can see her whole life, right there.'

'Well, go on then.' I sat back with my arms folded.

'Her best relationship was obviously with her father and that's how she engages with the world, winning men over, manipulation. This isn't some come-on, it's a child showing off to get a reaction... because she can.'

'And what's my reaction?'

155

'Don't get weird on me, babe.' Mark cocked his head. 'I don't think this is going to be the only time you watch this video, no?'

'You're a smug wanker sometimes, you know that?'

He swung his legs up on to the coffee table with a grin. 'Moi? Don't tell me you're not thinking of "MrsDyer"... XXX?'

'Ha, fuck you.'

'Do you know much about her relationship with Emma?'

'Not as much as I'd like. She makes it difficult to ask questions. There's something weird there, definitely.'

'You can imagine it wouldn't have been easy being her daughter.' He indicated his head at the screen.

'Why?'

'What an ego to contend with.'

'You think she was jealous of her own daughter?' Saying the words brought a sour taste to my mouth, but it made sense.

'People like that... it's in their nature to be jealous of female competition, I think. It doesn't matter who it is.' He pulled a face. 'She's trouble.'

An idea struck me, and I leant forwards to restart the video.

Clare was in front of the camera, tilting the screen, looking down at something.

'She must have a laptop,' I said, knowing that I was on to something. 'That's a keyboard she's looking at, this must be a webcam.'

'Bet this isn't the first one she's made,' Mark added. 'Be interesting to see.'

'That's it. I can get the laptop.'

'Don't...'

'What?'

He looked me up and down in a way that reminded me of Tony. In the instant I thought of him I replayed Harriet's voicemail in my mind. I thought of my parents, my promise to come back and the knowledge that I would never keep it. But then, as always, it was easy to push it all away.

'She's trouble,' he said. 'Don't get me wrong, she's beautiful and... whatever, but she is trouble. Just don't do anything stupid; you don't know what she wants.'

'Can find out though?'

'This is about Emma, remember?' he said.

'Well, yeah.' I shut the laptop, unsettled at having to look at her face any longer. 'Yeah, I know.'

CHAPTER EIGHTEEN

It was freezing. The pavements and houses were encrusted with a thin sheet of ice.

I was going to get that laptop, I had decided. Whatever it took.

She may be erratic, hard to read, but at the end of the day she was a woman. It wasn't the most fashionable view to hold nowadays, but it made me feel more secure that, for all the intellect and madness in the world, I would always have the upper hand where physicality was concerned. Brute force was our last resort for superiority.

I had taken the tube to Marylebone and then walked the rest of the way to their house. As I walked up to it I thought I could hear faint voices carried on the wind, and it was only when I got closer I realized they were coming from inside. I could hear them through the front door, screaming at each other.

'Clare, stop it! Just... fucking... stop it!'

'Or what, huh? Or what? What are you going to do, Pat? Are you going to make me? Are you going to *make me*, like you do in your *work*?'

There was a pause.

'Exactly! Oh, what a fucking *man* you are!'

'Stop it.'

'Fuck you—'

'STOP IT!'

I crouched at the letterbox, my heart pounding. I heard a scuffle and something breaking. By the sound of it they were both in the kitchen, as it wasn't long before something else smashed, like glass being thrown.

'Jesus... Clare... fucking... stop!'

'Get out!'

'I'm not putting up with this shit any more! Not now! I have things to sort out, we... *we* have our fucking lives to sort out and you won't fucking grow up!'

She said something inaudible.

There were footsteps in the hallway. I stood up, sharply, lest I be caught listening, and heard a dull thud. Pat started shouting but Clare was screaming over him, hysterical.

'GET OUT! GET OUT, GET OUT!'

'YOU KNOW WHAT?' There was a bang, the sound of something hitting the floor, and Pat slamming a door. 'You know what? I will! Fine! Change the fucking locks again, why don't you?'

The front door was wrenched open and Pat stared at me with pure hatred in his eyes. One of his cheeks was red and he was unshaven. His rage may have been diluted a little by the surprise but for a second I readied myself for a blow.

'Fuck's sake.' He laughed. 'Of course! Of fucking course you're here!'

I tried not to glance over his shoulder too conspicuously, but I knew he had seen the movement. The hallway was empty. I couldn't see where Clare had gone, but behind Pat everything was still.

He brushed past me, shutting the front door, and headed towards his car. I noticed he was carrying his briefcase, and an extra coat.

'Have a good listen?' he snapped.

'Not much.'

'She's just…' He made a futile gesture at the house. 'Just when you think it's going to stop, she just goes and… fucking hell, why does she make everything so FUCKING DIFFICULT?'

He shouted the last two words, back towards the house.

I had seen this sort of behaviour before. They always blamed the other person, implied that they brought it on themselves. No doubt he'd be remorseful later. I felt my lip curling and looked away, back at the front door, wondering if Clare was all right.

'She won't open the door, not while we're both here,' Pat said, putting his briefcase in the boot. 'What do you want?'

'I wanted to ask you whether you had heard of some people, ask some more questions about Emma.'

'Hudson a dead-end then?' he said, opening the door of his Mercedes. 'Thought so… Come on.'

Irritated by the change in plan, I did as he asked and got into the passenger seat, not bothering to ask where we were going. He had calmed down too fast to be convincing, I thought as I watched him start the engine and reverse out. His breathing was normal and, aside from the redness and residue scars on his cheek, there was no indication of the violence that had taken place.

'Has she thrown you out before?' I asked, breaking the silence.

'That wasn't being "thrown out",' he replied, eyes front. 'She's changed the locks twice, barricaded the door a few times, but Em… Emma would let me in eventually, when she was home.'

I wondered what it was that made a daughter apologize for her father's behaviour, let him back in again and again.

Had she really hated her own mother that much? I glanced at Pat's knuckles but couldn't tell whether he had thrown a punch or not.

'What were you arguing about?'

'Who are you, a fucking marriage counsellor?' He indicated to go left, but then changed his mind and went right. 'Just... things. She's not... she's not coping very well. Maybe I'm not either, I don't know how these things work... You'd think there would be some rules to follow but they're all just bullshit. Denial, anger, acceptance... what fucked-up PhD student came up with that?'

I didn't know what to say.

'And yes, I know it was Kübler-Ross, thank you,' he continued. 'I'm just making a point. It's bullshit.'

I found it hard to control the level of disgust I felt when around him, so I tried to look out of the window as much as possible as he was speaking. My thoughts kept drifting back to the house. I wondered whether Pat knew about the videos she made. It gave me a strange thrill, knowing that I had seen his wife in such a way.

'Do you know if any of Emma's friends were called Matt? Matt Masters?'

'Doesn't ring a bell.'

'Kyle?'

'Kyle?'

'Browning.'

'Maybe... Doesn't mean anything to me though, she talked about different friends all the time.' He was trying to light a cigarette one-handed. 'I need a drink, you know. You want a drink? I know it's before midday but—'

'It's a bit early for me, thanks.'

'It's weird, when time doesn't mean anything any more.'

I stayed silent, looking out of the window at the shops. I could still hear him struggling with the lighter.

'It's not like *stages*,' he said. 'It doesn't change... it just goes on longer.'

I thought of Tony and I looked at Pat.

'It never fucking changes.'

I saw a red light.

'PAT!'

There was a screech as Pat slammed on the brakes. I flew forwards, jerking against my seatbelt, and I felt the car mount the pavement as it came to a halt. Through the windscreen there was a young couple staring at us from a bus stop, teenagers. That was all I was aware of for a while, meeting their eyes through the glass, and then I heard Pat swearing.

'Fuck... Fuck, shitting fuck...'

I became conscious of my breathing, the ragged inhaling and exhaling, and got out of the car on unsteady legs. I supported myself on the roof for a moment, but nothing seemed to be broken.

Pat got out of the car also, but I didn't look at him.

Traffic was still flying past and the wind went deep into my skin. My eyes seemed locked on my hands, resting against the metal. I pictured them spattered in blood from a body that had meshed with the frame of the car.

It was a long time before I looked up.

Pat was leaning against his door with his back to me.

'You all right?' I managed to say.

He didn't answer me.

I stood up straight and glanced at the couple at the bus stop, but they were talking to each other, bored with the fleeting drama. Pat's shoulders twitched and a hand came up to rub his eyes.

I swallowed. 'You all right?'

He sniffed, and turned around with his gaze cast down inside the car. 'Yep.'

'You want me to drive?'

His eyes were red, but he was looking past me now, at the road. There was something in his face that was almost wistful.

'You think it's all over,' he said.

'What?' I raised my eyebrows. 'It is now?'

'Never is, is it.' He snorted and got back in the car. 'Come on then.'

'I'll walk,' I said.

I walked all the way back to Marylebone. I could have caught a tube, but I felt like celebrating having the use of my legs. It was to get the laptop, I thought for a while, before I dismissed the idea as ridiculous and admitted to myself it was because I was curious.

Mark had laughed at me this morning, saying over a mug of coffee, 'She could strap you on and play you like a keytar.'

As the house came back into view I tried to rehearse what I wanted to say, how I was going to act. It seemed best to act dismissive, as if this sort of thing happened to me all the time. But it was hard not to give in to concern; agonize over whether there was going to be another bruise, another scar, or worse.

I knocked on the door and listened. When I looked through the letterbox I thought that one of the pictures on the wall looked crooked, but it may have always been like that.

There was music playing from somewhere.

I knocked again, and waited.

'Is Pat with you?' Her voice was low on the other side of the door.

I stepped forwards. 'No, just me.'

'Did he send you back?'

'No.'

There was a pause, and I heard the sound of the chain being slid out of place. The door opened but then she left it. I heard her walking back down the hall so I let myself in.

It was dark; either she hadn't opened the curtains or there was something over the windows in the living room. She had stopped in the kitchen doorway, having ignored me coming in, and shook her hair out of its ponytail. Her skirt was too short and her top too tight. Like Mark she didn't have a spare inch of fat on her, but unlike Mark she was starting to look like a caricature of a human. Her face was a painted skull, all lips and cheekbones.

'Are you all right?' I called.

Pushing herself away from the wall, she slid across the kitchen floor like a child stepping on to an ice-rink, high heels crunching over broken glass. When she turned there was an odd half-smile on her face and her arms were covered in red and purple marks.

'I'm fine... Fine.'

As I came forwards I saw a shoebox on the kitchen work surface. Scattered around it were dozens and dozens of photos; some of Emma, others of the whole family. The music I could hear was distorted, like someone playing a guitar solo backwards.

'I took those,' she said, doing a twirl over the shards. In high heels she was even taller and her speech quiet and fleeting. She was like a super-imposed image on reality, rather than anything solid. 'Would you like to see them?'

'Um... OK, sure.' It was difficult to interact with her when she was like this. I felt reduced to watching events unfold on a screen, unable to control any outcomes. 'I thought we needed to talk.'

'Oh God, are we breaking up?' She laughed at her own joke as she leant against the kitchen counter, eyes on the shoebox. 'What did you want to talk about?'

'Did you and Emma get along?'

'What sort of question is that?' she snapped.

'It's a valid question.'

'You can't think of anything more interesting to talk about?'

'Well, did you?' I said, brushing off the question.

'How is that even…?' She pushed the photos around the surface, as if she was making some collage. 'It doesn't matter now, anyway.'

'God, why can't you just say yes or no? You'd make this so much easier on yourself.'

'On *myself*? On you, you mean.'

'No, for fuck's sake, I—'

'I took all these, you know,' she said. 'When you have children you realize, I suppose, that they're the most… perfect form of self-expression you're ever going to get.'

My mouth went dry. 'What… What do you mean?'

'You could be the world's greatest painter, dancer, musician, whatever… But once you've had a child, that's it. Nothing else even comes close to…' She trailed off. 'I know what I'm trying to say.'

'Why did you give up dancing?' I asked.

'Freakishly tall,' she said, gathering up a handful of pictures and flicking through them. 'Their words, not mine.'

I didn't know what to say to that.

'It's useful for modelling, if you want to turn up and have people take photos and give you free stuff for entertainment. Not so useful if you want to… do anything else, I suppose. But that's all people really want.'

'What?'

'An ornament.' She held some photos out to me. 'Some pretty, fucking… vacuous ornament. Of course, no one understands if you don't want that; they think that's all anyone would want to be.'

I took the photos but didn't take my eyes off her. 'What about Emma?'

'What about her?' She spat the words out, glaring at me. There was another bruise, always on her forehead or her cheeks. 'I can't tell you anything you want to know.'

'Did you get along?'

'She's my daughter.'

'That's not an answer.'

'Well, it's my fucking answer.'

I seized on to something controversial to say, something that would provoke her. 'Were you jealous of her?'

She swiped another water glass off the side and hurled it.

I leapt back into the doorway as it smashed at my feet, dropping the photos.

'Get out!' she hissed.

'Like fuck,' I said. 'Were you jealous of her because she had the chance to do the things you couldn't? Is that right?'

'You think you're so clever, well, you know what…' She was coming towards me and she skidded a little on the glass. I wondered if she was on something. 'You don't know anything!'

'Then tell me something I don't know!' I shouted back, my heart beginning to race with how close she was.

'You're not listening!'

There were tears in her eyes suddenly and she turned away with a hand over her face. Her shoulders trembled for a moment but then it passed. She kicked some of the shards away from her feet and moved a photo across the floor with her toe, but didn't look back at me.

'Why did you send me that video?' I asked, feeling light-headed.

'I wanted…' She still didn't turn around but I saw her rub her eyes. 'I wanted to tell you the worst thing about myself.'

'I… I don't understand.'

'Who said I expect you to understand?'

She took a step towards the back door, locked her gaze on something and twirled, whipping her head around with her lips parted. I didn't find it hard to believe that she wasn't aware of the kitchen any more, or of me.

I took a cautious step towards her, where she was turning in circles on a clear patch of floor, and wanted to put a hand on her shoulder. When she danced it was as if she left this world. I had this idea that if I tried to touch her I would fall through her, like an apparition.

'*Don't.*'

I stopped, but I didn't want to.

She turned her head and stared me down, unblinking. 'Don't you *dare* touch me.'

Maybe, on some level, it was what I had been planning all along. I pulled her forwards, more roughly than I meant to, and kissed her. She jerked away for a second, surprisingly strong, and dragged us both sideways, her nails raking into my forearms.

She slapped me across the face, kissed me back and it felt like what I had been waiting for. For a moment, that was all that existed in my world. I gripped the tops of her arms, leaving marks over the ones that were there already, until I realized the insanity of what I was doing and let her go.

The music had stopped.

I expected her to hit me again, but there was a faraway look in her eyes and her lips were swollen red.

'I'm... fuck, I'm sorry,' I said.

She burst into tears.

CHAPTER NINETEEN

'I didn't really know what to do with them all, so I put them in here.'

I hovered for as long as I could before sitting down beside her on the sofa, linking my fingers to stop them twitching. It was strange, seeing a person's life reduced to nothing more than a shoebox on someone's knees. The evidence of my life probably wouldn't fill one.

'These ones are really old. She was only about eight.'

In the first two Emma was with her father, smiling a gap-toothed smile. Pat looked younger, much younger and less jaded. It made me wonder if he had always been like he was now, or whether being too long surrounded by the ugliness of people had turned him so hard.

'This was her on her sixth birthday, with my mum.'

I nodded, trying to ignore the way my leg was just touching hers and the brush of her fingers every time she gave me a photo. Her skin was warmer than I had expected it to be.

'I think she was about four in these ones. God, it seems so long ago now.'

I looked at the tiny dark-haired child and felt an uncomfortable lump in my throat. The girl playing in the garden had no idea it was possible to end up a dead young woman on a mortuary slab and I envied her that kind of blissful ignorance.

Clare handed me another. Her eyes were still red and puffy

from the half-hour she had spent crying in my arms on the kitchen floor. She looked too fragile to withstand this level of grief; I thought the sobbing was going to break her.

'This one was in France last year, and this one was her last birthday.'

I thought that she looked a lot older than a teenager, an unsettling thing for any parent. Trouble was written all over her, in the come-hither eyes and the self-assurance with which she held herself.

'She looks... happy,' I said.

I didn't think my real thoughts would have been appropriate.

'She was. I—' She halted mid-sentence.

I tensed.

'I'm sorry.' She shook her head. 'I'm sorry, I... I'm not sure I've done that before.'

'Done what?'

'Talked about her like that, in past tense.' Her laugh wasn't quite right. 'Silly, I suppose, all this time talking about her like she's on holiday or something.'

'My brother died the other day.' I put the photos down on my knees, and for the first time since it had happened it stopped feeling like something I had watched happen to someone else. 'He'd been in Afghanistan for so long it doesn't actually feel like anything's changed. It's pretty weird.'

'Wow, I'm really sorry.' For once, she sounded genuine. 'I'm surprised, you know, that you have a brother.'

'Sister too, and parents, like normal people.'

'Are they OK?'

'I...' I still hadn't called back. 'I don't know, to be honest.'

'Were you close, you and your brother?'

'No. Though that was my fault, really. Me and Harri, my

sister, we fucked up a lot. I mean *a lot*, you have no idea how much...' I kept talking, letting the words find their own way out. 'So it wasn't his fault, he just made us feel... bad, I suppose.'

She nodded, rubbing at the bruise on her forehead. I was almost overcome by the urge to touch her.

'I don't get it,' I said. 'Why do you...? How can you keep making these fucking excuses for him?'

A weary expression came over her face and she sighed. 'It's not his fault, I... Sometimes it's better to just feel something, I guess. Or something... different, at least.'

'I don't get it.'

'You might... Maybe.'

I wanted to kiss her again.

Across the room another mobile started ringing and she stood up. She looked at it for a moment, and when she chose to answer I could hear Pat's voice without even being on speakerphone.

Clare held the phone a few inches away from her ear as he started shouting. I made out the words 'fucking', 'liar' and 'bitch'. I had a fleeting vision of punching him in the face, over and over and over again...

'Save the phone call for your lawyer, *darling*,' she said.

Pat started to say something else, but she cut him off and put the phone down.

There was a sardonic glint in her eye.

She looked at me. 'You have to go. I have some... things to do.'

'What sort of things?'

She ignored me. It was always her conversation; never mine. 'If I call you, will you come back?'

I hesitated, but not for long enough to be convincing.

Asking her about what had just happened would be pointless, I could tell.

'Yes,' I said.

She smiled, but I wasn't sure if it was at me. 'OK.'

I stood up and held out the photos.

She took them, curling her fingers around mine for a moment. It was as if a mist had descended around her face; she wasn't there any more. I left without saying anything else, feeling as though something poisonous was crawling across my skin.

I shut the front door and stood on the driveway, taking deep breaths before walking back towards the road. I resisted looking back at the house; I felt as though she might have been watching.

My mobile started ringing as I reached the pavement, and when I was sure I was out of sight I answered it.

It was Pat.

'Nic,' he said, sounding as though he was breathing through his teeth. 'I need a favour, a personal one. I'll pay you more if need be.'

'I—' I cut myself off, remembering to act oblivious to whatever had happened on the phone with Clare. 'Yeah, sure. What sort of favour?'

'Had some visitors to my office... I think I'm going to be charged with assault. Possibly ABH, I don't know, God knows what she's made up. Nic...' He paused. 'Nic, this is serious, I need you to watch her.'

'Clare?'

'I need you to watch her. Even if I get out on bail I won't be able to go home.'

I slipped on a patch of ice. 'Um, sorry, I'm not getting you. I mean, I understand but... what are you—?'

'You don't know her, Nic. You don't know what she's... what she's capable of. I know you think you've got it all worked out and you're probably feeling very fucking superior, but she's losing the plot. She's losing the fucking plot and she's not safe. I *need* you to keep an eye on her and tell me what's going on.'

There were normal behaviour patterns in abusive relationships; scripts and clichés that were always followed. I had seen them in enough jobs. This wasn't normal. No matter how I ran through the scenarios in my head, I couldn't grasp what was going on. One moment they were both playing the roles I expected of them, then one or both of them turned everything back on its head.

It dawned on me what Emma must have felt like; being between two people who had spent almost two decades of marriage learning how to fuck each other up.

'How much?' I asked.

'Depends what you tell me. I'm serious. You have no fucking idea what she's like and you *have* to tell me what's happening.'

He didn't sound angry any more, I realized. He didn't sound unhinged, or jealous, or possessive. He sounded worried.

Part of me wanted to throw it back in his face, tell him how glad I was that he was finally getting some comeuppance, that not even an hour ago his wife had left scratch marks on my forearms as she had kissed me. But I didn't. There was a creeping feeling, a tiny fragment of doubt, which kept telling me I might be wrong.

I wasn't wrong, almost certainly wasn't, but I still had to get the laptop.

'OK,' I said slowly. 'OK, I'll do it.'

173

'Thanks. I'll send you my lawyer's number, just in case, but I've got to go.'

He hung up.

I stood still in the cold for a while, unsure of where to start, where this was even going any more. This evening, I thought, checking my watch, I was going to start with calling my parents back.

Mark was watching *Question Time* in the living room, so there was a comforting level of noise in the background as I paced in the kitchen for a while with the cordless phone. After about ten minutes I pressed the Call button, hoping that being forced into speaking would calm me down.

I leant against the kitchen worktop, my heart pounding. I still hadn't remembered to change my fucking watch. As I looked at it I felt uneasy, but couldn't pinpoint why. It made me think of Matt.

Harriet answered my parents' landline.

'Hello?'

In the living room I heard Mark laugh and shout something at the TV. There had been a bottle of brandy on the coffee table.

'Hi, Harri, it's me.'

She made a disbelieving noise down the line. 'So much for coming back, huh?'

'I'm sorry.'

'Do you want to speak to Mum?'

'No, I mean it. I'm really...' I swallowed. 'I'm really sorry and... I really miss him.'

She didn't say anything and I started absently picking up kitchen utensils and putting them down again.

'Is that what you called to say?' she said.

'You know... You know what really gets me?' I said, choking.

'What?'

'Neither of us... We didn't turn up for the... er...' I stabbed a fork into the granite as a few tears worked their way down my cheeks. 'When he got his wings... We didn't, neither of us... It's so... fucking...'

'I know what you mean.' Her voice was thick.

'I don't even... remember what the fucking excuse... was,' I said, sniffing.

'I was high, I suppose.' There was a pause, where she sounded as though she had walked into another room and shut the door. 'He wasn't a saint, Nic, he just... thought he was. *They* just think that.'

'Oh, come on,' I said, wiping my eyes. 'What the fuck's the point in being bitter about it now? We both... we both fucked it up.'

'Oh, shut up.'

'No, listen!' I snapped, managing to fight back the tears long enough to construct a sentence. 'It's not his fault he made us look like shit, he was just—'

'*Perfect*,' she spat.

'Why the fuck are you being like this?'

'Why the fuck are you trying to apologize to him? He's *dead*, Nic, a gravestone's not going to hear your fucking *apology*, so just deal with it. You think I haven't had to listen to *them*, going on and on about how they didn't fucking do enough for him? Well, maybe if they'd done less for him they wouldn't have left us to the shit!'

I stared across the kitchen at my reflection in the oven door. I couldn't think of anything to say. There was nothing I could say, not even in contradiction.

There was a long silence.

Harriet sniffed, and I was shocked to realize she had probably been crying.

'So I don't... I don't want to hear it,' she said. 'And I hope... I hope you're coming to the funeral because...'

'Of course I'll come, I just—'

'... we have to say something and if there's not one other person there who's fucking *sane* about this I—'

'Harri, don't cry...'

'I might fucking throw up.' She sniffed. 'Nic... I'll call you... back.'

'No, come on—'

The line went dead. I realized there were still tears running down my cheeks and I brushed them away. As I put the phone down on the side I noticed the brief silence before the TV kicked in again. Mark had probably muted it for the duration of the call.

I dashed some cold water on my face from the sink, and when I took the phone back out into the living room Mark was acting oblivious. I watched *Question Time* for a while from the back of the room, until he turned the sound down a little.

'Want to talk about it?' he said, without turning around.

I laughed, but everything still hurt. 'Na... Maybe later.'

'I'm sorry.'

Sighing heavily, I came around the sofa and slouched down next to him. 'It's all right. Well, you know... It's... one of those things.'

Mark reached over and gave the side of my neck an affectionate scratch, before turning the sound up again.

'Look at this dick on the panel,' he said, his lip curling at the TV screen. 'I don't know how the audience do it, how they don't just stand up and shout, You're a cunt! You're a racist cunt!'

I poured myself a glass of brandy and put the phone down on the coffee table, just in case. I didn't expect her to call back; she was too much like me. Fuck her, I thought. Fuck all of them.

CHAPTER TWENTY

I turned up at Mackie's house, unannounced, at an antagonistic time of morning. Before getting there I had tried phoning Matt's number, and Brinks's, but neither of them had answered. In a way, I almost wished they were both dead. It would save me the hassle of tracking them down every time I needed them.

After ringing the bell a few times I kept my finger on it, sending the shrill noise throughout the house until, finally, Mackie answered the door in a burgundy dressing gown.

It was amusing that he made an effort to look pleased to see me, but his knee-jerk expression of dread betrayed him before he was able to force a smile.

'Oh... Nic, hi.'

'Can we talk?'

'It's six in the shitting morning.'

'I know.'

I didn't move, and he retied the cord of his dressing gown.

'OK,' he said, ushering me in. 'I suppose you want a cuppa?'

'Wouldn't say no.'

I stopped in the hallway and looked up at the tribal mask, leering at me with square teeth. It was like a caricature of an old man's face, with too much hair and too wide a smile. It reminded me a little of the statue in Clare's living room. Why would anyone have things like that in their home? Things that so obviously wished ill on everything they saw?

'Don't wanna be rude, mate, but... I was kinda hoping to never see you again.' He laughed, nervously, as he pottered around the kitchen. 'You know, unless it was a social occasion or something...'

'I need a favour.'

'Fuck, I thought so.' He sighed and put the kettle on. His eyes were still puffy with sleep. 'Go on then, what is it?'

'You've worked for Felix Hudson before, haven't you?'

I took my eyes off the mask when I received no reply. He was staring at me, his mouth moving as if trying to find the appropriate words. He was a truly awful liar.

'Don't bother trying it on, I'm not actually asking you,' I said.

'Um... Once or twice.'

'No, quite a few times.' I put my hands in my pockets and wandered into the kitchen towards him. 'I only just realized that was where I recognized his name from.'

'So...' His eyes went from my pockets to the doorway, and then back to the kettle. I could almost see the images in his mind, trying to work out if he could throw the boiling water in my face before I reached him. 'Why do you want to know about Felix?'

'That's... none of your business,' I said, smiling. 'I just need to speak to him.'

'Speak to him?'

The kettle had started to growl over us.

'Yeah.' I raised my voice. 'Just speak to him.'

Mackie took the thing off the boil. 'Nic, mate, you never wanna "just speak" to anybody.'

'You make me sound so antisocial,' I said, enjoying his discomfort.

'Oh fucking hell, why do you wanna speak to him?'

'Business, weather, you know. Can you get ahold of him? Bet you have a number or two.'

'Just the one,' he said, motioning as if to make the tea but deciding not to bother. 'Nic, is there…? Is there anything else? I mean, *anything* else I can do? He'll fucking kill me. He doesn't mess around.'

'Neither do I. Who's in your kitchen?'

He rubbed a hand over his face and made an audible noise of distress. 'What do you want me to do? Do you want his number?'

'Can you call him and ask him to meet you somewhere?'

'Jesus Christ, no.'

'Did you forget the question before that?' I asked, taking a step forwards.

'Oh chill out! Fucking hell, OK, OK, Nic, just chill out, yeah? Where?' He backed away, retying the cord of his dressing gown again.

'Fetching colour,' I said.

'Where?'

'Somewhere he hangs out already? Somewhere that won't sound too obvious.'

'It's gonna sound obvious whatever I say, mate. I haven't even fucking seen him since the summer.'

'Look, I don't really give a shit,' I said, shrugging. 'Just let me know by the end of the day that you've sorted something out, right? I'll be on my mobile, and make sure it's soon.'

Mackie put his hands up, looking like a man cornered by the law who didn't have the fight to plead not guilty.

'Oh, don't look at me like that,' I said. 'How often have I ever asked you for anything?'

'Only takes the once, doesn't it?'

He had given up more easily than I had predicted, and I realized I needn't have been so menacing. I thought about the body in the stilettos, carrying it in pieces out through the front door behind me. I wanted to ask if he had been all right, but indicated my head back at the tribal mask instead.

'What is that thing?'

'I don't actually know. Found it on a stall somewhere.' He shook his head, the colour gone from his face.

'What does it mean?'

'No idea. I'm not that cultural really, it just... spoke to me, I guess.'

In my mind I could see the statue with no face. It looked like something Clare would have bought, rather than Pat. The idea of it speaking to anyone made me shudder, but it wasn't hard to see her in it.

While I was in the car I remembered to take Dad's watch off and put it back in the glove compartment, for next time. I looked at the Rolex, thought of Matt, and the more I stayed with the image the more it dawned on me that he had been lying. It wasn't right, the way he had kept checking the time, the crude note from Felix, the way his grief and fear were so staged, and the way he avoided Emma's name...

Stupid bint...

Bitch...

I needed to find Felix. That was the only way I stood a chance of understanding exactly what Matt was lying about.

I stopped calling the number he had given me, dropped my phone on to the dashboard and parked the car outside Edie's geometric oddity of a house. This morning I'd decided I couldn't put this off any longer.

I rang the doorbell.

After a short wait Scott opened the door without the chain on. I had hoped he wouldn't be the one to answer.

Up close he looked unnervingly like his mother, but with someone else's jawline. Everything from the lips upwards was the same, even down to the direct stare, which was even more striking on a child in their early teens.

'Hey, Scott,' I said, with a grim smile that would never have fooled Edie. 'Is your dad in?'

'He went out for more coffee but he's coming back. You a friend of his?'

I ran through what I knew about Edie's background. 'Um… yeah, I'm a friend of your mum's actually. We were at NYU together for a bit.'

'You come from New York?' His face lit up and he had the same smile. 'Cool.'

'Lived there for a bit. Obviously not long enough to pick up an accent.'

'You wanna wait for him?'

I could taste copper and my pockets felt heavy. 'Yeah, that would be great, thanks.'

As he let me inside I noticed he was wearing a T-shirt with a black and white picture on it. It was of a girl, crouched on a pavement wearing heart-shaped sunglasses, with a cigarette between her fingers. He had the effortless confidence of the upper middle-class. When I had been his age I had struggled to look adults in the eye; in some ways I still did.

The inside of the house had pieces of Edie everywhere, in the open-plan rooms, the overload of glass and the abstract ornaments made of twisted metal. Contrary to what I had expected, there were books everywhere, shelves and shelves of them.

'You wanna drink?' he asked me as he led me into the kitchen.

'Yeah, sure, what have you got?'

'No coffee till Dad gets back, but we've got juice, tea... some of Mum's gay tea, with fruit and stuff?'

I leant against one of the stools at the breakfast bar. 'Juice is cool, thanks.'

The discs were probably upstairs. The staircase ran up around the walls of the living room, one of those modern ones with no banisters. My heart started beating faster and I tried to calm it down.

'You seen your mum a lot recently?' I asked.

'Na, not much. She works a lot. Dad works too, but she works all the time.' He pushed a glass of orange juice across the breakfast bar. 'I haven't seen too much of her since Dad kicked her out.'

'Yeah, I heard... Sorry.'

He shrugged and hopped up on to one of the stools across from me. 'Was better than them getting mad at each other all the time.'

'What happened?'

'She threw a toaster at him, and then they told me to go to my room.' He smiled. 'Looking back, it was kinda funny. They find it funny now, anyway.'

There was something disturbingly well adjusted about him. Was this the head start that all rich kids had? Yeah, I could see him experimenting with drugs, smoking the odd spliff and maybe doing a few lines of coke at some parties, but I couldn't see children like Scott ever fucking up. Not fucking up how other children fucked up. It was impressive, the level of confidence that came with knowing you'd always have a financial safety net.

I liked him.

'Your dad has quite a library for an ex-pat,' I remarked.

'He's obsessed.' He rolled his eyes. 'He says you might as well take your stories with you, because no one can throw memories out when you're gone.'

'That's pretty cool,' I said.

'It's all right, he's a sap sometimes.'

I heard the front door open and tensed.

Scott didn't bother to get up, he just shouted, 'Dad, friend came round for you!'

I looked over my shoulder and Sidney could see me as soon as he closed the front door. He was rubbing his hands together, a plastic shopping bag hung over his wrist.

'Who, Scottie?'

'Some guy from New York.'

I stood up, slowly, and said, 'Yeah, I'm here about those discs Edie said you were going to lend me.'

There was a silence.

Sidney had put the bag down by his feet. I saw the momentary fear cross his face, and his eyes scan the room behind me for his son. He was a big guy, extremely tall and built like an American footballer. The enormous khaki winter coat he was wearing made him appear even larger.

'Scott,' he said. 'Are you all right?'

'Yeah, you got coffee?'

I smiled, hands in my pockets, one around the butt of an automatic. 'Yeah, Sid, let's have some coffee.'

If Scott had noticed anything, he wasn't showing it.

Sidney looked at me and raised his eyebrows.

I shrugged, indicating my head ever so slightly at his son.

'Yeah,' he said, his voice taut. 'You want coffee?'

'Would love one. Be good to catch up. You got those DVDs for me?'

'DVDs,' he repeated, picking up the bag again.

'The DVDs Edie said you'd have for me. Been looking for them for quite a while but you can't get them in the shops. They're quite the rarity. Some might even say the only ones of their kind?'

'Sounds cool,' Scott said.

'They're pretty cool.' I nodded over my shoulder in agreement, and smirked back at Sidney. 'I'll make the coffee, shall I?'

It didn't take him long; he understood completely. Coming forwards, he stopped in the doorway. I held out my hand for the bag while keeping the other in my pocket, and put it down on the side when he gave it to me. He kept looking at Scott, but I shook my head.

'How's Edie?' he asked.

'Good form.'

'I bet she is.'

'I'll put on the coffee, shall I?'

'No, I'll do it.'

He made to move behind the breakfast bar and I cut him off, making it appear as if I was just stretching my legs.

'Guys,' Scott said from behind me. 'I'll make the coffee, if you like?'

'Thanks, Scott, that would be great,' I said, not taking my eyes off Sidney. 'I'm just going to go with your dad to find these discs.'

He glared at me.

'Come on,' I said, still not taking my right hand out of my pocket. 'Lead the way.'

Sidney backed away and, with another glance at Scott,

turned back towards the living room. I walked about three or four paces behind him; he looked like the sort of person who had the strength to manhandle a gun off someone if he took them by surprise.

'Nice, Edie,' he murmured as he walked towards the stairs. 'Real nice.'

I lied, deciding to relieve Edie of the hassle. 'I'm not working for her. I'm on my own.'

'You're all scum, people like you. People like her.'

'Mind your language, there are children in the house.'

I dropped further behind him as we climbed the stairs, mindful of the sheer drop and lack of banister. At one point he paused suddenly, letting me come a step closer, and I halted.

'Don't even fucking think about it,' I said.

In the kitchen Scott had put the radio on.

Sidney started moving again.

'If you weren't a coward,' he said, rigid with hatred, 'and you fought me man to man, without your weapons, I would kill you.'

'Well, that's why it's called the great equalizer,' I said as we reached the top and I followed him into the bedroom. 'We can't all rely on natural selection.'

I felt as if I had gone into something of a trance, where our voices were magnified and everything else sounded as though I was listening to it from under water. It was a familiar state. For the first time in a while, I knew I was in control.

Edie's dressing table was still here, and as he opened the wardrobe I could see a lot of her clothes. She struck me as quite a difficult person to remove from a place; some trace of her would stay where she had been and that was probably how she wanted it.

Sidney crouched and took a handful of DVDs out from

under a plastic box of socks. There were numbers written across them in red marker pen.

'If I give you these, you won't hurt my son.'

I shook my head. 'He's a nice kid.'

His lip curled. 'Don't talk about him like that.'

I took the DVDs off him and put them in the pocket that didn't contain my gun.

'If this isn't all of them, you know I'll come back?'

'I'm not stupid. They're all there.'

I moved around the double bed and let him lead the way back out of the room, keeping a safe distance behind him again. At the top of the stairs he stopped again and I moved my feet into combat position.

'You know if you take those she'll get custody of Scott?' he said, turning to face me.

I swallowed. 'That's nothing to do with me, is it? And she is his mother, anyway.'

'Some people...' He looked down at his hands and he seemed to find it difficult to speak. 'She's a great person, but some people aren't meant to be mothers. She doesn't really want him, she just likes having possessions.'

We both listened to the radio for a second.

'Well...' I couldn't find a reply; the trancelike state of action had vanished and the DVDs felt cumbersome in my pocket. 'Like I said, it's none of my business.'

'It is, now.'

I took a step backwards. I had a mental image of him grabbing me by the collar of my coat and hurling me over the edge of the stairs. I could feel the impact, and knew I was too close to react in time.

The moment passed.

Sidney turned and carried on downstairs.

'Hey, how do you take your coffee?' Scott called from the kitchen when he saw us.

'He has to go, Scottie.' Sidney stood in the centre of the living room, between me and his son, and stared at me in a way that made me wonder from whom Scott had inherited that intimidating trait. 'Emergency at work.'

'Yeah,' I said, waving. 'Nice to meet you, Scott.'

'Oh... Bye.'

I'd been concerned about what he might have had to witness. I liked him.

Sidney crossed his arms, and didn't stop watching me until I had left the house. I thought I would feel a greater sense of achievement, having got the proof I needed to show Edie that I could still be relied on for professional integrity. But my first instinct, when I got back in the car and put the discs on the passenger seat, was to snap all of them in half.

CHAPTER TWENTY-ONE

When I stopped at home to drop the DVDs off I checked my phone again, trying to drink tea from a polystyrene cup. I had a text and a voicemail.

In the car I'd been thinking about watching Clare's video again.

I jogged up the remaining stairs and let myself in too quickly.

'Someone was proactive this morning,' Mark called from his bedroom by way of greeting.

'You ever work any more?' I replied, picking up a pencil and my notepad from under the sofa.

I found my laptop under the coffee table and opened the screen, feeling out of breath. It took a while to start up, but I typed in the link and waited for Mark to leave before letting it load.

'My hangover is fucking *apocalyptic*. Think it might be haunted.'

His voice was closer this time, and I looked behind me to see him standing with a mug by the kitchen door, still in his boxers and Kurt Cobain T-shirt. He was paler than usual and had a slight sheen of alcohol sweat, but he wore the look better than I ever did.

When I didn't reply he made a noise of distress and rubbed his forehead.

'You want some paracetamol or something?' I said, knowing that he would refuse.

'No, I'll just struggle through.'

'Well, stop fucking moaning.'

'I never said I'd struggle quietly.' He ran his hands through his hair, grimacing. 'I'm going for a shower, then we'll talk Christmas stuff, yeah?'

'Plan,' I said.

As he left the room with a weak thumbs-up, I smiled to myself. He must have been feeling rough, I thought. It was unusual for Mark not to ask what I was up to. I turned back to the laptop and refreshed the site.

Inspiration. That was why I was watching it again. I just felt like drawing something.

I could hear Mark dropping things in the bathroom, singing a Duran Duran song to himself.

As Clare appeared on the screen again, I sketched a rough outline of her body, but then screwed the paper up and decided to just draw her face instead. The adrenalin that had been coursing through my system since the encounter with Sidney and Scott started to ebb.

I looked up at the video every so often, reminded of how surprisingly strong she had been. She disguised it well, with her coy smile and displays of grace, but it was still there.

Drawing her eyes was easy, I realized, because there wasn't much in them. They glared up from the page, more life-like than I had expected them to be.

I glanced at the video, on repeat, and she was twirling.

As much as I wanted this job to be over, so much so that I had started to fantasize about the months before I got that phone call, I had started to live in the future, focusing on the times when I would get to see her again. I wanted to know what was making her tick. I wanted her to keep pushing me, keep provoking, until I had an excuse…

I started the video again.

It only seemed beautiful because she was, I reminded myself, desperately trying to regain some objectivity. Aside from her presence it felt no different to watching a mental patient crying whilst being led along by their carer, or a car slowing down by a children's playground. You watched it and maybe felt uneasy, but you never said anything, because even if it felt wrong, that was just the way things were.

I drew her jawline, sharper than Emma's had been, and the shadow that her cheekbones cast across her face.

I watched the video a few more times, but I couldn't see anything in detail in this light. Nothing that I had missed anyway. Every time I thought she was drawing me closer it felt as if I was still behind a pane of glass.

I looked down at the notepad on my lap and was surprised by how easy it had been to capture her essence on the page. With some unease, I saw that it was because she looked at home in 2D. She wasn't hard to draw because there didn't seem to be much humanity to capture. I had tried drawing Mark once, when he had nagged me to, but after a couple of days I had refused to try again. I knew him too well, all of his idiosyncrasies and his perfections and imperfections, to do him justice on paper.

She looked up at me from the page, and she still wasn't giving me any answers.

'Eh!' Mark called from the other room, announcing his presence in time for me to shut the laptop before he walked in. He still hadn't showered. 'Eh, look at this. I forgot to tell you.'

'What?' I put my notepad down.

He handed me a newspaper, folded back on to a particular page. 'About a quarter of the way down... You remember that address I sent you to when you were looking for that Kyle

191

Browning? The one in Shooters Hill? A body was found there – check it out.'

'Jesus…' I sat up straight.

Mark slouched over the back of the sofa. 'Just caught my eye, wondered if it was anyone you knew.'

Joseph O'Donoghue.

I didn't recognize the name, but I recognized the picture. I recognized the blond fringe hanging over the eyes and the genial smile.

Meds.

'Fuck,' I whispered.

'Oh God, you do know him?'

'I didn't know him, I… came across him when I went round there. He was…' My eyes focused on one word. 'Suicide?'

'Yeah, heroin overdose. Nasty shit.'

'But…' I started to feel sick. 'A heroin overdose?'

'Yeah, really sad.'

I put the newspaper down on top of the laptop, got out my phone and tried calling Matt's number again. There was nothing. Doubt was turning into comprehension. I knew I had to speak to Brinks; he was the only person I knew with easy access to CCTV footage.

The boy had a disarming smile, I remembered. He didn't take heroin; I remembered that as well.

'Mark, you… read books and stuff.' I looked up at him. '"Bring thee to meet his shadow." Where's that from?'

It hadn't seemed to matter before, the meaning of the words. But everything that had once been inconsequential mattered now; it was a mess, a fucking mess.

'Edgar Allen Poe… "Silence",' he said, amused. 'Um, random. Have I won a prize?'

'No, I... It's just something that someone said and it's been bothering me a bit. I knew it was Poe but... what's it about?'

'"Silence"? Well... It's about death, I suppose, like most of his stuff really.' He crossed his arms, eyes searching upwards for the answers. 'It's subjective, it all is, but you could say that Poe's life was just a sequence of deaths of people he loved.'

'Jesus... Optimistic guy.'

'Well, isn't it the same for all of us really?' He shrugged. 'If you're connected to someone you're always signing up to having to watch one another die. It's in our nature. I mean, you and me, we're not going to live for ever. So which one of us is gonna go first?'

I swallowed. 'Guess I've never thought about it.'

'Well, that's what Poe is talking about. Um, the shadow inside him—'

'"No power hath he of evil in himself"?'

He stared at me, looking tired, concerned. 'Nic, are you OK?'

I shrugged, shook my head, spread my hands, watching him follow the pointless gestures.

'I don't know,' I said.

'I'm going to take that shower, all right?' He gave my shoulders a squeeze, like a boxing coach. 'Keep your cool, man. Keep your cool.'

'"I ain't got time to bleed,"' I replied, snorting.

Mark smiled and wandered away into the bathroom, sniffing. When he had locked the door I hid my notepad under the sofa after looking at the picture one more time, and then left the flat again at a run.

I saw a car with blacked-out windows stop a little way down the road. The men who got out recognized me straight away, and Ronnie O'Connell slammed the passenger door with a smile.

'Caruana, you elusive bastard, where have you been then?'

Usually I heard Ronnie before I saw him. He came bounding around the car and clapped me on the shoulder with a strength that would have sent me flying if I hadn't been prepared for the impact.

He was a big man, broad and darkly handsome. The Italian in his features wasn't as diluted as mine; he had browner skin and the authentic dark eyes. If he didn't speak and betray his lack of accent he could be mistaken for the real thing; the mythical gangster of seventies films.

'Just working,' I said.

'You haven't been in touch for a while. Was Cassie OK?'

I only vaguely remembered the blonde Norwegian girl. It had been at least six months since I had used their services. I remembered that she had a sweet laugh, and a liking for handcuffs.

'Yeah, God, yeah, she was fine. It was nothing like that, I've just been really fucking busy, you know.'

'Tell me about it!' He rolled his eyes and indicated at the two other men to start walking. 'Come on, walk and talk with me, Nic.'

We started walking a few paces behind his accomplices. I recognized them as his usual security. The name Ben came to mind with the tallest one, but I couldn't be sure.

'So what's up?' Ronnie said, lighting a cigarette with some difficulty.

'It's about Felix Hudson,' I said.

He leant back a little and watched the windows of a taxi going by. 'Hudson?'

'You know of him?'

'Yeah, who doesn't? Why are you asking after him?'

'Just business.'

'Business!' He laughed. 'Cheeky fucker, just remember I know what sort of business you do. Now, why are you asking about Hudson?'

'I want to know if he hangs out at the Underground.'

'You know I can't tell you that.'

'A source says he does.'

'Ha, a *source*. And you thought you'd come to me for confirmation?' He shook his head and blew smoke out of his nose. 'No way, Nic. You're a stand-up guy but I'm not stupid. You know Edie would fucking castrate me if I started talking about stuff like that.'

'Aw, come on, Ron—'

'No.' He pointed at me this time, eyes following his hand. 'Tell me it's not fucking obvious that you're only asking me because you know Edie would tell you to get fucked.'

'I'll tell you what it's about—'

'Not interested, I can't help you.' He looked away with finality. 'God, Nic, you know you have our loyalty after all you've helped us with… but come on, basic confidentiality and all that. Noel will only tell you the same so don't think about going around me, eh?'

I had foreseen this reaction and he wasn't someone open to persuasion. It had been worth a try.

'It's OK,' I said, slowing the pace. 'I can ask elsewhere.'

'Not in the club, you can't.' Ronnie's eyes met mine and he didn't have to raise his voice to convey the threat. 'Don't ask questions in there or it'll come back to us and then *I promise* it will come back to you.'

It wasn't an empty threat, and I wouldn't mess with him for any price.

Brinks it was then.

Fucking joy.

'Wait, wait.' Ronnie stopped and threw his cigarette away. 'Eh, fellas, wait!'

Ben and the other guy halted in unison and we all followed Ronnie's gaze across the road. I couldn't see anything, but he had obviously spotted something or someone of interest. He left my side and stepped off the pavement.

'Oi! Oi, you!'

There was a small group of boys on the opposite pavement, standing outside a kebab shop and smoking. I guessed they were Turkish, and they looked in their early twenties. Only one of them looked up, until Ronnie shouted again.

'Hey!' He spread his hands. 'Long time no fucking see!'

If I wasn't mistaken, one of the youngsters noticed him then. He took a step back from his friends, who were looking confused, and dropped his cigarette.

Ronnie laughed and it made me tense. 'Fancy a chat?'

To my surprise, the young guy let out a cry and broke into a sprint.

Ronnie started running also, punching a fist down on to the bonnet of a car that had to slam on the brakes. The rest of the street watched in bemusement as his two bodyguards followed him and, compelled by curiosity, I started after them.

I soon overtook the other two, coming up behind Ronnie.

'Come on, you fuck,' he was muttering as he powered after his prey. 'Come here.'

My face was stinging.

It felt good to run again, but out of respect I didn't pass Ronnie.

They rounded a corner, down a narrow alley between a pub and a shop of some kind, and I saw the guy make a leap up a chain-link fence. He made it about halfway up before Ronnie grabbed his ankles and wrenched him off, backwards through the air until he landed, with a yelp, on the ground.

The other two, bringing up the rear, stopped behind me. One of them, the one with the moustache whose name escaped me, put his hands on his knees, gasping.

Ronnie didn't appear out of breath. He gave the guy on the ground an unceremonious kick in the ribs and turned to me, beaming.

'Who's he?' I asked.

'Well, it's a great story, really funny,' he said, directing his speech at the Turkish boy. 'See, this guy here, he actually owed me three thousand pounds. I gave him two months to pay it back... three months ago.'

He burst into hysterical laughter and slapped me across the back. The harsh sound reverberated off both walls and became louder, ringing inside my ears. Ben's expression didn't change, but the Turkish guy had started shaking so violently that he looked as though he was suffering convulsions.

'Isn't that fucking hilarious?' Ronnie said.

'Pretty funny.'

'I lol-ed myself off my fucking chair.'

'Lol?' I smiled. 'Down with the kids?'

He made a rap gesture with his fingers. ''S how I flow.'

'Damn, your kids must wish they could *be* you.'

'You know what they say,' he said. 'You do anything to make your kids laugh, and if it embarrasses them you do it even more. You should hear me at Ryan's football. He loves it.'

It was hard to imagine him as a father, I thought, as Ronnie turned his attention back to the Turkish guy.

'You know who this is?' Ronnie gestured at me, speaking

in that drawn-out way that British people do with foreigners. 'You know him? He fuck you up, yeah? He going to fuck you up? Then you have money, yes?'

I looked down at him. He was in his twenties and wasn't wearing a wedding ring. Hopefully, I thought, there weren't too many family members to be traumatized. If I was really lucky he wouldn't even have a girlfriend, or siblings.

He met my eyes and I shrugged at him, not sure what I was trying to say with the gesture.

'Honours?' Ronnie said, making a sweeping motion with his arm. 'Go on, you know you want to.'

It was hard to turn him down; he was one of my most lucrative employers. I didn't want to, not least because it meant getting forensic all over the street. But it didn't matter, not really. To my knowledge, I didn't have a file aside from what had happened to me as a minor. If I did, I wouldn't be here.

'Please...' he said, the Turkish guy. 'Please... no.'

I glanced back at the road but Ben and his colleague were standing closer together, blocking us from view. It was getting late and I had little interest in who this poor fucker owed money to.

'Please... I'll get your money!'

I nodded at Ronnie, thinking that I could put on a bit of a show and get it over with quickly.

He stepped back.

'Please...'

I wanted the guy to stop talking and jabbed him in the throat, cutting off the words before they even reached air. It was so fast that for a while his hands flailed, struggling to locate the source of his pain before he started clutching his neck.

When I landed the first blow I aimed for his face, trying to knock him out. He fell sideways and I kicked him in the ribs once, twice, before he rolled over on to his stomach.

'That's what I'm talkin' about,' Ronnie said.

I loosened my coat, so that I had more freedom, and brought my heel down on to his lower back, my mind blank aside from the familiar actions. Something cracked. I stamped on his wrist. All I could hear was the grinding of his body jerking against the concrete. It would have been easier with a cricket bat.

It was awkward to punch him from this angle so I started kicking him again. There was no resistance, no cowering, no attempt to get me to stop. He had passed out.

'Gently, fucking *gently*,' someone said.

I wiped some sweat from under my fringe and realized my hands were shaking. One final kick and I forced my muscles to a halt. I didn't think he was dead, but it was hard to tell.

The expression on Ben's face made me worry I had overdone it.

A faint gurgling sound came from deep in the back of the guy's throat, and I relaxed.

Ronnie raised his eyebrows at me. 'You sure you don't want that drink?'

'No, I'm all right,' I said, breathing hard. 'Happy?'

'I'll owe you some on the house?'

'Hey, fuckers!'

We all turned in unison, and saw six of them, standing at the end of the alleyway. A few had bats. One or two had kebab knives.

Fuck, I thought. He was Turkish.

Their leader, the one with the thickest eyebrows and the most forbidding weapon, stepped forwards. 'Eh, you think we wouldn't catch up with you. What about you, *fat boy*?'

The last part seemed to be directed at one of Ronnie's bodyguards; the one who was still out of breath.

'You don't mess with one of us.' The Turkish man pointed his blade. 'I swear to God, I'll mess up your fucking faces. How about… for every bruise I find on his body, I take a limb, yes?'

'Guys…' Ronnie spread his hands, moving away from the body on the ground with a strained expression of calm. 'I don't have any business with you.'

They laughed and took a few paces towards us. 'You do now, fuckers.'

'Guys—'

One of the knives scraped theatrically along the wall, and for a fleeting second I wondered if any bodies had ever ended up in their kebabs.

'I cut your feet off first, yes?'

I'd had enough. I took out my automatic and pointed it at their heads. 'Make *this* your fucking business!'

Three of them ran. They were the sensible ones. I wasn't in the mood for taking threats.

'You! Yeah, you three!' I made towards the ones who'd stayed, my aim steady. 'Drop them. Drop your *fucking* weapons!'

Two blades and a bat hit the ground. I kicked them away, grabbed their leader by the back of his neck and dragged him back towards their fallen comrade, keeping my gun trained on the other two.

'All of you, on your knees, against the wall.'

The other two moved slowly.

I cracked their leader's head into the brickwork and hurried them along by pointing my gun at them again.

'Move!'

One of them had already started crying, but they did as I ordered. When they were all on their knees facing the wall, and I was satisfied that they were neutralized, I turned back to Ronnie.

'Right, let's go.'

His bodyguards were wide-eyed, spooked as fuck.

But Ronnie wasn't done yet. He strode forwards, lip curling, and held out his hand for my gun.

'Fucking mess with me...' he was muttering.

'Ron, come on, let's go,' I said, pretending I hadn't noticed his gesture.

'Not a fucking chance. Gimme that.'

'Ron—'

He glared at me, and I gave him the gun.

The guy to the far right still hadn't stopped crying, so hysterical that he hacked a mouthful of bile on to the wall.

'Please...' he said.

The word was like a parasite, buzzing around my head. Every time, it was *please*... You'd think that people begging for their lives would make the effort to be more convincing; not so fucking obvious in their lack of worth. I knew it would have annoyed Ronnie too.

Ronnie walked up to him and held my gun against the back of his head.

'Fuck's sake, Ron, what are you gonna do?' I protested.

'You're about to die,' Ronnie said, ignoring me and addressing the guy kneeling by the wall. 'You can't think of anything better to say?'

If anything, his sobbing just intensified.

'Come on!' Ronnie snapped. 'Let's say... whoever has the best last words gets to live?'

Nothing.

Just a line of trembling shoulders.

I realized I had been holding my breath, willing Ronnie to leave them. Across the alleyway, his two bodyguards were still watching.

Ronnie just shrugged, disappointed with their silence. 'Fine.'

There was a crack, as the butt of my gun met the back of a skull. The first man, the one who had needed to get hold of himself, crumpled backwards on to the pavement. Without pausing, Ronnie knocked out the second, and by the time he came to the last one the novelty seemed to have worn off and he was starting to look bored.

I leapt on the chance to defuse the atmosphere. 'Let's go!'

He ignored me, addressing the last man who was conscious. 'You going to make sure your friend pays his money?'

The man turned his head a little and I saw the eyebrows move as he spoke, and a small trickle of blood running down his nose. 'He's my brother.'

'Really?' Ronnie nodded. 'Well, family fuck-ups are a bitch.'

He shot him through the back of the neck and he fell to the ground.

I put my hands behind my head.

Ronnie stepped back as blood crept towards his shoes, and tucked my gun away under his coat.

The red brick, and the man lying next to it, were stained with a fierce arc of black.

When Ronnie finally looked at me his expression was challenging.

'Problem?' he said.

I contemplated saying something, maybe voicing my irritation over the use of my gun, but then shook my head.

'Good.' He walked past me towards the main road, leaving me amongst the bodies. 'If you're sore about the gun, I'll buy you a new one. Wanna come for a drink, champ?'

I stayed in the alley, drained by the brutal waste of such violence. 'No thanks, maybe another time.'

The three of them left.

After a while, I followed them, heading back to my car.

A double-decker bus roared its way past.

At first I thought the sensation of my mobile ringing in my pocket was some leftover effect of the adrenalin, but then I came to my senses and answered it without looking at the caller ID. 'Hello?'

'Is this, um... Nic?'

It was a lady's voice, slurring a little. I took the phone away from my ear and saw Clare's name. 'Er, yeah. Sorry, this isn't Clare, is it?'

'No no, um... Look, I'm really sorry but we didn't know who else to call. She said not to call her husband or whatever and she said to call Nic, so...'

'What's going on?'

'I'm *so* sorry. We just went out to this club and... we drank a lot, took some stuff, and Clare's in a really bad way, she's a bit off her face. She just really needs someone to come pick her up...'

I looked at my watch. 'What's your name?'

'Um, Steph.'

'Where are you?'

'West End. This club called Gecko, you know it, right?'

'No, but... I'll come find you. Can you wait outside or something?'

'Yeah yeah, God, thanks. *So* sorry about this!'

'Fine, whatever. I'll be there in a... well, soon.'

I ended the call.

Sometimes violence calmed me. I didn't like that it did, but I rarely had a choice in the matter. Mark would have told me to stop worrying, that it was natural to enjoy something that I had chosen to spend my life doing. He was usually right. Maybe it wasn't me? Maybe it was the rest of the world that had the wrong idea?

I started walking back to my car, envisioning the Turkish men waking up next to their dead brother and feeling demoralized. Everything had gone into soft focus. Whether I liked it or not, I did feel calmer.

CHAPTER TWENTY-TWO

It took me almost half an hour to find the club, and most of that was spent trying to park. In the end, I decided to take my chances and left my car across the road from the place the lady had mentioned.

There was a queue, even at this time. I hadn't seen a more sorry line of people for a while, dressed in next to nothing and shivering.

They had said they would be outside.

'Nic?'

I looked to my right and a brunette in a low-cut pink dress was approaching me, struggling in ridiculous heels. She was extremely tall, and pretty, in an obvious and available sort of way.

'Yeah?'

'Who we called?'

'Um, assume so. Are you Steph?'

'Oh, thank God.' She took my arm and led me away from the club with difficulty. 'We didn't know what to do, who to call... I mean, neither of us can exactly *carry* her and we couldn't get a taxi... We didn't want to leave her anywhere.'

'What happened?'

'We went out, and we invited her cos, like, she's going through a hard time and we thought she could have some fun, right?'

'Right...'

She was talking fast and her eyes were too wide.

'And we took these pills, it was stupid, right, but I know the guy and we've never had any problem… We didn't know who to call. She just told us to call Nic, so we did. I mean, I know she's married, right, but she said he's been arrested or something?'

We rounded a corner and there were two women on a bench, opposite a row of taxis. There was another brunette, in a blue dress, who had the sense to be wearing something warm over it. Lying at an angle, covered with a coat and with her head in her friend's lap, was Clare.

'And you didn't call an ambulance?' I snapped at Steph.

'We um…' She exchanged a sheepish glance with the other brunette. 'It's the pills.'

Clare stirred and one of her heels fell off. Her legs were bare and the coat didn't cover them.

'Fuck's sake,' I muttered, crouching down. 'Clare, can you hear me?'

'I don't know whether she had a bad reaction to the E or if she's just wasted,' the other brunette said. 'We've done it before and she's been fine.'

'Yeah, thanks, that's *helpful*,' I replied without looking at her. 'Clare, it's Nic. Can you hear me?'

She tried to open her eyes fully and murmured something; her fringe was stuck to the sweat on her forehead.

'Jesus…' I rolled my eyes.

The two of them were watching me, waiting for me to remove their problem.

'Look, I'll take her home,' I said. 'Can she walk at all?'

'Um… not really.'

'OK.' I stood back with my hands on my hips, and gestured at Steph. 'Can you put her shoe back on? I'm gonna carry her to the car.'

Steph did as she was told. The other lady helped Clare sit up and I took one of her arms around my neck. At her height I thought she'd weigh more, but when I lifted her it didn't take much strain. She opened her eyes for a moment, struggled to focus and then shut them again, her head resting against my chest.

There was a sequinned bag hanging from her neck and Steph tucked it away. 'Is she going to be OK?'

'I think she's only drunk,' I said.

'Um, my coat...' Steph took a step forwards.

I glared at her. 'I've no doubt she'll make sure you get it back. You were fucking stupid, giving her pills when she's like this.'

They looked at each other. They would probably go back into the club, I realized. They didn't care, not really.

I left them and took Clare back past the club and across the road to my car. I supported her against the side of the vehicle to open the back door.

'Clare, can you... fucking wake up a bit?'

When I threatened to lower her to the ground she responded, and managed to get inside the car. She pulled the coat tighter around herself, kicked her shoes on to the floor and curled up across the back seats. Even with the scars, it was so out of character for her to seem this vulnerable.

I watched her for a moment, and took off my jacket to put across her legs.

The air was bitter, full of dim music and other people laughing.

By the time I had hurried around the car and got into the driver's seat I was already shivering. I went to start the engine and looked in the overhead mirror. She was asleep, a hand up by her face and her lips parted.

Anything could have happened, I thought, glancing back at the club.

There was an indistinct noise behind me and I turned back. 'You all right? Clare?'

She was still asleep.

'You're all right,' I said as I started the car.

The jolt of the car coming to a halt outside the house woke her up. I got out, wincing against the cold, and when I opened the rear door she was trying to sit up.

'Where...?'

'You're at home.'

The coat fell off her; she was wearing a short black dress.

'... You?'

'You got your friends to call me, remember?'

She tried to form an expression of disbelief but didn't manage it. I held out a hand but she ignored it, choosing to struggle by herself instead. She eased herself to the edge of the seat, put her bare feet down on the road and realized she didn't have her shoes.

'Um... there.' I pointed at the footwell and the high heels. 'You sure you can walk in those?'

'I'm... fine.' She reached down, managed to reach one of the shoes, and came back up looking disoriented. 'I don't... feel very...'

I took a step back as she retched and vomited a stream of stale alcohol on to the road. She started to apologize but threw up again, her shoulders trembling and her shoulder blades showing through the criss-cross straps across her back.

I was glad she had waited until we had got home.

Clare had brought her feet back up off the road, holding her forehead in both hands.

'You OK?' I said.

She sniffed and wiped her mouth on the back of her hand, but didn't look at me. 'Sorry... I don't... do this.'

'Come on...'

'I can do it,' she said, leaning down to get the other shoe.

'No. You really can't.'

She ignored me.

'And can you decide soon? Because it's really fucking cold,' I added. My eyelids were growing heavy.

For a while she sat on the edge of the seat looking down, trying to work out how much effort it would take to put on the shoes and walk to the house by herself. She sniffed again, brushed her fringe out of her eyes and held out an arm.

'OK.'

I picked her up again and felt her tense.

'Sorry,' she said as I kicked the door shut. 'How embarrassing...'

'You're fine, I've seen worse.'

I avoided her eyes as I carried her up to the front door, the hand holding her shoes draped around my shoulder.

'There's a key... somewhere...'

She fumbled with her bag and I put her down, carefully, so that she could unlock the door. She still couldn't support herself and I held her up with one arm as we stepped inside. Her skin seemed yellowed in the harsh light.

'I'm OK, you can... just go.'

'Don't be stupid, you can't stand up.'

'I'm... not stupid.'

'Look, go to bed and I'll get you some water.'

She wavered at the stairs.

'Fuck's sake,' I said, picking her up again.

'I don't... I meant when I said I don't... do this. At least not for a while.' She dropped one of the shoes as I took her upstairs but I ignored it. 'Used to do it all the time… I was the… life and party.'

It was the first time I had noticed the lines around her eyes.

I nudged open the bedroom door and set her down. 'Stay here, I'll get some water.'

Clare sat on the edge of the bed, holding the one shoe in her lap; the soles of her feet were blackened by the pavement and road. A few tears had worked their way out and smudged her eyeliner. Without looking at me she brushed her hair off her face and fixed it up in a tight bun again.

'Hey, I don't mind,' I said. 'You look fine.'

She didn't answer.

I went downstairs and picked up the other shoe on the way. While I was in the kitchen I rested it on the side, running some water from the tap and filling a glass. The black suede was tarnished and scraped away by the tarmac.

It was nearing one in the morning.

While I was here I could find her laptop, I thought, but that was for later. I didn't have to do that now.

I picked up the water and the shoe and went back upstairs. In Pat's absence, the house was quieter than I had ever heard it. As I passed Emma's room I thought of going in for another search, but that could wait until later too.

Clare was sat where I had left her, looking at the high heel in her lap as if it was her life's shoebox.

I tried to picture what would be in hers.

'Thanks.' She took the water with a shaking hand and popped a breath mint from the bedside table. 'I'm… God, I'm so sorry. It's so… disgusting.'

I put the other shoe down by the wardrobe with the mirrored doors. 'It doesn't matter, really.'

'I thought going out... would... do something,' she said, between gulps of water.

I stood for a second, but then sat down next to her. She wasn't looking at me anyway.

'Sleep it off. You'll feel... well, you'll probably feel shit in the morning.'

'It's true, you know,' she said. 'My friends... They didn't say I was the life and soul... they said I *was*... I *was* the party. Nic, I... when Emma...'

'What?'

'Nothing... Nothing important.'

She put the glass of water on the floor and leant her head against my shoulder, wiping the tears off her cheeks. It seemed to calm her down.

'It's weird, that you seem nice,' she said.

I laughed.

'No, I'm serious... I'd like to know what made you hate people so much.'

'Well, I'd like to know what made you hate yourself so much.'

'Hm, well... You first.'

With a coy smile, she took her head off my shoulder and curled up at the end of the bed. Her eyes were closed, but she seemed to be listening.

I didn't even know where to begin.

She prodded me with her toe. 'Go on.'

I pushed her foot away with a smile, realizing that I would have to share in order to get any worthwhile information out of her.

'I killed someone, this kid, when I was seventeen. It was an accident; they had the knife.' I met her eyes to judge her level of shock, but they were still closed. I wasn't sure whether she

211

had fallen asleep but I carried on regardless. 'I spent a while in juvie, then transferred to an adult prison for a year, then got out as I was apparently no longer a threat to society. My parents... well, my dad never forgave me for it. I think he's always thought it was my fault.'

She sat up against the headboard, sniffing. 'That's terrible.'

'It's just one of those things, it was an... accident. I mean, I thought I was only punching him to get him off me, I didn't realize...' I frowned, unable to comprehend why she looked so distressed. 'Come on, it's not like I was a medical student or someone who was gonna change the world in some way. Sadder things have happened.'

'No, I just... I guess I never thought about... how you would get into what you do, you know.' She fiddled with the straps of her dress, observing where they had left red welts against her skin. 'I'm sorry.'

'Your turn.'

I knew she wasn't going to tell me anything in return, but it was worth a try.

She smiled at me, rubbed some smudged eyeliner from underneath her eye and shifted forwards. Her vision didn't look entirely focused; she wouldn't even be close to sober until tomorrow evening.

Despite all this, when she went to kiss me, I let her.

That was all I had wanted, really, I realized. Maybe it was all she had wanted too, as she dropped the pretence of a heart-to-heart and came closer to press her body against mine. She tasted like mint and faintly of spirit. Nothing about her was soft, not as I remembered from the mortuary. She was made up of sharp edges and corners.

She kissed me harder, sighed against my lips, and hooked her legs around my waist. Following her lead, I ran my hand up her leg towards the hem of her dress. All I could think about was touching her, every inch of her, possessing all of that strength and that madness and making her need me as much as I needed her. But she pushed me away. Not far, but far enough away to tell me my place.

'No,' she said, biting my lip.

The images that had been playing through my head were dashed. I was so hard, aching at the prospect of holding her and fucking her and doing something that made sense to me.

But this wasn't about me, I realized. It was about her; it was always about her.

Her fingers curled around my wrists and I let her force me on to my back, grinding her hips against me, and her eyes locked on to mine as if she was daring me to challenge her.

Every move she made sent spasms through my veins.

'Clare...' I breathed, one of my hands entwined in her hair.

She was kissing my neck, her hair falling loose and brushing against my forearms. 'No.'

'Why—'

'No.'

She pulled away a few inches with her eyes half shut, and I could feel her exhales on my skin. A faint gloss of sweat had reappeared on her forehead and the hand that wasn't pinning my wrist to the bed was between her legs.

I fought for breath. 'Fuck...'

She sat up, letting me go, and smiled at me in a way that mocked my desperation to be in control. Without taking her eyes off me she loosened the straps on her shoulders and let the dress fall to her waist.

I pulled myself up and she was still touching herself, the back of her knuckles grazing my erection as if I was nothing more than her toy. I'd let her do anything, because she felt so good, so *fucking* good, but, like everyone else, I realized that the most I could hope for were the scraps she chose to throw down from her table.

Her skin was hot underneath my hands, her breasts firm under my tongue. I could hardly see her clearly any more.

She groaned and pulled my lips back to hers, running her tongue along my teeth as she rocked against her own hand. The pressure was unbearable. In my mind I forced her down beneath me and made her tell me everything, made her say my name as though it meant something to her.

Instead, she took my hand off her thigh and guided it between her legs and past her underwear.

'Mmm…' She shut her eyes tight as she directed me, bucking her hips against every thrust.

It was the biggest kick, how wet she was, how she started gasping at the sensation of my fingertips working around her clit. Suddenly she had taken my wrist again, her features clenched, arched against me as if she might just die if I wasn't inside her. She let out the smallest cry as the rest of her body jerked against me, her lips parted, and then she opened her eyes.

They were flecked with green.

A bead of sweat ran down the side of my face.

'Don't go,' she said.

I brushed my thumb along her cheek, the flushed skin and the sheen of perspiration. I didn't get it. I didn't fucking get what she wanted the world to give her.

'Please, don't go,' she said, clinging to me as if she meant it.

Like a keytar, I thought. Obviously, I was going to stay.

CHAPTER TWENTY-THREE

There was a note on the bedside table when I woke up, in a feminine italic handwriting.

'Gone to work early. Sweat it out! Thanks xxx'

In a way, I was glad. I couldn't imagine that either of us would have wanted an awkward morning conversation. After she had begged me not go she had undressed and fallen asleep next to me. It had taken hours for me to relax enough to follow suit, confused and tired and agonizingly turned on.

In a perverse way, I decided, it was some kind of progress.

Getting out of bed, I dressed quickly and went downstairs. When I switched on my phone I had a voicemail from Brinks and a voicemail from Mackie. I decided to blank Brinks for a while, leaving him to be the one holding out for a reply for once. Besides, I wasn't in the mood for his whining. Mackie could wait a bit too.

She'd left the laptop on the kitchen work surface.

I took a moment to listen for any sound outside, over the beating of my heart, and opened it. After a few seconds the desktop had loaded, and I did a search for video files.

'Fucking yes,' I said under my breath.

There was a list of videos, some of which had names like 'Emma's birthday 2005' and 'Maldives 2002'. Some, however, had nothing but generic webcam titles; things like 'Clare Dyer – Webcam video – 16:45 20/09/10'. Despite my curiosity I knew I couldn't afford to watch anything now. I went on to the internet and uploaded everything to a storage site under my login, glanced at the clock on the wall and shut the laptop without leaving any trace of it having been used.

Exhilarated by the success, I dropped my bag and sprinted back upstairs into Emma's room. This may be my only chance, I thought. Don't fuck it up.

I hadn't noticed when I'd woken up that the landing still smelt dimly of alcohol.

Looking around the room, I tried to work out what sort of person Emma was, what would make a girl develop a chronic addiction to disappointing her parents. What would have turned her into the sort of person who kept letting her father back into the house to spite her mother?

All I could remember of her face was Pat's glare.

I searched through the drawers of her dressing table, where I had found her diary, and found payslips from a restaurant, bank statements, letters from college, a pile of photos that looked as though they had missed out on being stuck around the edges of her mirror.

I looked up at my reflection for a moment, at the grey shadows under my eyes, and lost myself to the recollection of the night before. I couldn't shake it from the forefront of my mind. Was that going to be it? All I was allowed of her?

It bothered me, how much it was hampering my ability to think straight.

I gathered up all the papers and photographs, anything that looked as if it could be relevant, and took them downstairs. When I had put them in my bag I went into the living room and pulled down the shoeboxes on the top shelf. I left the photos of Emma that Clare had been looking through, but I took the rest. It wasn't as if they were going to be missed, and even if they were it didn't matter. The worst consequence I could foresee would be her disapproval.

There was still a footprint in the centre of the door on Shooters Hill. I was smoking furiously, fighting back the creeping anxiety that had been festering in my stomach since the moment I had woken up.

It took a while for someone to answer, but I recognized the girl who did. She was a platinum blonde, thinner than Harriet and with even less warmth in her face, dressed in a see-through mesh shirt and jeans.

It was the girl I'd last seen slumped against a headboard with a needle in her arm.

Like I give a fuck.

'What do you want?' she said.

'Is anyone else in?' I asked. 'I was here before looking for Kyle.'

There was a flicker of recognition, but it didn't seem to concern her. 'He's not here, hasn't been here for a while... just said I could stay until his rent ran out.'

'So you live here?'

'Looks like. Who are you?'

'My name's Nic, I'm a private investigator.' I dropped the cigarette and crushed it under my shoe. 'I wanted to talk to you about a boy called Joe O'Donoghue. Meds, you might have known him as.'

'I know... I knew Meds.' She smiled. 'Took all sorts but the good stuff.'

'Can I talk to you?'

'Whatever. Don't think I'll be able to tell you much.'

She let me in and slouched down on to a threadbare chair in the living room. It looked bigger without the people lying all over the floor, but it stank of stale food from half-empty take-out boxes. An inch of dust coated all the surfaces and a vase of dead flowers stood in the corner.

'What's your name?' I asked, sitting on the arm of a leather sofa before realizing this was where Matt's photo had been taken.

'Daisy.'

'Daisy?'

'Yes. Is that OK?'

'How old are you?'

'Nineteen – why do you care?'

'Just... shouldn't you be living with your parents or at uni or something?'

Her bony hands were steady as she lit herself a cigarette, and she gave a short laugh. 'Uni? Whatever. Who has that kind of money? And my mum and dad are a schizo and a dead-end alkie. So thanks for your concern, but I think I'm OK here.'

There was a fierce layer of red lipstick painted across her lips and she wasn't wearing a bra under the mesh shirt. When she spoke she showed a set of shockingly white and straight teeth.

'Did you know Meds well?'

'He was nice. Not always trying to get a piece of you, you know. Total fucking square, but that wasn't his fault with his condition, you know.'

'Did you know Emma Dyer?' I asked on the fly.

Her eyes widened a little. 'Ems? God, they said she died... Thought she hadn't been round for ages.'

'Who said she died?'

'Oh, Matt told us. Kyle was pretty beaten-up about it, but between you and me, Matt was just as bad. He was fucking head over heels... sucker for a posh bird, you know. She liked her coke but she was a bit of *lady*, if you know what I mean. Guys love that shit. Anyway... it was pretty sad.'

'Matt had a thing for Emma?'

'Yeah, really bad. Almost fucking tragic. He kept all these photos of her from parties and stuff, stuck with her and Kyle like a puppy, but she wasn't having any of it. She really did like our Kyle, but I suppose Matt—' As if she hadn't liked where the sentence was going, she cut herself off and inclined her head suddenly. 'Eh, do I get anything for talking to you?'

I shrugged. 'You want money?'

'Yeah, that would be safe, thanks. Just a thought.'

I glanced around the room again and noticed that the shelf above the derelict fireplace was covered in statues of birds, birds of all different types and sizes.

'Are they yours?' I pointed at them, smiling.

'I put them away for parties.' She shrugged, but seemed a little embarrassed. 'I like birds, you know. They're nicer than people.'

'So, were you here when Meds died?'

'Yeah, there was a party going on. Only me and a few girls and their guys, you know. But you wanna speak to Matt about that; I think Matt was the last one to speak to him. Said Meds was doing some smack upstairs, but I haven't seen him since.'

'Matt?'

'Yeah. Matt came by to pick up some stuff and asked if Meds was about. Went upstairs, came down, said Meds was shooting up and... well, rest is history. One of the girls goes up and the idiot has only gone and overdone it. Probably cos he never did it before, you know, too paranoid about his injections and his blood sugar and all that.'

The filthy fucking liar. I saw him looking at his watch, going through the motions of his victim act and lying through

219

his teeth the whole fucking time… I had told Meds not to mention talking to me, but he had had no way of knowing just how much danger he could have put himself in.

'It's sad,' she said, taking a drag.

'Do you know where Matt is now?'

'Not a clue. Like I said, haven't seen him since. Probably doesn't even know.'

'Fuck…'

'Are you OK? I know, it's sad, right.'

'I… No. Yeah, it's pretty sad.' I felt sick, hungry, thirsty, tired…

'You're a nice-looking guy,' she said, levering herself off the sofa and on to the floor, where she sat cross-legged and started preparing some lines of coke. '*Nic*. You want some coke?'

'No, thanks.'

'Sorry, I haven't got anything stronger. This is Kyle's leftover stuff.'

'No, I mean…'

She looked up at me as she crushed the powder into lines across a grubby hand-mirror. There were a few millimetres of brunette roots at her scalp, and she seemed endearingly oblivious to the way her nipples poked through the holes in the netting.

'Fine, fuck it,' I said, putting my bag down and sitting on the floor opposite her.

She smiled.

My hypocrisy tasted bitter on my tongue, but it felt better than trying to do the right thing by everyone.

With a practised motion, she snorted two of the lines and handed me the mirror. As I looked at them, trying not to think about what Harriet would say, she stood up and walked past me to turn on a battered CD player in the corner.

'Do you like Nirvana?' she called back.

I snorted the other two lines and grimaced as they burnt the insides of my nostrils. 'They're all right…'

'"Grandma, take me home," ha!' She turned it on, and when she came to sit back down she collapsed gawkily across my lap. 'Oh, and this, right here, this is gonna cost you a couple of hundred. You got a problem with that?'

She weighed barely over a hundred pounds. Fuck knows how many other guys she had slept with.

'Nope, no problem.'

'Groovy.'

The coke kicked in a few minutes after that, when we were naked and fucking on the living-room floor. Up close and on her hands and knees in front of me, I noticed that she had a sparrow tattooed on the back of her neck. She turned on to her back, spreading her legs, and there was the heart on her pelvis. Nothing written across it; just a blank heart.

Daisy was a pretty name.

Afterwards, when she had let me come across her chest and she had wiped it off and we had snorted another two lines of coke, she told me that her mum was in another psychiatric ward. She also told me that she used to know where Matt's parents lived and that the way to tell the difference between common city pigeons and wood pigeons was the heavier build and the white collar around the wood pigeon's neck.

'They don't have the collars when they're younger… it's like they earn them. They're like the priests of the bird world, you know,' she said, laughing to herself as I lay there trying to forget anything that existed before and after my trip to this house. 'I'd like to come back as a bird, you know, if we come back after we've died. My dad used to put food out for the birds every day... we had finches and crows and stuff, and he'd never miss a day. Huh, never gave a shit about us, but no matter how drunk he was he never missed a day for the birds. Even when they did things like crap all over his car he'd never stop putting the food out.'

'So you'd come back as a bird, yeah?'

'Totally. What would you come back as?'

'Someone religious,' I said. 'Or a cat.'

'Haha, good one.' She laughed. 'Just try not to kill me, yeah? It would really put a downer on my flying around and sitting on feeders all day.'

I snorted. 'It's a deal.'

'Pinky swear?'

'What the fuck?'

She held out her hand and linked her little finger around mine. I didn't know whether it was the coke making me laugh, but at that moment I couldn't remember finding anything so fucking funny.

CHAPTER TWENTY-FOUR

At Mark's request I stopped at a Tesco on the way home to pick up some food, or as he put it, 'Something other than vodka, port and that bit of Brie you've been living on. Maybe something green that's not mould or jelly? Ta, Nic.'

Painful air whipped around the corners and up the ramps, catching us all in the wind tunnel.

I dumped a load of shopping bags in the boot and failed to notice the Mercedes approaching up the ramp of the car park until I reversed out, and it cut me up with a wail of brakes.

'*Christ!* Fuck's sake!'

Fuming, I stormed out of the car, praying for the opportunity to get in someone's face. It wasn't until I saw him getting out of the driver's seat that I realized it was Pat's Mercedes.

'Hey! What the *fuck*?'

'*You*,' he snarled, coming around the car.

Something feral in his expression made me stop in time to lessen the blow when he tried to punch me in the stomach. I grabbed his wrists as I was thrown onto the back of the car.

'Jesus, Pat...'

'You think I'm fucking stupid? Is that it?'

'What?'

'I said to keep an eye on her, but from what I hear you've been getting a bit too fucking involved.'

I forced his hands away from my throat and kicked him in the shins, making him step back. My ribs ached a little but it would be an easy lie to tell, even with the constant replaying of the night before behind my eyes: Clare grinding against me, gripping my hand between her legs as she made herself come...

'She was off her head at a nightclub and I took her home, what the fuck's your problem?'

'I had someone watching the house! You didn't leave!'

'I slept on the sofa – she'd taken a bad fucking E! What, you'd rather I left her there and let her over-drink or pass out or choke to death, is that what you're saying?'

He was breathing hard, but I seemed to have got through enough to make him think twice before punching me again.

'Nic, I'm not an idiot,' he said. 'You want her and you think she wants you, but the thing is, with her, *everyone* thinks that. That's why she's so great, isn't it? That's why everyone falls for her. She makes you think she's there to be fucking rescued and I hate to piss all over your parade, but that's just how she is. If you're smart you'll watch, fucking *observe*, but do anything else and I swear—'

'Why do you care?' I snapped. 'Every time I come round there she's beaten up in some way, you think I haven't fucking noticed?'

'God, you're so fucking *dense*.'

'Well, explain it to me!' I shouted, taking a step forwards. 'Everyone's telling me I don't understand or that I've got the wrong idea, so go on, *Pat*, explain it to me! Explain why she's always got bruises and she's covered from head to toe in scratches and cigarette burns, and why she's had you charged with assault, and that time you put her in hospital with—'

'I what?'

'Yeah, I know. I talk to people. I'm not the only one who's noticed.'

He didn't seem able to find the words. There was nothing

224

he could say when he was faced with the image of himself through everyone else's eyes.

'She dropped the charges, after she gave her statement. She dropped them.'

'Well, good for you,' I sneered.

'So... what?' he said. 'So you came to find out who killed my little girl, and on the way you've decided your fucking mission is to save my wife?'

I didn't say anything but I started to shiver again.

Pat shook his head at me. 'You don't think, after seventeen years, that I might have worked out how to do that for myself?'

'No,' I said, no longer caring that he was my employer or that I was letting my petty dislike get in the way of basic professionalism. 'You know what I think? I think you're the fucking problem.'

I expected anything else, but not laughter. He had to turn away, venting his hysterics into the back of his hand. It wrongfooted me, made me feel as if, again, some crucial point had just soared a thousand feet over my head.

'Jesus... I'm her problem? That's it? Trust me, I fucking *wish* that I was. In fact, I wish that she only had one fucking problem! *I'm* her problem... God, how much sweeter life would have been.'

'If you love her so much then how can you talk about her like that? How can you fucking *do* it?'

'*Yes!*' He lurched forwards, taking hold of my arm with a fist hovering in front of my face. 'Yes, *that's* right, I fucking love her. You have no idea how much, or how much *fucked-up* shit I've had to deal with, but I love her and I *know* her.'

I was readying myself for the blow, but it didn't come. He just hissed at me.

225

'I'll believe you when you say nothing happened last night, because she's too good for you and she knows that... She's screwed up but she's got standards.'

I refused to let him see that I was stung by the element of truth in his words.

'But...' he said. 'If I find out that anything's happened, that you've overstepped, then I will fuck you up. I will fuck you up even more than she will.'

He let me go and smoothed down the cuffs of his jacket. I didn't know whether I entirely hated him; I hated him, but I also hated him because he had her. That was what bothered me most of all.

Pat leant against the bonnet of his car for a moment and sniffed. 'She's not all right, is she?'

'She was just wasted.'

'No, but she talks to you, I know she's talked to you.'

'She's...' I ended up shrugging, wishing, as ever, that I knew enough to say more. 'I don't think this is the best time to try and judge what's normal and what's not. I think... she's getting by, but she needs help. Maybe she should talk to someone, someone like—'

'She'd never do it. I tried before when—' He cut himself off. 'She won't.'

I zipped my coat right up to my chin. 'Did she not become a ballerina because she was too tall?'

'*Freakishly* tall... She told you that?' He nodded. 'Yeah. When she was nineteen, before we had Emma. That's when they said that to her.'

I shrugged.

'I can't go back to the house yet,' he said. 'I'm gonna try calling. Are you...? Has anything happened?'

'I've got some solid leads. It's just gonna take some time.' I was glad he had finally asked something I could give a stock answer to.

'OK.' He stood up and opened up the driver's door again. 'Look… I meant what I said. You won't come out the other side, I *fucking* mean it.'

I nodded.

As he got into his car, it struck me what an odd thing that had been to say.

I will fuck you up even more than she will.

Pat's Mercedes pulled away and turned left to exit the car park. I watched it go and got back into my own car, thinking about the webcam videos and how many I would be able to watch before I had to answer Mackie's voicemail.

I let myself in with the tonne of shopping bags and listened for any signs of life, but Mark didn't seem to be home.

The message from Mackie told me he had scheduled a meeting with Felix Hudson tonight at the Underground. I knew it would be fucking about with Ronnie, and had a good chance of getting back to Edie, but I was in a reckless mood and decided to find a way around that at the time. All I needed was a decent visual and hopefully a car to follow.

With an hour or so to spare I sat down with the laptop and the photos and papers I had taken from the house.

For one stupid moment I considered calling Harriet and telling her I had spent the morning snorting lines of coke off a hooker's hand-mirror, just to make her feel better, but I didn't think she would appreciate the humour.

As my desktop loaded I took a pile of photos and shuffled through them. There were a few family photos, from holidays and Emma's Holy Communion. Then there were some older ones.

I stopped at a photo of Clare, posing outside the Royal School of Ballet. She looked older than Emma had been; she must have been about eighteen. She was wearing jeans and a simple white top, and had more weight on her face. When she smiled she looked softer, sweeter somehow. She was beautiful now, I thought, but she had been far more beautiful then, when her beauty hadn't deformed her, when she didn't look as though she had learnt to use it to break other people down.

In another photo she was with Pat, looking the same age and surrounded by people. When I turned it over the familiar handwriting said 'Jenny's party '94'. She was wearing a silver masquerade mask over a black party dress. Pat was wearing one too. I could only see their eyes, and their arms around each other.

'Emma's 1st birthday '95'. Clare was sitting on a living-room floor that I didn't recognize, feeding Emma from a bottle. Her hair was in plaits and she wasn't looking at the camera; she was looking down at Emma in her lap with an expression similar to the one I had seen when she was dancing. Probably love, I thought. I had to put the photos down.

I fired up the internet and logged in to the storage site, wanting Mark to come home and provide some sort of objectivity.

Starting from the most recent, I opened the video and waited. Part of me was excited, too excited for my liking, and part of me was filled with dread.

I heard a key in the front door and scrambled forwards to pause it.

'Honey, I'm...!' Mark spotted the shopping bags in the hallway as he shut the door. 'Ooh, vegetables. Halle-fucking-lujah.'

'Hey, shut up and come watch this!'

'So demanding.' He leapt over the back of the sofa and landed neatly next to me, still wearing his coat and shoes. 'Wow, you got the laptop then?'

'Copied all the video files, just watching them back in reverse.'

He glanced back over his shoulder. 'Can I put the frozens away?'

'There's no— No, shut up and fucking watch.'

'No popcorn? No—'

I punched him in the leg and pressed Play while he was still laughing. As I leant forwards to see the screen better he took the wad of photos off the table and started flicking through them.

This video was set in the same dance studio as the first one she had sent me. I assumed that it was where she worked. The date was only a few days ago.

'She was prettier when she was younger, wasn't she?' Mark said.

I smiled to myself.

'I don't mean that in a "because she's younger" kind of way,' he added. 'But she looks nicer, she looks like...'

'Think you mean happier.'

'Yeah, that'll be the one,' he said, sounding downcast.

Clare entered the frame with a graceful twirl, her hair flying about her and wearing a red dress and white tights that looked designed for dancing. I wondered if this was what she did in the gaps between teaching other people, created these fantasies so that she could take a look at them afterwards and pretend she was performing for someone other than herself.

She turned on the spot for a while, one leg alternating between kicking out to propel her round and tucking inwards towards her ankle. It was what she seemed best at, the spinning around in circles.

I counted six turns to the sultry music in the background, before she stopped, pushing out with her hands as if to drive the camera away, and steadying herself before circling the studio on the tips of her toes. Her arms whirled and she launched into a flying leap.

'Look at this,' Mark said, passing me a picture as his eyes flickered between the photos and the computer screen. 'Emma's 14th '08'.

I took it and held it up so that I wouldn't have to take my eyes off the screen. It was of Clare with Emma, in the kitchen I knew so well. At a glance it was just Clare and Emma, standing side by side, blonde next to brunette.

'Yeah?' I said, watching Clare lower herself into a curtsey.

'Isn't it funny that she's kind of... trying to out-pose her? Whose birthday is it? Who's that a photo of? It's not a photo of Emma, is it?'

I looked at the photo again. He was right, as he usually was. It was probably meant to be a birthday picture, the sort of picture that was a chance for someone like Clare to show off her daughter. But it wasn't like that at all. Clare was the one facing the camera, the one with the unnervingly direct stare, as if, standing there next to her daughter, all she could feel was the loss of the person she used to be.

'Nic...'

'No, I see it.'

'No, look.'

I did look, just in time to see Clare smash her forehead into the mirrored wall. She jerked away, held her head as she leant against the glass, and then sent her face crashing into the mirror again.

'*Jesus.*' I felt sick.

'Shitting... hell...'

She walked back to the centre of the frame on her tiptoes; keeping her balance with one arm while her other hand gripped her forehead. Her hair covered any bruising, but when she twirled, offbeat, towards the camera again, she was crying. It was a very controlled crying, I thought, as if she had learnt to cry while still looking attractive.

Her arms made the motion of wings as she knelt down in front of the lens, her cheeks shining with tears. She covered her eyes, like the heroine in a Shakespearian tragedy, and the video stopped rolling.

We sat there for a while in dumb silence.

I still felt like I was about to throw up.

'That just happened, right?' I said.

'For sure... Got to say, I expected a lot, but I didn't see that coming.' He rewound the video enough for us to watch that moment again.

Clare spun towards the mirror, hesitated for a moment and then, with a ferocity that shocked me, smashed her forehead into the glass. If I had head-butted someone like that I would have given myself borderline concussion. Watching it, I could almost feel the impact against my skull.

'God.' Mark leant forwards with his chin on his hands. 'That's... Hm.'

I wasn't used to him being rendered speechless. 'Hm?'

'It's interesting.'

'That's all you've got to say? "Interesting"?'

'Well, what would you call it?'

'Fucked-up.'

He raised his eyebrows, as if chiding me for my lack of imagination.

'And where did you stay last night?' he asked.

'With a girl,' I half lied.

'Yeah? Who?'

'She's called Daisy.' I grinned at how absurd it was going to sound. 'She... likes birds.'

Deciding not to pursue that particular subject, Mark shrugged and stood up. 'It's interesting.'

While he was in the kitchen putting some shopping away, I rewound the video and watched it again.

'Wait! Wait for me!' Mark shouted when he heard the music, darting back into the room to lean on the back of the sofa. 'Right, go.'

We watched it through again in silence. I thought about the time she had asked me to hit her and the bruise on her face. Had this been where it had come from? I looked at the date; it looked likely.

It's not his fault, you know.

I put a hand to my mouth.

Sometimes it's better to just feel something, I guess. Or something... different, at least.

'Fuck,' I said, under my breath.

'What?'

Well, I'd like to know what made you hate yourself so much.

'Nic, what?'

'I don't think he hits her,' I said, the realization flooding me with nausea. 'That's why Emma always let Pat back in the house. It was because it wasn't him... It was her.'

Mum on one of her head-fucks...

Mark could afford to look so morbidly intrigued; he wasn't the one who had made so many judgements. I rewound the video, played it again, watched her hesitate for that tiny

232

second before trying to crack her own head open, fists clenching against the glass, the straps of her dress loosening and falling across the cuts at the tops of her arms.

I had been so stupid, so fucking blinkered.

'Controversial shit,' Mark said. 'You want a drink?'

I glanced at the clock and stood up sharply. 'Can't, got a meeting.'

CHAPTER TWENTY-FIVE

Mark had been sitting on the living-room floor making a rough collage out of the stolen photos and paperwork when I'd left to meet Mackie. He had also let me borrow a spare firearm, which had felt alien in my hands.

If I made more of my spare time between jobs, like Mark did, then the Underground would probably be where I would spend most of it.

A regal-looking redhead called Portia let me in. I was glad it was her and not the same girl as last time, or Ronnie, even if he did owe me a favour. Hopefully he wasn't working here tonight and I would be able to avoid him without any fuss.

I ordered a sparkling water that I could at least pass off as a gin and tonic, and leant against the bar.

Some sort of modern jazz was playing, and a girl that I recognized was on stage dancing in a red G-string. Knowing this place, the stones lining the straps of her stilettos would be diamonds.

Mackie was sitting near the stage; I spotted his wispy hairline.

He glanced back at me once and looked away quickly.

My mobile vibrated.

WILL TALK, THEN LEAVE. MEET ME AT THE CAR AFTER, PARKED OUT BACK. M.

'Caruana.'

I turned and Noel Braben, joint manager and Ronnie's

234

partner in all other illegitimate escapades, was leaning on the bar. It was almost confirmation that I wouldn't run into Ronnie and have to explain myself.

'Braben.'

Noel was a good two or three inches shorter than me, with a weathered face and heavy eyebrows, but the expression in his blue eyes always suggested that he had just told the most hilarious anecdote.

It was odd, seeing such forceful personalities as him and Ronnie work so easily under Edie. But it suited them. They had free rein of the club and enough spare time on their hands to pursue their more lucrative ventures into drugs.

'That's a fetching mullet you're rocking,' he said.

'It's not a fucking mullet, and what did you come as? Where did you get that suit?'

'It's Yves Saint Laurent, I'll have you know.'

'Nice, was it delivered by Tardis?'

'Ah, shut up, Bono.'

We both sipped our drinks.

'Haven't been around for a bit?' Noel said. 'Was Cassie all right?'

'God, yeah, Cassie was fine. Been busy with work.' I kept an eye on Mackie but he was still alone. 'Business good?'

'Mental. Christmas time.' He rubbed his hands together. 'Girls keep asking for time off though, which is... annoying. Edie's a fucking soft touch with them but, you know, they can't have everything...'

'How's Caroline?'

'Dunno.' He pulled a face. 'Separated and all.'

'Fuck, sorry.'

As he waved away the platitude I noticed that he wasn't wearing his wedding ring any more. I'd met Caroline once or twice; she was a fiercely pretty and quick-witted accountant with red hair. Listening to any exchange between her and Noel was like listening to sarcasm made into an Olympic event.

'It's only a phase, I'm sure,' he said. 'She'll be back. Are you just watching or do you want me to sort you out a lovely lady?'

'Just chilling.'

'Wicked.' He put a hand on my shoulder. 'Gonna entertain, good to see you.'

When he left me I started getting tense. Mackie was still sitting alone. The girl on stage had finished her dance and gone into one of the private rooms off the floor of the main club.

The jazz had been replaced by something more classical. If I wasn't mistaken the next girl on stage in the white lace was Seven, the Japanese girl. I couldn't help smiling to myself. She was something else, but then I suppose you had to be, working for these guys. They only hired the best.

'I could tell you some stories about that sweet Japanese type.'

The man standing behind me at the bar was someone I knew I had seen before, but I couldn't place where. He looked too young to have the bald head that he did, and had a scar down his left cheek. When he spoke a gold tooth kept winking at me.

'So could I,' I replied, taking it slow with the sparkling water.

'Do you know what she is most partial to?'

'I remember she liked handcuffs.'

The man was wearing a beige golfing jumper and had a neat moustache. He seemed friendly enough, but the combination of features unnerved me.

'One of her favourite films, *American Psycho*.' He grinned. 'She likes to re-enact scenes. You know it well?'

Mark and I had quoted it every day for at least a month after we had last watched it. One night when we were hammered on brandy Mark had let slip that once, in the middle of hacking some poor guy to death in Russia, he hadn't been able to resist screaming, 'Try getting a reservation at Dorsia now!' I had laughed for three days.

I raised my eyebrows, smiling. 'Do you like Huey Lewis and the News?'

'So catchy,' the man said, raising his glass.

'Which scenes?' I asked.

'Bathroom.'

'Video camera?'

'And coat hangers.'

'Ha, sick.'

I could believe it of her, I thought, but then there wasn't much that these girls wouldn't cater for. It didn't mean they liked it, they just did it. They were clean, and they were safe, but they were there to fulfil a fetish and to be agreeable. What he was describing was most likely his fantasy rather than hers.

I saw Clare's forehead smashing into the wall, and my lip curled.

'"Is evil something you are? Or something you do?"'

I turned back to him again – I'd been hoping that at that point he would have left me alone. 'Sorry?'

'Shame on you. Novel's best line.'

'My flatmate would know, he has more of a memory for quotes than me.'

'So, what do you think?'

'What?'

'Is evil something you are? Or something you do?'

I smiled, but his eyes were dead above the golfing jumper and I hadn't seen him blink once. 'I'll have to let you know after a few more G and Ts.'

'I like your style. Have a good night, sir.'

The man put his glass down, bared his teeth at me and left the bar. I was glad he had gone. I looked around the club for Noel, making a mental note to ask who he was, but when I did I noticed that Mackie had gone.

'Shit...' I put my glass down, checked my phone but saw nothing. 'Fuck's sake, Mackie.'

I walked to the front of the club and back again, scanned the blurred faces for any sign of him, but there was nothing. As I came back towards the bar I bumped into Noel again, who clapped me on the arm.

'You all right, Nic?'

'You haven't seen Mackie Woolstenholme, have you? You know, Mackie?'

'Damn, spotted him earlier but didn't speak to him. I'll keep an eye out.'

'Thanks...'

'Hudson's a character, isn't he?'

I stared. 'What?'

'Hudson. Saw you two chinwagging. He's a funny guy, a proper livewire.'

'Oh Jesus...' I felt as if my stomach had been pitted.

'You all right?'

'No... Yes, I mean, yes, I've just got to go. Thanks, mate.'

Leaving him looking bemused by my sudden exit, I made a run for the club doors. Outside I skidded on the wet pavements, rounded the far corner in the drizzle and saw Mackie's red Ford parked under the solitary lamppost.

I jogged up to it, saw Mackie in the driver's seat, and got

into the car beside him, snapping, 'You could have given me some fucking warning. I—'

I froze.

His throat was cut.

My first instinct should have been to get out, but I couldn't take my eyes off him, the relentless cascade of blood, so much of it, running down the inside of his coat, on to his trousers, into the footwell.

The cut was so deep that his head looked almost severed from his body.

His eyes were still open.

When I came to my senses I checked the back seats and scrambled out of the door with such force that I fell and scraped my shin on the road. I shut the door, then opened it again and turned the headlights off.

My heart pounding, I started to sprint away from the car, but stopped when I remembered that my fingerprints were all over the door handle. I went back, wiped away what I could and tried not to look too closely at Mackie's vacant stare.

'Oh Jesus, Mack... Jesus...'

I opened the door and searched for his driving licence, wallet and any other identifying documents. As I jogged him his head seemed to move independently of his body. I looked through the back window of the car and the windscreen, but there was no one else around.

Once I had taken his wallet, I shut the door and left by the other end of the road, taking the long route to my car. There was no file, I kept telling myself. I had no file, no shoebox... But I couldn't risk it.

I stopped and got out my mobile.

*

I was watching both ends of the road when Mark arrived in the passenger seat of a brutal 4x4. It belonged to Roman Katz, an ageless Russian man with lips that reminded me of a dead fish and skin so pale that I could see all the veins in his hands. He freaked the fuck out of me, but he was a good friend of Mark's and, from what I knew of him, someone who was useful to have at the end of a phone in a crisis.

The two of them were wearing identical black coats with fur-lined hoods.

Katz had started up the Ford after lining the seats with plastic bags and pushing Mackie's body on to the next seat. He moved without ceremony, with no reaction, not even to the amount of blood.

'You know this man well?' he asked me around his elegantly poised cigarette, before he shut the door.

'I knew him, yeah. I suppose we weren't really friends.'

'It can still be strange. People are but associates, but when they are gone it feels similar like... always losing your car keys, I think.'

At least, I thought, Mackie hadn't died wearing a pair of stilettos. The last time I'd seen him he'd been so pitiful in his resignation; he had known this was going to happen, that he was going to die, and he hadn't bothered to make a fuss.

Katz drove behind me, with Mackie propped up in the next seat, while Mark followed us in Katz's 4x4. He hadn't asked me what had happened and took my basic explanation at face value, though I expected he would ask more questions later.

'We were going to go out for a drink,' he said. 'But this was as good a social occasion as any.'

'Yeah, sorry to drag you guys out.'

'No, I'm serious. Roman is like you, he doesn't know how not to work.'

We parked up outside a landfill, covered the Ford in petrol and set fire to it. I could taste copper on my tongue again and I felt light-headed suddenly, but I was sure it wasn't guilt. I couldn't stop watching the car through the thick plumes of smoke being carried off towards the M25, searching for the outline of Mackie's body as if I expected him to come walking straight out of the wreckage.

I stared, mesmerized, until Katz announced that he was going to go home to his wife. He never raised his voice when he spoke, and he spoke slowly, as if he expected others to strain to listen rather than exert himself in any way.

'I owe Mark many favours,' he told me, shaking my hand with the sensation of wet lettuce leaves. 'It is of no inconvenience to me. Besides, a healthy fireplace at Christmas, it is good for the soul, do you not think?'

He chuckled to himself, let go of my hand and got into his 4x4. After a brief exchange with Mark in Russian he left us alone, shivering, by the landfill.

'I fucking hate that guy,' I said.

'*Every* time...'

'I know, I know, he looks worse than he is.'

'You know who it was?' Mark asked as we leant against the bonnet of my car, watching the flames. 'Who offed him?'

'Hm...' I sighed. 'It was Hudson. I only took my eyes off him for a moment... God, tonight was such a fuck-up, you have no idea. This whole thing... *Such* a fuck-up.'

'What's going on with you?' He ruffled the back of my hair. 'This Clare thing... moving flat... Felix Hudson near cutting people's heads off... I wish you'd fucking tell me.'

When I tried to reply I realized that I was crying. The boot had flown open, hanging in the air like the tail of a helicopter. The burning shell of the car looked to me like rotor blades and the roar of the tall flames sounded like vehicles, like shouting, like gunshots, like warfare.

I rubbed my cheeks with both hands but the tears kept coming.

'Sorry,' I said.

Mark lit a cigarette with one hand, ruffled my hair a bit more, and didn't say anything. It was nice of him to spare me the embarrassment of a proper acknowledgement.

I held the emotion behind glassy eyes for what felt like a long time, maybe half an hour or something, and the only thing I managed to say was, 'I miss him.' If I'd said any more everything would have come crashing out.

Mark handed me the packet of cigarettes.

The air around us was warm but the smell was acrid. The smoke was starting to hurt my eyes and scrape against the back of my throat every time I inhaled.

'Not Mackie,' I said. 'I don't miss... Mackie. You know, I was talking about—'

'No.' Mark smiled, putting an arm around my shoulders and squeezing. 'No, I got that, thanks.'

I turned around and smoked my cigarette facing the roof of my car.

The helicopter burned in the corner of my eye.

CHAPTER TWENTY-SIX

'Hi, darling, it's me... Obviously, haha!'

After watching Clare's other video from the studio a few more times by myself, I started watching the others. My clothes and hair smelt of smoke, but I was too tired to think about taking a shower before morning.

The picture of her I had drawn was lying beside my laptop, watching me.

There were so many webcam videos, but the next one I clicked on seemed to have been filmed on Emma's last birthday. Clare was sitting on her sofa in the living room, wearing a green dress against a golden tan, and her hair cut a little shorter than I was used to.

I was so tired that my concentration was lapsing, and I started the video again after a few seconds, having dozed off against my headboard.

Clare smiled again. 'Hi, darling, it's me... Obviously, haha!'

I wished I had known her when she was normal. Or at least, when she had been able to smile like that. I noticed that the scars I was used to seeing all over her arms had been covered with make-up.

'Your dad is going to make one of these too... I'm a bit of a scaredy-cat with computers and stuff but he says we can email it... We both hope you're having the best time on holiday! I just wanted to say... happy birthday on your actual birthday, so happy birthday, darling!'

I looked at the date, and it was less than three months ago.

'We both miss you so much, and can't wait for you to come back so you can have your presents and...' She paused, fiddled with her hair and laughed. 'You know, I've done like ten of these and your dad is getting super annoyed that I keep messing up so I should probably try and finish this one.'

I turned the volume down so that Mark wouldn't hear me watching the videos through the walls. The collage he had made on the floor of the living room was still there, like a perverse family tree. He had kept Mackie's documents too; he didn't tell me what he had done with them but I knew he had a fascination with other people's history. Unlike me, he liked to think of everyone he came across in his work as individuals; he liked to know their stories.

'When you were first born... and Dad said I shouldn't tell you this, but I'm going to come clean. When you were first born, I dropped you off the back of a table... Haha, no, really, I did! I came in and I had these shopping bags and I put your carrier down on the kitchen table and...' She hesitated. 'It was like slow motion, like I couldn't get there in time... You just... fell off, and then you were upside down on the floor.'

The hard drive was getting too hot, and I balanced the laptop across my knees.

'You probably don't even get why it's a big deal to me, but when you have kids... Sorry' – she put up her hands – '*if* you have kids... you'll get it. I thought I was going to faint and cry and go mad all at once, I couldn't get over to you quick enough... And you were fine. It was so stupid of me, you were fine.'

It was harder to watch than the video in the dance studio.

Her speech wavered, and she looked up over the camera and laughed, such an unfamiliar sound.

'Now your dad is looking at me thinking, "Oh God, now she's going to cry…" But it's true. I was so scared I was going to lose you and… I suppose why I'm telling you this story is because I'm trying to say that I love you… more than anything, and you're the best thing in my life, darling. You're probably rolling your eyes and saying, God, she reads too many sappy books, like you usually do, but it's true. And I don't know what I'd do without you. So… have a great birthday and when you get back we'll party like it's not 1999, right?'

She wiped her eyes and glanced from the camera to the space above it.

'OK… Your go? Was that OK?'

The video froze and she was still smiling.

I dragged the cursor back and listened to her saying it again.

… is because I'm trying to say that I love you… more than anything, and you're the best thing in my life, darling…

I put a hand over my eyes.

And I don't know what I'd do without you. So…

What Pat had told me in that pub in Victoria made sense. In my job there was never a before and after picture. I had never been able to see how people had got from one place to another in their lives. Not like this.

Your go? Was that OK?

All I could see in her expression was something she would never be able to get back. She had answered the door, I had shaken her hand and thought that her eyes were full of sadness… and now the woman in this video from three months ago might as well have been someone else.

Try not to worry too much. You know, I'm sure she's fine.

That was what I had said to her that night, before I'd left. I'd actually fucking said that. I couldn't believe how ridiculous it sounded now.

She'd call if she was.

I knew I had said sorry to them before, I remembered doing so. I hadn't meant it though, or understood what I was saying.

It was half past three in the morning and I couldn't look at the end frame of that video any more.

I clicked on the next one.

This time it was Pat sitting on the sofa, still wearing a suit but looking strikingly younger before grief had aged him. He was frowning, the lens was jumping a little, and then he laughed. 'Clare, it's a bloody webcam, not Concorde... Look... there, *there*, press that!'

Clare was laughing as the picture came in and out of focus. 'OK, OK, I've got it!'

'Getting it?'

'Got it.'

'Right.' Pat gave the camera a thumbs-up and sarcastic smile. 'Hey, M&M, how's it going? I think your mum may have tested the memory capacity enough already so I'll keep it short... Um, happy birthday. Big sixteen... don't have sex. No, seriously.'

I felt like the biggest dickhead in the world. It had been so much easier to despise him for who I thought he was than feel sorry for him for what he'd lost.

'Anyway, M&M, we miss you bunches. Really, I've bought that motorbike with flames up the side and everything, so you'd better come home quickly, you hear me? Before I take up mountain climbing or something... Good stuff. I love you, it's *obscene* how much, quite frankly. So stay safe, *not* in that way, and we'll see you when you get back.' His gaze flicked upwards and he smirked. '*That's* how it's done.'

I thought of him calling Emma's mobile, over and over again so that he could hear her voice.

'Oh, shut your face,' I heard Clare say.

'They call me one-take Pat.'

'Ha ha!'

Unable to watch any more, I shut the laptop and put it on the floor beside the bed. I looked at the picture for a while, but it inspired nothing. I switched the lamp off but it felt like a futile gesture; I doubted that I was going to be able to sleep.

My pillow smelt of smoke.

The bar didn't have any windows, and aside from the weak candles the majority of the lights came from the green neon sign in the corner that reminded me of the dodgy places you found in mid-America. Over in a strange adjoining room were a white grand piano and a fireplace, with two old-fashioned patterned chairs.

I sat down in front of the bar, but there was no barman. When I started looking around one of the two men sitting the other side of the room stood up and walked behind the bar. He spoke with a Dutch accent and was wearing a brown waistcoat.

'What are you looking for?'

'Just a whiskey, Irish if you've got some.'

'Let me see...' He turned away and searched the spirit shelf.

While he was looking, I took the opportunity to size up the rest of the bar. The barman had been sitting with a middle-aged man in a crumpled white shirt to my right, and there were two women playing pool to my left.

'Double?'

'Please.' I got out my wallet as he handed me the glass. 'How much?'

He shrugged. 'Call it five pounds? Leave it anywhere.'

'Anywhere? Not... the till?'

'Man, I don't work here.' He spread his hands with an apathetic expression, and returned to his companion.

I left a five-pound note by the till.

Tchaikovsky was playing.

When I turned around on my barstool to face the rest of the bar the two women playing pool had gone. I wondered if someone was on the grand piano, and slid off the stool to go and stand in the archway separating the rooms.

Mark was dancing between the chairs with Clare, a waltz. She was wearing her red ballet dress.

I went to sip my whiskey but it had disappeared from my hand.

'You can't take drinks outside,' a familiar voice said. 'Isn't she beautiful?'

I looked sideways and the companion of the man in the brown waistcoat had come to stand next to me. It was only up close that I realized it was Mackie.

'What... What are you doing here?' I asked.

'This isn't real,' he said, smiling. 'Remember?'

I watched Mark and Clare, dancing around and around and around...

'She is beautiful.'

'Hm,' I agreed.

'Pity you can't see her face any more.'

I looked closer. Clare's face was a grey, empty space. No features, no shadows. Her skin was that of a statue, that thing in her living room.

When I looked back to Mackie I found myself looking at the gap-toothed tribal mask.

'Fuck!'

I pushed him away and his head lolled from his shoulders. He staggered backwards, his jugular and vocal cords severed and exposed, pulsing blood down his front. With some difficulty, he reached up and pulled his head back on to his shoulders, his voice echoing from behind the mask.

'God,' he said, with a mild annoyance. 'Now look what you've made her do.'

Clare was standing right in front of me, and I could see her face again.

I jerked away, tried to push her back but she grabbed the front of my shirt, whirled me around and threw me backwards on to the floor between the chairs. From the floor I could see under the piano: white-skinned feet were pressing against the pedals.

Mark was gone.

Clare stood over me, glaring. 'I'm so tired of dancing to her song.'

Back under the piano I saw blood running down the legs, on to the bare feet.

'No, please…' I backed away. 'I fucking hate Tchaikovsky!'

She threw a handful of soil in my face.

I woke up, choking, with a hand over my mouth.

There wasn't any soil. It was seven in the morning and it was still too dark to see the outlines of anything familiar in my room. I could hear that Mark was awake though, wandering around the kitchen with the kettle boiling.

I sat up, trying to remember what the fuck had happened in my dream. All I could remember was Clare's face, and saying something about Tchaikovsky… something about… feet.

Shaking my head, I switched the light on, thinking about Clare's face, Clare when she was young…

Mark was singing along to an eighties disco tune in a comedy voice.

I snorted, and remembered him and Clare dancing around a room.

Clare's face...

Something that had been playing on my mind clicked into place. The thing about Emma that I hadn't liked, that calculating confidence I had assumed was inherited from her father, didn't actually remind me of Pat at all. It reminded me of Clare.

Unsettled by the realization, I swung my legs over the side of the bed and switched on my phone.

I had forgotten about the voicemail from Brinks. I didn't want to speak to him, but I needed to ask him about CCTV footage from around Shooters Hill to try and help clarify what had really happened with Matt and Meds.

I called 901 and listened to the new message.

'Nic, it's me. It's Geoff... Brinks...'

The first thing that struck me was that he sounded even more hysterical than usual. Always a good sign if I was in the mood for entertainment. If Brinks had been into theatre he could have acted out his own one-man tragedy, I was sure of it.

'I'm fucked, mate, I'm... fucked. I need to see you, please. I *need* to see you!'

I started laughing. I couldn't help it. The relentless wailing was too reminiscent of a teenage girl for me to take it seriously.

'Nic, please call me back, I need to speak to you, please! Please, we need to talk, just talk, I need to talk to someone... I... Fuck, I'm desperate, Nic, I'm *desperate*!'

My laughter was audible now. Brinks kept on whining, getting higher and higher in pitch until I could barely understand the separate words any more. After a night like the last, this was exactly the sort of thing I had needed to hear.

I didn't even bother to finish the message before standing up from the bed and slamming open my bedroom door.

'Mark! Mark, you've got to listen this!'

'Morning...'

I walked into the kitchen waving the phone in his direction, trying to find the option to put it on speakerphone.

'Something funny?' he asked through a mouthful of toast.

'Christ, come here, listen... It'll kill you! It'll fucking kill you!'

CHAPTER TWENTY-SEVEN

The collage was still on the floor.

When Mark had gone out to meet someone for breakfast, after quoting his favourite parts of Brinks's voicemail at me once more time, I sat down by the coffee table and surveyed what he had done.

'*I neeeeeed you!*' Mark had shouted from the door. 'Haha, *fucking* genius.'

I started laughing to myself again.

Being the pedant that he was, Mark had grouped the photos at the top in chronological order. Any paperwork and miscellaneous pieces were underneath them. When he had felt so inclined he had scribbled a note and put it next to the item with an arrow, so it could be followed up later.

Things like 'What is this number?' and 'Who is this girl?'

I recognized Daisy in one of the photos that had been stuck around the mirror; she and Emma were striking a moody pose and pouting over the tops of their drinks. I hoped she had been nineteen, I thought, with a pang of unease. Emma hadn't inherited Clare's habit of writing the place and date on the back of every picture, so they were harder to group.

Emma had won an award at school for taking part in a national maths tournament. I wondered if it had bothered Clare, that her daughter's natural flair hadn't been for sports and athletics.

What is this number?

He had bookmarked a page of Emma's diary. I hadn't thought anything of it before. She hadn't written anything about that day; the only entry was the number, on its own. I suppose it did look a little strange, even if it hadn't seemed extraordinary enough to take notice of before.

I stood up to get the cordless phone and sat back down to key in the number. Outside I could hear hailstones clattering against the windows.

A lady picked up, and said, 'Hello, Maternity.'

I faltered. 'I'm... sorry?'

'Maternity?'

'I...' I hadn't planned what to say beyond this point, and even if I had I wouldn't have been prepared for this. 'Sorry, which hospital is this?'

'Er, Royal Free. Sorry, love, are you looking for another department?'

'This is Maternity?'

'Yes, love. Can I put you through to somewhere else?'

'Um... no, no that's fine. Think I've got the wrong number altogether, thanks.'

'No worries, my dear.'

I hung up but couldn't get off the floor. Outside there was a clanging sound of the bins being collected, and I blinked myself out of my reverie. I went through a list of names in my head: Danny? Kyle? Matt? If Emma had been pregnant, then whose was it? Had she called them for an abortion or a scan? Had she kept it? Who knew? Who knew and hadn't told me?

I decided against talking to Jenny Hillier first, on the assumption that she would still be traumatized from our last meeting. It crossed my mind to phone Danny, but I wasn't sure he would know anything.

Instead, I stood up, took the photo of Emma with Daisy, and decided to go back to the house in Shooters Hill.

Grandma, take me home. It came into my head every time I thought of her now.

Daisy answered the door holding a baby on her hip, wearing jeans and a white bra-top that showed her stomach. She looked surprised to see me and shifted the child on to her other side.

Inside the house I could hear something heavy playing.

'Well, hello. Couldn't keep away?'

I stared at the baby.

'Calm down,' she said with some scorn. 'He's my nephew, I'm babysitting.'

'I need to talk to you about Emma.'

'How are you, Daisy?' she said as she let me inside, answering the question herself. 'I'm fine, thanks. How are you? Lovely weather we're having, right? Getting into the Christmas flipping spirit?'

'Um, sorry. How are you?'

'Fuck off. Dandy.'

I stood in the same place as last time as she crossed the room to turn Radiohead down to a volume more compatible with discussion, before sitting on the sofa with her nephew on her knees.

'Are you really nineteen?' I asked.

She rolled her eyes in a way that reminded me so much of Harriet. 'What did you wanna talk to me about?'

'Why didn't you tell me that Emma was pregnant?'

Moments passed. Daisy was looking at the baby, bouncing him on her knee gently.

'His name's Michael. Isn't that a great name?'

'Don't fuck me around. Why didn't you tell me?'

'Hey, mind your fucking language, OK?' She raised her eyebrows at me. 'Well, honestly? I didn't tell you because it was none of your damn business. It's hers. Anyway, it doesn't matter, cos she got rid of it.'

I noticed that she had cleaned the house. The empty food containers were gone and it smelt fresher. It was nice that she made the effort for children.

'When did she get rid of it?'

'Few weeks before she died. I don't think many people knew. Me, maybe a few of her girlfriends, and Kyle, possibly Matt. She would *never* have told her parents, she said her dad would literally kill someone.'

'Whose was it?'

She shrugged.

'Daisy—'

'What? So what that I'm not entirely comfortable talking about my friend's business with some guy I don't even know!'

'You knew me well enough to fuck me.'

If she hadn't been holding Michael I guessed she would have stood up and gone for me. She looked the sort. I like a healthy amount of aggression in a girl, and Daisy came across as the sort of person who had never taken a milligram of bullshit in her life.

'I knew you well enough to know you were lonely with money to throw away. So go fuck yourself with a serrated edge, yeah?'

'You think that because you've got your fucking nephew here you can pull off this bullshit?' I took a step forwards. 'I don't know at what point I gave the impression I'm the sort of guy you can fuck around, but trust me, you have ten seconds to tell me who the father was, or—'

255

'Or what?' she snapped.

'Or you'll get to know me much better. One, two, three—'

'I don't know.'

'*Four*—'

'She didn't know!'

Michael started crying and she took him off her knees and propped him up against the back of the sofa.

'Really?' I said.

'She didn't know. She said it was probably Kyle's, but it could have been Matt's. I mean, she only slept with him as a one-time thing, she said they were both wasted, but it could have been.' She looked me up and down. 'You want to back the hell off now?'

I did as she said, and sat down.

'I'm a trained kick-boxer, you know.'

'That would have been' – I smirked – 'useful.'

'Yeah, well, Kyle was a black-belt in nothing and I saw him *floor* you, remember? I could have totally made you my bitch.'

'Do you know anything else?'

'Not really. That's the whole story from beginning to end. She got pregnant and then got rid of it. I mean, she was sixteen, what else was she going to do? It's no life for anybody at that age.'

I had worked out that Clare must have been in her early twenties when she'd had Emma; twenty-one or twenty-two. That had seemed young to me at the time. I wasn't even thirty and I still felt too young to cope with anything adult. It was debatable whether any of us felt grown up, I thought. I suspected we all just became better at faking it.

'Did she ever talk to you about her parents?' I asked.

'She was scared shitless of her dad, but only in the way that every little rich girl is scared of their dad. She was always

256

worried about him finding out about the things she was into, drinking, coke... sex. You know. I always used to tell her that it was a good thing her dad gave a shit.'

'Her mum?'

'She...'

Michael was staring at me.

Daisy ran her fingers through his fine patches of hair, smiling.

'Hey, Mikey, that's Nic,' she said. 'Say hi!'

I wasn't sure what to do, so I waved.

'Sweet, but I was kinda talking to him,' she said, laughing at me. 'Um, her mum... It was weird. She hated her. I mean, not just the usual way that people moaned about their parents, Ems really hated her.'

Every time this was reiterated to me I felt a rush of sympathy for Clare. It couldn't have been easy for Emma, dealing with the way her mother was, but all the same I couldn't help but think that maybe Clare's heart had been in the right place.

'What did she used to say?'

Daisy played with her hair and shrugged. 'Well... she just hated her. I didn't know much about her, Ems said she was a model and a dance teacher or whatever. Ballet? Is that right?'

I nodded.

'I couldn't even tell you anything specific, I just remember whenever she talked about her mum she was like, "I hate her. I fucking hate her." I used to tell her she probably didn't mean that but she was quite stubborn, she would always say, "No, I mean it. I hate her."'

I stayed silent and let Daisy stay with the monologue.

'Maybe she found it hard to live up to? I mean, a *model*. Must be harsh, you must feel like a right skank next to her. I couldn't deal with it, all your boyfriends checking out your mum and stuff!' She laughed. 'I'd find it harsh, anyway.'

'Is that all you can remember?'

'You know how it is, you don't remember random conversations very well. Ooh...'

'What?'

'Ems said her mum did hit her once, like properly hard, there was a mark and everything. They were having a fight and she just freaked out, hit her right around the face. I didn't think it was that big a deal. I mean, my parents gave me a slap load of times, but it was a big thing to Ems, I think. Don't think she was used to it.'

I had almost reached the point where I didn't want to know anything else about Clare. The more I found out about her, the harder it became to see the reasons for anything she did.

'Thanks,' I said. 'You want anything?'

She pulled a face and glanced at Michael. 'Not while he's here. It would be a bit weird.'

'No, I mean, for *talking* to me. A hundred for the info?'

'Oh? Hell yeah, thanks!'

I liked her. Something about the way she spoke made me laugh. I wouldn't have hurt her, and I wished that she didn't think I could.

I stood up, when something occurred to me that made me stop.

'So, you and Emma were friends?' I said. 'But you were sleeping with her boyfriend?'

'All right, *vicar*, not when she was alive!' Daisy shook her head, looking scandalized. 'Never. Only after... He gave me a place to stay, drugs, whatever. The sex thing, it's just not that friggin' sacred to me, that's all.'

258

'All right.' I didn't expect she cared much for my opinion of her.

'So are you gonna come back and visit, or is this *adiós*?'

I shrugged. 'Well, I think Mikey likes me.'

Michael gurgled as she picked him up and sat him on her bony knees again.

I handed her some notes and she winked at me.

'Whatever. You never know. You might come back tomorrow and I'll have gone to Timbuktu.'

'Are you going to be all right here?'

'*Yes*. Christ on a Boris bike, it's not *that* bad. Where do you live? I bet you come from a right swanky borough?'

'Just a flat in the West End.'

'Hiding from the hipsters?' She sniffed. 'Due respect, but you don't look trendy enough.'

'Well, if you're gone when I come back, I guess I'll see you when I'm a cat.'

'Stay the hell off my feeder, bitch.'

CHAPTER TWENTY-EIGHT

If it was anyone but Clare, I asked myself while I was sitting in the car, would I tell her? Yes. The answer was obvious. I would have told any other employer without hesitation that their daughter had been pregnant without their knowledge. It was my job, after all.

None of this made it easier. I wished I didn't know either of them well enough to predict the effects this information would have.

It took almost half an hour, but eventually I got out of the car, walked up to the house and rang the doorbell.

Nothing.

I crouched and looked through the letterbox.

Lights out.

Nothing.

At least this had made the hardest decision for me. Instead of telling Clare first, I'd tell Pat. I backed away, in case I could see any lights in the upstairs windows, but she wasn't there.

Relieved, I went back to the car, and heard heavy footfalls against the pavement. Clare was jogging past the houses across the road, looking even thinner in tracksuit bottoms, and I watched her until she spotted me.

I crossed the road again and waited by the house.

It was the first time I had ever seen her without make-up, I realized. That was why she looked so different.

'Hi,' she said as she stopped beside me and took out her keys. 'What's up?'

'Is this a good time?'

'Um… yeah, I guess. Has something happened?'

'Well, I'm making progress, but… You're probably going to want to sit down.'

Her fringe was stuck to her forehead and the back of her shirt was damp and painted against her shoulder blades. When she finally managed to unlock the door I noticed that she was shaking.

'Five miles,' she said when she followed my eyeline. 'Stupid, I didn't take any water with me. So… you want me to sit down?'

'Well—'

'I'm fine standing, thanks.' She took off her trainers and socks in the hallway, and walked into the kitchen to run herself a glass of water. 'Go for it. Shoot. Really, there's pretty much nothing you can say that's going to surprise me now.'

I raised my eyebrows as I came forward, replaying the list of ways in which I thought it would be easier to tell her. But clever phraseology wasn't going to help.

She downed the first glass of water and poured another, pulling her hair out of its ponytail. 'Go on. I mean it.'

'Emma was pregnant.'

I felt as if I hadn't said it right, as if one of the other phrases I had chosen would have been better, but I repeated it anyway.

'Emma was pregnant.'

She put the glass of water down and wiped a drop from the rim. 'Oh.'

'I'm sorry.'

'No, right… I asked for it. Um, how long?'

'What?'

'How… far along was she?'

'Oh.' I swallowed. 'No, she *was* pregnant. She had a termination a few weeks before she died. I don't know how far along she was, I assume less than twenty weeks.'

Her lower lip trembled and her hand was still clasped around the glass of water. 'How did you find out? I mean, how many people knew?'

I put my bag down, glad that I could still talk about it in a formal way. 'I found the number of the Royal Free's Maternity Ward in her diary. A few of her friends knew.'

'A few?'

'About three.'

'A few, and she didn't tell us?'

I spread my hands. 'She was just scared. She was only—'

'*Don't* tell me what she was!' she snapped.

Her hands were still shaking as she pinched the bridge of her nose. If I hadn't been so close, if I hadn't wanted to cross the room and hold her, I would have found it a perversely fascinating experiment. I was watching how many emotional blows one person could withstand before the wheels of their mind fell off completely.

'Whose was it? Was it… Danny's?'

'It wasn't Danny's. I don't actually know.'

'You're lying.'

'Honestly, I don't—'

'Stop protecting me! She's not *yours* to protect me from!'

'Clare—'

'Whose was it?'

'Just calm down…'

'Oh, please!' She laughed at me hysterically. 'Stop talking like you think you know me! You think that spending half a damn night here makes you *special*?'

'I'm saying calm down.'

'Whose was it?'

'I don't—'

'You think you have the right to decide what's for *my own good*? You think you know me that well?'

'No, I—'

'You want to know more about me? Fine. *Fine!*' She took off the white shirt, threw it down and started taking down the tracksuit bottoms. 'Take a good look! This is me, right here!'

She turned, so I could see the cuts forming rough train tracks down her biceps and the scars along her hipbones and ribs. She raised her arms, showing her wrists, and screwed her hair up into a ball at the back of her head to display the bruises along her hairline usually hidden by her fringe.

'These, that's me! These ones here, that's me too!'

I stood speechless while she rattled off the list with a trembling voice.

'So fuck you! Fuck you and everything you *think* you know! It's rubbish! You have no *idea*!'

I took a step back, captivated, a frantic erection pressing against the inside of my jeans, unable to even think about trying to stop her.

'Look, *look*!' Locking on to me with her gaze, she took a knife out of the holder and casually slid the blade across her forearm, with the attitude of someone ripping a plaster off a scab. '*This* is what I like. *This* is what you don't *fucking* understand! This is all me.'

Blood ran off her arm and on to the floor.

I opened my mouth to speak but nothing came out. My stomach clenched with horror.

'Clare—'

'So, Nic. How do you like me now?' She laughed, and did it again.

'Clare, stop it!'

'No!'

As I started towards her she pointed the knife at me with a playful glint in her eye. The cuts in her arm looked deep and they were bleeding quite heavily, but she hadn't acknowledged any pain. As with the mirror, she had learnt to hurt herself without tarnishing her outward beauty.

'Clare…' I said, trying to stay calm but knowing this had gone too far. 'Clare, *think* about it. I'm warning you, don't do this.'

'I said, so how do you like me now, *Nic*?'

I hesitated, eyes on the knife. Talking to her was useless. She didn't want someone to talk to her, but I tried one more time anyway, just so that I could tell myself that I had, that I wasn't just looking for an excuse.

'Clare, put the knife down.'

'Make me.'

I stepped forwards and I saw her start a little. When I made to go left she followed me and I grabbed her wrist. She pushed back, shocking me again with how strong she was, but I took hold of her other wrist and felt my hand slide against blood.

'Yes!' She was laughing. 'Like that!'

We whirled around and I tried to keep the knife away from us. She cracked her head into mine and I threw her backwards into the table, gritting my teeth through the pain. Everything went white for a moment. I slammed her wrist against the wood until she dropped the knife.

It fell with a clatter and she was still laughing.

Her blood was all over my shirt, all over my hands. Her body was heaving, sweat from her jog running down the curve between her breasts.

'Go on,' she was saying, 'you want to help, then *go on*!'

264

She slapped me and I slapped her back. The cry that came out of her was like nothing I had ever heard. Incensed, I picked her up and forced her back on to the tabletop. She slapped me again, harder. When she resisted I grabbed a fistful of her hair and then we were kissing. I tasted blood on my tongue as I undid my jeans and when we parted her lips were swollen red.

My coat hit the floor and one of the straps of her bra snapped as she ripped it off her shoulders. She tried to pull away across the table but I dragged her back towards me by her hips and the back of her head hit the table.

I pulled the crotch of her knickers roughly to one side and then I was inside her, and she was so fucking hot, and for a moment she stopped fighting me. She lay there, eyes closed, her chest bouncing with each thrust, gasping, lost...

Suddenly she had opened her eyes and wrapped her legs around my waist, pulling herself up, biting my lip, raking her nails across my back and making me leave bruises on her arms with my grip.

'Oh fuck, yes, like that... like *that*...'

She started pulling me closer with her heels, groaning into my neck, and I could feel her body becoming tense in my arms.

My breathing was ragged. I stopped and she slipped off the table.

'What! No...'

I turned her around, ripped her underwear down and held her bloodied arms behind her. She started crying out, shuddering against my grasp, her face turned sideways against the hard surface as her features tightened and then released.

Her moans were still echoing around the kitchen by the time I came. My legs felt weak and the room blurred in and out of focus in front of my eyes as relief, the likes of which I hadn't felt for years, flooded my veins. My heartbeat was knocking around my skull.

I let go of her, stepped back and was only vaguely aware of the semen running down the insides of her legs.

The silence seemed wrong now.

It was only when I started to feel everything more keenly, like the scratches across my back, that I realized how much blood there was. It was on my clothes, my hands, imprinted around her wrists, her arms, along her hips…

I did up my jeans and leant against the work surface, finding it hard to stand for myself.

Clare had sat down on the floor with her knees pulled into her chest and her head resting against the table leg. The knife was lying not far behind her, under the table where she had dropped it.

I couldn't analyse the expression on her face. She was watching something far away.

My first instinct was to apologize, but it would sound ludicrous.

'You know… people don't seem to understand it,' she said.

Thank God she had spoken first.

'It would actually be more acceptable if I… drank too much or smoked or did, you know, something more fashionable.' She smiled at me. 'People don't seem to get that it's only another way of making yourself feel something else, just for a bit. So why is everyone else considered normal and I'm the one that's screwed up?'

'I think you're right,' I said.

'I thought you would get it. If I just explained it right.'

'How long have you… you know?'

'I've always done it, it's just…' She shrugged. 'It's just what I do.'

266

'Why did you start?'

'When they told me I'd never go professional. I carried on for a bit, and then I got pregnant with Emma and got married, and that was it.' When I didn't reply she looked up at me and laughed. 'No, really. That's the whole story.'

'So Pat… never…?'

'No.' For a moment she looked sad. 'No, he wouldn't even hurt me if I asked him to. But he's just always let people think what they want. I suppose it's easier than trying to explain. She… Emma always hated that people thought that. It was my fault, I guess.'

'So… when he put you in hospital…?'

'Did my mum tell you that?' she said with a trace of a smile. 'No, I… I fell down the stairs. Well, I didn't *fall* down the stairs, I… kinda meant to. It's OK, you can think it's weird. It is probably weird… I think.'

I felt profoundly stupid, for everything I had believed, all the scenarios I had made up in my head.

She looked smaller than she was, sitting down there by the table.

I crossed the kitchen and sat on the floor beside her, sighing.

'I'm sorry,' I said.

'Are you kidding?' She snorted, rubbing her eyes. 'All I wanted was to not think about it for a while. It feels *so good* to not think about it… I'm fine, just… please, don't talk to me for a moment.'

A couple of minutes went by, and she shifted closer, buried her face in the crook of my neck. I didn't want to leave. I didn't want to wash the blood off.

CHAPTER TWENTY-NINE

Brinks's house looked even more tragic than usual. I wasn't sure why, maybe it was the weather, or the hilarity of the message he had left me. I still laughed thinking about it. Mark had sent me a text as I was leaving Clare's house that said nothing but I NEEEEEEEEEEEEED YOU! HAHA M XXX.

My skin felt raw. I knew I should have been thinking about Felix Hudson, but all I could think about was when I could go back to Clare's house again. In a way, I had almost believed that having sex with her would put an end to it, make it easier to stop obsessing over every aspect of her life, over knowing her better, knowing her completely. But it had made things worse. Now the moments in between touching her were nothing but interludes to me; time to be endured until I could invent another reason.

I went to the side gate out of habit, through the garden and in through the back door. Brinks was in his kitchen, sitting at his table, and didn't look up at me as I came in.

'There's no need,' he said, blowing across the top of a bottle of beer. 'She's gone.'

I shut the door, taking in how much thinner he looked. 'I'm sorry.'

'No, you're not.'

Annoyed that I couldn't immediately drag the discussion to business, I put my bag down. 'What happened?'

'She called work... They said I wasn't there.'

'Jesus, Geoff, why didn't you just tell her?'

'Well, how the fuck do you tell her? Oh, hey, sweetheart, I've been fired and the only way I might escape jail is to carry on selling people out who are even more fucking dangerous than my colleagues... Oh, *merry Christmas*!'

'Surely she would have preferred the truth, though? She might have stayed?'

'Well, that's easy for you to say, isn't it? Monsieur fucking Hindsight.' He gestured at the fridge. 'Get me another beer while you're up, will you?'

'You haven't had enough?'

'Do you *live* to fucking torment me?'

'Fine, Jesus... Fine.'

I crossed the room, took another bottle out of the fridge and handed it to him. There wasn't much food in there, I noticed; a few eggs and some fruit that had gone bad.

'So what happened?' I asked again, guessing that he would have that interminable urge to talk about it.

'I thought it would be louder,' he said, never looking at me when he spoke. 'When people leave, end things... I thought it would be louder, but she didn't shout at all, didn't make a scene. That's one of the reasons I loved... love her so much. She never was one to cause a scene, for drama or throwing wine in your face in fancy restaurants, you know, that kind of shit. She just asked me to explain myself... so I did. She took her ring off, put it on the side' – he indicated across the room with his bottle, to where I presumed it still was – 'and then she just left, took the kids to her parents' place.'

Brinks's wife sounded dignified, I thought. But when I began to consider what sort of woman would allow herself to marry someone like him, the glimmer of respect dissipated.

You couldn't tell that anyone had vacated the house from

the state of the kitchen. There were still no photos. No defining features at all. Much like Brinks, who even the most astute of individuals would struggle to distinguish in a line-up.

'You think she'll come back?' I asked, bored with asking him questions.

He shook his head. 'I've blown it, Nic. I fucked up. Big time.'

'What about your kids?'

'She's a decent person, she didn't tell them. I imagine I'll still be able to see them... at... weekends, or something.' He sniffed and wiped his hand over his face.

Don't cry, I prayed. Don't you dare fucking cry, you bastard.

'Women aren't everything,' I said, with a poor attempt at a smile.

'Yeah? Never heard you mention one. No offence, but I assumed you were bent, mate.'

I shrugged, ignoring the slight.

'I wish... I actually wish I was like you sometimes, ain't that fucking funny?' he said, smiling, drunk.

'Oh yeah?'

'Young, single, no responsibilities... maybe just the no responsibilities. Don't get me wrong, I liked having a proper profession and being married and I love my kids more than anything, you have no idea how much I love my kids, but... Well, you always want what you don't have.'

'I don't want kids.'

'No one in their right mind would,' he agreed. 'But if you do, you wouldn't change it for anything.'

'Seems too much hassle.'

'It is, when it hasn't happened yet.'

Getting tired of standing up, I joined him at the table.

'You know anyone in there I can work with?' I asked.

'A few. I can give you one or two names.' He smirked at me. 'Or you could just do what you did with me, eh? Get them young, reel them in.'

When he spoke his cheeks disappeared between his teeth, sucked into his jaws. His buttoned shirt had stains down it. Without thinking, I checked the zip of my coat in case he could see any of the blood on my clothes.

'You getting anywhere with that Emma Dyer girl?' he asked.

'A little bit. You?'

'Not really. Following legalities can hold you back somewhat. We let the taxi driver go, if that's what you're getting at?'

'It wasn't the taxi driver,' I said.

'Yeah, thanks, we worked that one out for ourselves.'

I frowned. 'You mentioned before there was no drug use?'

'Yeah, nothing. No alcohol either.'

Another reason why Matt's story didn't check out. *Coked out of our minds*, he had said...

I was sorry about Meds, and had thought about him more than I'd expected to since finding out about his death. I had started to hate Matt Masters, with a deep visceral hate that I could feel in my veins. It could only be a good thing.

'So why did you need to see me?' I asked. 'You sounded... in a bad way on the phone.'

'Yeah...' He was still speaking to his beer and it was starting to irritate me. 'I needed to talk to you, you know, about all this.'

'Yeah?'

'They were tipped off, my department. Someone told them about me, told them where to look, sent them *photos*. I was

271

so... fucking scared of going to prison that I never even thought about it.'

Any mention of photos brought me back to Hudson, even though the idea was ridiculous.

'I got a call to my house the other night,' he continued. 'They never said who they were, but it was funny... They said it was you who'd shopped me.'

His eyes were still on his beer.

I searched for something to say, rendered speechless.

'That was why I wanted to speak to you.'

I wished I could have thought of something more interesting to say, or more convincing, but all that came out was, 'What?'

The bottle cracked in half against my forehead.

I landed on my hands and knees, unable to see, coughing, hacking up nothing. My head had become nothing more than white pain. Brinks was shouting at me, but I couldn't hear him properly.

There was a gun in my bag, but I didn't know where my bag was.

I tried to stand, and Brinks punched me in the face.

I was on my back, blinking, still reeling from the impact of the bottle.

Brinks was ranting, pacing back and forth, alternate words leaping out at me but nothing making sense.

'*Fucking... life... mug... fucking...*'

I kicked him in the shin and crawled backwards into his hallway until I found some strength in my arms.

My bag...

As I managed to get on to my knees, Brinks caught up with me and kicked me square in the back. I turned and grappled with him, his hands around my throat and his teeth bared, grey and peppered with black fillings.

His fingers dug into my jugular, my heartbeat thudding against his hands.

I let go of his wrists and grabbed his head, jamming my thumbs into his eyes. He clutched them, howling, and I was free. Pushing back on my hands, I made it to my knees again, tried to stand but fell sideways against the stairs.

My head throbbed, draining all the life from my legs.

You're in trouble. It wasn't a voice, so much as an awareness going round and around my mind. You're in trouble.

I made a grab for the front door but it was locked, and Brinks cracked my forehead into it. Blood ran down the bridge of my nose. He grabbed the back of my coat and threw me on to my back on the stairs. I could fight him... I could if it wasn't for that fucking bottle.

'Ruin my life and *why*? WHY?' he was screaming at me.

My arms were shaking as I pushed myself up the stairs, away from him, six stairs up before he caught up with me and I kicked him again. I didn't know where I was going, just up.

I made it as far as the first landing. There was another flight of stairs and a corner. I couldn't do it. My arms gave way. If I passed out I was dead.

I was dead. The last blow against the door had done it.

How fucking sad, that I had never seen this coming.

Brinks was choking me.

My eyes clenched shut, trying to breathe, trying not to let his hideous face be the last thing I saw.

Would he do with me what I had done with so many other bodies? Would Mark be able to track him down? Probably not. Who knew?

His hands left my throat, like a tonne of weight being lifted off my chest. I was aware of breathing, air rushing in and out of my lungs, but when I opened my eyes I saw only the bottom of a picture hanging on the wall of the landing.

It was the first picture I'd seen in his house.

Feeling that I had been given a chance, I dragged myself up on to my elbows.

Brinks was at the bottom of the stairs, his legs at strange angles, like a crushed spider.

There was someone standing over me, I could see them in my peripheral vision.

I wasn't conscious enough to feel proper shock. I inclined my head, struggling to focus my vision. As I turned I smelt chloroform, saw glasses, and thankfully, with a wave of relief, everything went dark.

CHAPTER THIRTY

Disappointment was the first thing I remembered feeling when I came around. That, and a horrible attack of nausea. I'd almost hoped that had been it. Everything seemed like too much effort now, even breathing, through this level of pain.

I opened my eyes. I was lying in a hospital bed; I could feel the bars either side of me, but the ceiling wasn't right. It was dark, and too high.

When I moved my hands and tried to sit up I realized I was hooked-up to an IV line, going into the crook of my arm.

'It's important to get enough fluids,' someone said.

I started.

'When you have concussion.'

It was Felix Hudson, sitting next to me in a different coloured golfing jumper.

'Where are we?' I said, too tired to acknowledge fear.

'A safe place.' Felix smiled at me, creasing that scar across his cheek. 'Tristan used to be a medical student. You're being well looked after. He's outside if you start to feel woozy, the dust in here aggravates his asthma.'

'Tris…'

'You may recognize him. Though not well, I imagine.'

I found some moisture in my mouth. 'Your messenger boy?'

'He leaves my notes but he is much more than that. More qualified than you, I dare say. Did you like them, by the way?'

My coat was gone.

I lifted my head to get a better look round the room, but I felt sick and lay back down. There was a persistent nagging ache at the front of my skull.

'Why have you been following me?' I asked.

'I could ask you the same question.'

'Did you kill Emma Dyer?'

'Emma Dyer...' He said the name softly, as if she was a distant memory to him. 'She had such pretty cheekbones, a lovely structure.'

'Matt said you killed her.'

'I know.' He smiled. 'If you're as good as people say you are, you'll have worked out he was lying by now.'

I was too weak for conversation, so I just stared at him.

'Do you want me to tell you the story?'

Placing his accent was impossible. He was well spoken, could pass for a southerner, but he spoke with the self-conscious finesse of someone who had learnt English as a second language.

I gave the IV line a gentle tug, but knew I wouldn't stand a chance if I tried to make a run for it.

After a small hesitation, I met his eyes and nodded. 'OK, I'm listening... but I want you to answer a few questions.'

A nerve under his scar twitched. 'Of course.'

'Was it you who sent photos to Edie Franco?'

Twitch. 'Yes.'

'And told Geoff Brinks that it was me who grassed him up?'

'Yes.'

There was anger, at him, but mostly at myself, for allowing myself to feel this fear. Roman Katz scared me, with the way his lips moved like wrinkled leaves when he spoke, but this guy scared me more.

276

'Why?' I asked.

'Why do we do anything in life?' he replied, spreading his hands. 'For fun.'

'Huh, fun?'

'But it *is* fun. Your job is fun, just like mine. If I were to lean forwards right now and stick a knife through your throat, you wouldn't be able to react in time to stop me. You're not seriously telling me that isn't fun?'

My eyes flicked down to his hands, but they were folded across his knee. It annoyed me that he had seen my discomfort.

'Once you've listened, you leave me alone,' he said.

'What if you're not telling the truth and I can't leave you alone?'

He looked at his hands, at his perfectly manicured nails. A lot about his attitude reminded me of Mark, but without any of Mark's humanity. He answered my question with a question.

'Do you know what lye is?'

I swallowed. 'It's, er... a bleach, right?'

'If I or, more accurately, if Tristan were to pour it directly down your throat, it would corrode through the walls of the stomach. Your stomach acids would, effectively, do the rest of the work on your internal organs. I've never seen it injected before, but I imagine the results must be fascinating. I wonder, does it corrode straight through the walls of your veins?'

I felt sick, and looked at his hands again, thinking of Mackie's slit throat.

'Sounds... bracing,' I said, lip curling.

He smiled. 'People have been known to throw themselves through plate-glass windows in their death-throes after drinking it. Of course... there's nothing like that here.'

I thought of Matt, throwing himself through a window... The man outside, puffing on his inhaler. I imagined that the eyes behind his glasses were as blank and reflective as his lenses. I'd rather have died looking at Brinks than him, waiting for my own stomach acids to eat away at me.

'Go on then, keep talking,' I said.

'Matt wanted you to kill me, to make sure I never tracked him down and tied up the last of the loose ends. It's rather ingenious really, the complexity of the story he must have come up with to paint me as a scapegoat. What angle did he go for? A witness story? The people trafficking? Some kind of illicit affair?'

'Trafficking. He said she saw a nasty shipment and that you shot her when she wouldn't stop screaming.'

'Inventive. He had a talent for thinking on his feet.'

It crossed my mind that he might just kill me anyway, if he was all about the fun. After all, he had killed Mackie without hesitation. It was the sort of thing Mark would do, tell someone a story they would never be given the chance to remember.

'Why did he kill her?' I asked. 'Assuming he did kill her? It wasn't Kyle or anything?'

'No, no it wasn't Kyle… Matt killed her on one of their pick-ups, of a shipment. It was a shipment of *drugs*, I might add. Kyle told me they had been arguing in the car, about the girl being pregnant.'

I wondered how he would know that if he weren't telling the truth.

Keeping my eyes on his face, I gave the IV line another tug.

'Kyle told you?'

'He was… distraught. Matt would have hidden it but Kyle panicked, came running to me. Stupid boy, he should have known I would send them on their way. I found it almost insulting that they would ask for my help over such a petty domestic dispute.'

'What did Kyle say?'

'I don't think he was lying. He said they were arguing in the car. Apparently she had got rid of the child, and Matt reacted badly. He was convinced it was his, to the point of delusion… as Kyle put it. It escalated and when they got out of the car, she said some things that incensed him and he shot her.'

As I ran through the scene in my head, he sighed.

'Stupid, impetuous behaviour.'

'Impetuous…' I looked at him, grimacing as a spasm of pain crossed behind my eyes. 'Shooting a sixteen-year-old girl is *impetuous*?'

He shrugged. 'Extremely. But then I should never have trusted them to hide it properly. Kyle especially was weak. It was only a matter of time before I could see him tearing up the floorboards to reveal the beating of her hideous heart…'

I had no idea what he was talking about.

He grinned at me, mocking my ignorance, and continued. 'Disguising it as a sexual assault was so crude. Disgusting.'

'Why are you telling me this? What's in it for you?' I tugged on the IV line again, harder.

'Well, you'll leave me alone. Not that it hasn't been fun, Nic, but I could do without the trouble.'

A trickle of blood ran down my arm but he didn't notice. So long as he kept his hands where I could see them I had estimated I could either make a run for it, or deal with him before the nutcase outside heard anything.

I gritted my teeth against the headache. 'OK… So where's your proof?'

'Where's your faith?'

'Are you fucking joking?'

I believed him. I believed him more readily than I had believed

Matt. Everything that Daisy had said fell into place with his story. It made sense, whether he was going to kill me or not.

'Who do you believe?' One of his hands came off his knees and into his pocket.

It was too late to make a difference. I tightened my grip on the IV with a shaking hand, ignoring the blood, ready to rip it out.

'Is Brinks dead?' I asked.

The voice that answered came from behind me.

'I suspect a broken arm and fractured collarbone.'

I lashed out, instinctively, to my right.

Tristan caught my wrist, and gently waved a clear bottle. 'Careful, this is highly corrosive. Wouldn't want to spill it.'

Mackie's vacant eyes...

I couldn't stop watching the bottle, so close to my face. It was the first time I'd been able to take a good look at him and I was surprised. Tristan did look like a medical student; wiry, bespectacled, young and baby-faced but with an intellectual's frown.

He dropped my arm and peered at my head. 'Just checking your stitches... Oh, and that's going to scar, if you rip it out like that.'

I wiped the blood away, and when I touched my forehead I could feel the faint ridges in the spot where it had hit Brinks's front door. I felt short of breath, as if I was having an anxiety attack.

'If you're going to kill me,' I said, holding the crook of my arm, 'can you just get it over and done with?'

'You think I'd waste my expertise on a corpse?' He looked at me with disdain and wheeled the drip out of the way so that he could scrutinize my stitches more closely. 'Can you hold still?'

I jerked my head away from him. 'Can you get a bedside manner?'

I heard Hudson laugh. 'It would be more trouble to kill you.'

'You killed Mackie.'

'I don't have time for traitors, plus you're more useful to me... I'm counting on you to find Matt first. I've heard you have your ways.'

I glanced at Tristan.

Hudson leant forwards. 'I don't want to be enemies, Nic. I don't like making enemies.'

My stitches twinged whenever I tried to frown. If I agreed with him, at least for now, he might let me go. I remembered my bag, left at Brinks's house, and sat up.

'I need my bag,' I said. 'And my car.'

'We have your bag. Tris will drive you back.'

I dared to feel relief as the idea of there being a tomorrow, and a next week, began to materialize in my mind. 'Well, then I'd like to go now, please.'

'Do you think I'm telling the truth?'

'It makes sense.' I couldn't bring myself to agree wholeheartedly. 'As long as I can move back home without any more interesting mail.'

Tristan was indicating that he wanted to check the IV line, and I held out my arm.

'You need rest and an ice-pack,' he said.

'You don't *fucking* say?' I replied.

Hudson smiled. 'I'm glad we're on the same wavelength.'

It took almost forty-five minutes to drive back to Brinks's house, and for most of it I was blindfolded. Neither of us spoke until I could see again, and when I caught my reflection in the rear-view mirror I was almost luminous.

'Why did you drop out of medical school?' I asked.

Silence.

'Did you get convicted of something?'

He craned his neck to read a road sign and didn't reply.

'Just wondered…'

It puzzled me that someone who had had the chance of a real profession had ended up here, with me. I wondered how he had fucked everything up.

'What makes you think I dropped out?' he said.

I looked at him and he was smiling to himself, out through the windscreen. He had an odd, slightly autistic way of speaking.

'How did you meet Felix?' I asked.

Brinks's house came into sight.

'I'll drop you here,' he said. 'You shouldn't really be driving.'

'Yeah, thanks, I'll be fine.' I opened the door before the car had even stopped.

'Wait.'

I turned back; he was holding out an A4 envelope.

'What's that?'

'Your proof. I took them just in case.'

I took it off him and he reached over and shut the passenger door without a word. As I tried to say something the car pulled away. Not once had he bothered to meet my eyes.

I didn't look at the envelope until I got back to the flat. For a while I just sat down, without even taking off my coat and shoes. Then I stood up, pulled my suitcase down and left it lying open on my bed. When Mark came in I was folding shirts.

He stood in the doorway and went to say something about the suitcase, when his gaze alighted on me.

'Fucking *state* of you!' he exclaimed.

I was too tired to explain. 'Walked into a door.'

'Are they stitches?' He came forwards, peering at my face. I held out the unopened envelope.

'What's that?'

'Don't know, proof. You look first, I can't…' I shook my head, which was still aching. 'I almost don't want to know any more.'

He took the envelope and I avoided his concern by continuing to pack.

Taking the hint, he sat down and opened it.

After a few moments of pretending to be absorbed by a blazer, I heard him take a breath.

'What were you expecting to see?' he said.

'It's bad, isn't it?'

'I'd give it a solid twelve out of ten.'

'Fuck…' I took off my coat, sat down and held out my hand for the contents. 'Go on, hit me.'

When he didn't reply I looked at him; he was staring at my shirt. I had forgotten it was covered in bloodstains, along with my forearms. There was also a bruise from the IV line.

'Mark, it's fine, it's not even mine,' I said.

He raised his eyebrows and then handed me the A4 photos with a grimace. 'How's a bit of casual necrophilia in the afternoon?'

The first photo was taken from behind a metal structure. It looked as if they were still at the docks. Matt and Kyle were dragging a body towards the boot of a car, a body wearing a black and white striped top and boots. I could only see Matt's back but Kyle was crying.

The second and Emma was on the ground, between them, the bullet-hole in her forehead turned in the direction of the camera. Matt had a gun in his hand and was making some sort of gesture. Next photo he was undoing his jeans. I couldn't see his expression and I didn't want to.

As he was fucking her he had a hand around her jaw, watching her face as if she were still alive.

I looked away for a second, cleared my throat and continued.

Fast-forward through the pictures and Kyle was on his knees, at gunpoint, sobbing, between her legs. Emma was still facing the camera, impassive, dead, with her dad's eyes. Matt was looking at his watch, only half watching the gun he was pointing at Kyle.

The last shot and Matt was caught, mid-kick, the toe of his shoe flying towards her stomach, her jeans lying discarded next to the car. It was the only shot where I could see him properly, but his face seemed empty. He didn't look as if he had even broken into a sweat.

Kyle was sitting on the ground by the car, his knees pulled into his chest, still crying. Making him an accomplice guaranteed his silence.

'He asked me where my faith was,' I said, snorting. 'Jesus... So Felix Hudson was actually telling the truth.'

I looked at the photo of Matt, trousers around his ankles, hand around her jaw, and immediately started fantasizing about how slowly I was going to kill him. As I turned them face down and gave them back to Mark, I could feel my face contorting with disgust.

Nothing would ever make me look at the photos again.

Mark put them back in the envelope and smiled. 'Oh, you gonna "kill him dead".'

'"Dead man walking here."'

'So we can go home?'

'Soon as you pack.'

He reclined, leaning back on his elbows. 'Are you gonna tell me whose blood that is?'

'"I killed Paul Allen"' – I grinned, throwing in three pairs of jeans – '"with an axe."'

'Touché. Your business.'

CHAPTER THIRTY-ONE

I was surprised Edie agreed to see me. Either she didn't hold grudges for very long, or was just curious as to what I had to say. She met me in a bar not far from our old flat; it was nice to have moved back, even if I still found myself on the lookout for Tristan from time to time.

I expected to be waiting for a while but she wasn't late, for once. She was wearing a huge pair of sunglasses and the same shoes that she had thrown at me last time.

'Someone got better aim than me?' she remarked, brushing her fingertips across the bruise on my forehead.

'Girls just line up to throw shoes at my head.'

'That's what I like to hear.' She sat down and picked up the glass of red wine that I had ordered. 'Thanks, babe. We're not being watched, are we?'

'No, Jesus... Look, I know you have no reason to believe me but I'm not some informant. The guy was a source, I paid him for info, not the other way around. You think I don't make enough money without doing *that*?'

For a while she just watched me over the rim of the glass; then she took the sunglasses off. She didn't look as if she was angry, or was going to cut the conversation off and walk away. Instead, she smiled at me.

'Sid said you came round. Well, he didn't say your name but I guessed it was you.'

'I promise I wouldn't have hurt Scott.'

'No, I know you wouldn't. Sid didn't, so he was pretty mad... But does this mean you have something for me?'

I took the DVDs out of my coat and passed them across the table.

'That's all of them,' I said.

'For sure?'

'Certain. You don't have to pay me. Let's just call it an apology, for being stupid enough to get myself caught on camera in the first place.'

'You're not the only one who's been stupid enough to get caught on camera.' She put them in her handbag, smiling. 'Thanks. I mean it.'

'Scott's clever.'

'Yeah, he is.'

'Does he read a lot?'

She shrugged and sipped her wine. 'God knows. Maybe it's the wonders of the internet? Kids can get at anything nowadays.'

I thought of the walls of books, shelf upon shelf, and wondered how she couldn't know that. Sidney had probably been right, it made no difference whether it was her son or her car. I had known that at the time, but it was too late now; it wasn't as if I could take them back.

'Hey, something weird happened last night,' she said. 'This girl was in the club asking for you...'

'Another one wanting to throw a high heel at me?'

'No, I'm serious, she was called Daisy. Weird name... little blonde thing.'

My first instinct was to laugh. 'Daisy? Seriously?'

'Yeah, blonde, doesn't wear much, going into every bar round the West End asking everyone if they knew a Nic Caruana because she needed to speak to you. She said she'd been looking for two days.'

'Seriously?'

'Yeah, just going from place to place.' She raised her eyebrows. 'You haven't got some poor girl into trouble, have you?'

'What? No, no, not at all. Did she say what it was about?'

I couldn't make sense of the image; Daisy, walking from bar to bar and accosting everyone she met, for two days. I could believe it of her. She seemed crazy enough, bloody-minded enough.

'I don't know,' Edie said. 'You don't think I'd tell someone I know you personally? I kicked her out.'

'Damn...'

'You know her then? This *Daisy*?'

'Yeah, I...' I realized I had started standing up, and forced myself back down. 'Yeah, I know her.'

'Am I keeping you?'

I grinned. 'You jealous?'

'She wasn't a natural blonde.'

This time I did stand up. 'Sorry, I'd stay but this is really important.'

'I'm intrigued.' She stood up also and shook my hand. 'Thank you for these, Nic, and I hope she's worth it.'

'She's a mouthy little shite,' I said, as I moved around the table towards the door.

'Aren't all the best women?'

I didn't know what she wanted. I could only imagine that it was something to do with Matt and Kyle. As I ran up to the familiar front door, it occurred to me that I had wanted to come back anyway.

She answered the door with a roll of the eyes and dragged me inside by the sleeve of my coat. 'Well, you took your merry time, I've got blisters on my fucking heels!'

I stared at her. 'Have you actually been looking for me for two days?'

'Well…' She shrugged. 'You said West End, right? I figured you'd have to have gone out for a drink *sometime* but you know what, no one knows you. You didn't give me some fake name, did you?'

'No, sorry, that's just what they're meant to say.'

'Ha! Man of fucking *mystery*!' She punched my arm, swaying a little as she walked away from me into the living room and picked up one of the many half-drunk bottles I could see scattered about. 'I'm meant to be impressed, eh? You want a drink? I have… cider and… cider, with vodka?'

'It's midday.'

'Suit yourself. I ran out of brown, right. It sucks.'

With practised balance, she dropped to the floor, cross-legged, and lit a cigarette. She was wearing an oversized white shirt with a belt and red leg-warmers around her shins.

'Why were you looking for me?'

She laughed to herself, brushing her hair out of her eyes so she could take a drag. 'You think I'm joking, but I really did just go down all the roads, asking random people, going into bars and asking the barmen… Dense of me really, I mean, this is fucking *London*.'

'You found me though.' I bent down, trying to meet her eyes. 'Hey, why did you want to find me?'

'I'm not stupid,' she said, picking up her cider again and tapping ash into the tray by the sofa. 'I know that most people think I am, cos of how I dress or how I didn't finish college or anything, but I wanted to say that I'm fucking not. All right?'

I waited for her to stop drinking, and sat down on the floor with her. There were shadows under her eyes and her skin was blotchy with alcohol.

289

'You think Kyle and Matt killed her, don't you? I mean, I know you haven't said that, but that is why you're so interested in them, right?'

'Yeah.'

She pulled a face and concentrated too hard on her next drag. 'You sure?'

'Certain. Well, Matt killed her. Kyle was an accomplice, he helped cover it up.'

She nodded, quite violently, and kept nodding for a while. It was impressive, how well she took the confirmation, but she had never struck me as someone who would cry.

'And Meds?' she said.

'I suspect Matt worked out that he had spoken to me.'

'Shit... Was it over her getting rid of the kid?'

'Apparently. Well, Matt did it, and I think that's why.'

She fiddled with one of her leg-warmers. 'I really encouraged her, like, "Get rid of it, girl, you're too young." She was mega torn-up about it... I don't know if she would have kept the thing if we hadn't been so fucking hardline.'

'It's not your fault.'

'Well, who knows?'

'No, Daisy, look at me... It's not.'

Her eyes moved from my face to the mantelpiece behind me, scanning her array of figurines.

'I know where they are,' she said. 'Kyle called by the other day. He doesn't know I talked to you but he was picking up stuff.' She reached into the breast pocket of her shirt and handed me a Post-it. 'I wrote down the address as soon as he was gone; I'd have forgotten it otherwise. I have to drop round some money of his when the drugs sell on.'

I took the Post-it and watched her stubbing her cigarette out in the tray, unfinished. I pictured her, wandering around the West End with a name and a Post-it with an address on it, meeting all kinds of ridicule and bemusement. I didn't know what to make of her; whether she was remarkable or just fucking mental.

'Wow, thanks, this is—'

'You're not gonna arrest them though, are you? *Private* investigator...'

I started to lie, but knew she wouldn't buy it. 'No. No, I don't arrest people.'

She started nodding again.

'That doesn't bother you, does it?' I asked.

'Wouldn't have told ya if it did, would I? I suppose. It's just a weird thought. With Meds dead, and Emma, and now... Like, does killing everyone really make that massive a difference at the end of the day? It's not like it makes it better. It just means everyone's dead.'

'I just do what I'm paid for.' I kept hoping she might look at me again, but she didn't. 'It must make it better for who's paying.'

'I think' – another gulp of cider – 'you might be full of shit. But what do I know, right? I'm only young and naive and, well, you've got his address now and I spent two days looking for you so...'

I looked at the address. I thought of Clare, and Pat, and the photos.

'It's justice though, isn't it? It's proper justice.'

'I suppose I just wish... that I was stupid. Sorry, I wish I didn't know this much about you. You get me?'

'I get you.' I stood up. 'It really wasn't your fault. Matt's very... well, I wouldn't have been surprised if he'd done it anyway, even without that particular motive.'

'Road's closed now. No point going over what we don't

291

know.' She stretched her legs out into the space where I had been sitting.

I took out my wallet and offered her some notes.

'Na, it's all right.' She waved me away. 'It would feel like *I* was being paid to do it or something.'

'Well, take my number anyway, just in case.' I put the wallet away, regretting the offer, and gave her a card instead. 'This means a lot. It'll mean a lot to her parents, to me.'

'Safe. Well, I guess you're all *very* welcome.'

I didn't know why it stung so much, being refused acknowledgement, knowing that last time she had wanted me to come back and now I was certain she didn't. With a quick glance at the birds, I let myself back out and shut the door.

I called Pat.

CHAPTER THIRTY-TWO

I picked Pat up from Westminster and, with him belted into his seat and less likely to lose his cool, I told him everything.

Knowing what I did now, about what he let people think, I found myself almost warming to him. He was still conceited as hell and dripping with self-importance, but it was brave, what he had chosen to do.

'Pregnant,' he said. 'She never said a fucking word.'

'She was just scared you'd be angry.'

'Damn right, I'd have been angry, I'd have…' He shook his head. 'But I would have been on her side, you know.'

'It's hard, at her age. You feel like everyone's just waiting for you to fuck up.'

'You're more likely to remember than me.' He grimaced. 'Clare would have gone fucking ape-shit.'

The scale of her reaction had shocked me at the time. I could only imagine what she would have done had Emma told her.

'You know, she was a good mum, when she was on track with it,' he said, resting his elbow on the window. 'Her and Em didn't see eye to eye on a lot but it was just a clash of personalities. They wouldn't have been good friends, if you know what I mean, but she was good at being a mum.'

'I don't doubt that.'

'I just don't want you to get the wrong idea about her, because of how she is.'

It didn't go unnoticed, how he was protecting her reputation again. He couldn't stand anybody thinking badly of her.

'How did you guys meet?' I asked.

He smiled. 'She made the move on me in this pub. She was with a load of model friends or whatever, and when they left she just sat down next to me and said she wanted to stay and have another drink. So fucking young, only twenty. I was like a decade older than her but I was head over heels… obviously.'

'Have you gone back home yet?'

'I think she needs some more time.' He looked at his hands. 'She's so fucking exhausting sometimes, but I still don't know what I'd do without her.'

'You think you'll be all right? I mean, after this?' I stopped at some traffic lights just outside Clapham.

'I don't know. I don't know if she's ever been completely all right, that's the thing.' He thought about it for a bit, and then said, 'And I can't see any end. I can't think of any day in the future where I'm going to be *over it*.'

'It gets easier, so people tell me, eventually.' I snorted. 'But no, I get what you mean. They're probably talking shit, to be honest.'

'Reckon this will make me feel better though.'

'You and me, both.'

'Thanks for this.'

'It's just my job.'

I started counting the numbers on the terraced houses, relishing the idea of the looks on their faces. When I spotted number fifty-four, I pulled over and stopped the car. I heard Pat exhale.

'What are their names again?'

'Matt and Kyle.' I let myself out and gestured at the boot. 'You want anything?'

'Maybe later.' He smirked at me. 'I'll be fine with the basics for now.'

'You take downstairs then. I'll head straight up just in case.'

I walked up to the front door, a flimsy red thing with the kind of lock you see on garden sheds. With Pat shielding me from the road I took out my gun and silencer and shot it to pieces.

The door fell straight open when I shoulder-charged it, falling into a hallway and running directly up a narrow flight of stairs. I didn't even hear Pat come in; my eyes were on the next floor. It was the most common method of escape, taking a window from the second floor into the back garden.

I saw white walls, holes in the plaster, a bedroom door slamming shut. I sprinted towards it and kicked it open, right into Kyle's face.

He fell backwards on to the carpet, his shattered nose spewing blood down his front.

'Please! Please don't shoot!' he was screaming.

There were no weapons in his hands.

I fired a shot into the floor by his head to keep him down, and listened for Pat, coming up the stairs.

'Anything?' I called.

'No one down there.'

'WHERE'S MATT?' I shouted at Kyle, grabbing him by the hair and forcing the gun into his forehead.

'I don't know! He's not here!'

I glanced at Pat. 'Nothing?'

'No one down there.'

'Fuck!'

I let Kyle go, aimed a kick into the wall, saw a small bookshelf and threw the thing over. I sat down on the end of the single bed, shaking with anger, thinking of Matt's face, his smug lying face...

'Which one's this?' Pat asked, his gun aimed at Kyle's head.

'Kyle.' I looked up. 'Kyle, this is Pat Dyer.'

Kyle's eyes widened and he started to scrabble away across the floor, towards my feet. 'Fuck... Fuck, no. Please, I didn't kill her, I didn't mean for this to—'

Pat shot Kyle in the hand and blood hit my face. The bullet had gone through the back of his palm and into the floor. Kyle started screaming, so loud that I had to get down and grab him from behind to muffle the sound.

'Boot of the car,' I shouted at Pat, holding Kyle as still as I could. 'Get tape!'

Pat stared at Kyle for a while as if he hadn't heard me, and then turned and went back downstairs.

'Where's Matt?' I hissed.

When I took my hand away from his mouth he just kept screaming, so I forced him to be quiet and shouted at him again.

'WHERE'S MATT?'

'I don't... know. North... I don't... *oh God...*'

I let him cry to himself until Pat came back with the tape, and also a blowtorch. At the sight of him Kyle's struggling intensified, what was left of his left hand flailing in mid-air and getting blood all over me. I stood up and kicked him forwards on to the carpet, and in the few seconds he had free before Pat forced the tape over his mouth, he managed to say, 'No, I didn't! I *didn't!*'

It had crossed my mind in the car that he hadn't been the one to kill her, but in covering it up he had done himself no favours.

Pat sneered, 'You as good as did.'

I took a step back. His cheeks were sunken into his face. I couldn't help but see him on his knees between Emma's legs, at gunpoint, trousers round his ankles and tears running down his face...

I hadn't told Pat those details.

There was a horrible hacking sound from behind the gag as Pat taped Kyle's wrists behind his back. I let him get on with it and sat down at the end of the bed again. It wasn't as if I expected him to need any assistance.

He turned the blowtorch on and off a few times, dragged Kyle up and held it against his eye.

A vile smell reached me on the smoke, and I grimaced.

Kyle was thrashing in mid-air as Pat held him up, ignoring the noises coming from behind the tape. His jeans became dark as he pissed himself and urine trickled on to the floor.

I moved a little further down the bed.

'Wanna watch, Nic?'

'Na, you're all right.'

I'd heard the sound before, but it always surprised me, hearing someone's eyeball audibly popping.

I swallowed.

Kyle went limp as he passed out, and Pat dropped him to the floor. His right eye socket was a blackened hole, releasing a small trail of blood down his face. The air smelt like charred meat.

'I like the idea of my face being the last thing that fucker ever sees,' he said, sitting on the floor next to Kyle's prone form and taking out a packet of cigarettes. 'But he didn't kill her, did he?'

'Technically, no.'

'Smoke, Nic? Ha, ironic...'

'Yes, please.' I took the cigarette and nodded at Kyle. 'He

297

helped to cover it up, dispose of the body. But no, he didn't actually do it.'

'And he was her boyfriend, right?' He gestured with the lighter and I couldn't believe how calm he was.

'Yeah.'

'Hm.' He picked up the blowtorch again and blasted the flame against Kyle's neck, blistering the skin. 'I'll pay you half for this, if you like, as this has gone on a while. Half when you track down the other guy. Is that OK?'

I hadn't thought about the money for a while. 'God, yeah, that's fine. Don't worry about it.'

'I thought…' He gave Kyle's face a going-over, releasing a putrid coil of smoke, but he looked bored. 'I thought it would feel different.'

'What?' I exhaled towards the mould on the ceiling.

'This.' He snorted. 'Hey, shall I pop the other eye and see if that helps?'

I looked at Kyle's hand, at the hole and mess of broken tendons and pulsing blood where his palm used to be. Remembering what Felix Hudson had said, I agreed with Pat. This didn't feel like fun.

'I thought I'd feel like… like I really fucking wanted it,' he continued. 'But it… it just feels… God, it all feels pointless now. I mean, like Clare… she wouldn't be proud of me now, because it doesn't make a difference, does it? It doesn't bring…'

He sniffed, took a drag, red eyes blinking through an exhale of smoke.

'How old is this guy? Nineteen? … It doesn't bring her back,' he said.

It would have been better if it had been Matt, I realized. As it was, Kyle was nothing. He was a fuck-up, who had committed the worst of his crimes at gunpoint. He was just a mannequin for Pat to vent his rage on; a punch bag with a face drawn on it.

'Pat,' I said. 'Everyone I spoke to, Emma's friends and people like that, they all said that she really cared about what you thought. If I asked about her parents, they all said she got on with you.'

I thought I was about to see him cry as he nodded at me, taking the gesture in. But he just took a longer drag on his cigarette, and then stubbed it out on Kyle's arm.

He inhaled his own second-hand smoke. 'What did they say about Clare?'

It was depressing to witness, how much he cared, and how much she didn't.

I didn't reply quickly enough, and he looked crushed.

'They were just such different people,' he said, trying to justify my silence. 'Em was at a difficult age anyway. It was… Em once said to me that if Clare was a girl at school, she'd think she was a spoilt bitch.'

I wasn't sure whether to smile or not until he did, shaking his head.

'Spoilt bitch?'

'Spoilt *rich-bitch*. Shouldn't laugh really, but she was just being sixteen, you know. I think Clare wanted Em to be more like her and… well, when you're that age you want to be the opposite of anything your parents are. I understood it.' He nodded at me. 'Em probably didn't think I did, but I got it.'

We both looked to the window. There was no view; just the wall of the building next to it. Everything seemed so still.

I finished my cigarette, feeling numb inside, thinking about Matt.

Pat stood up.

'You done already?' I said.

He took out his gun and shot Kyle through the head.

Kyle jerked against the ground to the muffled whistle of the silencer.

I looked at him and swallowed. His face was almost unrecognizable as human. I felt nothing, but was unsure if I would have done the same.

It was probably better this way, rather than letting him live with all this. Looking at him now, at his emaciated frame, it was as if the memories had been physically eating away at his body, like parasites.

'I'm done,' Pat said, wiping his nose and putting his gun back inside his coat. 'I'd rather be having a fucking Scotch. Wouldn't you?'

I heard a noise downstairs, like the front door opening very quietly.

Pat didn't react for a moment but I was already down the stairs and out through the open door into the street. I could see his back, turning a corner into a passage behind gardens.

He must have been waiting there, hiding downstairs, waiting for the best moment to sneak out. He should have stayed where he was...

Every fibre of every muscle was straining, focusing on the back of his hoodie. My mind was full of the scenes of what we would do to him when I'd caught him, when I'd brought him back...

We tore across a road, at least two streets away from the house now.

Matt looked back, once, every fibre of every muscle straining for survival against the death that pursued him just as ruthlessly.

Did it bring her back?

It doesn't bring her back.

I shook the thought out of my head and felt rain on my face.

We were heading towards a secondary school, fenced off from the rest of the street.

Matt hit the chain-link fence at full speed and scrambled over. By the time I reached it he was tearing away across the school field and I had slowed down. I knew I could have climbed it, I knew I could have caught him, but I had slowed down, and then I stopped.

Through the mesh I saw him reach the other side of the field, scale the other fence and disappear.

I couldn't have caught him; he had had too much of a head-start.

It doesn't bring her back.

Why hadn't I just climbed the fucking fence? Because I hadn't wanted to? Because I couldn't have caught him anyway? Because, at the end of the day, who did the cataclysmic loss of life affect if neither Pat nor Clare really wanted it? It didn't affect anyone apart from me.

What difference did one more mangled body on a bedroom floor make?

I waited by the fence for a long time, shivering, as if I was still going to climb it.

CHAPTER THIRTY-THREE

Pat went back to his flat to pick up some things, and I drove around central London in a trance for a while, unsure whether to go home, or go drinking, hang out with Ronnie or Noel, someone I could talk bollocks with.

Any sense of achievement eluded me, especially when telling Pat that I had lost Matt had felt like such a lie.

When my mobile started ringing I pulled over, cutting up a furious motorcyclist who gave me the finger as he drove by. I wouldn't have bothered if it hadn't been Clare.

'Wanker,' I muttered as I answered the phone. 'Hello?'

I could hear that she was crying before she said anything. My hand went to my face and I checked in the overhead mirror if I still had any of Kyle's blood on me. I was wearing a change of clothes and we had washed the superficial stains off, but speaking to her made me paranoid.

'Clare?'

Silence.

'Clare, come on, talk to me.'

'Come over?'

It was strange that she phrased it as a question, as if she didn't know that I would drop everything and do as she asked.

'What's wrong?'

'*Please...*' She took a breath, but started sobbing again. 'Please, come over.'

I glowered out of the window as I replied, resenting the

way I was so willing to let myself be jerked around. 'OK. OK, I'll come over. Can you tell me what's wrong?'

She hung up on me.

'For *fuck's* sake!'

I dropped the phone into my open bag on the passenger seat and turned the car around into the wrong lane. A white van screeched to a halt beside me and I could hear the driver yelling at me, some grotesque fucker in a West Ham shirt who wound down the window and then opened his door.

I got out of the car, hating him on sight.

'Run me off the fucking road—' he was shouting.

'What?' I strode up to him and he was taller than me. '*What?*'

'You wanna start something, do ya?' He spat at the ground next to me. 'Come on then!'

I stared at him, took a blade out of my pocket, yanked his head to one side by his ear and sliced the lobe of the other clean off. I felt it come loose like a sliver of beef.

He made no sound as I shoved his heavy bulk away from me and walked back to my car. It was only after I had got back into the driver's seat and started the engine that he spotted the blood running down his shoulder. The shock on his face, as he tried to work out what I had done, almost made me laugh for a moment, before the familiar unease with my own actions kicked in. It made me calm, but it made me into someone I hadn't wanted to become; someone who enjoyed it.

It was tempting to scrape against his van as I pulled away, but it wasn't worth the inconvenience. I dropped the knife into the footwell and made a mental note to clean it off later.

My hands felt unsteady wrapped around the wheel.

Kyle's death hadn't even meant more than that van driver's ear. Matt's death wouldn't have done either.

'Dickhead,' I said out loud as it started to rain.

Music was playing inside. I had come to view that as a bad sign where she was concerned. She opened the door and her cheeks were brilliantly red, as if she had just rubbed mascara off them along with the tears.

Without saying a word she took hold of my coat and pulled my lips against hers. I wanted to say no, to retain some pride, an illusion of control. But I also wanted to believe that something I did would make things better; that I could be what she wanted. Just like Pat.

The door shut. I was backed into the wall.

'I knew you'd come.'

It should have bothered me more, but nothing felt better than her. She made it impossible to think about anything else.

I dropped my bag and my coat and pushed her back across the hallway. She pulled at the band of her trousers, smelling like strong perfume, kissing my neck, murmuring, 'Do it like you did last time.'

I could still feel the tears on her face.

'Hit me…'

'What?'

'Hit me again.' She took hold of my face with both hands and glared at me, one of her legs entwining around mine.

'Clare—'

'Do it!'

'No!' I pulled away and took a step back.

There was a silence. I don't know how I found the will to stay there. She shifted her weight from foot to foot, eyeing the space between us with suspicion, as if no one had ever taken a step back from her in her life.

She walked past me into the living room, I heard her

looking for something, and she met me back in the doorway with a fistful of notes, waving them in my face.

'Will this help?'

'Jesus...' I swatted her hand away, stung. 'What the fuck am I to you?'

'You're paid to help, right?' She started crying again, snapping at me through the tears. 'You're paid to hurt people and I'm *asking* you—'

'Clare, this is crazy!'

'You didn't mind last time!'

'No, fuck this shit.' I turned and picked up my bag and coat. 'Fuck you.'

'No! No, don't go!' She forced herself between me and the door, standing with her back against it and sobbing. 'Don't you dare go! Don't you *dare*!'

'Move.'

'No.'

'Get *out* of the way!'

'No!'

I grabbed her arm and she punched me, with surprising force. Using all my discipline, I refrained from doing the same. It was what she wanted me to do.

She pushed me, with both hands. 'You said you could help! You *said*!'

'Look, just move—'

'What you're paid to, right!' She slapped me and I almost tripped over the bottom stair. 'You do what you're paid to! If you won't I'll—'

'Stop it!'

'I'll—'

'You're being—'

This time she went for me with her nails and I caught her

305

with a blow to the jaw in my attempt to deflect them from my face. There wasn't much force behind it, but it was enough to make her stop. Her bottom lip started bleeding a little and she dabbed the blood away with her fingers.

I regretted it straight away, but at least the fight had left her.

'Is that what you wanted?' I said, shrugging. 'Is that all you wanted me for? Well, it's not that great, is it?'

In her eyes I could see that she was looking at a stranger. For once, something hadn't gone the way she had wanted. From the bewilderment in her expression I could see what Mark had meant; not getting her own way was alien to her.

The shock turned into embarrassment and, wiping the blood off her lip again, she turned away from me and sat down in the living room. She pulled her legs up on to the sofa as I came in and sat down opposite her, in the exact poses we had struck on the night we had met.

'Sorry,' I said.

'No… It's not like I didn't ask.' She tried to smile. 'You want to know a secret? Something I tried to tell you before?'

'What?'

'When Emma died… one of the first things I remember thinking, when I could think again…' She hid most of her face behind her hands. 'I thought, for a second, that I could go back. I mean… go back to how I was before. I was *glad*, for a second.'

As I was searching for something to say she succumbed to tears again, rubbing her eyes.

'It was only for a second.'

'I'm sure it's… normal.'

I didn't know if it was normal, if I was lying. I didn't know what was normal by her standards any more. Everything she said made me feel sorrow for her, and frustration that I couldn't do anything for her.

'No, you don't understand!' She stood up, shaking. 'I lost myself! I *lost* myself! I had a life, *my* life, and now I don't know... I thought I could get it back.'

I stayed sitting, wishing there was something I could say that would be enough for her. But what she wanted was fantasy. Pat was the lifelong mediator between her and reality and she hated him for it. I didn't know how he had done it for this long.

'You had a life,' I said. 'Emma wasn't some person who came along and stole it. You want to talk about fucking things up then, trust me, I'm an expert, but you didn't fuck things up. I mean, what would you have done differently?'

'I don't even know.' She spread her hands, almost laughing. 'Been someone... better?'

'Yeah, but all this didn't happen because you had a kid.'

'I... know,' she breathed through the tears. 'I know.'

Looking defeated, she turned the music off and sat down again.

'Well, what do you want? Seriously, Clare, what can anyone fucking *do*? If you just told someone what you want then—'

'I *told* you. I...'

The front door opened. In the time that it took for Pat to shut it again Clare had wiped her eyes and checked that her lip had stopped bleeding.

He looked at me from the doorway, pointedly, before he turned to Clare. 'Hey, I'm just picking up some stuff, is that OK?'

She nodded, barely meeting his gaze.

'I was just...' I retracted any gestures with my hands, trying

307

to appear as nonchalant as possible. 'I was just telling Clare everything I told you.'

He didn't take his eyes off Clare. 'Are you all right?'

It took a while for her to remember that she wasn't supposed to know about the pregnancy, that the last meeting between us could never have happened, and recovered well.

'It's a bit of a shock.' She shook her head. 'I'm starting to think we didn't really know her at all, did we?'

Thank God, I thought, resting my head on my hands.

'Are you OK to cash a cheque?' Pat asked me, indicating that he was going to the kitchen. 'I can write one out.'

I would have preferred cash but I didn't want to contradict him on anything at this point. 'Yeah, cheque is fine.'

'You're done?' Clare turned to me sharply.

'Not completely,' I said. 'I was just coming to that actually. We got one guy, but the other got away.'

'You got him?' She looked between me and Pat. 'When?'

'A couple of hours ago,' Pat said.

'You *got* him, a couple of hours ago.' She didn't manage to hide the expression of pure disgust that she shot in my direction. 'That's nice.'

Under normal circumstances I would have called her a fucking hypocrite, but with Pat there I just nodded. It seemed a strange attitude, only to advocate violence against yourself.

Pat also looked a little uncomfortable at the admission, and went to get my cheque.

'Have you come straight from wherever you just were?' she hissed. 'A *couple* of hours ago?'

'You didn't seem to give a damn where I was when you called begging me to come over.'

'You're so self-righteous.'

'*Me?*'

We both stopped talking as we heard Pat coming back. It felt more stable, more familiar, to return to this antagonism, but her agitation put me on edge. When she was like this she would do anything.

I stood up to take the cheque, and to my surprise Pat shook my hand.

'Thanks, Nic, let me know how it goes with... the other one.'

'No problem.'

Clare snorted to herself. 'Are you going to group hug or do you want some time alone?'

Pat sighed. 'Come on, Clare, what's your problem?'

'All this back-patting, like you're so proud of yourselves, well you know what?' She stood up, folding her arms with a flourish. 'I *knew* all of this, I knew about it days ago, darling.'

I felt like someone had grabbed me by the throat.

Pat's eyes narrowed. 'How?'

'Nic came and told me. Oh, and while we're on the subject, we had sex.' She grinned through a wave of her hair, partly at me, but mostly at Pat, as though she had been waiting for the perfect moment to say it. 'And it was *really* good.'

CHAPTER THIRTY-FOUR

It didn't cross my mind to try and deny it. Even though it confirmed my guilt, my instant reaction was to move away from Pat. He was staring at Clare, who was still smiling defiantly, glowing with bizarre elation.

He turned to me, the moment I had been dreading. Not since Brinks had smashed my head open had I been so sure that someone was going to kill me.

'You—'

'No, not him,' Clare cut in, taking a step forwards as if to block me from his view. '*I* wanted to. '

Pat was standing too close to the door for me to get out. All I could do was keep backing away across the room.

What the fuck was she doing?

What the fuck had she *done*?

Pat didn't say anything. He tortured people without making a sound. My gun was in a bin three streets away, where I had disposed of it, and his was inside his coat.

Clare cocked her head. 'Go on. Do something.'

With the jolt of revulsion, I realized what was going on, at the exact moment that Pat threw her to one side and lunged at me across the room.

'No!' she cried.

I almost grabbed the stone statue, but another ornament came to hand instead. The corner of the photo frame caught Pat's forehead. I dropped it and made a break for the door.

'Pat, wait!' I heard Clare shout.

I felt him grab the back of my jacket; he threw me sideways on to the floor. I scrambled up, managed to get into the kitchen and slam the door. It slowed him down, but not much. He came crashing into the other side and forced me backwards.

He was holding his gun.

'Don't!' Clare grabbed Pat's arm but he pushed her away without looking at her.

'Pat...' I said, trying to get him talking.

'Don't fucking talk to me.' His lip curled. 'It took me a while, but I trusted you towards the end, I actually *trusted* you.'

'Put it down, Pat!' Clare got between us, shaking, glancing back at me. 'Just put the gun down... Pat, it was me, it was me, it was *all* me, I promise, you don't need to shoot anyone—'

'Yeah, I bet you put up such a fucking fight,' he sneered at me.

'For God's sake!' She slapped the gun away, pushing her way forwards into his space. 'Pat, just listen!'

Clare had inadvertently blocked me from his view and I saw my chance.

I charged at him.

A shot went into one of the lights and glass rained down. I grabbed Pat's wrist, forcing the gun upwards and swiping at his head. For a second his gun was in my hand, but as Pat backhanded me across the face I lost my grip and it spun away across the floor.

Clare was crying, screaming at us to stop, but I couldn't make out the words. She had her hands to her head, watching us aghast, as if this was the last thing she had expected to happen.

311

Pat and I both went for the gun, grappling with each other, and I managed to crack his head into the granite work surface. As I made for Pat's automatic, just feet away, I felt a searing pain down my calf.

My left leg collapsed under me before I knew what had happened.

As I hit the tiles, I turned and saw a blade embedded in the muscle just above my ankle. Without thinking, I pulled it straight out, and the room blurred.

Clare cried out and darted forwards. 'Pat, no!'

Pat stepped over me.

I dragged myself to my feet using the kitchen worktop, and faced him as he pointed the gun at my head. The end of it looked like a black hole, the end of the fucking universe.

Clare ran into him, full force, and I heard the thud of the silencer.

I couldn't see hers, but I could see Pat's face, rigid with shock, suddenly devoid of any colour.

Even the back of my leg had gone numb.

One moment she was alive, her body still upright and moving with every breath, but then it looked as though the strength was simply whipped from her, leaving behind a mass of limbs and cells that could no longer carry out their function.

The legs that I had watched turn pirouettes buckled.

Pat caught her, went down with her, made sure the back of her head didn't hit the floor too hard, and only then could I see where the bullet had gone into the left side of her chest.

Her eyes were still open, blinking a little.

'No... Fuck, no...' Pat dropped the gun and keeled over her, his hands either side of her face as if trying to stop life escaping. 'No, baby... Baby, stay with me...'

312

It was like regaining consciousness, realizing that my mobile was in my bag.

'Wait!' I tried to put weight on the injured leg and it hurt so much that it brought tears to my eyes. 'Wait, I can call someone, wait!'

I limped down the hallway, my teeth clenched, hissing, 'Fuck fuck fuck fuck…' under my breath until I reached my bag. It took me a few seconds even to recognize my phone, I was so blinded with panic.

I picked it up and started to limp back towards the kitchen.

It was like a punch in the face, realizing that there was no way I could call an ambulance.

'Pat!' I called, coming back into the kitchen and pausing to regain some control over the agony. 'Pat, my car! We can—'

'*Shut up!*'

He looked up at me, tears streaming down his face.

'I can call my… I can call…'

He stroked her forehead.

It didn't seem real, watching her lying there, willing movement, a weak blink, a shallow breath… Air rushed in and out of my lungs. I had a vision of maybe carrying her to the car, getting her to a hospital, but it was fantasy. It would take longer than the minutes, the seconds, we had been left with.

Neither of us moved, for too long.

I stood with my phone, as if some solution was going to be offered to me.

Pat just brushed her hair back off her forehead, took hold of her hand and hovered his fingertips over the blood that had run down the front of her white shirt, searching for acknowledgement.

Her eyes were half open. Her lips, parted. I thought of Emma, the same expression facing the camera at the docks.

313

Pat let go of her hand and placed it across her stomach. His expression reminded me of Clare's that night at the mortuary; pain as if their souls had been ripped in two.

He picked up the gun and I ducked, shielding my face instinctively.

I waited, for the impact that felt similar to being punched, and when I dared to look at him again he was still pointing it at me.

He sighed.

'NO, FUCK, WAIT!' I shouted.

He put the gun against his temple and fired.

The inside of his head exploded over cupboards and drawers, and his body slumped backwards.

Blood ran down my ankle and into my shoe. My heartbeat was the only thing breaking the silence, but I could still hear my last words reverberating, as I had seen what he was going to do.

No, fuck, wait!

Feeling sick, unsteady, anaesthetized with shock, I crouched down and looked at her.

Was this it? Was this what she had wanted?

I reached out and rubbed some of Pat's blood off her forehead. The sensation of her skin under my fingertips seemed such a recent memory, but it didn't feel as if I could remember without that simmering well of hate; that anger, raging under the surface.

Of course this had been what she wanted, to push one of us too far.

I stood up, with some difficulty, and limped out of the kitchen, back towards the living room. When I was in there I sat down and called Mark.

*

'Are you OK?' Mark insisted on crouching down to look at my leg as soon as I let them inside.

Roman Katz went straight through to the kitchen with a nod and a casual muttered greeting. As much as I disliked him, I knew he was one of the only other people Mark would trust enough to come.

I sat down on the bottom stair, grimacing. 'It's all right, he missed the ankle, which is handy, cos you know I like those tendons.'

'No, I mean, are you OK?'

I shrugged.

'Does anyone else know you're here?'

'No. Pat had an alibi for the rest of today but I don't know what it was, we'd just come from a... job.'

'Cool,' he said.

I snorted.

He slapped a hand to his forehead. 'Sorry, that came out wrong. I mean, Cool, no one will come looking for Pat today...'

'No, I know.' I indicated my head back at the kitchen. 'You two gonna start wearing friendship bracelets soon?'

'What, and replace yours? We were just hanging out. Same country is a novelty for us, you know.' He eyed my leg. 'We're going to have to take you to hospital, I'm afraid.'

'Will he be all right here?'

'He's going to call some of his family.'

'Ha, they still use that term?'

'No, literal family.' He laughed. 'They're his brothers. Wait here, I'm just going to look...'

I remembered that I had Pat's cheque in my pocket, and rested my forehead on my hands. With him dead it was useless to me now. That was all I had got out of this in the end: a cheque that I couldn't cash and, as Daisy had said, a pointless body count.

Mark came back from the kitchen, shaking his head. 'God... That's going to take some puppetry. Your fingerprints and blood must be all over the place, so we're either going to have to clean the fuck out of this place or pull some major strings.'

Katz had followed him; he had a mildly amused expression on his face that I hated. He stood beside Mark with his hands in his pockets, looking as though he was in the midst of a pleasant sightseeing trip.

'Is that what you would call, in your country, a Shakespeare tragedy?' he asked me.

'Only if you find it *entertaining*,' I replied.

'You have an art for a scenic mess.'

Mark stood up and said something in Russian. They made a lot of gestures, towards the kitchen, towards the front door, at me. At one point Katz's tone softened and he almost smiled. Mark smiled back at him and said something that sounded like banter in return.

I cleared my throat.

'Roman's going to take you to the hospital,' Mark said.

'Seriously?'

The sarcasm came out before I could stop it, but Katz didn't look offended.

'We only have his car.' Mark spread his hands. 'Nic, you know better than anyone that I do this all the fucking time. This isn't his job and I'm more use to you here than sat in A&E.'

I couldn't think of anything worse than spending one-on-one time with Roman Katz, but I nodded anyway. 'Fine.'

'I'll come meet you when we're done here,' Mark said. 'Not soon, I imagine.'

Katz offered to take my arm around his shoulders but I insisted on standing for myself. I didn't look back at the kitchen again. It's not as if anything would have changed.

'I know what you want me to say,' Mark said. 'But I'm not going to tell you this isn't your fault.'

I didn't answer him on my way out.

CHAPTER THIRTY-FIVE

I thought it would have been serious enough to warrant a queue-jump, but apparently, now that the bleeding had stopped, we could afford to wait. Not surprisingly, we didn't have much to say to each other.

In front of us on another row of seats, two old ladies were talking. One of them, in a pink coat, had her left arm in a cast. Her friend, a taller, thinner woman wearing a blue cardigan, was talking her through her treatment.

'They'll have to cut those rings off,' she said.

'They're not taking my wedding ring.'

'They have to. If they don't, you'll lose your fingers, Lou. It's the swelling.'

'They're not taking it.'

'Why does it matter? You can still keep it.'

'But it'll look like I was never married.'

They lapsed into silence.

As long as I didn't move my leg I could ignore the pain with relative ease.

'You knew the woman well,' Katz said. 'That is what Mark said. I am sorry.'

'What do you actually do in Russia?' I asked, ignoring the statement.

'My family own restaurants. We own some here too, that is why my family are here for Christmas. Obviously, we do not only own restaurants...'

I nodded.

'What are you doing for Christmas Eve?' he asked. 'Apart from… convalescing? Recovery?'

'Dunno. When is it?'

'It is today.'

'Shit, right…' It hadn't even occurred to me. Days of the week had meant nothing recently. 'Probably just go home, hang out with Mark, maybe some other people if he's planned something. He's probably planned something or other… How did you meet Mark?'

Mark had never told me how he came to be working in Russia after his Oxford education. Despite the years we had known each other there were still a lot of holes in our respective histories.

'We met not very long ago – two years. He was working for friends of mine in Moscow.' Katz looked at his nails and I noticed, now that he had unzipped the coat with the fur-lined hood, that his shirt was inside-out. 'He is godfather to my youngest, Alex. My children like him very much.'

'Your shirt…' I gestured.

It only took one hesitation, but it made him human. It was the first time I had seen any evidence of it.

'Oh, I did not notice. When you are working fast you…' He trailed off, but didn't have enough of a natural grasp of English to turn it into a lie.

'No, I get it.' I nodded as the insight clicked into place. 'I don't mind, Mark sees whoever he likes.'

I wasn't sure what I thought of it, but I was surprised. He didn't seem like Mark's type, who, more often than not, tended to be male models. It seemed to bother Katz though. He frowned as he searched for the right phrasing.

'I believe in the sanctity of marriage.'

319

'So you're a non-practising believer?' I smiled. 'Don't worry, my family call themselves Catholics and we couldn't count a dozen Masses between us.'

I wondered why Mark hadn't told me. It wasn't as if he was discreet with anything or anyone else. Maybe it was because he knew that I didn't like Katz? Or because I knew Katz was married? Either way, it was still odd.

'Don't worry, I don't care, I wouldn't tell anyone,' I said.

'Thank you.'

The two ladies in front of us were still sat in silence. The one on the left was looking at her wedding ring, almost hidden by the purple skin.

'I wouldn't say I believed in marriage,' I said. 'But I've just seen the worst fucking advert for it, that's for sure. It's just... dangerous, getting to know someone that well, isn't it?'

After a while, I sat back in my chair and felt my pocket, reminding myself that the cheque was still there, thinking of the money that Clare had waved in my face.

My phone started vibrating.

I tried to stand up to answer it, but Katz stood up instead to give me some privacy.

'Hi, Harri,' I said.

'Hi, *how are you?* Whatever. So, Mum and Dad want to know if you're coming over for Christmas.'

'Are you there now?'

'Practically moved back in, haven't I. Well?'

I rolled my eyes. 'Why don't *they* ask me?'

'I don't know. I'm just the fucking go-between.' She sighed. 'Are you coming?'

I watched Katz reading the chlamydia leaflets pinned to the wall. Beside them were some posters about coping with diabetes, and another about the dangers of unprotected sex.

'Probably not, to be honest,' I said. 'I'm in A&E. My leg is a bit... stabbed.'

'Huh, surprise. But you're coming to the funeral, yeah?'

'Yeah, of course.'

'Sorry I was a dick to you... Last time, I was a bit of a dick. Dad was just on my back, you know. Made a change to see him disembowel someone else for once.'

'You shouldn't let him shit all over you, Harri. That's why he does it.'

She snorted. 'And you are such a classic example of that. The way you ran away last time, that was *scathing*, I mean, he couldn't get over it. I watched you, running away, and just thought, "There goes a guy who doesn't let people shit all over—"'

'OK, fuck off, you've made your point.'

Even on the phone she reminded me of Daisy. It was unnerving; the two of them had almost morphed into the same person in my head.

'What are you going to say at the thing?' she asked. 'If you don't do it then I'll have to say something and we all know that no one wants that...'

'Oh, fuck no, I'll play Rock Paper Scissors for it at the church?'

'No way, if I'm getting lumbered with throwing confetti all over his rose-tinted life then you definitely have to do it too.' She hesitated. 'Are you all right? You sound a bit... weird.'

My mind went blank on any kind of convincing lie. To me, the house I had left behind didn't seem to have existed. Like Katz had said, the sense of loss was like a nagging ache, diluted by the shock. Lost car keys.

'Just work stuff.' I grinned suddenly. 'Hey, I dare you to read the eulogy while high. Then afterwards everyone will try and work out why you stopped halfway through and became transfixed by the candles!'

'Ha-fucking-ha! Don't bail on me for the memorial, yeah?'

'I won't.'

I hung up, and managed to smile at Katz as he came to sit back down.

'Thanks for this,' I said. 'You know, coming, clearing up. It's... appreciated.'

'It is no problem. I owe Mark many things. As I said to him earlier, when you called for help, where I come from there is no favour that we do not do for our family or our country.'

'Sorry, we probably give the wrong impression. We're not related.'

'It does not matter. Mark said you are both his family and his country.'

The ladies in front of us got up to see the doctor on duty, and we were called not long after.

Katz dropped me at home after my leg had been dressed and bandaged, and Mark didn't get back until the early hours of the morning.

I'd fallen asleep on the sofa, watching the webcam videos, at around midnight, and woke up when I heard the front door shut.

My laptop was on standby on the coffee table.

In my dream I had been sat on the floor, against the mirror in Clare's dance studio. She had been dancing for me, back and forth, in black and white. The mirror had been cold against my back. It seemed impossible to comprehend, waking up and realizing that I would never touch her again.

I swung my legs over the edge of the sofa and rubbed my eyes as Mark sat down heavily. He smelt of bleach, and soap, and cigarettes. Mark never smoked unless he was stressed; it was one of the only ways I was able to discern problems.

'What's the line?' I asked through a yawn.

'You were never there. He killed her, then himself. That's it.'

'Any puppetry?'

'Not for now. We think it looks fairly convincing, especially given their… history.'

'Seriously, thanks.'

'I'm keeping a tally.'

'She wanted him to kill her,' I said. 'I kept thinking, why the fuck would she do that? Just tell him everything? But that was all she wanted really, she wanted one of us to lose it.'

'It's not your fault.'

'Oh, I know. She would have found a way eventually.'

'No, I mean, you couldn't have helped her.'

'Well…' I glanced at him. 'Road's closed. No point thinking about it now. Just need to find Matt and then I can forget all—'

'I don't think you should find Matt.'

He looked tired, and I didn't want to get into a debate with him. I still hadn't told him that I had effectively let Matt go, and I wasn't sure I ever would. I wasn't even sure that was what I had done… I could see the white cracks on the backs of his hands from the cleaning products. Deciding to tackle the issue later, I changed the subject.

'So how long have you and Katz been at it?'

'*At it?*' He grinned to himself, uncharacteristically coy. 'Mm, he said you knew. I don't know exactly, I suppose since we met, almost, but with living in different countries we don't see each other very often so…'

'You happy?'

He pulled a mocking face at me and I reddened.

'Well, I'm just checking,' I said. 'Being fucking *nice*.'

'No offence, Nic, but…' For the first time I could remember, he didn't have a response, and he picked at a tuft of his hair awkwardly. 'Just fuck off, Nic, OK?'

'Fine, nice evasion, real smooth.' I raised my eyebrows. 'Do you believe in marriage?'

He laughed at me. 'Bit of a loaded question, right now, isn't it? No, not really. If you have kids then you commit to something but I don't see any longevity in just the piece of paper. What's to respect about that?'

'No, I get you.'

'And yeah, I'm happy. You make the best of what you get. The world doesn't fucking move around how you feel, you just… make it work, somehow.' He shrugged. 'She wanted to die. She engineered it from the start. In fact, she probably thought you would do it for her, instead of Pat, am I right?'

'You're right.' The idea that she had only bothered with me because of my job, because she knew that I was so naturally inclined to violence, made me feel uncontrollably sad. 'Pat never laid a finger on her in her fucking life, and even now people are just going to believe the same. He hit her, he killed her… You know she threw herself down the stairs? It wasn't him who put her in hospital.'

Mark's expression was serene, even with his exhausted bloodshot eyes.

'Just let it go.'

'I *know*,' I said, touching the stitches by my hairline. 'I just need to… get it straight in my head.'

'OK.' He nodded at the clock over the fireplace. It was three-fifteen. 'Try and get some sleep, yeah?'

CHAPTER THIRTY-SIX

I had never heard Emma's voice before.

It seemed a bizarre thing to realize now; I had devoted this much time to her yet had never heard her say a thing. I had never seen her in motion either, only in photos, but hearing her voice was the most surprising thing.

'Mum, stop it. You're being a pure bitch!'

The first thing I heard her say. She was well spoken, and her clipped rhythm reminded me of Pat.

I rewound the video, listened for any sound of Mark returning, and started again.

My phone was on the sofa next to me. A couple of hours ago I'd had a text from a number I didn't recognize, saying, SORRY 4 BEING A MOODY BINT THE OTHER DAY. HOPE YR WELL N KICKING. DAISY X.

The Doors were playing, the same song that had been playing the first time she had danced in front of me. A red skirt, flaring with a spin, was the most vivid memory. That, and the way her mood could turn so quickly.

Would you like that?

Clare was posing in front of the webcam, adjusting the screen, looking as if she wasn't confident with using the device yet. Her hair was in plaits. She pushed the lens down so that her arms and chest were in shot, and sat back a little, watching herself.

The lights were down and the door was shut, but I could

see the rest of the living room, down to the end where the shelf was.

Clare looked at herself for a while, adjusting her hair and moving to different camera angles, and ran a small razorblade across the inside of her forearm. It was only a shallow cut, and she watched it until it started bleeding, checking how it came across on camera. There wasn't enough blood to make much impression on the lens; the lighting blurred it.

She stood up, struck some basic poses and turned a few circles. Smiling, she pulled up the hem of the dress to admire her legs.

The door of the living room slammed open, flooding the room with an abrupt onslaught of light.

'Mum, Danny's coming over.' Emma was standing in the doorway with her arms folded, her hair pulled back and wearing the same boots she'd been wearing the day she was murdered.

'OK, darling.' Clare went to turn the CD player off, not meeting her daughter's eyes.

'What the hell's this?'

'I'm just listening to music.'

Emma looked her up and down with scorn. 'I thought you said you'd stopped doing this.'

'Doing what?'

'That fucking shit all over your arm!'

Clare stood her ground but covered the cut. 'Don't use that language with me, young lady, not in my house!'

'It's so *embarrassing*.'

'Don't give me theatrics, Emma. I hope Danny's not staying over.'

'Mum, stop it. You're being a pure bitch!'

'Don't you dare speak to me like that!' She pointed at her.

326

'Don't you dare, or don't even think about Danny coming over!'

'Oh, what's the matter, can't take it when Dad's not here to defend you?' Emma took a step forward. 'You're sad, you know that? Who do you think you are, some emo teenager?'

'I mean it! He's not coming over if you carry on.'

Clare walked away, looking unsteady, but Emma followed her. Seeing them this close to each other only seemed to emphasize how much Emma looked like Pat; it was as if she had rejected her mother's genes as well as her traits and mannerisms.

I couldn't help but feel sorry for Clare. It was painful watching someone as fragile as her being verbally dismantled by one of the only people whose opinion she seemed to care about.

'No, you're pathetic! Living like you're this clichéd tortured fucking artist but you're *not*!'

'Emma, *shut up*.' Clare put her hands over her eyes, spitting out the words. 'Just shut up, go to your room...'

'Whatever, I'm going to Danny's—'

'Oh no, you're not!' Clare whirled around, her voice becoming shrill.

'Oh, go make up a dance routine, you fucking *has-been*.'

The first thing that came to hand was the statue. Clare dragged it off the shelf and before Emma could react she had swiped it at her head, catching her across the cheek. It was swung with such force that Emma had to grab hold of the doorway to keep herself upright, and she put a hand to her cheek with an expression of utter astonishment.

Clare burst into tears, dropping the statue on to the sofa.

'Oh God, oh darling, I'm so sorry—'

'Go to hell.' Emma backed away and disappeared from view into the hallway.

Clare followed, pleading through the tears. 'Please, darling, please, I'm sorry…'

'I *hate* you! Go carve the fucking Mona Lisa in your arm for all I fucking care!'

The front door slammed. Clare came back into the living room and sat down, crying, a loud, violent crying with heavy tears and swollen eyes. After a while she remembered the camera was still running, and came across on her knees to turn it off. She paused for a while beforehand, and I realized that she was watching herself again, observing how she looked while crying.

The last thing I saw was her tears in close up.

Even now, I couldn't take my eyes off her. Her beauty was so hard-edged; so aggressive that she used it to lash out at others while she lashed inwards at herself.

Mark came in, dropped shopping bags and let out an animated sigh. 'Jesus, who does Britain think it is, *Russia*?'

I considered shutting the laptop, hiding any evidence of having been watching the videos, but it was too late; he would hear and become suspicious. I chose to lie instead.

My leg twinged when I turned. 'Hey!'

'What you up to?'

'Just watching some stuff. You know, I'm thinking of picking up this lead I had for Matt…'

'Still looking for him?'

'I don't feel right unless I finish something. It should be finished, right?'

'No, sure thing.' Mark stood by the sofa, looking at the laptop, and gestured for it. 'Let's have a look?'

Glad that he seemed to be in agreement, I started the same video from the beginning, and we watched it through again. Every so often I glanced at Mark, to judge his expression, but he didn't look shocked by this one.

'It's sad,' he said as Clare switched the camera off. 'Here, can I check something?'

'Yeah, sure.' I picked up the laptop and passed it back to him, relieved that he hadn't found anything strange in my behaviour.

'This all of them?' he asked, tapping keys.

'Yeah.'

'Cool.' He shrugged and handed it back.

I went to return to the previous video, but the online file I had created was empty. Confused, I refreshed the page, then clicked back, then forwards, to try and find them. But there was nothing.

'What the *fuck*, Mark!'

'What?' He shrugged.

'You deleted them?' I stood up, shouting through the pain it caused. 'I fucking needed those!'

'For what, exactly?'

'For...' I couldn't think of a convincing answer, but I carried on shouting anyway, as if it would make a difference. 'You have no fucking right, *no* fucking right!'

'It's for your own good.'

'You patronizing fuck!' I spat.

'You weren't going to reform her, Nic!' He squared up to me, raising his voice. 'You weren't going to change her or help her or marry her and have two point five fucking children! She was a screwed-up woman, a beautiful screwed-up woman who knew how to make people as crazy as she was, *that's* what you need to get, OK? You weren't going to be her fucking saviour!'

I punched him but he deflected the blow.

'Nic, don't.'

I went for him again and this time he just stood there and took it. Hitting his stomach was like fighting a sheet of iron.

329

He grabbed me by the front of my shirt and threw me sideways into the wall. I rebounded with some force, caught him around the waist and took us both flying over the back of the sofa. My shoulder smacked against the corner of the coffee table as we hit the floor, and Mark came out on top, pinning me down.

I tried to get up but he wouldn't let me.

He pointed a finger in my face. 'I'm not having you sitting there and mythologizing her!'

'Get off!'

'I swear, I'll kick your fucking arse!'

I could have backtracked, but the scale of my overreaction had confirmed his theory. I couldn't even pinpoint why I was so angry, other than because he had taken away my only way of seeing her again.

All I could hear was our breathing.

Mark was glaring down at me, waiting for a response.

'Fine,' I said.

'Fine, what?'

'Fine, you're right.'

After a couple of seconds, he seemed pacified.

'Apology accepted,' he said, standing up and pulling me to my feet.

The back of my calf complained, and I had to sit back down again quickly. It struck me, with some regret, that we had never done that before; never even a raised voice, let alone a full-on fight.

Mark brushed himself down and stalked away without a word.

I had watched him work out before, seen the endless push-ups and pull-ups and hours of running that he insisted on doing any day he wasn't hung-over. He was fucking lethal, but it rarely occurred to me that if he wanted he could snuff me out like a candle.

I looked at the screen and the empty storage file, and called, 'Look, I'm sorry.'

He came back in with an empty mug in his hand. 'Do that again, I'll break something.'

He wasn't joking.

'Are you going to see Katz later?'

'Yeah, drop round some presents for the kids.' He sat on the arm of the sofa and glanced at the laptop. 'I just didn't think it was healthy.'

'No, you're right. It's just... she had this way of getting to you. I mean, how many people love someone so much that they would blow their own brains out instead of carry on living without them? I can't imagine it.'

'It's not something to envy.'

I smirked. 'You wouldn't blow your brains out for Roman Katz?'

He spread his hands. 'I'm kinda against the idea of sacrificing anything for anyone, if they wouldn't be willing to do the same in return.'

'Yeah, I get it.'

He ruffled my hair, and then stopped and checked his nails. 'I know it's hard, accepting that some people just don't change.'

I wondered who he was referring to.

'Is it that fucking wrong though?' I said. 'Wanting to find Matt? You want me to let him get away with it, after everything he's done?'

'It's not your fight any more. It's not going to change anything.'

'But—'

'Just let it go, Nic, *Jesus*!' He put a hand to the side of my face, elongating the words. 'Let. It. Go.'

I could see the scar across the curve of his top lip, where someone had swiped at him with a penknife three years ago. He was that close.

My phone vibrated on the sofa next to me, and I was surprised to see that the name on the message ID was Daisy's.

Mark stood up again and he was laughing.

'What?'

'Daisy... Well, fuck me.' He shook his head as he wandered back into the kitchen. 'Got to admit, I thought you'd made that one up.'

She was wearing a tweed poncho and nothing else. After a brutal fuck against the wall, on the stairs and on the sofa, Daisy put on some music and we lay on the floor smoking weed.

'If you'd told me you were gonna do that I'd have warmed up. You know, done some aerobic stretches, fucking Pilates...' She wrapped herself tighter in the tweed and rubbed her smudged lipstick. 'Nothing broken, it's all good.'

'What can I say? I'm glad you got in touch...'

'Well, I was curious. Did you off them then? Matt and Kyle?'

She sounded disturbingly matter-of-fact.

'Matt? No, he wasn't at that address. He went up north apparently. Does he have family up north, do you know?'

'Sorry, you're confusing me with someone constructing his family tree.' She ran a finger down the bridge of my nose. 'What are you, Italian or French or something?'

'Scottish-Italian.'

'Sweet. Least you could do is cook me dinner and all.' She

dug an elbow into me and turned on to her side. 'Is Nic your real name?'

'Yes.'

Her expression seemed to alternate between sardonic boredom and a persistent excitement. It didn't seem to bother her that she had run out of the hard-core drugs. If it had been Harriet she would have been rifling through the bathroom cupboards looking for a shower cleaner she could convert into a solvent.

'Yeah, but I bet you're a *filthy* liar.'

'It is. It's Nic Caruana; I can get people to vouch for it and everything.'

'Same people who can vouch for not knowing you, eh?' She blew smoke at me and shrugged. 'I don't give a flying one, really. Nic, Brian, whatever, I'll call you fucking Vanessa, if you like? ... What are you up to post-Christmas then?'

'I've got a funeral actually.'

'Oh yeah?'

'My brother's.'

'Fuck, sorry, man. I just talk and talk and *bleurgh* and you've actually got proper shit going on? How did he die?'

'Shot down in Afghanistan. He was a helicopter pilot.'

She whistled, writing words in the air with the smoke trail from her spliff. 'Wow. Hero.'

I hesitated, and she laughed.

'Ooh, favourite child, right? Tough shit, everyone has them. Seriously though, sorry, it must be... difficult, painful, I don't know. You're probably sick of people saying the same old same old...' She rested her head on my arm and fell silent for a bit.

I blinked, hard, starting to feel light-headed from the drugs. It felt good, these brief holidays from serious thought. It crossed my mind that Mark would like her.

'Are you OK?' I asked. 'You know, the rent's going to run out soon.'

'Then I'll be packing, won't I? I'm sick of this place anyway, and it feels weird with Meds dying upstairs and... I mostly sleep down here now anyway. I believe in ghosts, right, but I would freak the fuck out if I had to see him drifting about with his endless fucking insulin shots. He'd be the worst haunting ever.' She paused. 'I miss that lad a bit. I miss Ems something rotten... What a waste, man, what a waste.'

I had considered telling her about Pat and Clare, but decided there was little point. I kept thinking, 'Let it go. Let. It. Go.' It was a waste. She had no idea how much of a waste it had been.

I pulled her closer against me.

She let out a snort of amusement, but went along with it.

'How are you spending the holidays?' I said, on the verge of dropping off.

'Dunno, the usual?' She gestured a lot when she spoke, up into the air. 'I'll probably get pissed on WKD, watch *Love Actually* and cry.'

'Sounds fine to me.'

'Oh, and do a bit of a dancing in front of the mirror with a hairbrush.'

'Funny, I was going to do *exactly* the same thing.'

She punched me on the arm, laughing. 'Ha, you big gay.'

CHAPTER THIRTY-SEVEN

We arrived too late for introductions, but it gave me the excuse I needed to sit at the back unnoticed. There were flags everywhere, rows and rows of people wearing uniforms with medals pinned to their chests.

I saw Mark scanning the congregation for Harriet and my parents as we sat down; he had a David Attenboroughesque fascination with where I had come from, much like me with his background.

'He doesn't look much like you,' Mark whispered.

I followed his gaze to the picture of Tony, many rows in front, and was shocked by the recollection of his features. His face had become a blur to me in recent months. I tried to feel something, but couldn't. I even tried to recall specific memories, from the times when I was young and still fond of him, but they didn't work.

'Yeah, he looks like Mum,' I said. 'Got the blond hair. The fucking pretty boy, Harri used to call him.'

I tried to catch a glimpse of Harriet but gave up. My suit was irritating me.

An imposing man in military uniform cleared his throat to say something, and started reading a poem.

'"You risked your life for others, each and every day..."'

'Fuck's sake,' I muttered.

'What?'

'I just knew this was going to be shit.'

I got the impression that Mark hadn't believed me when I'd told him in the car why I hadn't wanted to come. He thought my reluctance was some kind of symptom of grief and not genuine resentment.

Harriet and I would never be afforded this level of air-brushing.

Mark looked perplexed.

'Talk about mythologizing,' I said, by way of explanation.

I could hear Mum crying already. It was an unfamiliar and distressing sound, dragged out of my memory. The last time I had heard Mum cry was when one of my uncles had died, her younger brother who lived in Inverness. I'd been young, ten or eleven, and only heard it through her bedroom wall. At that age I didn't even believe parents were capable of swearing, let along crying.

'"And we loved and respected your courage, more than you understood..."'

I could smell flowers and taste copper.

The man's voice reverberated against stone.

I felt like ripping one of the fake plastic wreaths out of someone's hands and strangling him with it.

I remembered the day it had happened and I had come home, shaking so much I was unable to even use my key. Tony had looked up and down the street, hand around the sleeve of my coat lest I make a run for it. 'Oh, Jesus Christ...' he had said, before dragging me inside.

I remembered being yanked up the stairs and into the bathroom, hauled into the bath and hosed down, being told over and over again, 'You don't tell Mum and Dad about this, you hear me? How could you have been so damn stupid! You don't tell anyone! You don't tell anyone!'

I remembered that he had washed the blood off, thrown

the clothes away and forced me to recite an alibi. I had cried until my head hurt, and did as he ordered. But when Dad got home from work I still told him everything.

Tony stopped speaking to me, and didn't start again for over three years, when I was out of incarceration. He didn't even visit, so total was his sense of betrayal. The way he had seen it, he had tried to help me and I had thrown it back in his face.

'"Your efforts will impact generations…"'

As far as my parents were concerned, any attempted cover-up had been mine, and they would never know any different. If I had known from a younger age that your job as a human being was just to lie like everyone else, then maybe my funeral would have stood a better chance of looking like this.

'"Through lives saved and all the good you did."'

There was a commotion at the front, muffled voices…

Mark sat up straighter to catch a glimpse of any drama.

Harriet was walking back up the aisle with a hand covering her eyes, ignoring the startled eyes following her. She was wearing a black dress and high heels that she didn't look used to walking in.

On her way out of the door she kicked over one of the stands holding the hymn books.

I hovered, half on and half off my seat, before following her at a jog.

Harriet had stormed off across the graveyard, pausing only to take her high heels off and throw one of them at a headstone. She lit a cigarette and sat down on a tomb with her back to me.

Shivering, I zipped my coat up over my suit and called out, 'Hey, I want my money back!'

She turned, and rolled her eyes.

'I was expecting pyrotechnics, to be honest,' I said, sitting on the tomb beside her. 'Gi's a cigarette?'

She handed me one and lit it for me.

I was surprised to see tears in her eyes.

'You OK?'

'Fuck, no...' She sniffed. 'I fucking *hate* him, Nic. I can't help it. Listening to all that just makes me feel *literally* sick. I couldn't stay.'

Of course she wasn't crying over Tony. Fury was the only thing that could get tears out of her, even as a child. It was as close to human feeling as she got.

'I like to think he'd rather we just went out and got hammered anyway.' I glanced down at the name of the man we were sitting on. 'Is this technically disrespecting the dead? Mr... Lionel Charles Carthew.'

Mark climbed on to the tomb next to me, lighting his own cigarette with an amused expression. 'Na, I think he likes the company.'

'Harri, this is Mark. Mark, this is Harri, my sister.'

Harriet craned her neck around me and stuck out a hand. 'Nice to meet you, finally. Sorry about this vomit-fest.'

'Na, I love a good funeral.' Mark took a drag and gave my shoulder a squeeze. 'And by funeral I might mean free buffet.'

'Free bar too, it's a bloody rave.' Harriet winked at me. 'He's cool.'

'So you're not saying anything?' I asked.

'No, the army lads have got it. Plus, I couldn't possibly finish a eulogy. I'd keep gagging on the smell of burning martyr.' She kicked her heels against the stone and I saw the beginning of a ladder by her big toe. 'Hey, how are things going with that married woman?'

I exchanged glances with Mark.

'Didn't really come to anything, Harri.'

'Sucks... It's true though, they never leave their wives, or husbands, whatever. You're better off well shot of anyone married, trust me.'

It was strange, thinking about Clare here. She belonged so solidly in fantasy that I couldn't superimpose her image on to anything real, like my family, or other locations. In a way, it made sense that in dying she had got what she wanted; she got to carry on as fantasy, without age, without failure...

I had kept the picture of her that I had drawn. That was all I had left. It was tucked into the back of another notepad, in a drawer, under another notepad. Just in case.

'God, I know,' I said. 'You have no fucking idea.'

I saw Mark smile to himself, but he said nothing else on the subject.

For the next half an hour the three of us chatted nonsense and finished a packet of cigarettes between us. Mark was the first to notice when people started coming out of the church.

The coffin came first, being carried to the car by his fellow pilots, ready to be driven to the military cemetery.

'You want a lift?' I asked Harriet, slipping down from the tomb on to the wet grass. 'It's no trouble.'

'Can't say no. It's got to be better than driving with Dad.'

I couldn't help checking her eyes as she answered me, searching them for any dilation out of habit, but there was nothing. I knew better than to draw attention to it, but I was impressed.

We walked back towards the congregation after Harriet found her shoes, and I started psyching myself up for an exchange with Dad. I hoped, if only for Mark's sake, that it wasn't too embarrassing.

'Don't worry, he'll probably go easy on you,' Harriet said, as if my thoughts were visible on my face. 'It was my turn to be the public disgrace today.'

'Thanks.'

'Just taking one for the team.'

I was surprised by how many people I didn't recognize. Even the ones out of uniform were strangers. I wasn't aware that Tony, or my parents, had known this many people.

I caught Dad's eyes through the crowd without meaning to, and grimaced rather than smiled.

'Did you bring garlic?' Harriet said to Mark, snorting.

'More like silver bullets...'

'I left my bag in the church, I'll be with you in a sec.' She patted me on the back, as if to wish me luck, and left us.

I watched Mark, looking people up and down with interest. I was glad he had agreed to come. Not just because he was driving and allowing me to get drunk, but because it was a relief to be around at least one person who I knew would keep their cool. He was unshakable; a total fucking lighthouse.

'Is that your mum?' he said, with a nod.

Mum was standing a few feet away, being accosted by two ladies who I assumed, from their Scottish accents, were friends of hers. In the moment of silence before she reached us I found myself face to face with Dad.

There was an awkward silence, but we managed to shake hands.

'You had nothing to say?' were the first words out of his mouth.

'No, I... It was great as it was.'

'We didn't think you were going to come. Harri said you didn't sound certain on the phone.'

'Yeah, well, you could have always called me yourself.'

He glared at me, went to move on, but spotted Mark.

'Are you going to introduce us, Nic?' he said.

'Dad, this is Mark. Mark, this is my dad.'

I could tell from Mark's smile that he hated him on sight, but it looked convincing enough to anyone else.

'Your friend from work?' Dad said.

'Yeah.'

'Is work OK?' He looked me over, taking in the suit and the Rolex replacing his watch on my wrist. 'You OK for money?'

I considered telling him where to get off, but it was never the right time or place. I could barely summon the anger towards his act any more; all I felt was pity.

'Thanks, but I'm fine.'

He nodded at me, and carried on.

Mark raised his eyebrows at me, but said nothing.

It struck me that, somewhere, both sets of parents must be organizing a funeral for Pat and Clare Dyer. Possessions would be dispersed and the house sold off. I couldn't imagine anyone else in that kitchen when all I remembered it for was the blood on my forearms and slow twirls over glass. I wondered who would take the statue, or whether someone with sense would smash it to fuck.

'You all right?' Mark said.

He probably thought too well of me for it to cross his mind that I would still be thinking about her. He expected me to be thinking about Tony, or my dad; about something more appropriate, but she was like a disease in the blood.

'Yeah... Yeah, fuck. Let's go. At least there's brandy at home.'

He grinned and put an arm around my shoulders as we walked towards the road. 'Brandy's for *heroes*, Mr Caruana...'

I laughed, searching my pockets for another packet of cigarettes as we passed another car flying the Union Jack.

'I hate carols,' I said, taking out my lighter. 'And you know what else? I fucking hate poetry too.'

Mark smiled, saluting the flag.

'Oi.' Harriet came up behind me and slapped me across the shoulder. 'This mate of yours is still in there, said he wants a word.'

I frowned. 'What?'

'When I went to get my bag there was a young guy hanging around. Glasses, kept needing an inhaler – ring any bells? Said he was there to remind you about something. I said you were outside, but—'

I was already running back towards the church, away from the cars and people and their bemused expressions. Freezing air stung my face until I'd sprinted inside, but inside there was nothing but silence and empty pews, an altar and a gold cross.

It had been difficult to sleep recently, with the nagging awareness that Tristan knew where I lived. I found myself searching for a glimpse of him out of our windows, on the tube, in the overhead mirror, looking through the windscreens of cars behind me...

I walked down the aisle, treading quietly, watching the figures painted on to the stained-glass windows. The men looked down on me, their expressions serene and their eyes, sad. In front of me was Tony's picture. *The fucking pretty boy.*

'Tris?' I said, listening for a reply amongst the echoes, a puff from an inhaler.

Nothing.

Let it go? Like fuck...

'Tris!' I raised my voice, feigning bravado to hide the unease. 'Come on!'

I reached the first row of pews and something had been left on the seats. Tony's eyes followed me as I sat down opposite a book of psalms, but he was the only witness. I picked up the white plastic bottle and peeled off the paper that had been taped around it, taking another glance around the church.

It was no use. He was gone. It was as if he didn't need exits. I half expected to see him watching me from the scenes painted on the windows.

The note said, *The Chinese enjoyed the spectacle of death, Jim had decided, as a way of reminding themselves of how precariously they were alive.*

Precarious, indeed. I smiled thinly.

It was a bottle of lye.

HANNA JAMESON

GIRL SEVEN

BOOK 2 IN THE
LONDON UNDERGROUND
SERIES

PROLOGUE

I could almost see my block of flats from his window, less than two streets away.

Outside the grey cloud melted into grey buildings. Inside I was wrapped in grey sheets with my legs wrapped around Jensen McNamara's head. I couldn't stand him, but he was passably attractive and there was nothing else to do. Everyone here was fucking, being fucked-over, getting fucked, on drink, on drugs, on a daily basis.

He was a talker, that was for sure.

'I fucking knew you wanted it... You know, right from that moment you were scaring those kids away and you caught my eyes through the window and you knew I was watching you but you didn't find it weird, did you? ...Most girls would find it weird, get scared by a guy looking at them like that, but not you...'

When a guy has his tongue between your legs there's really only one acceptable response.

'Mm.'

It could almost be mistaken for pleasure and I thought I'd heard the end of it. What the fuck else did he expect me to say?

'Go on, talk dirty to me!' he said.

I wondered if I could gag him. It could always be passed

off as erotic.

'Talk dirty to me, go on, I bet you can. I bet you can be a right nasty little bitch...'

It was funny listening to him for a while but I lost heart not long after that. Even my naturally tanned skin skin was starting to look grey, like the walls. Everything looked as though it might have been white once, before the flecks of dirt started spreading. I looked down and saw white streaks where some bodily fluid had cut through the grime on the inside of my right thigh.

I couldn't do this, not again, not now, not with this fucking running commentary...

'You can stop now,' I said, at the ceiling.

'What, babe?'

'I said you can stop now, it's fine.' I swung my legs away from him and over the side of the bed, pulling down the edges of my skirt. 'I'm not in the mood anyway.'

'What...babe?'

I gave him an exasperated look and stood up.

His hurt pride followed me all the way downstairs and through the doors into the humid air hanging over the estate outside. I walked back towards the tower block with my shoulders hunched and head up. Constantly dodging missiles thrown from the roof taught you to walk with your eyes to the sky.

I entered the stairwell and broken syringes crunched under my feet. No one touched the handrails now. Too many people had gripped it only to catch their hands on concealed needles.

A gang of kids passed me on the way down, reeking of something faecal.

'Oi, Jap, you got any fags?'

I was half-Japanese and half-English and couldn't be mistaken for either nationality, but the nickname had caught on months ago.

'No.' I didn't make eye-contact.

'Think there's been a fight upstairs, a big one.'

I looked around at them, eyes narrowed. There were three of them, bony and feral with a spattering of red marks down their arms. Even if they only looked thirteen I wouldn't stand a chance if they wanted to search me for money. I was barely taller than them.

'Yeah?' I raised my eyebrows.

They shifted.

'Couple of blokes went up, big geezers, like. They had blades like this,' said the eldest, holding his hands in the air a foot apart. 'We thought they were the filth for a second but then there was banging and shouting and all sorts. Someone's got carved-up big time. Look.'

The kid pointed and I followed his finger to the blood on the floor. It wasn't an unusual sight. It was fresh though; wet enough to catch the light.

My mind was with my parents and my sister as I carried-on up the stairs again.

'I wouldn't go up there. There might still be someone waiting.'

Nausea clouded my head, like I already knew.

I ignored them, avoiding the blood on the floor, trying not to think of the blood on the floor and my parents and my sister and 'blades like this'...

Fifth floor and I stopped.

Fifth floor and I didn't want to go further.

Fifth floor and I could see my front door, in pieces.

Fifth floor with the bile rising in my throat and all I could think of was my parents and my sister and the blood and 'blades like this'.

I could have turned around then, called for help downstairs and spared myself, but I didn't. My heart pounded into the silence, thumping on the inside of my skull as I moved forwards to ease myself through the wreckage of the door.

More blood on the carpet and my entire body shook.

Blood on the walls blurred as my eyes filled with tears.

I smelt copper and my eyes refocused on an arm, on the floor, an arm and a body, red matted hair and a five-year-old skull cleaved in two.

Bile hit the carpet with the blood, mine. My knees gave way, choking and shaking, hands over my eyes so hard that my cheekbones bruised but I could still see it, still see it and I would never stop seeing it.

I was out of the flat, scrabbling backwards through the blood as it covered my legs. There was blood on my hands, my hands over my eyes and blood on my face. On my feet, hanging onto the wall, onto the banister, forgetting the needles, and then down the stairs, so fast I was barely touching them...

I crashed through the doors on the bottom floor, back out onto the warm concrete. The three kids I had seen on the stairs were loitering, eyes wide and poised to run.

'You!' I pointed with a bloodied hand.

They ran.

I ran.

I was faster.

The nearest boy choked as I yanked him backwards by the hood of his jacket, hitting the tarmac with a strangled yelp and a dry slap before I dragged him up and threw him into the wall.

'YOU SAW THEM!'

4

He was thrashing, kicking, almost hanging in mid-air with my hands around this throat too tight.

'YOU SAW THEM! YOU FUCKING SAW THEM!'

I was screaming.

He was screaming.

The other kids were screaming, 'Fucking leave him alone! Leave off, what're you doing?'

I punched him, just to stop the noise, just because he was there. All I could see was the blood, and the arm, and the red matted hair and the five-year-old skull cleaved in two.

I let him go and he sank to the ground, cowering and holding his nose, red outlines around his throat and blood trickling through his fingers. The two other kids came forwards, slinking past me to pick him up and pull him away out of harm's reach.

'Crazy bitch...'

None of the blood was my own. It was all from my flat, my carpet, my parents and the five-year-old skull cleaved in two. I caught my reflection in a parked red Peugeot and couldn't recognise it.

Behind me was grey brick and in front of me blinding sky.

I could hear one of the kids on a phone, calling someone. Their voices were a meaningless hum in my ears, ringing with screams and later with sirens. I wanted it to stop, this relentless sound. I wanted to back into a corner and drown in silence.

The blood was still wet.

I didn't go back in, but when the police cars arrived it still hadn't dried. I sat on the kerb ignoring their questions, trying not to remember, trying to unsee it, but the blood was still on my hands, on my face, on my bare legs, and it wasn't mine.

I had been less than two streets away and the blood was still wet.

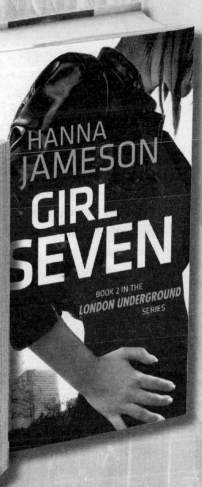

ABOUT
LONDON UNDERGROUND

The London Underground series is set in the bleak ganglands of southeast London. An upmarket club, The Underground, forms the centre of this amoral, violent, and moneyed world: this is where drug smugglers and corrupt officials discuss business over cocktails and cocaine; where hit men devise honey traps with the gorgeous girls who work the poles...

To discover more – and some tempting special offers – why not visit our website? www.headofzeus.com

MEET THE AUTHOR

Hanna Jameson started writing the London Underground series when she was just seventeen. She has travelled Europe, Japan and the USA with the Manic Street Preachers and Kasabian.

You can contact Hanna Jameson via twitter: #hannaninajameson